"S. D. Perry delivers the goods. . . . With real virtuosity *Unity* manages to be both the perfect ending and a new beginning all at the same time."

—Jackie Bundy, treknation.com

"A sweeping tale that packs action and drama in every one of its . . . pages."

—James Swallow, *Star Trek Monthly*

STAR TREK
DEEP SPACE NINE®

UNITY

S. D. PERRY

Based upon STAR TREK®
created by Gene Roddenberry
and STAR TREK: DEEP SPACE NINE
created by Rick Berman and Michael Piller

POCKET BOOKS
New York London Toronto Sydney Ashalla

POCKET BOOKS, a division of Simon & Schuster, Inc.
1230 Avenue of the Americas, New York, NY 10020

Originally published in hardcover in 2003 by Pocket Books

This book is published by Pocket Books, a division of Simon & Schuster, Inc., under exclusive license from Paramount Pictures.

For information address Pocket Books, 1230 Avenue of the Americas, New York, NY 10020

ISBN: 0-7434-9654-X

First Pocket Books paperback edition December 2004

10 9 8 7 6 5 4 3 2 1

Cover art by Cliff Nielsen

Manufactured in the United States of America

For Cyrus and Benjamin, the new boys.
And for big brother Jeremy.

In the meeting of the best in each
a higher unity of understanding is established.

—Norman Vincent Peale

ACKNOWLEDGMENTS

This book would not have been possible without the creative input of Marco Palmieri and Paula Block, nor without the talented authors who continued the *DS9* saga after *Avatar*: David Weddle and Jeffrey Lang, Keith R.A. DeCandido, David R. George III, Heather Jarman, Michael A. Martin and Andy Mangels, Robert Simpson, and J. G. Hertzler.

I'd like to thank my friends and family for their patience and support—the entire Perry clan, Gwen Herzstein, Curt and Joelle, Sera, Thad and Britta, Leslie and Paul, Doctors Goldmann and Cohen. Oh, and Tamara, of course.

I'd also like to thank Denise and Michael Okuda for their compilation and reference masterpieces, and the other ST writers I've met, who are all cool; we deserve more money, don'tcha think?

ACKNOWLEDGMENTS

LINEAR TIME

2376

JANUARY

• Following the end of the Dominion War, Chancellor Martok returns to Qo'noS to consolidate his power base as leader of the Klingon Empire. Upon his arrival, a coup d'état destroys the Great Hall in the First City, killing the entire Klingon High Council. With the aid of Federation Ambassador Worf and Lieutenant Ezri Dax, Martok defeats the coup, but at the cost of many lives close to him, including his wife, Sirella, and their two daughters.

• Starfleet Commander Tiris Jast, a Bolian female, is assigned to Starbase Deep Space 9 as first officer and commander of the *U.S.S. Defiant*. Also arriving around this time are Lieutenant Sam Bowers, the station's new tactical officer, formerly of the *U.S.S. Budapest,* and Ensign Prynn Tenmei, the *Defiant*'s new conn officer, formerly of the *U.S.S. Sentinel.* Due to personnel shortages in the aftermath of the war, Lieutenant (j.g.) Nog, already the station's chief operations officer, briefly doubles as DS9's chief of security.

• War-weary Starfleet renegade and Maquis survivor Ro Laren returns home to Bajor, having spent the final year of the Dominion War as leader of a group of independent fighters staging guerilla attacks against Dominion forces. In recognition of her actions on behalf of the Alpha Quadrant, the Bajoran Militia awards her the honorary commission of lieutenant in its special forces division, and gives her an administrative post at Militia headquarters.

• Captain Kasidy Yates begins building the house designed by her missing husband, Captain Benjamin Sisko, in the Kendra Valley province of Bajor.

• Bajoran First Minister Shakaar Edon spearheads initiatives to bring humanitarian aid to Cardassia Prime, and Deep Space 9 is designated official coordinator of those relief efforts.

• The autonomous covert organization Section 31 locates an abandoned Jem'Hadar hatchery on the planet Sindorin in the Badlands. A team led by Dr. Ethan Locken, a genetically enhanced human, is sent to study the hatchery for possible exploitation by the Federation.

• Hoping to come to grips with the loss of his father, Jake Sisko joins the archaeological dig at B'hala on Bajor, where he spends most of his time excavating and cataloguing ancient artifacts.

FEBRUARY

• Starfleet's attempts to extradite Ro Laren to face charges of treason to the Federation are met with resistance from Bajor. Unknown to Ro, Starfleet is further impeded from pursuing the matter by Captain Jean-Luc Picard, her former commanding officer, who lobbies Starfleet Command to drop its charges against Ro.

• In the Gamma Quadrant, Odo encounters resistance from the Great Link toward his insights into "solids," but perseveres. Wishing to discontinue the exploitation of the Jem'Hadar and to prove that they possess the potential to become something other than killing machines, Odo instructs the Vorta to begin searching for anomalous Jem'Hadar who do not need to take ketrecel-white, the health-stabilizing enzyme the Founders use to control their soldiers. Odo hopes to find one suitable to send to Deep Space 9 in order to realize the Jem'Hadar potential outside the Dominion.

• Ensign Thirishar ch'Thane, also known as Shar, formerly of the *U.S.S. Tamberlaine,* is assigned to Deep Space 9 as science officer.

• Unable to adjust to life on Bajor, Ro is assigned to Deep Space 9 as chief of station security.

MARCH

• As Cardassia Prime continues the long and difficult process of recovery, a new democratically elected provisional government, headed by Alon Ghemor, nephew of

Tekeny, rises to power. At the same time, an increasing number of the surviving population begin to rediscover their lost spirituality, turning to an ancient religion, the Oralian Way, that dates back to Cardassia's First Hebitian civilization.

• Shakaar begins a diplomatic tour of key Federation planets to lobby for Bajor's membership, which was approved more than two years earlier and subsequently declined by the Bajoran government at the urging of Benjamin Sisko.

• Dr. Ethan Locken breaks away from Section 31, assuming full personal control of the Jem'Hadar hatchery on Sindorin. Modeling himself on Khan Noonien Singh, Locken begins to plan the takeover of the Alpha Quadrant, with himself as leader of a genetically enhanced ruling class.

• In the Dominion, the Vorta's search for ketrecel-independent Jem'Hadar uncovers four. One of these is Taran'atar, a twenty-two-year-old "Honored Elder" who didn't fight in the war for the Alpha Quadrant. Odo selects him to become his cultural observer on DS9, with instructions to obey Kira Nerys and immerse himself in life aboard the station, until Odo calls him home.

• Deep Space 9 begins a series of upgrades to the station's infrastructure and defenses, as well as to the *Defiant*. The *U.S.S. Aldebaran* is assigned to DS9 to stand in for the *Defiant* as the Bajoran system's first line of defense.

• Acting on sensor readings provided by the Klingons, the *U.S.S. Enterprise* goes into the Badlands to investigate the possible presence of the Breen. On board as a mission specialist is Commander Elias Vaughn, a centenarian human and Starfleet special operations officer, who is contemplating retirement.

• On Cardassia, Elim Garak sends an autobiographical letter to Dr. Julian Bashir on DS9.

• Members of the Petraw species posing as ancient Iconians begin making overtures to governments and other interested parties throughout the Alpha Quadrant, offering the secrets of Iconian gateway technology to the highest bidder.

• Prylar Istani Reyla, working at the dig in B'hala, unearths an ancient prophetic text by the heretic Ohalu. While more historically accurate than any of the accepted prophecies, the book appears to refute the orthodox interpretation of the Prophets as gods. It further foretells the birth of the Avatar, the second child of the Emissary, for whom it says ten thousand people are fated to die before the birth. The Vedek Assembly attempts to suppress the Ohalu prophecies by censuring Istani and demanding that she turn over the text to them.

APRIL

• Prylar Istani seeks out Jake Sisko at B'hala and entrusts him with a fragment of the Ohalu prophecies, one that describes a son who is destined to enter the Celestial Temple and return with a lost herald. Believing the prophecy describes the return of his father, Jake sets out to fulfill it by entering the wormhole alone in a shuttle obtained from Quark, without telling friends or family.

• Istani comes to DS9 to inform Kasidy Yates about the prophecy of the Avatar, but is murdered before she can contact Yates.

• A Jem'Hadar ship carrying Taran'atar leaves Dominion space for Deep Space 9. It is followed and attacked by four ships of renegade Jem'Hadar, who seek to redeem themselves for their failure to conquer the Alpha Quadrant by sparking a new war. Though one of the attacking ships is destroyed and Taran'atar's ship is disabled, the other three succeed in reaching DS9. Taran'atar's vessel arrives in time to help thwart the attack, but his ship is destroyed, the *Aldebaran* is lost with all hands, and over seventy people on the station die in the attack, including Commander Jast.

• Unknown to anyone on Deep Space 9, several of the renegade Jem'Hadar beam aboard the station before their ship is vaporized, and remain shrouded while they attempt to destroy DS9 from within. Taran'atar beams aboard as well, and, also shrouded, systematically begins eliminating the rogue Jem'Hadar without alerting the station residents.

• In the Badlands, the *Enterprise* discovers the Cardassian freighter *Kamal,* trapped in the plasma storms for over thirty years. Aboard the dead ship, Vaughn discovers and experiences the lost Orb of Memory, which he recovers for return to Bajor.

• After learning of the attack on Deep Space 9, Admiral William Ross assembles a task force of Federation, Klingon, and Romulan ships to enter the Gamma Quadrant and, if necessary, respond with force to the new Dominion aggression.

• Shar senses one of the shrouded renegade Jem'Hadar on the station, Third Kitana'klan. In order to give his accomplices time to carry out the destruction of DS9, Kitana'klan claims to be the observer sent by Odo, and that he acted to stop renegades from carrying out an attack not sanctioned by the Founders.

• Ro discovers the Ohalu prophecies hidden aboard the station and learns that Istani's murderer was a vedek sent by Vedek Yevir Linjarin to stop Istani from releasing the heretical text. Shocked by the prophecy of the Avatar but even more appalled by the actions of Vedek Yevir and his supporters, Kira uploads the Ohalu prophecies onto the Bajoran comnet, making them public.

• The *Enterprise* arrives at DS9 with the Orb of Memory. Shortly thereafter, Kitana'klan attacks Doctor Julian Bashir and sabotages the station's fusion core before he is stopped by Kira, Vaughn, and Taran'atar. Kira succeeds in ejecting the core before the station is destroyed.

• The Allied task force arrives at Deep Space 9, and Taran'atar explains the truth about the attack against the station and his assignment. As proof, he gives Kira his credentials: a message from Odo inviting the Federation and its Allies to renew their exploration of the Gamma Quadrant—if they agree not to violate Dominion space.

• Due in part to his Orb experience on the *Kamal,* Vaughn requests a transfer to DS9, replacing Jast as first officer, and begins plans to test the Dominion's sincerity by taking the *Defiant* on an exploratory voyage into the Gamma Quadrant.

• After an encounter with the newly recovered Orb of Memory, Kira learns that the prophecy of the Avatar has already been fulfilled. Taking Vedek Yevir, Kasidy Yates, and Ro Laren to Bajor, she reveals previously unknown catacombs beneath B'hala, in which are interred ten thousand people who over the millennia gave their lives to protect the Ohalu prophecies.

• Lieutenant Ezri Dax, forced to take command of the *Defiant* during the Jem'Hadar attack, begins to actively experiment in the use of the Dax symbiont's past lives, sometimes involuntarily. Hoping to discover her true potential as a joined Trill, she transfers to command, becoming second officer of the station and Vaughn's executive aboard the *Defiant.*

• As punishment for placing her own judgment regarding the spiritual well-being of Bajor above the judgment of the Vedek Assembly, Kira is Attainted, formally cast out of the Bajoran community of faith.

• Jake's shuttle encounters some anomalous activity in the wormhole that disables his ship but propels it more than a hundred parsecs into the Gamma Quadrant. He is rescued by the *Even Odds,* a ship of fortune hunters—retrievers of valuable artifacts and antiquities. Though their business prevents them from ferrying Jake directly back to the wormhole, Jake is invited to remain aboard for the months it will take them to reach Ee, a free port where Jake may be able to obtain passage back to the Alpha Quadrant. Jake joins the crew, and in the process, decides the prophecy was wrong and resigns himself to a life without his father.

• Nog devises a solution to the station's lost fusion core: replace it with the one from Empok Nor, DS9's long-abandoned twin station in the Trivas system. With the aid of the Starfleet Corps of Engineers and a task force of nine ships, Nog has Empok Nor towed to the Bajoran system, and its fusion core is transferred to DS9.

• Bashir is contacted by Cole, a member of Section 31. Cole apprises Bashir of Ethan Locken's activities on Sindorin, and recruits Bashir to help stop him. With the help of Ro, Dax, and Taran'atar, Bashir succeeds, but fails to prevent Section 31 from recovering Locken's data, or to bring back evidence capable of exposing the organization. Bashir is also aided surreptitiously by Vaughn, who reveals he is part of a small Starfleet group that has been working against Section 31 for decades.

• Kira begins to experience how difficult the Attainder will make her life among her fellow Bajorans. At the same time, Shakaar, on his way back to Bajor, shows the first signs of atypical behavior.

• It becomes common knowledge that Elias Vaughn is the father of Prynn Tenmei. The two have been estranged for seven years, ever since Prynn's mother, Commander Ruriko Tenmei, was lost on a mission while under Vaughn's command.

• Quark is approached by Malic, a member of the Orion Syndicate, who blackmails Quark into acting as a negotiator in the Syndicate's bid for control of the Iconian gateways.

• Kasidy Yates and Joseph Sisko learn that Jake has disappeared, and the search begins to find him.

• Quark seeks out Ro's help with his blackmail problem. Ro tells him to go ahead with the negotiations for the Orion Syndicate, but to bring her along disguised as a dabo girl so she can get useful intelligence on the Syndicate's operations.

• Vaughn takes the *Defiant* through the wormhole to deploy a subspace communications relay at the Gamma terminus, facilitating communication between the two quadrants.

MAY

• Hoping to accelerate the bidding on the Iconian gateways, the Petraw open all of them at once, in every quadrant of the galaxy, creating chaos. In the Delta Quadrant, a Malon tanker under attack by a Hirogen jettisons its radioactive cargo into one such gateway, which leads directly to the independent human settlement of Europa Nova in the Bajor sector, putting the colony of three million people at risk.

• Deep Space 9 is assigned the task of evacuating Europa Nova. Kira leads a task force of numerous Starfleet and Bajoran ships, and together they successfully evacuate the colonists to Bajor and the station, as well as the Jarada homeworld. The task force also gets aid from a Cardassian warship, the *Trager,* commanded by Gul Macet, who closely resembles his missing blood relative, Gul Dukat. Unlike Dukat, Macet was a member of Legate Damar's resistance during the war and his offer of aid is genuine, a gesture that Cardassia is at last ready to begin working harmoniously with its neighbors.

• Among the evacuees to DS9 is Federation Councillor Charivretha zh'Thane of Andor, the *zhavey* (mother) of Shar, who had been on Europa Nova for talks with the government when the crisis broke out. On the station, zh'Thane uses the opportunity to remind Shar of his responsibilities to Andor, where he is expected to return soon to fulfill his obligation to produce children, a culturally mandated necessity in order to delay the gradual extinction of the biologically troubled Andorian people. Shar is resistant.

• On Farius Prime, Quark's negotiations on behalf of the Orion Syndicate deteriorate when his family connection to Nog, a Starfleet officer currently attempting to deactivate the gateways, is revealed. At gunpoint, Quark admits that he is, in fact, working with station security, at which point Ro abandons her dabo girl disguise, and engineers their escape from Malic's ship, with the aid of a hostage: Treir, one of Malic's slaves. Once safely back on DS9, Quark convinces Treir to accept a job as his new dabo girl.

• In an attempt to prevent irreversible damage to Europa Nova, Kira takes the runabout *Euphrates* through the gateway into the Delta Quadrant, where she and Taran'atar are forced to fight the Hirogen hunter on the dead Malon tanker before they can plug the gateway using the *Euphrates*. Taran'atar is nearly killed in the battle, but prevails, giving Kira the time she needs to save Europa Nova, even though it means sacrificing herself on the irraditated surface of a nearby planet. Taran'atar succeeds in making it back to the Alpha Quadrant, and Kira is saved by the appearance of another Iconian gateway on the planet's surface.

• Passing through the gateway, Kira inexplicably finds herself on Bajor, thirty thousand years in the past, and becomes caught up in a battle between two warring republics. The experience forces her to confront her own self-doubts as commander of DS9. The appearance of another gateway beneath the surface takes her back to the present, to an Iconian outpost outside the Milky Way galaxy. With the help of the outpost's custodian, Kira returns to Deep Space 9, uncertain if her experiences in Bajor's past truly happened, or if they were a vision from the Prophets.

• Fleet Admiral Leonard James Akaar comes to Deep Space 9 to join Councillor zh'Thane in observing Bajor's handling of the Europani crisis. He is also representing Starfleet as part of a larger diplomatic delegation assembling to work out the details of Bajor's admittance into the Federation.

JUNE

• Shar's three bondmates arrive on the station in a last-ditch attempt by his *zhavey* to get him to return to Andor. The attempt fails, though Shar vows to rejoin his bondmates when he returns from the Gamma Quadrant in three months.

• Under the command of Vaughn, and with Dax, Bashir, Nog, Tenmei, and Bowers among the crew, the *Defiant* sets out on its trailblazing mission into the Gamma Quadrant.

• Prylar Eivos Calan visits Yates on Bajor and gives her a jevonite figurine originally intended as a gift for Jake. He also informs Yates of the growing schisms in the Vedek Assembly resulting from the upload of the Ohalu prophecies.

• On DS9, Akaar formally informs Kira that a summit meeting will commence on the station to answer Bajor's petition to join the Federation. Kira assigns Ro to oversee security on the station during the summit, despite Akaar's reservations about Ro, relating to her rocky Starfleet career.

• Six days into their voyage, the *Defiant* makes first contact with the Vahni Vahltupali. The crew spends several days with the Vahni, during which a mysterious energy pulse shatters the Vahni's moon, creating seismic chaos on the homeworld and killing some three thousand people before the *Defiant* can prevent further devastation. Those efforts cost the life of Ensign Gerda Roness. The *Defiant* tracks the pulse back to its origin, and discovers that the pulse is the effect of a vast alien intelligence pushing its way into the universe through an aperture on the surface of a dead planet. In order to save the Vahni, Vaughn facilitates the entity's passage into this universe, an act which allows the entity to reorganize the matter of the dead planet into a suitable receptacle for its mind. In the process, the shuttlecraft *Chaffee* is destroyed, and Vaughn and Prynn reconcile.

• On DS9, Treir talks Quark into hiring his first dabo boy, a Bajoran man named Hetik.

• The Federation delegation meets with Shakaar. Among the members is Hiziki Gard, a member of the Trill ambassador's entourage and security liaison for the delegates. After a few days of the summit, Shakaar announces publicly that Bajor's renewed application for Federation membership has been approved. There are still weeks of talks to go through before the signing ceremony. Quark and Ro are the only ones not happy with the news, as Ro finds it unlikely that she'll be accepted back into Starfleet when the Bajoran Militia is absorbed into it; and the Federation's moneyless economy means Quark's bar will have to close.

JULY

• The *Defiant* encounters an energy web created by a species called the Cheka, causing tremendous damage to the ship. They are aided by the Cheka's enemies, the Yrythny, who take the *Defiant* to their homeworld to help the crew facilitate repairs. The Yrythny, it is learned, were genetically engineered in the distant past and possess a biological "turn key" the Cheka wish to exploit, but can only do so by harvesting the Yrythny's gestational forms. Complicating the situation is a caste struggle within Yrythny society, bordering on civil war.

While the *Defiant* goes offworld to obtain materials needed to develop a practical defense against the Cheka traps peppering that region of space, Dax remains on the Yrythny homeworld with Shar, convinced that she can mediate the Yrythny's internal disputes.

• Shakaar returns to Bajor to deal with various administrative issues in preparation for the signing ceremony. The delegates from the Federation remain in the system to continue working out the details of the transition.

• Macet and the *Trager* return to DS9 with Ambassador Natima Lang to formally initiate the normalization of relations between Cardassia and Bajor. As a symbolic gesture, they bequeath to Bajor the recovered art of the late Tora Ziyal, daughter of Cardassian Gul Dukat and Bajoran Tora Naprem, who dreamed in life of bringing her two worlds closer together. The art is put on permanent display in Garak's old tailor shop on the station's Promenade.

• Quark and Ro go on a date.

• Lower-caste Yrythny militants set in motion a plan to give the Cheka viable Yrythny eggs in exchange for weapons the militants can use in the violent overthrow of the Yrythny ruling caste. The plan also includes betraying the *Defiant* crew so the Cheka can obtain the ship's cloaking device. The plan is thwarted, Dax mediates an imperfect but workable solution to the Yrythny's caste conflict, and a Yrythny lower-caste delegate who befriended Shar bequeaths him the gift of a number of nonviable Yrythny eggs, whose genetic turn key may offer a real solution to the Andorian crisis.

• Shakaar delegates the Cardassian talks to his second minister, Asarem Wadeen, who takes a surprisingly confrontational and obstructionist position in the negotiations. Kira investigates, and learns that Asarem actually wants a meaningful, lasting peace with Cardassia, but was ordered by Shakaar to scuttle the talks. Kira confronts Shakaar and is confounded by his increasingly uncharacteristic behavior, but cannot expose his duplicity without putting Bajor's entry into the Federation at risk.

• Shathrissía zh'Cheen, one of Shar's bondmates, grows increasingly despondent over Shar's refusal to come home, and commits suicide aboard the station.

• The *Defiant* discovers a supremely ancient and mysterious alien artifact on the edge of a star system in the Gamma Quadrant, partly out of phase with the space-time continuum. Contact with the artifact connects an away team consisting of Bashir, Dax, and Nog with alternate realities in which their lives turned out differently. This results in a physiological "resetting" of those crewmembers: Bashir loses his genetic enhancements; Ezri rejects the Dax symbiont, necessitating its removal; and Nog's leg, shot off during the Dominion War, grows back. Only by returning to the artifact, which is paradoxically called both a "cathedral" and "anathema" by two nearby civilizations in conflict over it, can the away team be restored. In the process they each gain a new level of self-awareness.

• In the Gamma Quadrant, the *Even Odds* reaches the planet Ee, where Jake meets a Trelian named Wex, who is seeking a local healer and spiritualist. Together they encounter Kai Opaka Sulan of Bajor, missing for seven years. Opaka interprets Jake's arrival as a sign from the Prophets that she is to return to Bajor, and joins him aboard the *Even Odds* for the journey home.

AUGUST

• On Earth, Joseph Sisko, who has grown increasingly despondent over the loss of his son and grandson, collapses.

• The religious schism over the Ohalu prophecies continues to spread, and a group calling itself the Ohalavaru (Ohalu's truthseekers) begins making appeals and staging public demonstrations in an attempt to force the Vedek Assembly to rescind the Attainder of Kira Nerys.

• Quark and Ro go on a second date. They resolve to leave the station and go into business together when the Federation changeover goes into effect.

• Vedek Yevir, troubled by recent events, looks for an unorthodox solution to the discontinued peace talks with Cardassia. Inspired by what he perceives to be a convergence of signs—the jevonite figurine passed on to him by Kasidy Yates, the example of Tora Ziyal, and a half-Cardassian child belonging to one of the Ohalavaru—Yevir convinces Gul Macet to take him to Cardassia. There he makes contact with the Oralian Way for the purpose of creating true peace through their worlds' spiritualists.

• On Cardassia, Elim Garak leads Yevir and Cleric Ekosha of the Oralian Way into the devastated subbasement of one of the Obsidian Order's old storage facilities. There

Yevir recovers the last four of the Bajoran Orbs missing since the Occupation, with which Yevir wins the support of the Bajoran people in accepting his peace initiative with Cardassia.

• The signing ceremony to formally admit Bajor into the Federation is held on Deep Space 9. Before First Minister Shakaar can thumb the agreement, he is shot dead by Trill delegate Hiziki Gard, who flees the scene by beaming out, leaving the station in chaos.

• On Earth, Judith Sisko, half-sister of Benjamin Sisko, goes to New Orleans to help her father, Joseph, recuperate. She is joined at Kasidy Yates's request by the O'Briens, who conspire with Judith to convince Joseph that he mustn't allow his grief to consume him, and that he is soon to be a grandfather again to a child that will need him. Joseph's strength of spirit recovers, and he asks the O'Briens to take him to Bajor to be with Kasidy when her baby is born.

• On an uninhabited planet in the Gamma Quadrant, the *Defiant* discovers the crashed wrecks from a battle between a Borg ship and a Dominion ship. The Dominion ship has one survivor, a young Founder marooned since the ship crashed. Nog and Bowers eventually win her trust, and convince her to join them aboard the *Defiant* so they can take her back with them. The Borg ship, which is actually the assimilated Starfleet vessel *U.S.S. Valkyrie,* lost seven years prior, also has one survivor: the drone that was once Commander Ruriko Tenmei, Prynn's mother. Vaughn becomes obsessed with trying to restore her immediately, and his judgment is called into question.

Dax succeeds in helping him regain his perspective, but when Vaughn comes to believe that Ruriko is about to assimilate their daughter, he kills her with a phaser. The necessary act renews the rift between Vaughn and Prynn.

• In the aftermath of Shakaar's assassination, Asarem Wadeen is hastily sworn in as the new First Minister of Bajor. A report from the *U.S.S. Gryphon,* which has been standing in for the *Defiant* during the latter ship's mission to the Gamma Quadrant, gives Asarem reason to believe that Gard is on a cloaked ship to Trill. Kira is ordered to join the *Gryphon* in apprehending the assassin.

• Ro becomes convinced that Gard has not fled the station, but is in fact still somewhere on board. With Taran'atar's help, she captures him, and it is soon learned that Shakaar was the host-victim of an alien parasite, a member of a species that once attempted to take over the Federation. Realizing that *Gryphon*'s pursuit is a deception, most likely engineered by another parasite on board with plans to retaliate against Trill, Akaar warns Kira aboard *Gryphon,* who incorrectly concludes that the parasite is Captain Elaine Mello, the ship's C.O. Kira stages a takeover of the ship, only to learn that she has been deliberately misled by the *Gryphon*'s first officer, Commander Alejandro Montenegro, the true parasite host. In the battle to regain control of the ship, Captain Mello is killed, but Kira succeeds in killing Montenegro and thwarting the parasite's plan. Shortly thereafter, Kira is contacted by General Taulin Cyl of the Trill Defense Ministry, who informs her that he has information about the parasites, which are still a clear and present danger not only to Bajor, but the entire Federation.

• On DS9, a parasite enters the body of Gul Macet.

• In the Gamma Quadrant, the *Even Odds* is detoured by a troubled Tosk to a class-M planet in the Idran system, which Opaka senses is the source of a tremendous residual concentration of *pagh,* spiritual life-energy. Working together, Jake and Opaka trigger an ancient mechanism that retrieves from subspace the lost Eav'oq civilization, natives of Idran and followers of the Prophets, who fled into subspace millennia ago to escape the Ascendants, violently aggressive religious zealots seeking the location of the wormhole. As the Eav'oq return, the Idran system instantaneously shifts three light-years back to its original position, with the Gamma terminus of the wormhole now inside it. As Jake, Opaka, and Wex set out for the wormhole in Tosk's ship, the craft begins to break apart. The passengers are rescued by a Jem'Hadar ship commanded by the newest clone of the Vorta Weyoun.

• As the *Defiant* nears the Gamma terminus of the wormhole, the crew is shocked to learn of the physical rearrangement of local space, and even more surprised when Weyoun's ship makes contact to exchange the Founder aboard *Defiant* for Jake, Opaka, and Wex.

SEPTEMBER

PROLOGUE

SOMETHING WAS HAPPENING, OR HAD HAPPENED, OR WAS going to happen. He couldn't see it but he knew, and hoped that They would lead him to understand when it was time. He'd seen that They would.

There were aspects of him that knew time to pass, the way he'd always understood it. And there were other realities, beyond linear tempo, in which he easily achieved the kinds of comprehension that his highest mind had once blindly, vainly groped for. These realities were outside of his experience as corporeal, let alone as Benjamin Sisko, and he cherished them as the closest he could come to reaching a real awareness of Them, of Their vision. There were other places, far more of them, where he wasn't even a child trying to learn, but a particle of an atom that was lost and always would be in a universe of complexities.

It had been strange at first, existing in the Temple, the awe he felt often bordering on terror . . . but he'd progressed, learned a kind of patience that only the nearly eternal could grasp, that kept the bulk of his consciousness focused. Patience and peace were linked more tightly than he had ever imagined, and mostly he was at peace. They had many questions, and were eager to understand. He wanted to learn, to teach and be taught. The possibilities were infinite.

But still . . . still, when he experienced himself as whole within the Temple, he remembered that the other reality kept grinding along without him, time passing, things changing. As wondrous, as amazing as his experience was, there was no warm hand to hold his own, no eager laugh to match his. No beloved to share his thoughts with, to be shared with in turn. These things, a thousand others, big and small—the smile in his boy's eyes, a soft breeze at sunset, the good, rich smell of garlic in butter—these were home, and he wished for it. And now there was this *something*, this thing that no facet of him could see, that They couldn't or wouldn't explain. It was important. It was change, and though he didn't know what it was, he knew that everything would be different when it was through.

He would watch. He would be patient. He would be ready.

I

Captain's Log, supplemental.

We discovered the loss of the Gamma Quadrant's subspace communications relay at the same time we became aware of the massive, apparently sudden shift of matter and space in the 1A-2E sections of the Gamma Quadrant's Idran sector (see initial entry, Stardate 53679.4), which sensors suggest occurred eighty-five hours ago. Presumably, our relay was destroyed during said celestial event, which has effectively moved the Idran system approximately three light-years closer to the wormhole.

Having maintained communication silence with DS9 since our encounter on undesignated class-M planet two weeks ago (coordinates available with clearance above Level 16), we were unaware of our inability to communicate with the station, or of the spatial shift which caused the relay loss until Ensign ch'Thane ran a standard frequency diagnostic, approximately one hour ago. Shortly afterward, we encountered a Dominion vessel, Starfleet classification 232. Weyoun, the Vorta commander—a clone whose predecessors were known to much of this crew—had no explanation for the anomalous event that altered the area around the wormhole's Gamma terminus. He seemed as mystified as us.

Our encounter with the Dominion ship was brief but amiable. An exchange was made—the female changeling recently retrieved left us to return to her people, and three of Weyoun's passengers boarded the Defiant *for passage back to the Alpha Quadrant: Opaka Sulan, former kai of Bajor, absent for approximately seven years; Wex, a female native to the Gamma Quadrant, of the Trelian species, traveling with Opaka Sulan; and Jacob Sisko, Federation citizen and son of Captain Benjamin Sisko. The younger Sisko has been missing from the Alpha Quadrant for five months. After making brief statements to myself and the crew of how they came to be on Weyoun's ship, the trio offered an explanation of the spatial shift, which apparently coincided with the sudden corporeal appearance of a species called the Eav'oq (Idran system, see accompanying [obsolete?] chart). The Eav'oq are a sentient species native to a class-M planet of the Idran system, but have been absent for a lengthy span of time. Sisko and the others' statements are now being officially recorded.*

Vaughn paused, lightly tapping the recorder patch with the tip of one finger. The unexpected rearrangement of space around the wormhole had been a startling discovery, was undoubtedly a scientific wonder that would be studied for generations to come . . . and yet he couldn't work up any real interest, let alone enthusiasm. It was as though it was just one awe-inspiring experience too many; with all that had happened during their months in the Gamma Quadrant, his mind, body, and spirit were simply saturated with miracles and emotional traumas; the dramatic rotation of local space . . .

. . . It just doesn't matter. One more huge thing in this universe that doesn't have anything to do with me.

Right, a part of him commented, searching to hurt. *Everything has to be relevant to* your *life.*

Wonderful. It wasn't enough that he was miserable; it seemed he was determined to wallow in it.

Around him, the bridge hummed with muted mechanical life, the crew working quietly at their stations . . . but there was an anticipation in the air, no question. The bridge had settled back to work after the return of Jake Sisko and his traveling companions, once Nog and Dax had whisked the trio away to make statements, but the *Defiant* was now only minutes away from the wormhole. His crew was more than ready to go home.

And why wouldn't they be? Vaughn thought randomly. *Home is where the heart is, after all.*

The thought was a painful one. Back to the ship's log, he decided, feeling morose and irritated with himself for feeling it. What else to say? Though he'd probably write a summary report back at DS9, this would be the last entry for their mission, their grand adventure into the Gamma Quadrant. *A personal comment about our successes? A sum-up observation of the places we've been, the species and individuals we met and interacted with?*

Three months. They'd been exploring the Gamma Quadrant for just over three months, with all its highs and lows; the gentle Vahni Vahltupali and what the Prentara had accidentally unleashed upon them, the tragic death of Ensign Gerda Roness, the Yrythny and Cheka, the D'Naali and Nyazen. All of the amazing places they'd been, the wonders and horrors they'd seen . . . and for him, all of it overshadowed by the events of a single moment, of a second that had changed him forever, a touch of his hand and the blast of a phaser . . .

"Approaching the wormhole, Commander," Prynn said, as if to remind him of what he'd lost. Her voice was cool, inflectionless.

Vaughn looked up at his conn officer, who had returned to duty only minutes earlier, saw her rigid back and high shoulders, and welcomed the numbness creeping through him again. In the days since Ruriko's death, it had been getting harder and harder to maintain it.

"Take us in," he said, speaking as carefully as his daughter had. Ezri Dax had returned to the bridge after seeing to their passengers and he could feel her gaze on him, watching their interchange. He deliberately avoided looking back at her, not wanting to see the sympathy in her eyes; it might disrupt the numbness, and as insidious, as frightening as that lack of feeling was, it was surely better than the alternative.

He pressed the recorder patch again, still watching Prynn's stiff posture, feeling as close to nothing as he could manage. "We are returning to Deep Space 9 after ninety-four days in the Gamma Quadrant," he said, his voice low. "The successes and reversals of this mission are on record."

Successes and reversals. It sounded so organized, so neat and clean. He watched his daughter's deft movements as she piloted the *Defiant* into position, wondering if she would ever speak to him again. She was so bright, such a whole, lovely person . . . and with so many problems that he had caused, directly or indirectly, he didn't know how to begin mending the most recent—and surely most devastating—of his mistakes. He'd had to kill Ruriko, there'd been no other choice. But to have done it in front of Prynn . . .

He felt a rush of suppressed feeling wash through him, of sorrow and guilt, the wave of emotion coinciding perfectly with the dramatic opening of the wormhole, blue-white light blossoming across the viewscreen even as his gut spasmed in regret. He shut the feeling down before it could get any farther, clearing his throat, touching his combadge and speaking without much thought as to what he was going to say, only sure that he had to retrieve that numbness as quickly as possible. Work, he had to work.

"Engineering."

There was a brief pause, then Nog's response, a choppy yes-sir. He sounded pleasantly out of breath, as though he'd been laughing . . . and in the background, Vaughn could hear Jake Sisko's confirmation, a tapering chuckle. It seemed that their last-minute passengers had finished making their statements.

"Update on warp core diagnostic, Lieutenant," Vaughn said briskly.

"The initial specs are filed, sir. I already . . . ah, everything is in proper condition, though we'll want to run a more extensive diagnostic once we get back—"

"Fine," Vaughn said, remembering that Nog had told him just that only a few hours earlier. Vaughn thought about saying something else to the lieutenant, perhaps apologizing for the memory lapse, perhaps telling Nog he was on duty, that Jake shouldn't be in engineering . . . but only touched his combadge again, severing communication. Nog was happy to have his friend back. And after all that they'd been through these past months, Vaughn's crew, his "Corps of Discovery"—and wasn't that an ironic title, now? Hadn't he been optimistic?—deserved whatever small pleasures they could find.

The *Defiant* swam through the dashing, stretching lights of the wormhole, Shar dutifully calling out a list of routine sensory figures that Vaughn barely heard, except to note that the strange rotation of space in the Gamma Quadrant apparently hadn't changed anything inside the wormhole. He looked wearily around the bridge, saw the same weariness wherever he looked, in spite of the obvious impatience to be home. Bashir was at the environmental control station and Dax leaned against the bulkhead next to him, her arms folded, not officially on duty. The couple was talking about Kira's likely reaction to the return of the kai, to Jake . . . and though they were both visibly pleased to have found the missing adventurers, they also looked worn, ready to be done with their own adventuring for a while. At sciences, Ensign ch'Thane wore the blankly impassive face he'd worn more and more often in past weeks, the excited and curious expression that once defined him now mostly a thing of the past. Lieutenant Bowers, at tactical, seemed a million klicks away, his gaze distant. And Prynn was . . . she was dealing with a lot of things, Vaughn expected, catching a glimpse of her expressionless profile as she checked a reading.

Watching her estranged father murder her invalid mother is probably at the top of the list . . .

Ruriko was Borg. *She would have killed Prynn if you hadn't acted.*

That hurtful part of him was bitterly amused at the attempt to rationalize. *And I'm sure Prynn will take that into consideration every time the scene replays itself in her mind, haunting her nightmares.* Watching her mother die at his hands.

He felt nothing but tired, now, thinking these things. Numb and struggling to stay numb, exhausted and desperately in need of something he didn't know . . . and going home, to a place that had never been his home. His heart had nowhere to be still, to rest.

Ahead of them, the brilliant spray of light swirled into an immense aperture, opening into the darkness of the other side. Vaughn straightened up from his slump, readying himself. There was a lot to do before he could be alone. Without the subspace array to call ahead, their sudden homecoming would be a surprise. It'd be fairly late on the station, 2300 at least, but a group debriefing as well as a private one with Kira would have to be arranged . . . and with L.J., if he was still around. The *Defiant* hadn't been in contact with the station since their discovery of the lost Borg ship on that "undesignated" class-M planet, Vaughn not wanting to send such potentially explosive information through subspace, even directed . . . and although there didn't appear to be any immediate threat from the Borg, Starfleet would need to be briefed promptly, particularly about the possibility of an information exchange between the Dominion and the Federation; the strange little Vorta who had rescued Opaka and young Mr. Sisko hadn't dismissed the idea outright, at least.

L.J. Akaar's open-ended mission to the station had been to act as Starfleet representative to help negotiate the details of Bajor's entry into the Federation. Assuming nothing had changed since Vaughn's last update from Colonel Kira, L.J. should still be there, and Vaughn suspected that Akaar would want to deal with the Borg-Dominion development personally.

Beyond that, there were reports to be filed, info downloaded, standard diagnostics for the ship and medical checks on the crew with station equipment. And with Bajor on the verge of signing into the Federation, there were weeks, months of work ahead, of helping to organize the changeover. Akaar had already made it clear that he expected Vaughn to take a leading role with the transition of Bajoran Militia personnel into Starfleet, no small task . . .

Vaughn felt a new heaviness around his heart as ahead of them, the Alpha terminus to the wormhole began to swirl into existence. Even with their history, trying to explain what had happened with Ruriko to L.J., particularly after the Admiral had warned him about serving with his own daughter in the field . . . it was going to be a struggle to maintain any kind of professionalism. It would be embarrassing, and he was immediately ashamed that he cared, *as if I should be worried about saving face in light of what's happened—*

"Entering the Alpha Quadrant . . . *Commander*."

Vaughn snapped to attention at Shar's tone of voice, the reason for the Andorian's surprise visible only a split second later, appearing on the viewscreen like an impossible dream. A bad one.

"Full stop," Vaughn said, in reflex. Prynn instantly brought the *Defiant* to a halt, the wormhole's brilliant light closing down behind them a second later.

"There are four Cardassian warships, *Galor*-class, holding position ten thousand meters from the wormhole's event horizon," Shar said. "Seven more between us and the station. Sensors are showing at least nine others scattered throughout the system. Three of those are holding positions proximate to Bajor."

Shar blinked at his screen, looking up in confusion. "They've just armed, Commander. All of them."

The crew stared at the screen, their faces as shocked as Vaughn felt. It appeared that their adventure wasn't quite at an end, after all.

". . . and that's when the first officer called down, and told us we couldn't transport out," Jake said. "And the Drang were on their way. They were these big mouth-breathing lizards, all teeth and muscle."

Nog shook his head in amazement. Jake had been as busy by himself as the *Defiant* had been, all those months he'd been gone . . . and traveling with a troop of treasure hunters, no less! If he hadn't been so glad to see Jake, he might have been overwhelmed by the jealousy. "So you hid. And that's when you found the, ah, 'janeega' box? The rare one?"

"Giani'aga," Jake said, nodding as he leaned back in his chair. They were more or less alone in this part of engineering. Permenter was writing a report on the upper level, Leishman and Senkowski were checking inventory in the storage racks next door; the machines surrounding the small table where Jake and Nog sat were quietly running yet another diagnostic that wasn't really necessary. They'd be back at the station before it was complete, and he'd have to run another one using DS9's computers, anyway . . . but he didn't want Commander Vaughn or anyone else to think he was just sitting around swapping stories with Jake. Which, since there was no real work to be had, he was.

And it's great, terrific, wonderful, Nog thought happily. Seeing Jake again . . . he seemed older, somehow, but he also had the same bright smile that was so contagious, the same gleam in his eye that Nog had grown up knowing so well. It was like his face was a balm on Nog's tired nerves, a reminder that there were good things in the universe, good, solid things.

"We sold the box, on Ee," Jake said. "That's where I met the Tosk, and Wex, too . . . she took us to Opaka. She's kind of strange, but she's been nothing but helpful . . ."

He trailed off, then seemed to shrug ever so slightly. "Tosk was Hunted, and now he's gone. I said good-bye to the *Even Odds* when I realized . . . when I realized I wasn't cut out to be a fortune hunter."

He smiled a little, a humorless smile. "It's like everything I did while I was gone was all a lead up to finding Opaka and taking her to the Eav'oq planet. And now I'm taking her back to Bajor. Just like the prophecy said."

Though Jake's voice was casual, Nog caught the slight strain in tone, a tension he wasn't familiar with coming from Jake. Anger? More like frustration.

Because he thought he'd be bringing his father home, Nog thought. *And instead, more Bajoran religious stuff.*

Jake had never been bitter about it—that because of his father, his life had basically been dominated by Bajor and the Prophets—or at least not that Nog had ever been able to tell, but things were different now that Captain Sisko was gone. Jake didn't even believe in the Bajoran religion . . . or, well, not as a follower, anyway; it was kind of impossible not to believe in it, considering all the evidence about the wormhole and the beings that lived there, what they were capable of. It must have been hard for Jake, deciding to follow some prophecy that strongly implied he'd see his father again, only to have it mean something else entirely. It was too bad there wasn't anyone to file suit against.

Nog bared his teeth at Jake in a wide grin, determined not to let his friend dwell on anything bad. "Well, we'll be back at the station in a few minutes, and then you can go see Captain Yates. She missed you a lot. I saw her before we left, and she was worried, but I told her you were okay. I knew it, too."

Jake smiled back at him. "How?"

Nog shrugged, noting that the engines were powering down, *must be switching to thrusters*. "Just did," he said, hesitating a second before saying what he really wanted to say. "I wish . . . I wish you'd told me, though. Where you were going."

"Me, too," Jake said. "It was stupid, running off without saying anything. And I am sorry. Though if it's any consolation, you're the only one I seriously considered telling."

Nog was glad to hear it, and was about to say as much when his combadge chirped.

"Nog, get to the bridge," Vaughn said, his tone commanding, but also taut with barely hidden concern. Something was wrong . . . and they weren't switching to thrusters, either, Nog realized; the engines had shut down. *"Have your people standing by for orders . . . and get someone to secure the passengers in quarters. We've got a situation."*

"Acknowledged," Nog said, his eyes wide. He looked at Jake, saw the same expression as his friend nodded, standing up.

"I'll do it. I know the drill," Jake said, and Nog nodded in turn, relieved. Wex and Opaka had retired to guest quarters after giving their statements, but someone would have to make sure they stayed put. Jake was always dependable in a crisis.

They both headed for the door, Nog calling directions to Permenter, feeling a too-familiar tightening of his stomach. Hadn't they been through enough? The *Defiant* had to be out of the wormhole by now, only a few minutes from the station; what situation could possibly have come up here, now, that could cause Commander Vaughn to use his battle-ready voice?

Jake knew better than to keep him, only glancing a farewell as they split at the lift, Jake veering fore and to starboard as Nog stepped aboard and asked for Deck One.

Maybe something shorted out, he thought hopefully, stepping off the lift a few seconds later and moving briskly down the corridor that led to the bridge. The door opened. *Maybe—*

Maybe there was a fleet of Cardassian ships parked in front of them. Nog stared at the main screen, barely aware that he was still moving until Sam Bowers's voice caught him.

". . . unable to contact the station. The Cardassians are jamming our transmissions. . . . We're being hailed." Sam looked up at Vaughn. "It's the *Trager,* sir. Gul Akellen Macet in command."

"Onscreen," Vaughn said, as Nog took his place at the engineering station, reflexively calling up a sensor read.

Macet's face swam into view, and Nog shifted nervously, working to concentrate on the statistics that played out across his screen.

"Commander Vaughn," Macet said, his slick, smooth voice and faintly predatory smile awakening unpleasant memories. He still looked too much like his thankfully deceased cousin, Gul Skrain Dukat. *"Welcome home."*

Nog glanced around, saw the doctor and Ezri frowning at the screen, saw Commander Vaughn's jaw tighten ever so slightly.

"Gul Macet," Vaughn began. "Your presence here is unexpected. And, according to the data from my ship's sensors, quite provocative. May I ask exactly what brings you here?"

"It's quite simple, Commander," Macet said. *"We've been anticipating the* Defiant*'s return for several days now, and have made preparations for its safe arrival."*

"How thoughtful," Vaughn said. "But the last time I was here, the Cardassian military—or rather, what's *left* of it—had no authority in this system."

The commander's indirect reminder of how the Cardassian fleet had fared during the war was a definite slap. Nog's discomfort level shot up as Vaughn rose from his chair.

"Yet here you are, commanding what can only be described as an occupation force, and preventing us from communicating with our base," Vaughn continued, his voice rising slightly. "I therefore demand—"

"You are in no position to demand anything, Commander," Macet interrupted calmly. *"I have the* Defiant *surrounded and targeted. You will surrender your ship to me, or I will destroy it."*

Vaughn's tone cooled. "I don't respond well to threats on the best of days. So it's only fair for me to warn you that this *isn't* the best of days."

"Then let us not waste each other's time posturing, Commander. You will stand down immediately and prepare to be boarded, or I will order my ships to open fire."

As shocked as he was, Nog felt some small, deep sense of satisfaction that Macet had turned out as treacherous as Dukat. The resemblance had always seemed like too much of a coincidence.

Never mind that. We're going to war again . . . but how? The Cardassians had to have been planning this move for months, to have overrun the Bajoran system so quickly. But with what resources? The ships in front of them probably made up half of what was left of the Cardassian war machine. *None of this makes any sense.*

"Under the terms of interstellar treaty, I formally request that you allow me to speak to Colonel Kira," Vaughn said. To Nog's ear, he was starting to sound strained.

"That will not be possible," Macet said. *"And you are trying my patience, Commander."*

Vaughn's shoulders suddenly sagged. He settled back heavily into the command chair, looking truly old for the first time since Nog had met him, as if he could no longer carry the weight of his hundred-plus years. It was somehow as shocking as Macet's crazy demands.

"Will you guarantee the safety of my crew?" Vaughn asked quietly.

"If your crew cooperates fully, they have nothing to fear."

"Give me time to prepare them."

Nog swallowed hard. It was an act, it had to be.

"One minute," Macet said. He then nodded to someone off screen, and the transmission was severed. The gul vanished and the battle-scarred Cardassian fleet reappeared, hanging in the dark, Macet's *Trager* on point.

Vaughn straightened and spun around in his chair, all signs of defeat and weariness gone, his voice clear and level. "Are they running a total comm block?"

Nog relaxed. Of *course* it was an act, and an effective one. *It's his age,* he decided. *Too many people still make the mistake of thinking "old" means "weak."* Himself included, it seemed.

Responding to Vaughn, Bowers nodded. "Visual, audio, text," he said. "They've got a wall up for anything not on their frequency."

Vaughn looked at Nog. "Any chance we can break in on their comm cycle?"

Nog studied the sensor reads. He sighed inwardly, reading the channel switches, the rapid band rotation. There was just enough space around the station not to interfere with internal transmissions, and beyond that . . . "total" wasn't a strong enough word for the blackout. "If I had time to pin it down, maybe," he said. "But they'd be able to shut us out almost immediately, we'd have two or three seconds, at most. Sir."

Vaughn nodded. "All right. The way I see it, we attempt to get clear under cloak and try to make contact with Starfleet . . . but we do it making a run past the station, acquire as much intelligence as our sensors can manage. Ezri?"

Dax was frowning, her arms tightly crossed. She glanced at Bashir before answering. "I agree," she said. "We can't let them take the *Defiant*. And we might learn something to help plan our next move."

"Then let's do this," Vaughn said. "Nog, see that everything's on line, and watch for my signal to cloak. Sam, prepare to raise shields and charge phasers if we're forced to become visible. Tenmei, set course zero-eight-zero mark two-five and be ready to jump at full impulse on my command. We'll have to circle farther away from the station before we can begin our run, we may get boxed in otherwise. . . . Macet's ship is equipped with Dominion sensors, so the cloaking device may not protect us for long. Be prepared to go to warp once we clear the station."

Vaughn hesitated and added, "We'll need you at the top of your game, Ensign."

Prynn didn't acknowledge his comment, only turned back to the flight controls.

As Vaughn called out instructions, Nog signaled to Permenter and Leishman to stand by the cloaking device and sit on impulse, and put Senkowski on shields, not offering any explanation; there wasn't time, and even if there had been, he didn't have much of an explanation to give them. He felt like he'd been plunged into an unfamiliar holosuite program that he hadn't ordered. Everything seemed speeded up and wrong. Only a few minutes ago he'd been listening to Jake's story about the Drang treasure caverns, looking forward to a night in his own bed, a dinner that didn't come in a packet, perhaps a celebratory homecoming root beer at Vic's beforehand . . .

. . . and now we're going to play whip-dodge against a fleet of armed Cardassian ships, in order to find out the extent to which the station has been compromised. The thought conjured up images of Uncle Quark and Colonel Kira. Nog gritted his teeth against the distraction, focusing instead on Vaughn.

"*Trager* is hailing us," Bowers said.

Vaughn sagged in his chair, resuming his defeated posture, and nodded to Bowers, who tapped up Macet's dangerous countenance. Nog's fingers hovered over the cloaking device relay, his gaze fixed on the commander.

"Your time is up, Commander," Macet said. *"Do you surrender?"*

"You really give me no choice," Vaughn said. "If you'll stand by, I'll have my engineer send out our stats. Nog?"

As he said Nog's name, he nodded sharply. Nog stabbed at the controls, watched the read that told him the cloak was active as the *Defiant* darted away, out of Macet's sight and into the vast dark, circling toward home.

2

THE CARDASSIAN SHIPS IN FRONT OF THEM SWEPT UP AND offscreen in a dizzying blur, the *Defiant* cutting starboard, dropping beneath Macet's ship. Prynn let herself relax into the controls with a deep breath, making her muscles unknot in spite of the high, tight thrum of her nerves. As their ship fell away into empty space, so did thoughts of her mother, worries about what was happening on the station, the confusion and anger that her father represented for her now. There was nothing else in her mind, nothing but her and the ship and movement.

"They're sweeping, antiproton, tachyon, and chroniton," Shar said. "Sensor arrays concentrated on an area between zero-seven-five mark four-zero and mark six-five, z-plus thirty-eight degrees."

Too high, they're looking too high.

"Let me know if they find us," Vaughn said, a touch of humor in his voice. Prynn filed Shar's information, ignoring her father's voice. She only needed numbers and facts and her own hands, her own honed instincts.

"Cardassian ships spreading into a defensive pattern between us and the station," Bowers said.

Evek Arrangement, Prynn decided, without looking at her console. A Cardassian standard. A second later, Shar called off a series of designations, the numbers confirming it. Five ships in a kind of slanted wheel shape, maximum coverage to perform a sensory sweep, and to act as a kind of loose barrier; flying through it would pass a cloaked ship close enough to at least one of the five for a read, and with the ships on a constant rotation of outward sweeps, bypassing such a formation could prove difficult.

Shar rattled off a new string of numbers, then another. Except for three, all of the Cardassian ships were grouping into Evek formations, surrounding the station.

"Shar, establish sweep patterns on formation at two-seven-five mark ten," Vaughn said. Prynn would have chosen the same. He meant to go in as close as possible, pass between the lower docking pylons and the fusion reactor—the riskiest, and therefore least likely, approach. At least, from a Cardassian standpoint. It was the one area that would receive only partial coverage from their sweeps.

"Dropping to two-seven-five mark ten," Prynn said, not needing Vaughn to tell her what to do. Her voice was distant to her ears, her attention entirely focused on the unfolding dark in front of her and the rapidly shifting numbers on the panel at her fingertips. The ship responded to the slightest adjustments of her hands like an extension of her will, the power of the act as exhilarating and awesome as it had been her first day solo at the Academy.

"Nog, how close are we to breaching the block?" Vaughn asked. Prynn reflexively looked for herself, not hearing Nog's response as she calculated, *speed, distance, allowance for impulse cut . . .* two minutes, give or take. Assuming the Cardassians didn't manage to stop them.

". . . let me know the instant we're through," Vaughn said. "Dax, work with the secondary comm bank, see if you can boost our signal to the station . . . and have a text ready to send, in case we have to abort before we can make contact."

"They're hailing again," Bowers said.

Vaughn didn't have to tell Sam to ignore it. "Mister ch'Thane, feed whatever you've got on the sweeps to navigation, with your recommendation. Tenmei, pick us a hole."

She could hear the pleasure in his voice and felt a flush of cold anger, in spite of the fact that she was surely just as excited to be in action. What right did he have to be enjoying anything, after—

—let it go. Fly.

She flew, watching the reads as Shar's calculations dropped onto the screen. There, at three-one-four mark five, intervals of . . . four seconds clear, seven-second sweep, then four clear again. The other two openings Shar had pinpointed had shorter sweeps but only offered windows of two and a half seconds. It was going to be tight, very tight, but she could do it. She *would* do it, she had the reflexes and the training and the nerve.

The *Defiant* moved closer to the station, where Prynn could see the *U.S.S. Gryphon* docked at an upper pylon. Its silver-white hull was streaked black with battle damage, but there was no way to know how recently she'd come under fire. Behind Prynn, Vaughn continued to call out orders—stand by to drop cloak, to send text, to raise shields. She concentrated on her mark as she swept the *Defiant* up toward the reactor at ninety degrees, preparing to cut impulse and go to warp once they'd coasted through, Shar's sensors taking in whatever they could. Forty, forty-one seconds from contact and the flying was fine, she was as good as her reputation and as messed up as her life usually was, it was one sure thing to be proud of, to hang on to . . .

Bowers's voice cut through that good feeling, turning it to dust.

"Target group falling out of formation."

Shar was confirming, and Prynn barely had time to register the new numbers that were pouring onto her screen before she had to move. Three of the Cardassian fighters at the reactor group were spreading out, dropping slowly toward the *Defiant* as it sped upward.

Rate of acceleration, projected course, estimated sensory movement— Twenty seconds to contact with the station, give or take; and only eleven or twelve seconds before they were made.

Unless.

Prynn scanned the numbers, saw what she wanted, as much a leap of trained intuition as anything. She didn't have time to calculate it to a certainty, but there was a one-, one-and-a-half-second opening at zero-zero-seven mark one, she was sure of it.

"Ch'Thane, report," Vaughn snapped.

"Their sensors will find us in the next ten seconds," Shar said, his voice mild and relaxed. The calm in crisis of a trained Andorian.

"Tenmei—" the commander started.

"There's a hole," she said sharply, hoping to hell that she was right. "I can get us through."

Vaughn didn't hesitate. "Then do it."

Prynn rotated the *Defiant*, set her mark, the controls

warm beneath her fingers. She was going to shoot between two of the descending ships at an angle, twisting at precisely the right instant to avoid their sensory sweeps and curving in to avoid the sweeps of the two stationary ships, both cruisers, situated near two of the station's lower pylons. The *Defiant* was going to have to pass extremely close to one of the dropping fighters to catch the opening. If she made a mistake—

They'll see us. Or crash into us.

Bad thinking, she let it go. She wouldn't make a mistake.

Just another few seconds, and each ticked down in her mind like a pounding hammer, the Cardassian ships rushing toward the viewscreen, blotting out the darkness, her gaze steady on the numbers, her fingers steady at the helm—

—and they moved, all three of the descending ships turning. Changing sweep patterns.

Prynn hissed through her teeth, forcing her hands not to jump, reflexively pushing the controls with the gentlest of touches . . . and the *Defiant* blew past them, twisted and arced, clearing the closest vessel with barely enough distance to avoid bouncing off their shields.

Prynn's cocksure attitude went down in flames. Good piloting or no, the Cardassians had them.

Almost as one, the three ships ceased their descent, the two cruisers near the pylons turning to face the rapidly approaching *Defiant*. Prynn ignored them, focused on controlling their advance, slowing to quarter impulse, her chest tight with frustration. They were still seconds from breaking through.

"Sir, signal from the station," Bowers announced. "It's Colonel Kira. She's ordering us to stand down."

"Cut the engines," Vaughn snapped. "Full stop."

Prynn hesitated, then did as he asked, still too dismayed by the outcome to register what Bowers had said.

Six or seven seconds, we would have been through, she thought, her jaw clenching. *At most.*

"Detecting EMP generator readings coming from the ships at one-three-five mark thirty and mark forty," Shar said. "And . . . both of the cruisers have powered their spiral wave disruptors and fixed on the *Defiant*."

Prynn's heart skipped a beat.

"What the hell's going on?" Vaughn asked quietly. "Sam, are you sure it's the colonel?"

"Voiceprint confirmed," Bowers said. "The Cardassians opened a comm window."

Prynn sensed Vaughn rising to his feet. "All right, drop cloak," he said, "and put her on screen."

As the cloak dissolved, Ezri realized she was holding her breath and let it out. If it really was Kira, they might finally get some answers. And if it wasn't, if it was some trick of Macet's . . .

Too late to second-guess now, she thought, moving to Vaughn's side. *Too late for any outcome but this one.* If she'd learned anything since moving to command, it was that hindsight could be devastating for a leader.

Before she could take the thought any further, Kira appeared on the viewscreen, in a tight shot of ops on board the station. At her side, dwarfing her, stood Admiral Akaar.

"Colonel?" Vaughn began. "Admiral? I hope you'll pardon my bluntness, but do you mind telling me—"

"Commander," Akaar interrupted. *"Who is your daughter named for?"*

"Excuse me?"

"Answer the question, Commander."

Vaughn blinked. "T'Prynn of Vulcan."

"And have you spoken with T'Prynn since becoming first officer of Deep Space 9?"

"You know perfectly well Commander T'Prynn died almost thirty years ago," Vaughn said, his frown deepening.

He's challenging Vaughn to prove his identity, Ezri thought. *But why?*

"Yes," Akaar continued. *"At Raknal V."*

"No, in deep space, during a mission against renegade Ktarians. T'Prynn was never at Raknal."

That appeared to satisfy Akaar, who turned to Kira. But instead of offering an explanation, the colonel said, *"Doctor."*

Ezri felt Julian move alongside her. "Yes, Colonel?"

"I don't think I ever thanked you properly for the care you gave me during my pregnancy."

Julian nodded. "You're, ah, very welcome, Colonel."

"That was your first Bajoran delivery, wasn't it?"

Julian folded his arms. "I didn't deliver Kirayoshi, Colonel. He was delivered by a Bajoran midwife, Y'Pora."

"But it was in the Infirmary."

"No, in one of the station's guest quarters. It was set up as a traditional Bajoran birthing room."

"Doctor," Akaar said.

"Yes, sir?"

"Please step directly behind Lieutenant Dax."

Julian did as ordered, everyone on the bridge watching closely.

"Examine the back of her neck, please."

Vaughn's attention snapped back toward the viewscreen.

The reference to the back of her neck . . . Ezri wondered if he knew what was happening. *Then at least one of us would.*

"What am I looking for?" Julian asked. His familiar fingers slid through her hair.

Akaar was looking directly at her. "You will know it if you see it."

After a long moment of careful examination, Julian sighed. "I don't see anything."

"Look carefully. Feel the skin."

Julian's fingers were gentle, as always.

"There's nothing unusual about Lieutenant Dax's neck, Admiral," Julian said.

Akaar and Kira both relaxed visibly. *"That'll do, Doctor, thank you,"* Kira said. *"Sorry about the precautions, but we had to be sure. Welcome home, to all of you."* She looked haggard and tense, the lines of her face tight, but she also wore a small, crooked smile that did Ezri's heart good. Whatever was happening, Kira was Kira, and it was good to see her.

"You'll need to examine the rest of the crew," Vaughn said, addressing Kira. It wasn't a question.

Kira nodded. Her smile faded, her gaze darkening. *"Once you dock. Take port one. The* Cardassians *will be handling the examinations."*

Vaughn raised an eyebrow. "That's interesting," he said. "I take it we can expect a briefing?"

"Once you're cleared, yes. . . . Tell the crew not to resist the exams, or any security measures you find in place. I'll explain when I get there."

She smiled again, this one less sardonic. *"You may be sorry afterward, but it's good to have you back,"* she said, and the screen went blank. A second later, Macet appeared.

He didn't appear to be angry or pleased. Ezri thought he actually seemed relieved.

"Well played, Commander," the Cardassian said, his expression tight but not unpleasant. *"I have ordered my ships to stand down. You may dock at will."*

"Thank you," Vaughn said. "Will I see you aboard the station?"

Macet nodded. *"I will be there presently. Macet out."*

The view onscreen returned to stars and ships, to the station itself. To home, where something had gone very wrong.

Jake, Wex, and Opaka were called up to the bridge shortly after the *Defiant* docked, and were walked to the airlock a few minutes later along with most of the bridge crew. Leading the way—and surrounding them, and bringing up the rear—were a number of Cardassian soldiers, armed and silent.

A handful of Cardassian medics and techs were waiting for the disembarking crew just outside the airlock, holding unfamiliar medical equipment. A female Cardassian in civvies was in charge, identifying herself simply as Vlu, and she politely but firmly explained what would happen—that except for the officers and passengers, the rest of the crew would stay aboard the ship for the moment, that it would be easier for her people to run their security scans in a "contained" environment . . . though she didn't explain what needed scanning, exactly. Jake could see that although the commander wasn't entirely comfortable with it—and after hearing a hastily whispered abridged version of their homecoming from Nog, Jake could understand why—Vaughn went along, making it clear that they would all cooperate.

More Cardassian soldiers and medics boarded the *Defiant* for the unspecified security check as Jake and the others waited their turn to be scanned, lining one wall of the corridor outside the airlock. Jake was looked over by a young male medic who frowned a lot, read off his vitals, and ran cool, scaly fingers over the back of Jake's neck before nodding him away, to stand with the others who'd already been checked. No questions were answered, no information about the scans given. It was decidedly creepy, but no stranger than some of what he'd been doing in the past six months. Being among old friends again definitely made it more bearable.

Jake stood with Nog, Wex, and Opaka, watching as Ezri walked over to join them, using her fingers to comb her short hair down in the back after having it ruffled (for the second time, apparently) by one of the medics. Dr. Bashir was close behind, frowning thoughtfully as Ezri took his hand. Except for Wex and Opaka, who watched the scans silently, they all spent a few useless moments guessing at what they were being checked for as more officers were waved toward them. Dr. Bashir said he recognized at least two of the programs being used by the subsonic pulses they emitted, naming them both with impossibly long medical terms that Jake instantly forgot—though basically, they were to scan for physical abnormalities. The most popular guess was that some sort of illness had come to the station. Ensign Juarez, someone Jake hadn't met before, proposed that perhaps a ship carrying the disease had docked at DS9, and now all incoming ships were being checked over.

"So . . . maybe the Cardassians are immune?" Jake said. "And that's why they're running this . . . lockdown?"

"That would make sense," Ezri said, nodding.

"They're looking for abnormality, though, they're not

running standard viral or bacteriological checks," Bashir said. "That would suggest an advanced stage . . . or something else entirely."

"Do you think it could have something to do with what happened to us, with the cathedral artifact?" Nog asked the doctor, somewhat anxiously. "Maybe when we were changed . . ."

"I very much doubt it," he said. "After our second encounter with the artifact, we were returned to the same physical states we'd been before."

At Jake's puzzled look, Nog briefly filled him in on a Gamma adventure that he, Ezri, and Bashir had been involved in, one that had actually altered them physically for a time. As interesting as it was, Jake found it hard to pay attention. Now that he was actually back on the station, he was too busy taking in the environment, feeling like he was in a dream but also in hyper-reality, both at once.

It was beyond weird, to be back after almost half a year in the Gamma Quadrant, even without the unnerving greeting. The air was so familiar, cool and clean, the lights so perfectly muted, the architecture beautifully bland . . . and yet it was all different, too. *He* was different, maybe. Whether or not that was a good thing . . . he thought it was, but wasn't sure, either. His own Gamma Quadrant experiences had altered his perspective in ways he didn't entirely understand yet.

It's good to be home, though. Maybe Kasidy would come to the station to meet him, so he could spend some time just existing again in familiar territory. But then, she might be close enough to her due date that she shouldn't be traveling; he'd have to call her and see. The communications blackout probably wouldn't be a problem; along with being the son of the Emissary, being friends with the station's commander had its advantages, and considering her own status, he couldn't imagine Kas being turned down for anything.

Nog wrapped up his story as Commander Vaughn joined them. Bashir told him what he'd noticed about the scanning devices, but Vaughn seemed distant, saying only that they should wait for Kira. He kept glancing over at two young ensigns standing together several meters away, the Andorian science officer and a dark-haired human woman he hadn't met yet. Jake thought that the woman, at least, was consciously ignoring the commander. Quite an age difference for lovers, Jake thought, but decided in the same thought that they weren't. Whatever the relationship was, there wasn't any romance to it.

He noticed that Wex and Opaka were standing with a pair of Bajoran deputies—additional security, Jake assumed—Opaka smiling gently as they bombarded her with questions and stories. Wex only observed, taking it all in, and though Jake had never been entirely at ease around her—the slender gray alien's manner was somewhat stiff, almost to the point of unfriendly—he felt sorry for her, now . . . stuck in a strange new place with people she didn't know, caught up in some kind of security crackdown. She had followed Opaka home, she claimed, to learn from her—apparently, spiritual pilgrimages were an integral part of life among her kind—but she definitely hadn't signed up for being poked and prodded by Cardassians in the midst of some kind of plague alert.

Jake moved closer to her, smiling. "So, how do you like the Alpha Quadrant so far?"

"It's . . . different," she said, brushing a length of pale hair behind one tiny ear. She seemed as distant as

Commander Vaughn, her liquid black gaze fixed to the end of the connecting corridor that led into the station proper.

"Once this is all sorted out, you'll be able to go to Bajor, with Opaka," Jake said. "And me, probably. I owe Kas—Kasidy, the one I told you about—I owe her a visit. Besides, she'll probably need me pretty soon, she's going to have a baby any time now . . ."

At the look on Wex's face, Jake faltered, turning to see what it was that had so completely seized her attention—and grinned widely. Kira Nerys was striding down the hall to meet them, nodding to the Cardassian medics as they finished with the last few crewmembers . . . and when she saw Jake, she stopped in her tracks.

"Jake?" Almost a whisper.

Jake stepped forward, nodding, and she half ran to him, catching him in a huge embrace.

"Hi, Nerys," he managed, and she stepped back, grinning, searching his face with shining eyes.

"Where—how did they—oh, it's so good to see you, you have no idea," she said happily. An instant later she was frowning, her voice dropping half an octave.

"You had me so worried, Jake. Terrified. And Kas, she's been beside herself, and your grandfather . . . Jake, what happened?"

Jake started to answer, then simply looked toward Opaka, who was watching with her own mild smile of pleasure. "I had to give someone a ride," he said.

Kira followed his gaze and visibly paled, even as she laughed, a short, surprised sound. Her gaze welled up, but she managed to hold it together as the former kai stepped over to join them. Vaughn and the others held back, obviously aware that it was an emotional meeting for Kira; Jake even backed up a little as the two women faced one another, not wanting to intrude. He exchanged smiles with Ezri as Opaka and Kira embraced, Kira hanging on to the smaller woman as though her life depended on it.

"Oh," Kira breathed, "oh, thank the Prophets."

After what seemed a long time, it was the kai who stepped back first, reaching up to touch Kira's left ear, her eyes closing slightly. Watching, Jake thought there was something different about Kira's face, something he couldn't quite place . . . a new haircut, or . . .

Her earring. It's gone.

Opaka smiled again, letting go. "I'm happy to see you again, Kira, and I hope we'll have a chance to talk soon . . . but you obviously have business of some urgency to attend to." She nodded slightly toward the Cardassians. "And I should like to rest awhile. Perhaps we can meet later . . . ?"

Jake was impressed. For someone who claimed no political tendencies, Opaka Sulan was amazingly diplomatic.

"Yes, of course," Kira said, straightening. Her eyes were still overbright, but she was a colonel again, in control. Jake was surprised that she'd let herself show so much feeling in front of other people, though he supposed it wasn't every day one's long-missing spiritual icon came strolling through the door. If that wasn't a reason for an emotional reaction, nothing was.

Kira turned toward him again, but before she could speak, he realized that Opaka had the right idea. Kira had her hands full enough without having to deal with personal considerations. He glanced at Wex, deciding that a hurried introduction would have to do.

"Ah, Colonel Kira, this is Wex, from the Gamma Quadrant. She's a Trelian. She's here with the kai."

"Welcome to Deep Space 9, Wex," Kira said, raising her

chin slightly and squaring her shoulders, reminding Jake that the Trelian were a new species for the Alpha Quadrant. "I'm sorry that your arrival has come at such a turbulent time, but we'll do whatever we can to make your stay here comfortable. I'll see to it that one of our diplomatic aides is available to you for any questions or concerns you might have."

She nodded politely at the petite Trelian girl, who nodded woodenly in turn, her expression strangely blank.

"If it's all right, I'll take the kai and Wex to guest quarters, get them set up," Jake continued, and saw a flash of relief cross Kira's eyes.

"That'd be great, Jake. I'll come find you as soon as I have a moment. We can call Kas together."

She seemed to know what he was thinking, adding, "Even a blackout has exceptions. I wish I could explain . . ."

You and me both, Jake thought, but he shook his head reassuringly. "Hey, remember who you're talking to. You'll tell me about it when you can." She smiled again, reached out to squeeze his hand, but already, he could see that she was turning her thoughts to whatever crisis the station was dealing with, her gaze sharpening, her warm smile turning brisk as she let go. Jake took the cue. He tapped Nog's shoulder, exchanging a look with his friend that said they'd hook up later—Nog had already insisted that Jake bunk with him about fifty times—and, with a final smile at the *Defiant*'s crew, he gathered Wex and Opaka and started down the hall.

An armed Cardassian followed them at a discreet distance, though Jake ignored her. No matter what was going on, he was glad to be back.

* * *

Seeing Jake again, and Kai Opaka . . . Kira was stunned and overjoyed and hugely curious, and much, much too busy to investigate any of it, mentally, physically, emotionally. She compartmentalized the feelings, setting them aside as she welcomed her friends back—people she'd missed and cared about, people she respected. It was selfish, she knew, to be glad that they were now locked down with the rest of the station, but she *was* glad. She hadn't realized how lonely she'd been, how unsupported she'd felt in her work, but seeing all these familiar faces, confused by the circumstances but so open and friendly . . .

. . . *and Jake! And the kai!* It was impossible not to think about it. Jake was home, where he belonged . . . and her own personal reaction aside, as far as Kira was concerned, the former kai was every bit as important to Bajor as any one of the Orbs. Especially now.

After getting an all-clear from Vlu, Kira asked Vaughn and the *Defiant*'s other senior officers—Julian, Ezri, Nog, Shar, Merimark, and Sam Bowers—to accompany her, promising a debriefing to the remaining crew members within the hour. They started toward the wardroom, Kira asking that they hold their questions for the time being—as much for the opportunity to collect herself as for the fact that the wardroom was heavily shielded—and though her thoughts edged back toward the briefing, on who was waiting for them and what needed to be said, she couldn't suppress the new lightness in her step.

Things on Bajor, *for* Bajor, had been rough lately, but everything would be different now; Opaka coming home changed things, giving Kira real hope for the first time since Shakaar had been killed. She and Opaka had never been especially close personally, but the respect and religious awe she felt for the older woman was beyond what she'd ever felt for anyone, even the Emissary. Kai Opaka had been Bajor's spiritual guide through much of the Occupation; she had sacrificed everything to take care of her people in that bleak time, including the life of her own son . . . and she had never wavered in her faith, never turned to anger or violence, never doubted that the Prophets would somehow provide.

And she's back, she's back and the Orbs are home, and the whole planet will welcome her return. She'll lead us all through what's happening, with the Prophets' help . . .

. . . except . . . the Attainder.

Kira felt the absence of her earring, and the reflexive despair that came with it—but let it go, let it die before the memory of Opaka's smile when she'd reached for Kira's *pagh*. Opaka Sulan would never turn anyone away.

As they reached the wardroom, Kira realized that she was doing an extremely poor job of setting anything aside, reminding her that she was tired, that life had been one crisis after another for what seemed like months. She thought of Shakaar, of what Asarem wanted, of what General Cyl had told her on their way back from Trill . . . and with the firm reminder of what was at stake, her mind was focused once more as the doors to the wardroom slid open in front of them.

Except for Ro, the others were already waiting, and stood as Kira made introductions. Starfleet Admiral Akaar knew everyone, as did Councillor zh'Thane, Andor's representative on the Federation Council. Out of respect for the ambassador and her family, Kira hadn't asked zh'Thane to attend the meeting. Charivretha zh'Thane had been of great help in their crisis so far, smoothing the Federation's suddenly troubled relations with Bajor, but her presence at the

Defiant's briefing wasn't necessary . . . and besides, it would be her first interactive contact with her offspring, Shar, in months, their first since his betrothed's suicide. Inappropriate or no, however, it seemed she'd taken it upon herself to be present.

For what good it's doing, for either of them. Though she tried not to, Kira could see the strain between Ensign ch'Thane and his *zhavey,* the lack of eye contact, the careful distancing after a brief, unemotional greeting. From the quick, sympathetic looks exchanged among the rest of the *Defiant* crew, it appeared that Shar's private tragedy had become common knowledge. Whatever they might be feeling, however, the ambassador and the ensign controlled themselves well, much to Kira's relief. Starfleet and diplomatic training might rechannel the Andorian tendency toward violence under stress, but nothing could change the biology.

The only formal introduction that needed to be made was that of General Taulin Cyl, an older, white-haired man from the Trill Defense Ministry, whom the Trill Ambassador had sent in his stead. Upon learning of the general's arrival at the station Seljin Gandres had been visibly relieved to turn the whole crisis over to Cyl. Privately, Kira was surprised at the ambassador's reluctance to take part in what was happening, but Cyl seemed to have a better grasp of the situation, anyway.

Kira noticed the surprise and unease with which Dax reacted to the introduction of General Cyl. Kira couldn't even imagine how strange it must be, for either of them; on their journey back from Trill, Cyl had informed Kira privately of his previous connection to Dax, several host lifetimes before. One of Dax's previous hosts had been the mother of a woman who became a host of the Cyl symbiont. Confusing, to be sure. Kira knew that the Trill frowned on symbiont reassociations through new hosts, but it hadn't seemed to bother Jadzia much, and Ezri apparently felt the same. As for Cyl . . .

Kira watched Cyl's expression as he regarded Ezri, gazing at her with the intimacy of history, and the grim seriousness of the threat they now faced. She hoped there wouldn't be any problems between them. With what they were up against, no one could afford a personal crisis.

Ro walked in as they were all seating themselves, followed by Gul Macet, who nodded to Kira as he entered the room. He took a place standing near the door, from where he could watch everyone during the proceedings, keeping his distance. Kira didn't envy him his situation; his forces were here at the Federation's request for help, yet he was surrounded by people whose first instinct was to mistrust him simply because he was Cardassian.

Ro Laren took a chair near Shar's, her usually sharp expression softening slightly as she nodded to him and to the other returning officers. She carefully set the padds she'd carried in on the table in front of her, keeping her hands on them as though they might suddenly disappear. Kira knew the feeling; nothing was as it seemed, anymore.

Everyone was present, and though it had been only minutes since they'd left the docking ring, it already felt like too long. Kira took a deep breath, picked the most obvious starting point, and began to speak.

3

The excitement and worry of their homecoming had worn off, and Ezri's weary mind had been elsewhere; she had been watching Shar and his mother, and thinking about getting a decent meal, and considering what crisis had occurred to warrant the *Defiant*'s reception—she was concerned, but not overly so; a health quarantine was nothing to scoff at, but they'd handled them before—and then Kira introduced the general and everything else fell off her sensors, her attention fixing on the older Trill.

Cyl. Once upon a time it had been Neema, daughter of Audrid Dax and Jayvin Vod, a stubborn, brilliant child who, as an adult, had joined to the Cyl symbiont. There had been a period of estrangement between mother and daughter, a bitter one, over lies Audrid had told regarding Jayvin Vod's death . . . And they had finally mended things after eight years of not talking, after Audrid had sent Neema a letter with the truth. But once Audrid had died, Trill custom demanded that any relationships from the symbiont's previous host-life be abandoned.

When was Torias, ninety-one, ninety-two years ago? It had been a long time. For Dax, four lifetimes.

And now Cyl was here. Ezri was unable to look away from him as she took a seat next to Julian. *A general, at least three times my host age. How many lives has Cyl lived since Neema? How many memories of hers come to Taulin's mind, when he looks at the universe, when he forms his thoughts and opinions?*

It was strange, but Ezri actually felt a trace of pride looking at him, at the deep lines on his well-weathered face, imagining how Neema's directness must have helped his military career. Strange, and . . . inappropriate? She didn't know what the emotional protocol was for something like this. Though Audrid and Neema's relationship had changed dramatically, both from their estrangement and Neema's joining to Cyl, they had still been mother and daughter . . . and this was the first time Dax had come across any of its host-children's subsequent lives. It was disorienting, to say the least, more proof that the Symbiosis Commission's rules against such reassociations held merit.

So, what is he doing here? The general certainly hadn't been surprised to see her . . . and though both Jadzia and Ezri had found their attitudes about the reassociation taboo relaxing somewhat, she couldn't imagine that a general in the homeworld military wouldn't be concerned about ignoring such a rule.

"Past host relationship?" Julian whispered, nodding toward Cyl, more a statement than a question.

"My—Audrid's daughter," Ezri whispered back. "Neema was Cyl's host."

Julian knew about Dax's children, of course, but she apparently hadn't ever mentioned Neema's symbiont by name. He looked at Cyl with newfound interest, but said nothing. Everyone else had also fallen silent, watching as Kira leaned over and rested her hands on the table, her expression harried and grim.

"So you're all aware, these proceedings are being recorded," Kira said. "Holoconferencing isn't currently available with the security restrictions, and there are several people who weren't able to make it to this briefing on such short notice. Now, I hope you'll all forgive me, but I'm going to forgo the formalities and get to the point. The situation is this: Seven days ago, First Minister Shakaar Edon was assassinated here on the station, just as he was about to sign Bajor into the Federation."

Ezri blinked, her attention finally pulled away from Taulin Cyl, a half-dozen questions pushing for priority through her astonishment. Obviously aware of the statement's impact, Kira held up one hand and quickly continued.

"The assassin was a member of the Trill ambassador's entourage, a Trill named Hiziki Gard."

Ezri froze.

Gard? No. It couldn't be . . .

"After shooting the first minister, Gard beamed out from the Promenade. Sensor readings suggested that he had fled the station for Trill, and I immediately left with the *U.S.S. Gryphon,* in pursuit."

Ezri felt a flush of real anger. Kira and Shakaar had been lovers for a time, shortly after he'd been elected Bajor's first minister; he'd been a good man, and a good friend to her. And as independent as she was, as convinced as she was that she was autonomous, Kira needed her friends, perhaps more than most. Ezri knew, through Jadzia and herself, that Kira had spent years trying to overcome her own defenses, built up from a childhood brutalized by the Cardassian Occupation, to learn how to let people in . . . but very few actually made it inside, and the loss of any one of them was devastating.

"While we were on our way to Trill, Lieutenant Ro tracked down Gard, still in hiding on the station," Kira said, "and between his interrogation and the autopsy data on the first minister, it was discovered that Shakaar had been taken over by a parasitic alien, presumably at some time in his travels through the Federation earlier this year. He was no longer Shakaar Edon."

Ezri's breath caught, her hands curling into fists as dark memories flooded her mind like water. She shot a look at Cyl, saw that he was watching her, his expression affirming the truth of it, explaining his presence. It explained everything, the knowledge hitting her deep.

. . . after so long . . .

Dax had hoped never to hear of the parasites again, had actually dared to believe that the threat had passed. A parasite had killed Jayvin Vod, Audrid's husband and Neema's father . . . a parasite that the Trill Symbiosis Commission had covered up just over a century earlier, the lies about which had been the cause of Audrid and Neema's long estrangement. Ezri felt a sudden chill, remembering what Audrid had experienced on the day of Jayvin's death—an icy darkness, running exhausted through a twisted black labyrinth, chased by the raging screams of what had once been her husband . . .

And now something else came back to her: memories of the Dax symbiont's personal ordeal during the "cathedral" encounter . . . which, she now realized, may have been a confrontation with its own reluctance to probe deeper into that earlier parasite incident.

"These parasites are known to both the Federation and apparently Trill, though very little data is available," Kira continued. "What information there is, we've encrypted into a file that has been made accessible to each of your personal clearance codes. I suggest you all read it as soon as possible . . . but for the sake of this briefing, I'll give you an abbreviated rundown.

"What we know at this time is that they have a limited group consciousness, but are capable of individual action. Unjoined, they're small and mobile, and use a chemistry similar to that of a Trill symbiont in order to subjugate their hosts. Their goal appears to be the destruction of Trill. We know that they thoroughly dominate their unwilling carriers and are difficult to detect through medical scans. We don't know how many there are, or where they're currently based, but we must assume through their actions thus far that they are uninterested in pursuing a diplomatic course."

"The Starfleet conspiracy," Vaughn said, glancing between Kira and Akaar. Ezri looked around the table, saw that she wasn't the only one who'd never heard of it . . . and that Cyl's gaze had dropped, his expression carefully blank.

The admiral nodded. "We have been reevaluating the data on the parasites' last incursion twelve years ago, in which they attempted to take over the Federation by infiltrating Starfleet," he said. "Knowing what we do now, we can see that their redeployment of Starfleet personnel and forces at that time was putting a great deal of firepower specifically within striking distance of Trill."

"And we now have reason to believe this latest incursion was initiated with the same goal," Kira said. "Only this time their plan of attack was to entrench themselves first on a single world on the verge of Federation admission.

"Prior to the assassination of Shakaar, another parasite

had taken over the first officer of the *Gryphon*. It manufactured evidence to suggest that Gard had fled for Trill. It did this in order to take *Gryphon* there and use the ship to cause widespread destruction. Fortunately, we were able to stop it at the edge of Trill space, though not without . . . sustaining losses on board."

She took a deep breath, then went on. "Before it was stopped, the parasite talked to me. It said that its species meant to change things on Bajor and in the Federation, and made it clear that they despise Trill, though it was less than specific about why. General Cyl has explained that he represents a group on Trill that has been preparing for the parasite threat for some time, and that this group began to suspect Shakaar's takeover at a point when it was already too late to save him. For the present, we are accepting the general's word that Trill's secrecy and the operation to assassinate Shakaar were unavoidable."

Which means they haven't been able to get through to anyone on Trill who's willing to talk, not yet, Ezri thought. Cyl turned his gaze on Kira, his expression still bland, but Ezri understood what Kira hadn't said: When all this was over, the Trill government could expect Bajor to demand a full investigation into Trill's handling of the crisis. From Akaar's neutral expression, Ezri had no doubt that the Federation was with Bajor on this. Not that Ezri would blame them. Trill's need to keep secrets, time and again . . . it was their undoing.

Only now we're dragging other planets in with us.

Kira went on. "Once the immediate threat to Trill was neutralized, Starfleet and Federation officials met with General Cyl and the Bajoran Chamber of Ministers and proposed this quarantine. With Bajor's go-ahead, and with the generous assistance of the Cardassian military," she added, nodding at Macet, "we've instituted the lockdown of Bajoran space in the hopes of containing the threat. At this time, however, with the exception of government officials and key Federation personnel, it's generally believed that the security measures we've taken are related only to the assassination. We've made it known that there's a vague possibility of anti-Federation terrorist activity, nothing specific, we don't want to cause a panic—but more important, because the nature of the threat involves the total appropriation of individual identities, we don't know at this time who can be trusted. So it's vital that the truth doesn't get out. We've found six infected people on board this station thus far, all of whom are currently in medical stasis."

Kira looked around the table. "Admiral Akaar, General Cyl, Dr. Girani, and Lieutenant Ro all have statements to make regarding what's been done and what needs to be done. You may want to hold questions until everyone has spoken. Admiral?"

Akaar unfolded his large frame from his seat, nodding at Kira. "As the colonel has already stated, the Federation and Starfleet have instituted a class-one lockdown of Bajoran space. Bajor's new first minister, Asarem Wadeen, agreed—with understandable reluctance—to support the Federation's efforts on Bajor's behalf, but there is some civil unrest both here and on the planet."

Ezri nodded inwardly. How could there not be? As far as Bajor knew, they'd lost their popular First Minister to an assassin while he was under Federation protection, apparently while in the act of signing Bajor into the UFP.

"Five days ago, a parasite attacked Gul Macet, here on the station," Akaar continued. "But it was ultimately unable to take hold over his system. Preliminary data suggests that

Cardassians are immune to this species, possibly through a biochemical discrepancy . . . which may explain Shakaar's apparent reluctance to forge ties between Bajor and Cardassia in the last weeks of his life."

Jake was right, Ezri thought numbly. *The Cardassians are here because they're immune.*

The admiral stated it aloud. "Because of their resistance to parasitic infection, the Cardassians are ideally suited to help enforce the lockdown and assume point in the detection process." Akaar then looked directly at Vaughn. "We attempted to contact *Defiant*, but when we learned the GQ relay had gone dark, we had to begin preparing for the possibility that one or more persons aboard the ship had been infected prior to its departure from Deep Space 9, and that it would return as an enemy vessel."

That explained Macet's unwillingness to reason. Vaughn nodded, looking over at the Gul. "No hard feelings, I hope." Macet inclined his head, but did not otherwise respond.

Akaar continued: "Several Federation starships have been deployed to secure adjacent sectors—but they will not be docking here. Their purpose will be to stand by in case an emergency evacuation becomes necessary."

Ezri saw Vaughn's gaze sharpen, saw that Kira's jaw had gone tight, and understood immediately. Next to her, Julian shifted uneasily. Akaar hadn't said it, but he hadn't needed to, either.

Not just for emergency evac. If the infestation were to get out of control . . . Containment was necessary, at any cost.

"Just prior to and sometime after the assassination, a small number of ships departed the station," Akaar continued. "We have sent transports after each one, and have managed to find and scan the crews of all but four, three of those transports bound for Bajor. The shuttle passenger lists were accurate, but a number of the people we are attempting to track work and live in remote agricultural communities, so it's taking some time. The fourth ship was a civilian freighter headed for Andevian II at warp, we were not able to contact them before they slipped into the Badlands . . . but they were reached yesterday, and have agreed to remain quarantined until a Federation ship can rendezvous with them to perform examinations. So far, there have been no new cases of infection reported."

"What about ships that left here after Shakaar's return to Bajor?" Vaughn asked, his expression suggesting that he didn't really want to know. Shakaar Edon had been back in Bajoran space for months, and had been to the station a number of times. "And those he was in contact with on Bajor?"

Akaar glanced expressionlessly at Ro, who looked down at one of the padds in front of her before answering. "We're doing what we can to meet with the people he had personal connections to on Bajor; fortunately, as First Minister, his movements were well-documented, and those who were with him on a day-to-day basis have tested negative, including his own personal assistant. We now believe the parasites are either slow to spread, or their numbers are small. As for the departures from here . . . what can be done to follow up on them is being done, but of more immediate concern is the number of Bajoran civilians we've been unable to track down."

"How many?" Vaughn asked.

"Including the three shuttles that left around the time of Shakaar's death . . . there are one hundred and seven civilians currently unaccounted for," Ro said.

One hundred and seven. Ezri felt sick.

"Right now, there are several different search-and-screen teams working the surface, under General Lenaris's supervision," Akaar said. "And though we have tried to keep their presence as low profile as possible, the citizens have become aware that there are Cardassian ties to the process; we have met with resistance to voluntary scanning procedures. Commander Vaughn, I would like you to assist General Lenaris and coordinate additional teams."

"Understood," Vaughn said, the flicker of despair in his gaze there and gone almost too fast to see. Knowing what he'd been going through since the death of Prynn's mother, Ezri caught it, and felt her heart go out to him. "Of course. Do we know yet how they breed?"

"Dr. Girani has reviewed the available data," Akaar said. "Doctor?"

As Girani stood up, Ezri felt the memories again, too clear for an event a hundred years gone, recalled the words of the parasite that had worn her husband's body for one terrible night, its hateful litany screamed and echoing in her helmet. It had called itself the Taker of Gist, and had insisted that it was paving the way for many, that however long it took, nothing would stop them from destroying their enemies.

They finally made it . . . and we are the enemy, Ezri thought helplessly, as the doctor began to speak.

Girani had a number of interesting things to say, but Ro had already heard them, at the briefing that Kira had held when the *Gryphon* had returned to the station. Ro found herself tuning out the repeated information, watching the *Defiant*'s crew instead as they struggled to digest the crisis and its implications.

Vaughn was entirely focused, his quick gaze missing nothing. Dr. Bashir was paying close attention, as well, though Ezri Dax seemed to be in a state of mild shock. Nog seemed fairly shocked as well, with that trace of Ferengi nervousness that seemed to come at the slightest hint of danger. Ro didn't really know Bowers or Merimark, though both looked tired and unhappy, as one might expect.

Shar's attention was completely focused on the doctor, so much so that it seemed obvious he was avoiding his mother's gaze . . . and the Andorian councillor was doing the same, her countenance carefully poised, rapt to the doctor's words. Ro had never been particularly at ease with emotional matters, her own or anyone else's, but she decided to make a point of approaching Shar with a sympathetic ear, when there was time. She remembered the conversation they'd had after he'd translated the Ohalu text, how interested he'd been in her motivations for not following the religion of her people . . . and after learning the facts of his own private rebellion, she finally understood why. Andorian biology was fragile and complicated, and by leaving the station when he had, Shar had caused incredible stress to his three bondmates and his mother; Shar, it seemed, had gone against his sacred duty to marry and procreate, a necessity to the slowly dying Andorian species . . . and one of his mates had killed herself while he'd been away, apparently convinced that her own life was worth nothing without the children their rigidly structured culture demanded. It was tragic, but unlike his own mother—who had apparently dragged his bondmates to the station in the first place, hoping to make her child return to Andor—Ro didn't think it was Shar's fault; the girl had been unstable. Ro liked Shar, he was the first real friend she'd made on the station, and she hoped she could offer him some kind of support.

". . . the only visible sign that someone is infected is a tiny barb that protrudes from the back of the neck," Girani was saying, quoting almost directly from the *Enterprise*'s files. "However, in two of the cases we found on the station, the barb had been plastimasked to the skin, making it impossible to detect on sight."

Ro had read the reports several times. The Federation's only extended contact with the parasites had been during the coup at Starfleet HQ on Earth over a decade ago, in which several key officers had been infected. Jean-Luc Picard and Will Riker had been instrumental in stopping it. The conspiracy had been rather widespread, a number of key Starfleet personnel infected throughout Federation space, but Starfleet had managed to keep it quiet, dealing with the matter internally. It had all happened well before her own struggling stint on the *Enterprise*.

Girani continued. "As the colonel said, while they can act individually, there's reason to believe that they prefer to operate in numerous hives or colonies, with one central creature controlling the actions of those surrounding it—a mother parasite, if you will. She breeds a small colony inside her carrier, then sends her offspring to find their own hosts. The mother transmits direction and purpose to her spawn telepathically. We've hypothesized that such a female can communicate with the other females within range. But at what range, we don't know."

But we do know there's a good chance that there's a female on board, Ro thought grimly, remembering the attack on Macet. So far, the only cases on the station had been infected with the sexless, sterile offspring, Shakaar included. They'd been assuming that he had smuggled one of the females to Bajor from wherever he'd been infected.

"Have there been any attempts at surgical removal?" Bashir asked.

Girani shook her head. "It would kill the host. Starfleet's Dr. Beverly Crusher documented the complex neurological connections, chemical and physical, that would make such an attempt impossible beyond a certain point; her notes are in the file. Data from Shakaar's autopsy and Gard's own testimony also suggest that there can be no separation beyond a certain window, probably a matter of three to four weeks for humans and Bajorans, based on the sim runs. This window may vary from species to species—longer in some, much shorter in others.

"When the mother parasite on Earth was killed, the 'soldier' parasites were then easily removed from their respective hosts. We don't understand the exact reason at this time. We *do* know that those who carry the mother parasites can't be saved, the internal damage is too great, and these hosts became dependent on the mother for survival.

"Each parasite has the ability to access the short-term memory of a host, creating further difficulty in detection . . . though long-term memory is beyond their reach, which is another way they can be spotted."

Akaar broke in. "Finding them is difficult; subduing them even more so. We know that low-level phaser fire has no effect. Because they have the ability to neutralize pain receptors in the host body, and control adrenaline levels, anyone infected by one of these parasites can resist physical trauma . . . and is capable of enhanced physical strength, at least for short periods."

No kidding. All six parasite cases on the station had fought when they'd been detected. One had managed to break a security officer's arm and two ribs before the med techs could sedate it; a second had given Corporal Hava a concussion.

Dr. Bashir had a few more technical questions for Girani about the isoboramine connection, the neurotransmitter that was apparently shared by both Trill symbiont and parasite, most of which Ro couldn't follow. From the slight frowns around the table, she figured she wasn't the only one left behind by the medical jargon . . . though she noticed that both of the Trill present seemed to be following along without much trouble. Girani answered as best she could, but it was apparent that research on the parasites was still in its earliest stages. That much, everyone could understand.

Girani seated herself and Cyl gave his brief, noncommittal speech: There had been a chance encounter with some kind of a parasite nearly a century before, a joint Starfleet-Trill science expedition that had resulted in several deaths—but the Trill files on the event had been lost, nothing was definite about the symbiont-parasite connection, he had come to investigate on Trill's behalf and to offer his assistance. He offered up a few "theoretical" ideas about how the parasites might communicate with one another if there was, in fact, some relation between them and the symbionts beyond a similar genetic code, and then took his seat again.

Just as with the first time she'd heard it, Ro was convinced that he wasn't being entirely forthcoming, but she had nothing solid on which to base her suspicions. Kira had told her that the general had appeared just before the *Gryphon*'s return to DS9, claiming, as Gard had, that the parasites wanted to destroy Trill. Their motivation still hadn't been explained to Ro's satisfaction. The Starfleet file on the century-old incident wasn't particularly helpful, nor was Gard, and the general would say only that the parasitic threat to Trill was part of an ancient mythology, so ancient that no one could remember the circumstances surrounding it. As Quark would say, an utter load of—

"Lieutenant?" Kira asked, and Ro realized that she was asking it for the second time, that everyone was watching her.

So much for making an impression. Ro quickly stood and gave her report, referring to the padds at hand a number of times, though she knew the information without looking. She wanted to be as precise as possible, particularly with Akaar looking on; his doubts about her still ran deep. Usually that didn't bother her, she was used to Starfleet brass looking down on her past, but he had been particularly blatant about it, especially since their confrontation in ops, when she'd discovered Gard's hiding place. Akaar had loudly and publicly doubted her assertion that Gard was still on the station, and had been less than thrilled to be proved wrong.

Ro went over the security measures currently in place on the station, explaining the sweep process she had set up, cross-scanning station residents by several rotating criteria. It seemed to be effective so far, although the sweeps would have to be ongoing throughout the crisis unless they could create a better scan procedure . . . or institute a real lockdown, quarantining those who'd tested clean, not a possibility if they meant to keep the situation classified. There were three official incidents of "civil unrest" on the Promenade to report, all due to the Cardassian presence—two shouting matches and one thankfully bloodless scuffle between a Cardassian soldier and a trio of youthful Bajorans. The only good to come out of the lockdown was that there'd been no further tension at the Bajoran temple; in her opinion, the stresses between the "new religion" and the old continued to seethe under the surface of things, but for the time being, the Ohalavaru had stopped their scattered demonstrations. Perhaps they were still trying to digest Vedek Yevir's dramatic recovery of the last missing Orbs, presented just before Shakaar was murdered—practically assuring the conservative vedek's election to kai—or perhaps they were simply like the rest of Bajor, shocked and in mourning over their loss.

Ro finished with an update on the tracking difficulties being experienced by the investigation teams on Bajor. She'd conferred with General Lenaris just before the briefing, and he could only report that progress was slow; they'd managed to locate and clear only three more civilians in the past two days. Someone had started a rumor that the Cardassians were around because Cardassia was joining the Federation, and that their military was already being absorbed into Starfleet—a complete falsehood that was making it nearly impossible to get anything done. Federation inquiries about the whereabouts of private citizens were not being well received.

Ro waited for questions.

"What about Gard?" Ezri asked, her tone somewhat sharp.

"He still refuses to talk, beyond what he's already told us," Ro said. *Except to Cyl*, she added mentally, though she couldn't prove it. The general was being given "latitude" in the investigation, which meant he'd interviewed Gard without surveilance or an escort. The general had been to see the assassin twice, but had insisted both times that Gard hadn't revealed any new information . . . which only added to Ro's conviction that he was holding back.

No one else had anything for her. Relieved, Ro sat, aware that Akaar was watching her with a critical gaze. He really was starting to irritate her. She'd already made public her decision to resign from the Bajoran Militia, she wouldn't be joining Starfleet when and if Bajor finally signed into the Federation; what more did he want?

"Here's where I think we should go from here," Kira said, taking the floor again. "As the admiral suggested, Commander Vaughn, I'd like to see you lead the Bajoran surface check. I'm sure General Lenaris would be more than happy to assist you with whatever resources you require."

Vaughn nodded, saying nothing.

"Dr. Bashir, Drs. Girani and Tarses have already recommended that you take over the medical research into the parasite-host relationship. They'll assist, of course, and continue to manage the station's medical facilities."

Bashir nodded. "I'd like to start by looking into the apparent Cardassian immunity," he said.

"Good," Kira said. "I'll see that you have a few volunteers standing by. Ensign ch'Thane, Lieutenant Nog—we need to develop more effective scanning equipment for the station, and if possible, for ship-to-surface use on Bajor. Nog, see if there's something you can do with the *Defiant*'s sensors, if there's any chance of creating a long-range-scan process. Get a team on it. And Shar, I'll need you to coordinate with Lieutenants Ro and Nog, and Dr. Bashir, to improve the equipment we already have and to keep everyone apprised of new biological information as it comes in.

"Medical, sciences, security, and engineering are going to have to work together closely on this. We all are. And it goes without saying, we must do what we can to contain this information for as long as possible—tell your people only what they need to know. It's going to get out, but even a day might make a difference."

She turned her slightly haunted gaze to Ezri. "Dax, perhaps you and the general could try talking to Gard again. He might be more receptive; he told Lieutenant Ro that he had some interaction with one of your past hosts."

Ezri frowned into the middle distance and nodded.

Interesting, Ro thought. Whatever Dax's connection to Gard, Ezri clearly wasn't eager to renew it. Ro wondered if he'd been the same duplicitous bastard then as now. She and Gard had been friendly to the point of flirting for days before the assassination; in his guise of arranging security for the Trill ambassador and other Federation delegates, he'd duped her along with everyone else.

"In any case, see if you can access anything on the possibility of a historical connection between the symbionts and parasites," Kira said. "We'll arrange a directed link to Trill's comnet, and I'm sure the general and Ambassador Gandres will both be glad to help. The general has assured us that he's already scoured the files, but I'd like to go at this from every possible angle."

Every possible angle, Ro thought, as Kira finished with the assignments. It seemed that Kira had done just that, covering all the options they had. The colonel asked Bowers to go with Vaughn to Bajor . . . and then the meeting was over, and Ro was wondering what they had missed.

Security, Starfleet backup, medical, equipment changes . . . Ro couldn't help thinking that they'd forgotten something, something important. Maybe it was just the situation itself, so sudden and strange and full of variables, that gave her such a feeling of unrest.

Or maybe it's the fact that we barely know what we're up against, and they may have infected half of Bajor by now. Hyperbole, maybe, but it was also frighteningly possible.

The assembled group pushed away from the conference table, breaking into smaller groups—Nog and Shar, Vaughn and Bowers and Akaar, Cyl and Dax. Kira, Macet, and Councillor zh'Thane started talking to the two doctors. Ro realized she had no one she needed to coordinate with, at least not immediately, and didn't feel like it was the time to go through welcome-back formalities; everyone had things to do. Nodding acknowledgment to the people who noticed her leaving, she gathered her padds and slipped out, deciding that it might be a good time to visit Quark. She owed him, anyway, he'd been trying to get hold of her all week, and except for planting the story about possible assassin rings with him, she hadn't had time to talk.

Besides, she decided, heading for the Promenade, between the symbiont-parasite connection and Cardassia joining the Federation, there seemed to be a lot of rumors flying around . . . and Quark was just the man to see about a rumor.

Nog walked over to Shar as soon as the meeting broke up, all too aware that the Andorian's mother was only a few meters away. In Shar's position, he'd definitely want someone to rescue him . . . and after hearing about the parasites, Nog wouldn't exactly mind some friendly, uninfected company, either.

"I thought I'd head back to the *Defiant* right after I get something to eat," he said, cutting a glance at the Federation ambassador. She was talking to Kira and the doctors about something or other. "You know, look things over, start thinking about how we can alter the sensor array. I mean, I could do it with the computer, but it's never the same just looking at the schematics. Why don't you come with me? I could use an idea man."

Shar was also looking at his mother. His *zhavey*, as he called her.

"I'd best not, sir," he said slowly. "I believe I have personal business to attend to."

When was the last time he called me "sir"? Shar must have been seriously shaken by his mother's less than enthusiastic reception. Nog couldn't imagine getting such a cold greeting from anyone in his family, after so long away; even Uncle Quark would work up enough enthusiasm to yell at him about something.

Nog gave it one more shot. The *Defiant*'s replicators had been out for weeks, forcing all of them to get used to field rations . . . and he, for one, had been dreaming of the perfect meal for much of that time. "We just got back. Don't you at least want to have some real food before—" Nog tried to think of a delicate way to put it, but could only come up with one of Vic's quips. "—before you, ah, face the music?" He wasn't sure of the exact meaning, but the context seemed right.

Shar blinked, then tried on a smile. As usual, it looked almost genuine, but Nog knew better; culturally, Andorians generally only smiled as a manipulative tool, and Shar was still working out the humor/affection possibilities.

"Thank you, Nog. I appreciate your offer, but I really must decline. Later, perhaps."

Even as Shar spoke, Councillor zh'Thane broke away from her conversation and moved to join them. "Lieutenant. Thirishar."

Nog nodded at her, doing his best not to grin in welcome. Unlike on Andor, a wide smile was an ingratiating trait on Ferenginar, expressing a willingness to do business or to encourage enthusiasm, but he still remembered a few of the rules of the Academy's xeno-etiquette class . . . chief among them, Don't offend Federation Council members.

"Ma'am," he said politely, but her attention was already fixed on her son.

"I wonder if we might speak in private," she said, her voice and manner as cool as her expression. "Perhaps you would escort me to your quarters?"

"Yes, *Zhavey,*" Shar said dutifully. He'd also gone entirely cool, not a glimmer of expression on his dusky blue face. "Please excuse me, Lieutenant."

"Sure, of course," Nog said, and bowed his head at zh'Thane, but she was already walking away, Shar right behind her. Nog winced internally. Unless he'd misread the situation, Shar was in for a tough time.

Seems like we all are, Nog thought, the reality of the parasite predicament still not quite . . . well, real. It had all been dropped on them in one enormous *swoop,* as Vic might say; Nog hadn't even adjusted to being back in the Alpha Quadrant, yet. Over dinner, he'd work out a plan, come up with a team, figure out where to start . . . for now, he just desperately wanted a decent plate of food, as much for the time to let the situation settle in as for the taste of an unpackaged meal.

Nog shuddered. Parasites that attached themselves to people's brains. If there was anything more horrible or disgusting, he couldn't imagine it.

Fresh toasted tube grubs, he thought suddenly, and felt his mouth watering. Maybe a spore-jelly fritter on the side . . . and a root-beer float for dessert. Perfect.

The *Defiant* would have to wait another half hour. Nog quickly said his good-byes and hurried off to eat.

4

THE ANDORIAN COUNCILLOR HAD GONE TO SPEAK WITH Shar, and Girani had left to find Tarses, to organize what research they had. There would be a team meeting in the lab within the hour . . . but at the moment, Julian was more interested in what was going on with Ezri. She and the Trill general had immediately come together as the meeting broke up, standing close, their voices low and urgent. It was all Julian could do not to eavesdrop, as Kira discussed disregarding a standard report schedule; certainly one of the drawbacks of having enhanced hearing.

Ezri's body language while watching him speak; the look they exchanged when Kira said that Shakaar had no longer been Shakaar; the way they were acting now. There was a shared knowledge there, Julian was sure of it, but one that neither had felt compelled to express during the meeting. Personal, or related to the parasite infections, or both? He wondered if she would share it with him, too . . . as close as they'd become, he couldn't imagine her keeping anything from him, but he didn't want to assume, either. There were vast stretches of her past that he still knew very little about.

". . . and let Girani handle the logs, too," Kira was saying. "We need your talents full-time."

"Of course," Julian said, his attention moving back to Kira. He reflexively assessed the darkness beneath her eyes, the hectic tone of her skin, her uneven breathing pattern. "How long has it been since you've slept? For more than twenty minutes?"

She did her best not to look irritated, but it was in her voice. "I'm fine."

"How long?" Julian asked firmly.

Kira sighed. "Thirty, thirty-two hours."

Knowing her as he did, Julian added another ten. "You have one more hour to delegate your responsibilities, and then you're confined to quarters for six hours, minimum. Preferably eight. And I *will* pull medical discretion if you make an issue of it."

He half expected her to fight him regardless, but Kira only nodded. "Fine. I'm too tired to argue with you." She smiled faintly. "I'm glad you're here, Julian."

"It's good to be home," he said, and meant it. It wasn't the restful break he'd wanted after so many weeks in the Gamma Quadrant, but it was home. And as horrifying as the details of this parasite infection were, he couldn't help feeling a pique of professional excitement. If there was a medical solution, he'd find it.

Kira moved to speak with Akaar, and Julian was finally able to turn his full attention to Ezri and Taulin Cyl. He approached them directly, aware that he was probably interrupting but too curious to stay away . . . and too honest to listen in, much as he might wish to.

". . . much did you tell him?" Ezri was saying, her voice hushed.

"Only what he needed to know," Cyl answered.

"Did you know what was going to happen?"

The general shook his head, started to say something—and then looked up and saw Julian. He straightened, nodding almost casually at the doctor before speaking to Ezri again.

"Tomorrow morning, then," he said. "I'll need to speak with Ambassador Gandres again tonight, and I imagine you'll want to get some rest before we talk to Gard. Perhaps . . . eight hundred hours, at the security office?"

Ezri followed his gaze, and smiled when she saw Julian, but he could see the strain behind it—not just from the barely perceptible tightening at the corners of her mouth and eyes, but also because he knew and loved her. She was distressed, and at something beyond the news of the parasite infiltration.

"Julian. Ah, Taulin, this is my . . . very good friend, Julian Bashir. He also knew my predecessor, Jadzia Dax."

Kira had introduced the general to everyone before the meeting, but Ezri's introduction obviously carried a more personal meaning. Cyl smiled warmly at Julian, extending one chill hand for him to shake.

"A pleasure," Cyl said. "And I hope we can meet again in less formal circumstances. But for now, if you'll both excuse me . . ."

A slight bow, and he was gone, Ezri watching him intently as he strode for the door.

"Audrid's daughter," Julian said mildly, hoping to coax more information. "Weren't . . . didn't you once tell me that Audrid and Neema were estranged for some time?"

Ezri nodded, glancing around at the emptying conference room. "Let's walk," she said quietly.

Together, they headed toward the habitat ring, walking closely but not touching. Ezri chewed at her lower lip, troubled, collecting her thoughts. Julian held his peace, knowing that she would tell him when she was ready—and as they neared the lift, she started to speak, her voice low and even.

"A little over a hundred years ago, Audrid Dax was married to a man named Jayvin Vod, another joined Trill," she said. "She was on the Trill Symbiosis Commission, a doctor and a specialist in symbiont biology, and Jayvin was a professor of xenobiology. . . . We had two children, Neema and Gran. They were very young when Jayvin died."

Julian took her hand as they stepped into the lift, holding it lightly, saying nothing. She had slipped into first person without realizing it, something she rarely did anymore.

"The commission was contacted by Starfleet sometime around Stardate 12 . . . something. Hard to remember exactly. They had news about a comet that was headed toward Trill. It was due to pass us in thirty years or so, there wasn't a danger of collision . . . but a Starfleet probe had brought back data concerning a unique biosignature located within the comet, a biosignature that closely resembled that of a joined Trill. Starfleet didn't know that at the time, hardly anyone knew that we were a joined species, then, but they knew that the reading was similar to that of a particular few of us. They asked if we would be interested in joining a scientific investigation of the comet.

"On Trill, the debates about the simultaneous evolution of host and symbiont had been raging for decades by then, so Starfleet's invitation was accepted with no little enthusiasm . . . though it was kept quiet. The commission wanted to see what was there before they said or did anything. And between the political connections and the science backgrounds, Jayvin and I were selected as the logical choices to join the landing party."

The lift had come to a stop, but Ezri hardly seemed to notice as they stepped off, continuing their slow walk, Julian leading them toward his quarters. He noted that there were very few people about, although it wasn't all that late. Most of them seemed to be in a hurry, too, walking quickly to wherever they were going.

"We were beamed aboard a Federation ship a few days later, and made it to the comet in short order," Ezri went on. "Myself and Jayvin, as well as four human men, all Starfleet, took a shuttle to the surface—there was kelbonite present, we couldn't transport—and started to take our readings, following the faint biosignature into the comet's winding caves."

Ezri seemed to shiver slightly. "Even in the envirosuits, it was cold," she said softly. "Cold and dark and airless. There were these veins of bioluminescent ice all throughout the caves, and we—Jayvin and I—detected a symbiont pulse in one of them, an electrical flash that unjoined symbionts discharge when they're communicating with each other. We were thrilled, though we kept it to ourselves. Like I said, no one outside of Trill knew about the symbionts. We wanted to protect them . . . and we thought, we hoped that we were about to find one, thirty years from home, coming from some distant world to tell us about ourselves, about our history. We even had a cover story worked out if we found a symbiont, that it was a primitive life-form from Trill's ancient past. The Starfleet scientists wouldn't know that it was intelligent . . . if I remember correctly, their equipment hadn't even picked up the communication pulse in the ice floe."

Julian felt his muscles tensing. "It was a parasite, wasn't it?"

Ezri looked up at him, her blue gaze far away. "Yes. We made it to a chamber, deep inside the comet, and found what we thought was a symbiont pool, like the Mak'ala pools, only a small one, filled with that greenish glowing ice. Jayvin was so excited when we picked up the life reading inside . . . not a symbiont, it was smaller, the shape different, but genetically the match was near perfect."

She looked away, folding her arms tightly. "It tried to communicate with us, with me first, I think, and then with Jayvin. There was this intense pain, like a knife sliding into my head . . . but it stopped after a second or two. Jayvin was closer to the pool. The alarms in his suit all started to go off, and he leaned over the pool, and . . . and it broke through the ice and then broke through his face shield, and in a matter of seconds, he wasn't Jayvin anymore.

"I remember screaming his name. He grabbed one of the men's phasers and killed three of the Starfleet team, just like that. He injured the team leader as well. I thought he was dead, too, though he survived—it was Fleet Captain Christopher Pike—but I was already running."

They'd reached his quarters and stepped inside, Ezri still speaking in a low monotone, remembering. Julian didn't interrupt to ask about Pike, a legend in Starfleet, though he was amazed anew at how many exceptional people Dax had interacted with through its lifetimes. They moved to the padded seat by the window and sat facing one another, both of them intent on her story.

"It came after me," she said. "For what seemed like hours, I stumbled through the caves, trying to find a way out . . . and the creature followed, speaking to me in Jayvin's voice, saying terrible things, horrible . . ."

For the first time since she'd started, Ezri seemed to feel what she was saying, her gaze turning wet, her chin trembling. She blinked back tears, looking at Julian but seeing something else.

"I heard him dying. Not Jayvin; I think, I *hope* he was gone as soon as the parasite took him—but the symbiont, Vod. I heard this thing, this *monster* ripping its memories to pieces, somehow breaking apart the continuity of Vod's lifetimes. Finding the anger and pain in each host's separate voice, and using those feelings, that rage, to express itself."

"What did it say?" Julian asked gently.

Ezri took a deep breath. "That it was coming. That it was leading the way for its species, to find *us,* to find Trill . . . maybe humans, too, I don't know, but it definitely knew about the Trill. It called us 'the weak ones' and said that its kind would obliterate us."

Julian frowned. "How did it know about you? About the Trill?"

"I don't know," Ezri said. "And I was too busy trying to survive to ask it any questions . . . but it was a nightmare, listening to what was left of my husband spew out that thing's hatred, in Jayvin's voice. It seemed to go on forever. Finally, it managed to corner me, I was caught in a dead end . . . but before it could act, Pike showed up and knocked it out.

"Somehow, we carried Jayvin's body back to the shuttle, and Pike got us back to the Federation ship. We warped for Trill immediately. I wasn't able to tell much from the Federation's equipment beyond seeing the parasite itself, clutching at Jayvin's brain stem . . . and though I knew it was unlikely, I held out hope that Vod might still be alive and whole."

Julian nodded. The unexpected loss of a host was a tragedy, of course, but to the people of Trill, the loss of a symbiont was beyond tragic. Lifetimes of memories, gone. . . .

"When we got home there was a transplant team standing by, and a waiting host. The symbiosis between Jayvin and Vod was lost, both were dying . . . but knowing what I'd seen and heard on that comet, I couldn't let Vod be transplanted. I ordered a scan of its neural patterns . . ."

". . . and they had joined," Julian finished. "The parasite and Vod."

Ezri nodded, almost angrily. "There was no choice, we had to let it die. We covered it up, of course. Starfleet wasn't happy with us, either—we immediately sent ships to destroy the comet, and disposed of the parasite and Vod. I didn't have anything to do with the decision, but I can't say I was surprised, either. We still had our damn secret to keep, that we were a joined species . . . and we had another secret to keep from our own people, about a genetic connection between our symbionts and that . . . that *thing*. I thought that looking for the connection would become a priority for the Trill, that the other members of the Commission and the government would want to find out what they could, to prevent a future attack . . . but I was wrong. They buried it, and I went along."

"What about Pike?" Julian asked. "Didn't he know what had happened?"

"Yes, and he didn't approve of Trill's actions, but he did what he could for us. He had enough pull with his superiors to keep the whole matter classified. We agreed, he and I, to exchange what information we could find, but nothing like that ever came up again.

"I tried to contact him more than once, but he had that accident a year later, and disappeared soon after that . . . and as far as I've known, there's been no further contact with the parasites since."

"Except this incident at Starfleet HQ," Julian said.

Ezri shook her head slightly. "Today's the first I've heard of it. I guess they were determined to keep it quiet, too."

"And Cyl?"

Ezri actually smiled a little, but there was no humor in it. "Right. That was the point of my story to begin with, wasn't it? When it happened, I told the children that their father had been killed . . . but that the Vod symbiont was still living. I thought it would make things easier for them, and maybe it did, for a while—but when she got a little older, Neema found out. She was a smart girl, she got hold of my personal access code and went digging. She discovered that Vod had been allowed to die, at my recommendation."

"The cause of your estrangement," Julian said.

"Yes. We didn't talk for something like eight years, during which time her brother Gran died of an unrelated illness, and Neema was joined to Cyl. I was too guilt-ridden to approach her, guilt that I let turn into self-righteous anger, for her prying into commission business . . . but when I retired—"

Ezri blinked, seeming almost startled. "When *Audrid* retired, she wrote a letter to Neema, explaining everything and taking her rightful share of responsibility for the rift between them. Neema accepted Audrid's apology, and they were actually starting to mend their relationship, by the time Audrid died . . ."

She looked at Julian. "Dax went on to Torias, and Neema . . . I never knew what happened to her, or Cyl. But she's the only person outside the TSC and the governing council who knew the true circumstances, the only one Dax ever told."

And now me. Julian reached out and touched her soft cheek, feeling a surge of love for her . . . and more than a trace of fear. If the parasites could take hold so quickly and completely of a joined Trill, she wasn't safe. No Trill was, but apparently the parasites hadn't reached Trill, not yet. Ezri would be especially vulnerable.

"Did Cyl tell you how he became involved in all this?" he asked.

"There wasn't time," Ezri said. "But he knows more than he's telling, and I think he'll talk to me about it tomorrow morning, when we see Gard."

"May I ask . . . how is it you know Gard?"

Ezri sighed. She looked worn and weary. She met his eyes and offered up a strange smile, one that he couldn't remember seeing on her face before.

"He killed me," she said.

They didn't speak until they were almost back at Shar's quarters, *Zhavey* walking stiff and silent at his side. As they reached the corridor that led to his rooms, she paused, turning to face him.

"Thavanichent and Vindizhei both await our arrival," she said.

Shar heard the unspoken, that Shathrissía also waited, and didn't answer. He'd avoided dwelling on it, dreading the mental picture of Dizhei and Anichent expecting him, watching over Thriss's cold and lifeless form, but he could avoid it no longer. It was Andorian tradition; until the surviving bondmates could mourn together at their fallen member's side, there would be no death rites.

Assuming that they were still in contact with their offspring, it wasn't uncommon for one's own *zhavey* to attend such things, though Shar had entertained vague hopes of meeting, of mourning with his bondmates alone. His *zhavey*, however, was not one to withdraw over minor considerations such as privacy . . . though she also wasn't one to struggle with words, which she seemed to be doing, standing there, frowning as her gaze wandered in thought. Shar waited.

"I know of your *tezha* with Shathrissía," she said finally.

Shar closed his eyes. Of course. Perhaps Thriss had confessed it before she'd died, or perhaps his astute *zhavey* had drawn her own conclusions after Thriss's death. It had been one of his most cherished memories, so perfect in his mind's eye that he brought it out only rarely, afraid that it would lose its tender glow; now the *tezha* was his true shame, the one shame that he could not deny or rationalize. That his beloved Thriss had killed herself was terrible enough, for all of them; that she had apparently done it because she'd fallen into despair over his choice to leave . . . that was still something he hadn't chosen to accept as his own. He'd promised to go back to Andor after the Gamma Quadrant mission, to bond with his three mates and produce offspring as they all wanted, as their society demanded; Thriss could have waited, she could have decided to live.

Except . . . could she? To have bonded with her privately, to have secretly embraced the physical, chemical, and emotional ties of *tezha*—that had made them closer to one another than to Diz or Anichent. The ritual was supposed to be performed by all four at their *shelthreth,* to bind them as mates, but he and Thriss hadn't waited. If they had, would it have prevented her death? Would she have been better able to cope with his absence? There was no way to tell.

But I was trying to save us all, a part of him protested. *I had reason to leave.*

Yes, and does it matter, now? His own mind answered, quieting the rational. His self-righteousness had no place in mourning the loss of their *zh'yi.*

"Do they know?" Shar asked quietly. There was no need to specify who.

His mother looked worn, much more than when he'd last seen her, the lines of her face more defined. For the first time in his memory, she seemed old. "Of course they know, my *chei,*" she said. "They've always known."

Shar could think of nothing to say. The painful inevitability of his position was what it was. He'd known for weeks that he would have this conversation, that he would have to face his surviving bondmates and his *zhavey* . . . and he'd suspected that some, perhaps much of the blame for Thriss's suicide might be directed toward him. But he could only be sorry, and sad that she was gone. Beyond that, they—Dizhei and Anichent—would have to tell him what he could do to help.

And where can I turn for help? he thought, staring into his *zhavey*'s eyes, she who bore him, seeing the anger and frustration and pain there, feeling threads of his own. *Haven't I lost anything?* He'd loved Thriss, had wanted to stay with her always, and would miss her until the end of his days. Did he not have a right to pain?

Zhavey seemed to be waiting for something, searching

his face, but whatever she saw, it wasn't what she wanted. Her mouth pressed to a thin line, she started for his quarters again. Shar followed, feeling that he could barely carry the weight of his own limbs.

The door slid open, a comforting blast of warm, humid air enveloping them as they stepped inside. Dizhei and Anichent were waiting, seated in the dining area, both draped in the loose robes of ritual mourning. He saw another, folded neatly on the table, and felt heavier, the weight of unhappiness bearing down on him as he looked to his promised mates. Both rose at once, Anichent stepping forward immediately, Dizhei only a step behind.

A welcome shock ran through him as they silently embraced him, both touching his face and hair, accepting him home. The weight lifted a bit, allowing him to breathe, to feel gratitude and some small hope in his sorrow. Shar hadn't realized how afraid he'd been until then, that they would shun him or turn away, holding him accountable for what had happened to poor Thriss. His feelings of doubt, of self-reproach and fear, were swept away in the caresses of his beloveds.

After too short a time, the embrace ended. His bondmates stepped away, Anichent still holding his hand, Dizhei sitting again. His mother did the same, crossing behind Shar to sit on one of the plain benches of his room. Shar didn't know what to say, where to start, and so began with the most simple of truths.

"I'm sorry," he said, struggling to control the depths of feeling that the words inspired. "I am so sorry that she's gone."

Anichent held his hand tightly . . . and Shar could see the bleared glassiness of his gaze, the telltale sign of sedation. "As are we, Thirishar."

"She couldn't wait any longer," Dizhei said, and was there a trace of the accusatory in her voice? "She was afraid that you would stay away. Or that you wouldn't go with us when you did return."

"With reason," *Zhavey* said. She didn't sound accusatory, only tired. "His responsibilities to the Federation will keep him here."

Both of his mates watched him, a dawning expression of hurt on Anichent's face, a flicker of anger on Dizhei's.

"Only for a short time," Shar said. "I said I would return to Andor when I got back, and I mean to, if . . ." He trailed off, *if you'll still have me* dying before it reached his lips.

"When?" Dizhei asked, her voice, always warm and loving, now chill, unknown. "When, exactly?"

Shar felt helpless. "I . . . don't know. I'll leave as soon as I can. I'll—they need me here now, but I won't wait for permission to leave. We can decide now, all of us. A matter of days. Perhaps a few weeks. At most."

Dizhei, his rational, reasonable, forgiving *sh'za,* looked at Anichent with an expression of vast sorrow . . . and scorn. Anichent let go of Shar's hand and shuffled back to his seat, sitting heavily. Had he been sedated since her death? The question wasn't worth asking; of course he had been. Both had fasted, too, living on injections and water, he could see it in the narrowness of face and frame, had felt it when they'd touched him. It was expected of those in mourning . . . and as terrible as Shar had felt, he hadn't needed drugs, hadn't stopped eating or sleeping, determined to act as a proper Starfleet science officer. Fresh pain unfurled inside of him.

"You see? *Zhadi* was right," Dizhei said, nodding toward the Andorian councillor, talking to Anichent. "Even after what's happened, even *now*."

She stared again at Shar, her gaze pleading, her fists clenched at her sides. "There were four of us, and now there are three. Do you care that we wait on your decision? That the waiting drove Thriss to her death? What is there to decide, if you love us as you say?"

He deserved her anger, deserved everything she was saying and more, but he couldn't stop himself any longer, he had to say something in his defense. "We're dying, my *sh'za*. Our people's solution prolongs the inevitable, you know it as well as I. The pressure on our young to bond and mate, to keep our entire race alive, is too much—"

"*You've* resisted it," Dizhei interrupted.

Shar ignored her, desperate to make her see, hoping that somehow this time she *would* see. He'd argued it so many times, and so many times they had tried to understand. "—and Thriss succumbed to that pressure, and still, *still,* we'll be extinguished if we don't change, if we don't find a better way. You know our only chance is to seek new answers, you *know* it—and I may have found something."

Shar turned to Anichent, eager for understanding, for a look of hope in his beloved's anguished, drugged gaze. "In my travels, I encountered a people called the Yrythny. Their eggs hold a genetic key to creating life, after any pattern that is introduced into the sequence—I can show you, I was given samples and I think there's a real chance that we can apply the technology to our own biology, that we can overcome the chromosomal flaws that are killing us all . . ."

At the look on Anichent's face, Shar trailed off. He saw such great sadness there, such pain . . . and understanding, the understanding he'd so desperately wanted.

"That's wonderful," Anichent said, his words slurring lightly. "I'm proud of you, Shar."

He was, too, Shar could see it . . . but he could also see

that it didn't lessen his anguish, not at all. Thriss was gone, she was gone and no matter what possibilities he'd found in the Yrythny sample, she would not be a part of their lives anymore.

Shar felt a sudden, nearly uncontrollable rage, for and at himself, at Thriss, at his *zhavey,* at any and all who existed apart from him . . . and let it go, exhaling a deep hiss, his muscles, antennae, his *mind* gritting against the desire to lash out. His bondmates and *zhavey* waited as he hissed again, forcing control over his biology, forcing himself not to rip and tear and grind.

His *zhavey* held her silence until he was past the worst of it, then spoke, saying what had to be said, each word like the end of all hope.

"I've spoken to the *Eveste* Elders," she said calmly. "And they've found three *zhen* candidates who appear to be suitable . . . and two *chan* who would be willing to step in. All have successfully mated within their own bonds at least once but are now free, and still in viable range."

Shar was *chan.* The pure shock of what she was suggesting hit him like ice, like dying. He turned to look at her, betrayed, his emotions rising once more—but the look on her face stilled him. There was no malice, no reproach there. She was doing what she could to salvage the lives of his bondmates, what she saw as her responsibility.

"Are you so surprised," she half asked him, her voice soft. "You resist the ritual. Your career obligations keep you away from home, from your duty and family; you choose to honor these obligations over your obligations to your mates and to your people. Someone will have to take Thriss's place, and though I know the prospect of mating with another stranger is not ideal, it is better than no mating at all . . . and you push so hard, Thirishar, you've made it so very clear that you will continue to resist . . . would you have your mates suffer the consequences?"

She met his gaze evenly. If she felt guilt over her proposal, over telling her *chei* that he was unnecessary, Shar couldn't see it.

"Perhaps I've failed to teach you properly," she said, standing, her tone defeated. "Or perhaps I've simply failed. Whatever the reason, I won't force your decision. I've done what I can. It is for the three of you to decide."

Without another word, she turned and walked out.

Shar turned and looked at his mates, at the dear faces of those he'd known since childhood, his betrothed since before he was old enough to understand what that meant—Anichent, his first love, his friend and intellectual companion for as long as he could remember; Dizhei, the soul of their union, the bright and responsible peacemaker who had taken care of them all—and they both looked away. They had already been offered freedom from his indecision, it seemed . . . and were, perhaps, contemplating it. Mating with two strangers might not be so much worse for them than mating with one . . . might, in fact, be better for them—to have partners who truly wanted to be there, who believed in the sanctity of procreation.

And can I blame them? How could he dare?

Dizhei picked up the folded mourning shroud and handed it to him silently, before turning and walking into his bedchamber. Anichent lingered a few seconds longer.

"Shar," he said gently, reaching out to take his hand again. "You could . . . you could come home with us, now. We love you. We could still make it work."

Shar's fingers were numb, unable to detect his beloved's hand in his. Go home, now. Find a replacement for Thriss, the irreplaceable, and watch the lovers he'd broken try to mend themselves. Or stay, and know that he was no longer a part of anything, that his lifelong family had moved on to fulfill their separate destinies . . . that there would be no child with his features or traits, ever, no proof that their love had ever existed.

He let go of Anichent's hand, unable to know anything beyond what was required of him now. Thriss, he was to see Thriss once more. He donned his robe and followed Dizhei into the darkness of his room, Anichent shuffling along behind.

Quark knew he complained about it often enough, but this time it was true; business was bad. In the course of a week, he'd gone from successful caterer and proprietor of Quark's Bar, Grill, Gaming House, and Holosuite Arcade (a wholly owned subsidiary of Quark Enterprises, Inc.) to barely scraping by, practically a charity case, and no one seemed to care. Morn certainly didn't. The bloated windbag had picked the perfect time to develop a contagious rash, and hadn't been in for two days; not only was there the loss of revenue to think about, Morn was one of the few patrons willing to listen to the woes of a man on the edge of destitution . . . probably as penance for his own near constant complaining. Without even his homely face to talk at, Quark was feeling very much alone.

My last days as the owner of Quark's, he thought wearily, looking out at the empty sea of tables from behind the bar. There were a few customers—a handful of *kanar*-drinking Cardassians, a couple of Starfleet enlisted men bravely shoveling through the night's special. Octavian Surprise, Quark called it, because Miscellaneous Leftover Stew just didn't sound as good. It was a depressing scene, to say the least, and it suited his mood perfectly.

That the Federation was about to drive him out of business was bad enough, those idiots with their lack of economy. Had he despaired? No. He had been prepared to go out with a profitable bang, serving up a celebration feast to the crowds of men and women watching as Shakaar signed Bajor into eternal servitude. Then it was off to the stars with Ro at his side, their ship's hold full of latinum from his mostly legal business dealings. The food had been prepped, the glasses polished, the servers standing by . . . and then death, chaos, and a kitchen full of unsalvageable party platters. Since then, Ro wouldn't return his messages, either, too involved with her job—the job she was leaving, no less—to bother spending time with the man she'd agreed to go away with. Well, tentatively agreed. She hadn't *disagreed.* And, yet again, had he despaired? No, he'd tried to look at the bright side, to make what he could of a bad situation. Shakaar's untimely death was Quark's reprieve, at least a temporary one—no Federation takeover, no loss of profits—but now everyone was either too preoccupied to drink or too scared to enjoy a night out. Even after the assassin was caught, too; everyone seemed to think there was some kind of conspiracy going on . . . and conspiracy equaled paranoia, which equaled an unwillingness to take risks—like, say, on a harmless game of dabo. Sure, people were still eating, but profits did not grow by food alone . . . and watching high-strung worker types come in and bolt down a quick meal before clearing out again was disheartening, a bleak vision of the DS9 to come. Even the holosuites weren't being booked.

The Federation, he thought, shaking his head. No-fun, do-gooding, play-by-the-rules self-righteously *dull.* For the first time in what seemed like years, there were no dabo tables running, no need for Treir or pretty boy Hetik to come in, and Quark had sent M'Pella home early; as nice as the scenery got when she was around in her dabo number, it wasn't worth paying to look at. Usually he had between four and six servers on, but with as dead as it had been, only Grimp and Frool were working, and neither had much work to do; he had them back in the kitchen, mucking out the clogged disposal—there was no way he was going to pay for repairs with the end of Quark's so close—and every few minutes he would stomp loudly behind the bar, making noise as if he were going to go into the kitchen, just in case they were leaning instead of cleaning. It gave him something to do, at least, besides dwell on his own lonely, miserable, practically profitless existence. . . .

Maybe not lonely, he thought, a slow smile spreading across his face as Ro Laren walked in. Stalked in, really, as she was wont to do, the vaguest hints of both a sneer and a frown on that lovely countenance, an expression that just screamed "Don't bother me." Much as he appreciated her gleaming, sarcastic smile, there was nothing as splendidly misanthropic as the look of Ro Laren at rest.

She spotted him and walked to the bar, Quark setting aside his inspired thoughts for a blank face as she approached. He'd seen her twice in the last week, and both times had been strictly business, trouble in the bar or on the Promenade, not even a personal aside. She'd been avoiding him, or at least ignoring him, but he still had his pride . . . that, and a deep, abiding fear of commitment. Ro Laren was an incredible woman, but then, he wasn't exactly diced *sleark* gut . . . and romance aside, was he actually prepared to go into business with her? The thought made him giddy and vaguely ill, in no particular order. The situation was complicated.

"Lieutenant," he said airily, as she swung one long, limber leg over a barstool and sat in front of him. "How nice of you to drop by. I mean, that you could be bothered to stop in at all. Truly an honor."

Ro smiled, that very same sarcastic twist that always melted his insides. "Come on, Quark. You know I've been busy."

"Busy slaving away at a job you're about to quit," Quark scoffed. "That makes a lot of sense. And excuse me, but didn't you already catch the assassin, that charming Mr. Gard?" Heavy on the sarcasm; Ro had obviously found Gard somewhat attractive, before he'd turned slavering hit man.

Ro shrugged, lowering her voice slightly. "I already told you. There's evidence of a conspiracy to keep Bajor out of the Federation. Gard is only one of them. We have to find out who else is involved, and who's next on their list."

"Don't hurry on my account," Quark said, scowling. "I still have to pack. Though you *could* let people know that the bar is safe. Until Bajor gets into the Federation, this is still an operational business . . . contrary to how it looks."

He nodded toward the group of Cardassians, quietly drinking. "Wouldn't hurt to get rid of them, either."

"They're who volunteered," Ro said. "You know Starfleet is still spread too thin to drop everything and come running."

Quark snorted. "Yeah, but the *Cardassians*?" He opened his eyes wide and tried to look stupid. "Hey, Bajor's First Minister has been assassinated? Let's invite Bajor's former oppressors to help out! That'll give the citizens a sense of security, don'tcha think?"

He shook his head, dropping back to a scowl. "Just

because they finally gave the Orbs back doesn't make them anyone's best friend."

"I know, I know," Ro said, sighing. "Wasn't my decision." She leaned in, her lanky upper body resting across the bar. "What are people saying about all this, anyway? Anything I should know about?"

It was Quark's turn to shrug. "What you'd expect; paranoia and grudge theories. The Cardassians are responsible, they brought back the Orbs as a distraction . . . ah, Hiziki Gard is a spy for the Dominion, they want to start another war . . . Asarem Wadeen is actually on the verge of a psychotic breakdown, the Federation is exploiting her . . . Starfleet is just putting on a big show to cover up their own bumbling incompetence for letting Shakaar—"

At the sudden tightening of her fine mouth, Quark cut himself off. Ro had organized station security for the induction ceremony. Hiziki Gard had been one of the Trill ambassador's people, she couldn't have known that he was an assassin . . . but she was a name and a face that could be blamed, and there were plenty willing to do so.

"Sorry," he said, and actually was.

"I know." She offered another half smile, though she dropped her gaze to the bar's polished surface. "Maybe that's why I've been working so hard. Trying to make up for not stopping it. Not that there's anything I can do . . . I don't know. I'll just be glad when this is all over."

It was as emotional as Ro got, at least around him, and it was obviously a struggle for her. It made him feel kind of . . . well, good. He saw that her hand was on the bar, and briefly considered touching it—but she sat back, the opportunity gone before he'd made up his mind. He wanted to say something, to ask her about leaving the station with him, but suddenly he wasn't so sure he wanted to hear the answer. They'd only talked about it once, and she *had* been drinking at the time, they both had. . . .

Opportunity plus instinct equals profit, the Ninth Rule. He'd already passed up the chance to touch her, and profit didn't always mean latinum. Just usually.

"Laren, when this is all over . . ." he started, hesitated, then took the plunge. "Are you still interested in the two of us, ah, working together? Investing together, I mean? In business, and, ah, traveling, and all that?"

"I've been thinking about that," she said, meeting his gaze again, and Quark felt a twitter in the general vicinity of his heart. "And I don't know, Quark. I'm still interested, don't get me wrong, but we're . . . it seems like a big commitment, don't you think?"

Quark wasn't sure if he should be insulted or relieved, feeling an odd mixture of both. They'd only been on a few dates, after all. And except for holding hands once or twice, they hadn't explored any real romantic aspects of their companionable relationship. What did she want? What did *he* want?

"We should both keep thinking about it," she continued, still staring into his eyes, her own sharp and true. "Or at least, I should . . . and I hope you will. Right now, though, there's too much going on for me to give your proposal the time it deserves."

"I didn't propose," Quark said hastily.

Ro grinned. "The proposed transaction," she said. "Is that all right with you?"

Relief won out, killing the instinct to offer up a glib response. "I . . . Yes, that's all right with me."

"Good." She sat back slightly, effectively ending the personal conversation. She glanced around the near empty bar, then down at the padds she was carrying. "So, any of those rumors going around seem reasonable to you?"

She needed work on her subtlety. "What are you looking for, exactly?" he asked.

"Nothing," she said. "Really. I'm just trying to keep an eye on things. Hoping to avoid trouble, you know."

Quark's eyes narrowed. There was something more to it than that, but . . .

"Has Nog contacted you yet?" Ro asked.

Quark blinked. "Was he supposed to?"

Ro arched one exquisite eyebrow. "The *Defiant* got in about an hour ago."

Quark was shocked, and more than slightly embarrassed. On DS9, he was the man in the know; he'd built his reputation on it. He had contacts, he had a line into ops and sensors at all the docking portals; how had he missed this? Maybe the communications block was actually as solid as the Federation was purporting . . . which suggested a much more serious situation than they were letting on. Even during the war, he'd never had difficulty getting through one of their standard blocks before.

"The, ah, debriefing just broke up, though," Ro added quickly, apparently mistaking his shame for hurt, that Nog hadn't come by yet. As sharp as she was, he wasn't an open book . . . and he still had a few resources she hadn't managed to shut down, though at the moment the thought made his head hurt; he was still paying off the portal sensors, which were evidently useless.

"Right," Quark said, forcing a grin. "That's fine, he's probably . . . right over there."

His wayward nephew had just stepped inside, and had stopped to talk to some passing stranger in the corridor, a short, gray girl with long white hair. The girl looked at

Quark with no expression, said something; Quark strained to catch it, but only heard the words "seems quiet." Nog laughed and shrugged, then walked on, heading toward Quark and Ro with a gleaming grin. The girl looked into the bar for a few seconds, then turned and wandered off down the Promenade, apparently uninterested in patronizing such an unpopular establishment.

"Uncle!" Nog said happily, nodding at Ro as he sat at the bar. "How have you been?"

"Terrible, as if you couldn't tell," Quark said, motioning at the empty tables. "Thanks to your Federation and their grand plans to turn me out. Who was that girl, anyway? What were you laughing about? Did you bring me anything?"

"It's nice to see you, too, Uncle," Nog said, still grinning, a vaguely forced affair. Quark saw with some disdain that he'd neglected his tooth filing since he'd been gone, the tips beginning to blunt.

"I'll leave you two to catch up," Ro said, standing.

"You don't have to," Quark said, putting on his practiced winning smile. "You just got here. I'll—I'll buy you a drink. Anything you like."

Nog gasped audibly, but Ro didn't seem to catch it.

"I'd like to, but I've got about a thousand things to do before I can call it a night," she said. "I don't expect I'll have much free time coming up, but I'll try to stop in for lunch or dinner, soon . . . and I'm glad we talked."

She smiled at Nog. "Welcome back, by the way," she said, and with a final nod at both of them, she stalked out. Quark gazed dreamily after her, thinking that he was also glad. They hadn't resolved anything, but knowing that she was as hesitant as he was to firm up plans made him feel much better, about everything. *That, and she said she'd been thinking about it . . . maybe while she was showering . . .*

He was a romantic, to be sure, but his lobes weren't *dead.*

"I had no idea it had gotten so serious," Nog breathed, staring at Quark. "Even Grilka had to pay for that cask of bloodwine."

Quark sighed, remembering his last great affair. "You know how much a Klingon can drink. I did give her a discount, though. . . ."

He shook himself, turning his attention to his nephew, his thoughts about Ro Laren and business and the Federation moving from the forefront of his mind . . . except for that nagging, shameful detail, that he hadn't known the *Defiant* was back. Contacts ran dry, but the failure of his docking information system, *and* his hardwire line to ops . . . they were top-of-the-line. Both had been working fine last week, and could only be bypassed by a full channel switch, a complete reprogram, something the station had never done before. Exactly how serious was this so-called conspiracy? And why didn't he know more about it?

Nog ordered food and Quark started questioning him about possible business ventures in the Gamma Quadrant, setting aside the concern until he had a chance to review the data privately. Maybe there was something big going on, something the Federation was keeping under wraps . . . and if there was, a man with good business sense and a big set of lobes would be just the man to find and exploit the opportunity there, one way or another.

He grinned at Nog while the boy ate, feeling hope again.

5

Jake and Wex had gone on to quarters of their own, which was just as well; Opaka Sulan was still absorbing what they'd heard along their walk to the living area of the station, supplied by a local vedek, a man named Capril, who'd recognized her as they'd passed his shrine. Capril had been only too eager to share the events of recent days . . . and, no doubt, from the excited shine in his fervent gaze, to spread the word of her own return. Much as she'd wished for time alone to readjust to Bajor, it seemed that events and attitudes weren't going to allow for it.

The Ohalu prophecies. The return of the Tears, thank the Prophets. The first minister, murdered. . . .

Opaka sat on the edge of an overstuffed chair provided with her rather opulent living area, thinking of how different Bajor was now, how different it was sure to become in the days ahead. Any one of the three events described by Capril would have far-reaching effects on the Bajoran people; two of them, at least, were positive changes to Opaka's view—obviously, the return of the Orbs, and the discovery of the Ohalu book . . . although the vedek hadn't been nearly so excited about the book. It seemed that the ancient tome of prophecies had caused something of a rift in the spiritual unity of the people. Capril had been quite adamant about the horror of it all, that this heretical text was turning the once faithful away from the Light of the Prophets.

Jake's prophecy, given to him at B'hala. The passage that had led the Emissary's son to her had been from this Ohalu book, she was certain of it. From what she'd been able to glean from Jake and now Capril, the Ohalu prophecies were all turning out to be true . . . and they didn't extol the Prophets as gods, but rather as teachers of alien origin. That this has caused a rift was understandable.

Before she'd left Bajor, she, too, would have disdained such a book as heresy . . . and she had little doubt that the vast majority of the Bajoran people did so now, clinging to their faith in the Prophets, afraid to expand their boundaries. But . . . in her eight years away, far from the gentle, daily routines of self-referential worship and meditation, what had she learned, if not that truth was a matter of perspective? Why couldn't the Prophets be gods *and* aliens? The Eav'oq, the race of Gamma Quadrant beings that she and Jake had been led to discover, called the Prophets "Siblings," seeing Them much as Ohalu apparently had—beings to learn from, not just to worship. Opaka knew the love of the Prophets, she had felt Their Touch, but that didn't necessarily mean that there was only one way to understand Them.

Strange times ahead, she was sure. The Cardassians had returned the sacred Orbs, inspired by a vedek she hadn't known before, one Yevir Linjarin. In spite of his lavish praise for Yevir, Capril had flushed when she'd asked him about this new vedek's history . . . and had then stumbled over her title, stuttering out the word "kai" as though it were poison. Opaka had smiled, and explained that she was only Opaka Sulan now, but Capril had not been eased . . . which suggested to her that Yevir Linjarin was favored to be the next kai. The title meant nothing to her personally anymore, and though it was not a position one retired from—a new kai was elected only when the old had passed to the Temple—she had no desire to interrupt the current evolution of Bajor's spiritual leadership. If the people wanted Yevir, they should have him.

Except . . . does he also fear the Ohalu text? She hoped not, hoped that a man who could bring the sacred Tears of the Prophets home, thus forming a union of peaceful intent between Bajor and Cardassia . . . Such a man would surely be open to new ideas, to change. Wouldn't he?

Opaka sighed, feeling overwhelmed by the circles within circles, unclear on what her role was to be, if any. The Prophets had brought her back for a reason, and she was willing to accept any responsibility that They had planned for her . . . but she was only mortal, and not such a young mortal, either. That Shakaar Edon had been killed, only moments after the Orbs were presented by Yevir, only months after this Ohalu book was discovered—it was difficult to accept so much so quickly. At least when Jake had helped her catch up on the years she'd been away, she'd had some time to think it over, to let the information become thought, to become the beginnings of memory. . . .

There was a signal at the door. Opaka stood, stretching her back as she walked to answer it, feeling every one of her years. It would be Kira Nerys, of course; still more information to digest, though she'd been expecting the visit. Even with all the trappings of chaos that had greeted the *Defiant*'s arrival, Opaka had seen and sensed the turmoil of the Bajoran woman's *pagh* . . . and the missing earring could not be overlooked.

The door slid open at Opaka's touch, and there she stood, smiling and anxious and obviously very tired. Opaka welcomed the colonel in, remembering Major Kira, the brash young resistance fighter who had struggled to contain her own violence once the fighting had stopped. Opaka hadn't known the major well, but had known so many like her . . . clinging to faith with the rabid intensity of the brutalized, growing to adulthood in an atmosphere of deprivation and destruction. Once the Occupation was over, the roots of struggle roughly cut away, these children had faced a loss of identity, had been left to find themselves in a new context, many of them so damaged by the old that they could barely see, let alone seek.

But not this woman, Opaka thought, smiling as the colonel sat down on the couch, the look of exhaustion she wore unable to disguise the strength of purpose that radiated from her fine features, from her straight shoulders and lifted chin. Opaka took the chair once more, facing Nerys, both women still smiling.

"You look well, Colonel. Tired, but well."

"Thank you, Kai."

"Call me Sulan," Opaka said gently. "If I may call you Nerys?"

The colonel's smile became easier, less forced. "Of course. I'm sorry it took so long for me to get here. I had to get some things organized . . . and I stopped by to see Jake Sisko. We called his stepmother together."

"I imagine she was very happy to hear from him," Opaka said.

"She was. It seems that Jake's grandfather is on his way to visit, too. Kind of a family reunion, for the birth." Nerys trailed off, her weariness showing, before focusing on Opaka again.

"It's so . . . I'm so happy to see you, Sulan. Bajor will be rallied by your homecoming, and so soon after . . . but so much has happened since you've been away, I'm not sure where to start."

"Jake was kind enough to fill me in on most of it, on our journey," Opaka said, trying to keep her tone light. As hard as it was to know some of the things Bajor had experienced, living through them must have taken great fortitude; she didn't want to open any recent wounds. "I know about B'hala, and the Reckoning . . . about Winn's election, and Bareil, and the Emissary's path, about Dukat and the war so recently waged. Our world has had a time of it, wouldn't you say?"

Nerys nodded, unsmiling. "There's more, Kai . . . Sulan. In the past few months, there have been developments . . ."

She frowned, searching, and Opaka cut in.

"I was approached by a vedek on my way here, Vedek Capril," Opaka said. "He told me about the return of the Orbs, and the first minister's death. I'm very sorry to hear about Shakaar. He walks with the Prophets, I'm sure."

Nerys nodded again, but didn't look at her. "I'm certain he does."

"Capril talked about a book, too, one that was found at B'hala," Opaka continued, curious at the subtle expressions that flickered across the colonel's face at the mention of it. "Thousands of years old, written by a man called Ohalu. Capril seems to believe that this book is dangerous."

Nerys met her gaze again—and was it guilt Opaka saw there? "It has caused problems," she said slowly. "There's a small but growing community of men and women who believe that this book offers a choice . . . a spirituality very different from that which the Vedek Assembly promotes."

Perhaps this explained the absence of her earring. Opaka wouldn't have thought it of Kira Nerys, a girl she'd known as deeply faithful, but as she'd said herself, things had been changing; perhaps she'd turned to this new way.

"What do you think, Nerys?" Opaka asked, no judgment in her tone or in her heart. "Do you think this book is heresy?"

The colonel gazed back at her a moment, then seemed to slump within herself, her shoulders sagging, her entire demeanor changing. It was like watching a dam break. "I . . . I don't know, Kai. I thought it was, at first . . . then the Assembly didn't want anyone to read it, they tried to have it destroyed, and I—I gave it to the people. It's my fault, I put it on the comnet because I thought—I really believed that it was no threat, that our faith was stronger, and I was so furious with Yevir, with what the Assembly had done and was trying to do. . . ."

Her voice cracked with fatigue and emotion, trembling with tears. "I was Attainted for it. I'm unwelcome in the public shrines, forbidden to share the faith, and now everything is so wrong, there's so much going wrong and I feel so alone. . . ."

Opaka went to her as she began to weep, understanding that there was nothing more that needed to be said, not now. Nerys was exhausted to the point of a breakdown, her tears the lost, hopeless tears of a small child, and Opaka did what she would have done for any crying child. She held her, rocked her, soothed her with meaningless words of comfort until Nerys's hitched breathing became deep and regular, the young woman falling into a heavy slumber.

After a time, Opaka stood and went to find a blanket,

pleased that she had given in to sleep, the only real cure for what was wrong . . . and glad, too, that she had cried. It gave Opaka real hope, that someone like Kira Nerys had traveled so far from her childhood of anger and defense, had become strong enough inside to admit despair. People who never cried were the weakest of all.

She found extra blankets on a shelf in the bedroom. After covering the colonel, her tear-streaked face at rest, Opaka sat and watched her for a time, thinking.

Attainted, by the Assembly, by this Vedek Yevir. For exposing Bajor to a piece of its own history . . . a religious text that defied the Assembly's beliefs. What kind of place had Bajor become, to be led by such people? And how would these leaders accept the news of the Eav'oq, the peaceful, beautiful beings on the other side of the Temple that also benefited from the love of the Prophets, but called them by a different name?

Bajor was on the brink of great change, there was no question. The question was whether or not the people were ready to go forward, if they were strong enough in spirit and faith to embrace something different from what they'd known.

"You are, child," Opaka whispered, and Nerys slept on, unaware, perhaps, that she represented what Bajor could be . . . at least to one old woman, who was returning to a home she knew but did not know, not anymore. All she could do—all anyone could do—was hope.

Ezri watched the Promenade, watched the small groups of morning people as they walked by the security office, their faces drawn and too pale. There was an air of anxiety that she could feel, that radiated from each man and woman who passed, mostly Bajoran—a sense that something vast and unpleasant was ahead, something that would leave no one untouched.

Most of them don't even know about the parasites. Is it the Federation, is that what they fear? Ezri wondered, leaning against a pillar outside the office. Only weeks after finally having their petition for UFP membership accepted, Bajor was dealing with the loss of their first minister and a lockdown of the severest order, at least partly patrolled by armed Cardassians. If she were a citizen of Bajor, she'd certainly be wondering if this was what they had to look forward to, as Federation members. It made her question whether or not Starfleet had the right idea, not telling the people the truth about the threat. The security reasons were sound, even necessary, but the trust issues being raised weren't exactly conducive to the bonding process.

Case in point. A pair of Cardassian soldiers stood near the entrance to Quark's, talking quietly, and the Bajorans that passed by either glared at them or looked away; there didn't seem to be a middle ground. Containment was necessary, but it was going to cost.

After a restless night mostly alone in Julian's bed—he'd stayed at the lab until very late—she'd arrived at the security office a few minutes early for her meeting with Cyl. A quick glance inside told her that Ro Laren was busy, surrounded by a number of padds, a frown deeply embedded across her brow. Not wanting to disturb her, Ezri had decided to wait outside. There wasn't enough time for a real distraction from the meeting with Gard, to hit Quark's for a warm drink or visit Ziyal's art exhibit in Garak's old shop—an exhibit that was plainly deserted—but she was disturbed enough by the Promenade's atmosphere that she was on the verge of bothering Ro, after all . . .

Taulin Cyl stepped off the nearest lift and walked toward her, wearing a reserved smile. Ezri reflexively matched it as they exchanged pleasantries, still not sure how to treat the symbiont of one of Dax's children. They lingered outside the security office, Ezri sensing his reluctance to get to business, feeling it herself. It seemed like they had a lot to talk about . . . so why was nothing coming to mind?

"You were trained as a psychologist?" Cyl asked, breaching the topic before she could think of anything. "And before that, you were in sciences, I gather. How many hosts since Audrid?"

"Five. Jadzia Dax was the science officer here, she was before me. I was a counselor, but since the end of the war, I've found myself drawn to command." She straightened her red collar, smiling. "Let's see . . . before Jadzia there was Curzon, he was a diplomat, I suppose you'd say—"

Cyl nodded, his expression wry. "I know about Curzon."

Ezri decided not to ask. A lot of people knew about Curzon, and a lot of what they knew wasn't exactly flattering. "There was a, ah, musician, briefly, before him . . . and a test pilot just after Audrid, Torias. What about you?"

"Three, since Neema," Cyl said. "A professor—forensic science, actually—and a xenobiologist. I'm a military advisor, now. Career. On a leave of absence, technically."

Ezri nodded, not sure how to ask what she wanted to ask, finally deciding to blurt it out and live with the consequences.

"Was Neema . . . did she do well?"

Cyl hesitated, then nodded slowly. "She lived to be very old, and very wise. She had two children late in life, both girls, and a husband who loved her—he also taught sciences at the Ganses University. Neither of their daughters joined, but she was very proud of them; Kiley, she was the oldest, became a professional dancer, part of the Balinsta troupe. And Toshin ran her own business, a consulting firm. Very successful, too."

Ezri was fascinated, hearing of grandchildren she'd never met . . . and relieved, that even after such turmoil between Audrid and her daughter, Neema had gone on to have children of her own.

"Neema . . . she missed Audrid for the rest of her years," Cyl said. "She had great respect for her mother."

The last was delivered almost shyly, a side to the aging general that Ezri wouldn't have expected. She smiled, pleased with his bare honesty, reminded once again of Neema.

"She also spent a lot of time trying to research the parasite that Audrid told her about," he added, lowering his voice slightly. "As did Reck, and Elista, Cyl's hosts since Neema . . . and me. We've never stopped looking."

Ezri nodded, feeling some guilt that Cyl had carried on with the search. She'd let it go, Dax moving on to Torias and then to other things. "Did you find anything?"

"Yes and no," Cyl said. "We found rumors, as I said last night—that there was some real connection between the parasites and the symbionts, a very long time ago. There aren't any government records, though, and none of my current contacts have been able to find a trace of shared history."

"Current contacts?" Ezri was surprised, but only for a few seconds. From Cyl's very presence, it seemed inevitable that there would be a fairly extensive network . . . and something he'd said a moment ago sunk in, about a leave of absence. Did the government even know he was here? "How many people know about this?"

"Not many, but enough to keep watch," Cyl answered, matter-of-factly. "You asked yesterday, if I knew this was coming . . . again, the answer is yes and no. I never doubted that we'd hear about the parasites again, even before their infiltration of Starfleet. There was already a watch group in place, though we were lucky to catch it; the attempt wasn't common knowledge, and Trill wasn't the obvious target. Since then, however, the watch has kept a constant vigil, keeping an eye on military movement in the quadrant, and monitoring incoming inquiries and outgoing files, anything pertaining to Trill security and defense. . . . There are a number of red flags we look out for, but we've never really gotten a hit—until just over five months ago, when someone on Shakaar Edon's ship started sending us the wrong kinds of questions. Shakaar was traveling through Federation territories at the time, lobbying for Bajor's admittance into the UFP . . . though we still haven't been able to pin down where he was prior to his first contact with Trill officials. It *was* Shakaar asking, though. One of our people insisted that he give his credentials before we sent him anything."

"Does the TSC know about you?" Ezri asked.

"Not officially."

"Then how did you manage to intercept Shakaar's queries? And why haven't you gone public?"

"I said not *officially,*" Cyl said. "We have a few low-level people inside . . . but as you may remember, the TSC wasn't all that excited about Audrid's discovery of the parasite, and the government backed them. Ambassador Gandres is a good example—I've been trying to talk him into going before the commission, demanding a united action, but he's terrified, doesn't want anything to do with any of this. He has his hopes pinned on the Federation making it all go away, and I have little doubt that the rest of our government is firmly behind him. As I said yesterday, I only told him what he needs to know . . . and he's fine with that."

"And the governing council? The TSC?"

"Those at the very top know about what's happening," Cyl said. "That's why I'm here."

Unofficially. Ezri felt a trace of disdain for the leaders of her homeworld, and tried to let it go. She hadn't behaved much better, as Audrid or since.

They're scared, that's all. Just as she had been, and still was. The very concept of being taken over by some malevolent creature . . . it was something that went beyond mortal terror, a fear that was primal and deep-seated, perhaps particular to a joined species . . . doomed to feel what the creature wanted you to feel, the host completely lost, forced to bond with the parasitic mind, its life memories torn away . . .

Cyl glanced into the security office, then back at her. "We should talk to Gard. He'll be able to tell you more about Shakaar."

Ezri frowned, feeling a sudden knot in her belly. "I thought—I thought he hasn't been talking, since his capture."

Cyl gazed at her evenly, his face a blank. "Gard is part of our organization. I thought you would have gathered that by now."

"I—no, I didn't know," Ezri stammered, not sure if he was telling her what it sounded like he was telling her. She might have suspected it, but that meant . . .

"Are you—did you send him to kill Shakaar?" she asked.

"No," Cyl said immediately, and though his tone was

firm and even, he dropped her gaze for a beat. "We needed Shakaar to be monitored, by someone who knew what to look for. Gard had the security credentials to escort Ambassador Gandres to Deep Space 9 for the signing, he volunteered for the job . . . and once he'd ascertained that the First Minister was infected—and well past the possibility of salvation—he made the decision himself."

"But you support that decision," Ezri said, not sure how to feel, what to do with the information.

"Don't you?" Cyl asked. "The letter that Audrid wrote to Neema . . . You know what they're capable of."

Ezri nodded absently. She knew. But assassination, hiding in an underground network, operating outside the government's line of sight . . . it just wasn't what the good guys *did.*

But the good guys were supposed to be the TSC, the council, people like Seljin Gandres—and they've done nothing. They destroyed evidence, they turn a blind eye to the issue, they avoid action. How else can the watchers function, with a government that doesn't want to participate?

But . . . if they don't want to help . . .

"What will happen to Gard?" she asked quietly.

Cyl's face seemed to harden slightly. "I've asked Gandres to lobby for his release, for remand back to Trill, but he refuses. The Council is behind him, they've already promised full cooperation with the 'investigation' into Shakaar's death, and that includes leaving Gard in Bajoran custody. President Maz agrees."

Gard was stuck with his assassin title, at least until the truth about the parasites came out . . . and afterward? There might be some leniency, considering the circumstances, but he would be prosecuted. He'd worked for an unrecognized and possibly illegal agency on Trill, he'd plotted and carried out the murder of another planet's leader, he'd planned to escape. Even knowing that Shakaar was infected, the Federation would have to do something, to show Bajor that they didn't allow such reckless disregard for the lives of its citizens.

So Gard is left taking the fall, even though this is something our people should have been prepared to handle without a shadow group resorting to such tactics. Gard must have known what could happen to him, if he were caught . . . and she wondered what kind of man he really was, to accept such a risk.

"Ready to speak with him?" Cyl asked.

Ezri nodded, wishing she felt as on top of things as she needed to be, feeling absolutely uncertain about everything.

Hiziki Gard was resting, lying on his back and staring up at the blank, featureless ceiling of his cell. It was cold, which he actually didn't mind—for a Trill, he'd always been prone to overheating—and he was bored, which he minded very much. Taulin Cyl had filled him in on the station's situation when he'd arrived from Trill, and updated him once . . . but past that, he'd had no visitors except Akaar, the aging Starfleet admiral, who'd attempted to intimidate him into revealing information. Ro Laren had tried to engage him on a few occasions since his capture, usually when she brought him meals, but he couldn't talk to her, not about what she wanted to know. He shouldn't have talked to Akaar, either, but at least the admiral had known about the parasites, from the comet incident . . . and there had been a Federation ship on its way to Trill at the time Akaar had come to him, a parasite in control.

Gard sighed. Nothing to do, nothing to see. The immediate disaster had been averted, the *Gryphon* stopped in time, and since he hadn't been authorized to talk, he'd kept his mouth shut since. Cyl was still trying to maneuver behind the scenes, to see how much Trill could help without becoming a focus for the investigation, and Gard didn't want to make things harder for him.

Goes with the territory, he thought idly, glancing at the seemingly open space at the front of his cell. He was a Gard, after all, and no Gard had ever bothered overmuch with self-interest, not when it came to doing what was right. The problem was, there was still a problem . . . and instead of making it home to plot the next course of action with his fellow watchers, he'd been caught. He'd been restless at first, and frustrated that there was nothing he could contribute to stop the rapidly unfolding crisis—but now he was just bored. No matter how bad things were, he wasn't going anywhere, he had nothing to say and no one to say it to. Being frustrated was a waste of energy.

The door to the outer security office opened. In walked Taulin Cyl and a short, attractive female Trill, slightly younger than Hiziki. Ro escorted them in, but after a few low words with the woman, she left them alone.

Gard stood, straightening his rumpled jacket, nodding politely at his visitors as they pulled chairs to the front of his cell. Once they were seated, he also sat, studying the woman. She was joined, and openly curious about him, studying him in turn. He knew her instantly. He'd kept tabs.

"I remember you," Ezri Dax said without preamble.

Gard nodded. A few years back, he'd heard that Dax's memories of Joran had resurfaced, memories that had been medically suppressed almost a century before. The mistaken matching of Joran Belar to the Dax symbiont had created a serial murderer, whom Gard had been sent to hunt down.

"You remember Verjyl Gard," Hiziki said. "My symbiont has a very long history of . . ." How to describe what he did? ". . . ah, seeking out criminal elements within Trill society."

"And without, so it seems," Dax said.

Cyl finally spoke up. "Gard has never done anything else. I'm surprised Audrid didn't know about him; the TSC called Gard in whenever there was evidence of a bad joining."

Bad. That's an understatement. Though it didn't happen often, a "bad" joining meant anything from suicide to serial murder. Throughout all of Gard's lifetimes, its hosts' specific training had always been to seek out these extremely rare joined killers. Cyl had approached a retired Verjyl Gard shortly before Gard had gone on to Hiziki, nearly twenty years ago . . . and both hosts had found merit in the loose organization of watchers, particularly considering the government's blatant denial of its necessity. In a way, the parasites represented the ultimate in joined killers.

Dax nodded. "There weren't any mismatches in my time on the board, though."

Gard said nothing. The TSC kept secrets from itself, too, but he saw no reason to disillusion her.

"How much do you know?" Gard asked, turning to the more immediate situation.

"All of it, I think," Dax said, and Cyl nodded. "You've been watching for the parasites, they finally showed up, and you came here to deal with it . . . but why kill Shakaar? Why not just turn him over to security, let the Federation in on it?"

"It's better that the reason for his assassination remains

unclear," Gard said. "The night before the signing ceremony, he sent seven separate coded messages to Bajor, from his private quarters here on the station. I think the parasites have taken root down there, and I also think they're organized enough that Shakaar's capture would have spurred them to action."

"What action?" Dax asked.

Gard shrugged. "Terrorism. Mass infection. At the very least, they might have gone deeper underground. Right now they suspect we know, but they can't be sure. That's my belief, anyway."

Dax looked back and forth between the two of them. "Do you really think that the Council and the TSC aren't capable of handling this information? About what your organization has been doing? Someone has to know something about this mysterious genetic link, and it might be key to figuring out how to deal with the parasites. If the Federation were to approach the president—"

"—then they'd be met by hysteria and denial," Cyl cut in. "I think it *is* a genetic thing, Ezri, in more ways than one. I saw it on your face, outside—something about the parasites creates an acute discord in our people, a revulsion, a fear so ingrained that no one wants to go near it."

"You both did, and the people who've watched with you," Dax said. "And I admit that there's something about the concept, something deeply disconcerting . . . but *I'm* not going to walk away from this."

"Audrid did," Cyl said, a trace of bitterness in his tone, so slight that he obviously wasn't aware of it. "And Dax's hosts since."

Dax flushed, but to her credit, she didn't look away. "I should have pushed harder, that's true. But I didn't know. And whatever mistakes I made, I'm here now."

Gard decided that he liked her. It was a rare person who could accept that they'd fallen short without trying to defend their actions in the same breath.

"I think most of it is the evolutionary connection," he said, drawing their attention toward himself, addressing Dax. "It's obvious to anyone with a DNA scanner that the parasites and our symbionts are related. We don't know precisely how, but it's also obvious that Trill doesn't want to know. They don't want to become central to this parasite investigation, don't want to be connected to these creatures, in any way."

Dax started to say something and then closed her mouth, her jaw clenching slightly. Yes, he definitely liked her. She had idealism, but had also been around long enough to understand the reality of how people dealt with fear and stress. As one of his hosts always liked to say, *Just because it's the truth doesn't mean anyone wants to know about it.*

After a moment, Dax sighed and looked at Cyl. "This isn't going to go away this time, you know. Even if we get past the immediate crisis without things getting any worse . . . Trill's leadership will have a lot to answer for, to Bajor and the Federation. I want to report this to Colonel Kira."

Cyl looked at Gard, who nodded once. She was right. Keeping secrets at this point was counterproductive, and if it meant exposing their watch organization, what of it? It had served its purpose. Trill might even thank them for it, one day . . . though he was no longer optimistic enough to hope for it. He hadn't been that optimistic in a long, long time.

"Any chance I could get out of here?" he asked, smiling because he doubted that there was, too restless not to ask. "Or at least get computer access? Limited, of course."

Dax smiled back at him. It was small, but sincere. "I'll see what I can do. Now, why don't you tell me how you knew that Shakaar was infected?"

Gard started in, going over the physical manifestations first, the slight trembling of the fingers, the tendency to rapid eye movements, a sudden propensity for Klingon and Ferengi cuisine—both of which included vermiform invertibrates. Ezri Dax sat and listened carefully, asking the right questions at the right time, and by the end of their little meeting, Gard felt like they might have a chance of getting things under control, after all. Dax was a ninth-host symbiont, and had lived long enough to be flexible; she'd do what was necessary, even if it meant compromising Trill's strangely insistent denial.

After they left, Gard lay back on his bunk, gazing unseeing at the ceiling once more, wondering if his suspicions about Trill's history would be proved right or wrong. If he was wrong, no harm done. If he was right, no Trill would be the same again . . . and their society as a whole might never recover from the truth.

6

After she tapped out from the holoconference, Kira sat back in her chair, absently drumming her fingers on the console in front of her. It seemed that for every step forward they made in dealing with the parasite crisis, less was being resolved.

It was definitely a mess, but surprisingly, Kira felt better equipped to handle it than she had for days, even weeks.

Maybe I should take up sleeping on couches, she thought, although she knew better. It had been the company, and the emotional release that had done it. She'd felt strangely light this morning, as if someone had scraped out her insides, washed them, and put them back in place. When she had finally woken, Opaka had been meditating in the adjacent room, so Kira had simply slipped out, hurrying back to her own quarters to shower and change. She didn't think the older woman would mind . . . and also felt a bit awkward after her display the night before, not sure if she should apologize, or pretend it hadn't happened, or what. A deeper part of her understood that all was well—

that she had needed to let down her barriers, and Opaka had been more than fine with letting her do so—but she still felt vaguely uncomfortable, as though she'd burdened the former kai with her tears and distress. Understanding didn't really help; some neuroses were harder to get past than others.

She'd cleaned up and gone on duty, only to be visited by Ezri and Cyl barely an hour after she made it to ops. Though it had already seemed clear that there was a genetic connection between the symbionts and the Trill, her conversation with Dax and Cyl had strengthened the foundation. The general's nameless underground watch operation had been organized enough to spot Shakaar and send Gard to investigate. This suggested that there was more information to be had on Trill . . . but it seemed that except for a select and dedicated few, Trill's government and people didn't want to know about any of it; that they would, in fact, be quite opposed to further investigation, possibly resisting Federation inquiries.

Kira had set up a four-way conference as soon as Ezri and the general left her office. Akaar, predictably, had been livid, as had Councillor zh'Thane, and both had given First Minister Asarem their assurances that the Federation would not be deterred from pursuing the full truth of the matter, no matter where the trail led.

Kira stared out into ops, thinking about the Federation. Asarem at least seemed satisfied that the UFP itself wasn't at fault for what had happened, and the Chamber of Ministers would follow her lead. Bajor's entry into the Federation was back on stable ground.

But Kira herself had doubts, more of them than she would have expected. Federation membership had been the goal for so long, but Bajor had been put through so much . . . and now the Federation had Starfleet locking things down, frightening the citizens and letting, *encouraging* Cardassian participation. Of course they were helping, extending resources and aid, putting themselves in a position to absorb the impact of a parasitic invasion . . . but never in her life had Kira felt so claustrophobic, either.

She shook it off, aware that she was projecting some of her anger and fear onto the Federation. The truth of it was, she was afraid that whatever relationship Bajor had with the UFP would be forever tainted by Shakaar's death. Seeing a man she had admired, had once loved, slain in front of her . . . She hadn't had time to address what it had done to her people, let alone to her personally.

And then there are the Cardassians, she thought, her gaze wandering to the two soldiers posted by the lift. Both stood very still, staring straight ahead; as with the others on board, they were doing their best to keep a low profile, keeping to themselves . . . but they couldn't help what they were, what they represented to Bajor. It made a difference that the Orbs had been brought home, and that Yevir was standing by the new Bajoran/Cardassian bond that had sealed their return; according to Asarem, that and the confusion over Shakaar's death were the only things keeping the people from attacking the small but incredibly visible Cardassian presence, on the surface and on the station. But even Kira felt a shiver of bad, angry feelings, seeing the small handfuls of soldiers scattered about, armed and expressionless . . . and *she* knew the real reason they had come. If only someone could get through to the people, could ease the escalating tensions . . .

Someone like Opaka.

Kira felt a flutter of hope, thinking of the former kai's calming influence. She'd talked to Asarem first thing, and both had agreed that the news of Opaka Sulan's return should get out as quickly as possible, to distract the populace from the ongoing parasite scans . . . scans still being passed off as security checks. *But if Opaka is willing to do more, to get everyone looking elsewhere . . . maybe even to encourage cooperation . . .*

Kira's combadge chirped. As she tapped it, still looking out, she saw Kaitlin Merimark turning toward her office wearing a perplexed expression.

"Colonel, Gul Macet has just called in," Merimark said. Her voice came a fraction of a second after she mouthed the words. "It seems a shuttle from Bajor has been intercepted just outside the planet's orbit . . . and the passengers are insisting that they be let through."

After yesterday's events, it sounded like Macet was erring on the side of caution. "Who are the passengers?"

"Ah, apparently there are three vedeks aboard . . . and one of them is Yevir Linjarin. He's . . . Gul Macet says Vedek Yevir has made it very clear that you'll want to speak to him."

Yevir? Kira felt an abrupt pounding at her temples. Shortly after the assassination, he and his entourage had taken the Orbs to Bajor, and she'd hoped not to hear from him for a while. He'd done a great thing for the people, certainly, but she couldn't help her personal feelings. She was consistently irritated by his self-righteousness, particularly in the face of her own loss; he continued to stand behind her Attainder with no doubts, acting as though she should accept the punishment meekly, accept that he somehow knew best. The current schism in the faith wasn't making things any better. He wasn't Winn Adami, thank the Prophets, his leanings truly spiritual rather than political, but that didn't mean he was flexible or empathetic.

And as if I don't have enough to contend with.

"Ask Macet to stand by, and have Yevir commed through to me," Kira said.

"Yes, sir."

Kira turned to the screen on her desk, waiting for Yevir, wondering how good the picture would be. Visuals had been sketchy since the lockdown. A few beats later, Yevir Linjarin popped onto the screen, surprisingly clear and obviously excited. He was flushed and smiling, a tuft of hair sticking up behind one ear as though he'd been running his hands through it, a nervous habit of his that she actually remembered from his days as a Militia officer aboard the station. She hadn't seen it in a long time.

"Colonel," Yevir said quickly. "I understand that Opaka Sulan and Jake Sisko are both on the station. Is this true?"

Not interested in small talk, it seemed. "Yes, Vedek. And I'm sure—"

"You *must* allow us to see them," Yevir said. "Myself and vedeks Bellis and Eran have come to welcome them home."

Kira did her best to look patient. "Vedek Yevir, are you aware that this station . . . that all Bajoran space, in fact, is currently at a lockdown status because of First Minister Shakaar's—"

"Yes, yes," Yevir interrupted again, his own impatience showing in his too-bright smile. "I understand. But surely this doesn't apply to Opaka Sulan, or the son of the Emissary . . . ? They belong on Bajor, and I'm here to see that they have proper escort. I haven't spoken to her directly about this, but I can assure you that First Minister Asarem will cooperate fully, with whatever security measures need to be taken. They *must* be allowed to come home."

"Vedek, are you certain that they wish to leave the station with you?" Kira asked mildly, aware that he couldn't possibly know. She wasn't in the mood to be lectured about what *must* be done.

Yevir's smile hardly wavered. "I'm sure that if I have a chance to see them, to explain to them . . . I have no doubt they'll want to return with us. Colonel, think of what this means for Bajor! In such turbulent times, the son of the Emissary returning our former kai to us . . . it's surely a gift from the Prophets."

Although his enthusiasm wasn't catching, the idea wasn't bad. Hadn't she just been thinking that Opaka might be able to divert attention from what the Federation was up to? It would undoubtedly be safer for them on Bajor than on the station, their status demanding Militia protection . . . and it would definitely be a gift to both Jake and Kas, particularly with Kas already past her due date.

She sighed inwardly, looking at Yevir's shining visage, then nodded. "Perhaps you're right, Vedek. If you'll stand by, I'll ask that Gul Macet escort your vessel to the station. There will have to be a security check—"

Yevir was beaming. "Of course. You're doing the right thing, Colonel."

Having gotten what he wanted, he tapped out, leaving her with a blank screen. She hadn't expected his gratitude . . . which, it seemed, had been a good call.

Kira arranged the escort and then glanced around her desk, at the reports she still needed to look over, remembering that she had to meet with Nog at 1000 hours to talk about the *Defiant,* reminding herself that she wanted to meet with Vaughn and Bowers before they left for Bajor. A half-dozen additional tasks came to mind, schedule coordinating and reports that were waiting to be filed . . . but it would all have to wait, at least for a few minutes. She wanted to stop by the lab, see how Julian was progressing . . . if he was getting a lot done, maybe working out the parasitic communication basics, she might have something to show Akaar at the next meeting. And, much as she would have liked to keep them around, she needed to tell Opaka and Jake that they now had a ride back to Bajor, if they were ready . . . and before they left, she wanted to tell Sulan how grateful she was for the peace she'd received the night before, however temporary. Opaka probably didn't need to hear it, but Kira needed to say it.

Julian inserted the tissue samples from Shakaar Edon's limbic system into the scanner and waited, tired from lack of sleep but too involved in what he was doing to allow himself to rest. The work was fascinating. His colleagues had done a competent initial rundown, but they hadn't followed through on the extent of the neurotransmitter/receptor control that the parasites wielded, particularly the acetylcholine levels.

While the samples were being tested, Julian picked up the padd with the serpentine receptor numbers, so involved with the delicate changes in the transmembrane structures that he didn't notice Kira until she was practically standing next to him.

"How are things going?" she asked.

Julian blinked up at her, ignoring the reflexive tug of impatience he felt at being interrupted. They were alone in the small mid-core lab, the majority of the team still working with the Cardassian volunteers in medical. "Good, I think. Nothing yet on the Cardassian immunity, but I've been able to better clarify how the parasites control their hosts."

Kira nodded. "How?"

Julian translated automatically, from how he understood it to how someone with a nonmedical background might. "Chemistry. They tap into the sites of synthesis for every neurotransmitter used in the host body and direct the flow of neuropeptides, which mediate sensory and emotional response."

"So it's mind control," Kira half asked.

"Yes, but they also dominate the host's acetylcholine levels—that's the transmitter used at the neuromuscular junction. It's a control that extends to every part of the carrier body."

"What about the time window?" Kira asked. "How long before the union becomes permanent?"

"Dr. Girani was right—it depends on the host species," Julian said carefully, thinking of Ezri's story from the night before, feeling a pang of random anxiety that he quickly stifled. Vod and his parasite had been inseparable by the time Audrid and Pike had returned to Trill, less than a day after they'd been joined. . . . and it could have happened in less time than that, as the Federation ship they were on hadn't had the equipment to properly monitor Vod. *Maybe it only took minutes. . . .*

Kira was waiting. "And how quickly the parasite can affect the specified mutation of each individual's synapses," he added. "A synapse is where the axon of the presynaptic neuron terminates on the postsynaptic neuron—"

At her rising frown, he cut himself off; he was more tired than he'd thought . . . or more anxious, but again, he carefully steered himself away from acknowledging the fact, noting that Kira had apparently heeded his advice about getting some rest. She still looked strained, but also about a thousand times less so than the day before.

"With Shakaar, twenty to thirty days, as Dr. Girani said," he said, getting back to her question. "It's a process. I can't say with any certainty that all Bajorans would have the same window—the first minister's is the only advanced case available—but the simulations do suggest it."

"And the hosts in stasis?" Kira asked. "They're stable, aren't they?" Julian saw her microexpression of distaste at having to use the word "host," thinking that he, too, disliked the term. "Victim" seemed more apt.

"They should be fine," Julian said. "They were all detected well within the window. We're watching them closely for any sign of advancement, but from what we've seen so far, stasis will hold indefinitely. Again, though, I should stress that each species the parasite encounters will probably react differently."

Kira studied him, her gaze unreadable. "How do you think the Trill species might react?"

Julian didn't answer immediately, wondering if Ezri had talked to her, wondering what he should say . . . and felt that pang of anxiety become the fear that he'd managed to put aside for the hours he'd been working. Ezri's story had frightened him, for entirely selfish reasons; he simply loved her too much not to worry.

He reminded himself that his overriding concern had to be finding a solution to the parasite crisis, that every bit of information needed to be available to those working on the problem . . . but except for the apparent rapidity of the symbiont-parasite bond, there weren't any useful particulars in the story of Audrid Dax that hadn't already been reported by Starfleet.

And I wouldn't betray her trust, in any case, he affirmed

to himself, a surge of protectiveness sweeping over him. He could talk to her later about what information she wanted to pass along, but he meant to support whatever decision she made.

"There's no scientific data available," he answered neutrally, and truthfully. "Because the Trill have evolved to host a similar life-form, I would hazard to guess that the time window might be much shorter . . . and that the parasite might be capable of bonding to the host and the symbiont."

Kira definitely knew something, he could see it in her sharp and careful gaze, but she chose to let it drop. "Have you found anything on how the parasites communicate?"

"Not yet. When Dr. Crusher encountered them, she documented the 'mother' or queen connection—that is, a single master female that commands those closest to her telepathically, and possibly with occasional bursts of pheromones—but until I can get a living specimen of one of these females, I won't know for sure. The scans of those in stasis suggest that the 'soldier' parasites are passive receivers . . . unless the psychic link is more evolved than we know. At this point, we can't be certain. There is some rudimentary evidence that suggests a high sensitivity to light, at least while not in a host body, but again, we don't understand yet how this might apply."

Kira nodded slowly. She seemed on the verge of asking more, her longing for useful information etched across her face, but she obviously didn't know what else to ask. They'd already agreed that he wouldn't waste time giving scheduled reports, instead going to her when he found anything with practical applications . . . but there was still a lot to do before they would get to that stage, and he was eager to get back to it.

As he thought it, the scanner beeped that it was finished with the samples.

"I'll leave you to it, then," she said, smiling slightly, as though recognizing his offhand impatience.

"And I'll let you know what I find," he said, tapping up the reads before Kira made it to the door, falling back into his fascination and his need to find answers. As he'd assumed, the limbic system's 5HT serotonin receptors had been dramatically altered, in a way that complemented the mutations of the CNS synthesis sites for most of the tyrosine transmitters. . . .

Julian let the work absorb him, engage him, and take away his fear, at least for a little while. Ezri was safe, and he would find the answers.

They had knelt by Thriss's stasis chamber throughout the long night, sharing their grief as much as they could, Shar feeling very much alone in his own despair . . . and in the morning, he'd done the right thing. It had ripped at his mind and spirit to do it, but it was best for both of his mates.

Dizhei and Anichent would return to Andor without him, to meet with the *zhen* mates who might carry their offspring, to choose one . . . and they would also meet with the *chans* his *zhavey* had found, his own possible replacement; the *chan* would add his gamete to Dizhei's, already fertilized by Anichent, then Dizhei would transfer the zygote to the *zhen*'s pouch.

Thriss, it should have been Thriss. He had dreamed of her often, gravid with child. She would have been beautiful.

When he'd put forth his decision, they had fought him . . . but not for long, and not very hard. It hurt him to see, but he felt no resentment. Whether he meant to or not, he had injured them, he had taken Thriss from their lives, stealing the future they had all imagined. The very least he could do was suggest that they start over with mates who had not behaved so badly.

It was not an ideal situation, for anyone; without Thriss, there was no ideal. But Dizhei and Anichent could still parent, at least, and perhaps care for one another through the worst of the pain that Shar and Thriss had created. And they had made him promise that if they couldn't find a compatible *chan,* Shar would return to Andor to fulfill his duty. At least there was that.

Shar sat on a plain bench in his living area and stared at the closed front door, exhausted, listening to the slow, deep breaths of Anichent, finally asleep in one of the padded chairs. Dizhei had gone to speak to Charivretha, to inform her of their decision and to see if immediate transport could be arranged. Shar had little doubt that it could be, even with the lockdown . . . and though he, too, was very tired, he resisted sleep, waiting for Dizhei's return. He'd had no desire to speak with his *zhavey*, and was grateful that his mate had volunteered.

She returned only seconds after he thought it, meeting his gaze as she walked in, dropping it almost immediately.

"We can leave now," she said quietly, moving to sit by him. She kept her voice low, gazing at Anichent, curled in his heavy sleep. "As soon as clearance is authorized, actually, but *Zhadi* said she'd already discussed the matter with Admiral Akaar and Colonel Kira, and there will be no delay. She's giving us the use of her private transport."

"And Thriss?" Shar asked, his voice dull to his own ears.

"We'll have her transported aboard," Dizhei said, finally looking him in the eye, holding it. "Would . . . Have you reconsidered your position? I'm sure that your *zhavey* could explain the necessity of your leave."

No explanation would be necessary, coming from a Federation ambassador . . . but Shar wasn't staying merely because he felt obligated; that was only a small part of why, and Dizhei knew it.

What's the human euphemism? A clean break. He would only remind them of what they'd lost.

Shar reached for her hand. "I think I should stay," he said.

Dizhei's fingers lay limp in his, and though her words were angry, her tone was as lifeless as her hand. "If punishing yourself is your reason, you punish us by it. We've all lost Thriss."

Yes, and some part of you will always blame me for it, Shar thought, understanding that for as wise as she was, Dizhei wouldn't accept that. She would insist that it wasn't true, but Shar had seen it in her, in the helpless anger that had stained last night's tears. Punishing himself was incidental.

"The decision is made," he said, and as she turned away, it was all he could do not to blurt out the truth—that he loved her, that he loved them both more than anything; that he wanted desperately to be with them, to run away and hide with them and cry for Thriss until there was no more sadness, forever.

What stopped him was also the truth. He could no longer afford the luxury of selfishness; his morality wouldn't permit it.

Without another word, Dizhei stood and walked to the bedchamber, picking up both her own and Anichent's traveling satchels on the way. She would pack, and wake Anichent, and though Shar would walk them to the airlock and embrace them and wish them well, they'd already said their farewells. Unspoken but no less powerful, their mourning for Thriss had said it all.

Someone signaled at the door. *Zhavey*. Shar pulled himself up, resigned to the shame in her eyes, and went to answer.

Prynn Tenmei was standing there, her arms tightly folded, her face pinched. She spoke in a rush, blurting out what she'd come for before he had a chance to register surprise.

"I'm sorry to bother you, Shar, but he—I mean my father just left for Bajor, and I ignored his messages, I didn't go to see him off . . . and I know you've been having kind of a hard time lately, and I thought . . ."

She saw past him, saw Anichent, and trailed off.

"I thought you might want to have lunch with me," she said, backing up a step. "But maybe another time would be better."

"Maybe," Shar said, strangely unable to remember how to be more polite about it. He searched for something pleasant to say, to send her along without offense, but could think of nothing at all.

Prynn lowered her voice, staring intently into his eyes. "Are you okay?"

Shar looked back at her, saw a real concern for him in her own dark gaze, and still could think of nothing to tell her, not sure how to answer. Was he okay? No, he thought not. But it wasn't the time to discuss it. He was fairly certain that there would never be a time to discuss it.

"Never mind," Prynn said, reading something off his face, somehow. "Find me later if you want to talk, okay? I'm sorry if I interrupted."

She reached out and touched his arm, then turned and

hurried down the corridor. Shar stood in the doorway looking after her, vaguely wondering how he might have handled the situation better, not sure if it was important. He thought he'd been doing well enough, but now had to wonder if he was in some kind of shock.

"Shar?"

Anichent's weary voice rose from behind him, calling him back to the shambles of his life. Shar stepped back from the door, letting it close, and went to sit with his lifelong friend and first love, to try and explain that it was time for him to go, that it was all over.

I caused this, he thought, looking into Anichent's worn countenance, hearing Dizhei rummaging through clothes in the next room, Thriss cold and silent and watching it all.

More than ever, he understood now that he couldn't go home with them, that he wouldn't survive it. All he had was his work. Whether or not that would sustain him was still to be seen.

7

His stopover at DS9 hadn't lasted very long. Jake had stayed up late, hoping to spend some time with Nog—who had been able to spare all of a half hour for a midnight drink, too busy working on some *Defiant* array thing to get away—had finally fallen asleep in the early hours, and had crawled out of bed a full ten minutes before Kira was knocking on his door. Yevir, the vedek he vaguely remembered meeting just before leaving for the wormhole, had apparently volunteered to give Jake's traveling party a ride to Bajor. And as soon as possible.

Much as he'd been hoping to stick around for a few days, catch up with Nog and Ez and station life, Kira seemed to think it was a good idea . . . and after yesterday's conversation with Kas, he *did* want to get to Bajor; she was hugely pregnant, and though her complaints were lighthearted, it sounded like she could actually use some help around the house.

Kira said that Yevir's shuttle would be ready to return to Bajor in an hour, then went off to find Opaka and Wex.

Feeling entirely out of touch with reality, Jake packed a bag. Traveling had always made him feel that way, the sudden change of environments making everything seem . . . not quite certain. Only yesterday, he'd been saying goodbye to Itu, the Eav'oq leader, just returned to corporeal existence after fifty millennia of subspace meditation. The farewell had been pleasant and calm; from there he'd almost been blown up by a malfunction in a Tosk transport, he had seen Weyoun while on board a Dominion ship, and had almost been blown up *again* by the Cardassians. Now, less than twenty-six hours later, he was on his way to Bajor, with the vedek who had apparently kicked Kira Nerys out of her religion; Nog *had* managed to catch him up on a thing or two, information he'd gotten directly from Quark. Even Nog agreed that it was a lot to get hit with on the first day home.

Speaking of. Nog had either gotten up early and returned to work, or he hadn't ever come in. Since Yevir's ship was docked only two locks down from the *Defiant,* Jake decided to stop in and see him on his way out.

On our *way out,* he thought, latching his slightly overstuffed bag. Kira said that she would urge Opaka and Wex to go, too; maybe it was a safety issue. Kas had mentioned something about a few Bajorans hanging around the house, ostensibly to offer their assistance in her last days of pregnancy . . . but maybe they were Militia.

Maybe Yevir is trying to protect us. Jake had gotten the impression from Kira that the vedek's visit was a welcome-back-important-people kind of thing, but perhaps that was only part of it . . . or maybe Kira was using Yevir's invitation to get them to the safety of Bajor. How would Opaka and Yevir get along, the former kai and the probably kai-to-be? Jake wondered if she knew yet that Yevir had been behind Kira's getting pushed out of the faith—Attainted, Nog had called it—and tried again to remember the smiling man he'd met at Quark's big party. Jake had been distracted, upset by the death of the prylar who had given him his scrap of prophecy, worried about how to approach Quark to buy a shuttle . . . though he remembered thinking that Yevir had seemed a little young to become kai, the big rumor going around. At some point, either Kira or Nog had told him that Yevir Linjarin had actually served on the station as one of the Militia crew, and that he'd had some kind of vision after meeting Jake's father a few years ago. Touched by the Prophets through the Emissary, Yevir had been quick to rise up through the ranks of the Vedek Assembly.

Interesting, but Jake had already decided that anyone who would banish Kira from practicing the religion she so loved was probably a jerk. He'd already heard about the Ohalu prophecies being uploaded to Bajor's net, first from the vedek who had stopped Opaka on the Promenade yesterday, then with more details at his midnight meeting with Nog. Jake was certain that the prophecy he'd been given, about returning through the wormhole with Opaka, was from the same book, and saw no reason at all that the people of Bajor shouldn't know what was in their history. As far as he was concerned, Kira had done the right thing.

I guess she's come to terms with Yevir, anyway, Jake thought, hefting his bag and heading out toward the Docking Ring. She obviously trusted the vedek enough to let him transport Opaka . . . and he *had* been responsible for bringing the missing Orbs home from Cardassia. Jake decided he would reserve judgment for later, when he had the time to actually think about anything.

His visit with Nog was brief. The Cardassians standing

security at the airlock wouldn't let him board, so Nog met him in the docking corridor, hyperspanner in hand, his round face flushed. He apologized about a thousand times for not breaking away earlier, which Jake brushed off. He was back in Bajoran space to stay for a while; they'd have a chance to catch up soon enough. Nog agreed to visit after the baby was born, and Jake promised him drinks at Vic's within a month. Nog vowed to tell everyone good-bye on his behalf, then reluctantly left Jake in the corridor. Jake watched the entry roll closed after him, then went to find Yevir's shuttle, glad that all was well between them.

There were another two Cardassian guards at the lock where he was to meet Opaka, Wex, and Yevir's group, both with scanning devices ready and waiting. Jake was the first to arrive, it seemed, and waited patiently while the taller of the two checked him over, presumably for weapons. It was odd that yesterday Dr. Bashir had been so sure the scans had been health-related; he was usually very precise about that kind of thing . . . though maybe they *had* been medically scanned, as possible carriers of infectious microbes or disease. The whole conspiracy to keep Bajor out of the Federation . . . Jake could understand why everyone was being so careful.

They'll get in, though, Jake thought confidently, picking his bag up after the second Cardassian finished searching it. The fact that the Federation was going through all this trouble, determined to make everything secure . . . Bajor was already in, the official paperwork just waiting until the conspirators were caught.

He saw Opaka appear at the end of the corridor, carrying her small bag over one shoulder. A trio of Bajoran station workers were following her, and Jake watched as she stopped midway down the hall, gently speaking to them, touching their hands, blessing them. All three went away happy.

Opaka smiled and waved when she saw Jake, and he returned it, surprised at how glad he was to see her. When he'd first found the former kai, he'd been disappointed and angry—he'd hoped to find his father, after all, not the spiritual icon who had named Ben Sisko the Emissary. And he'd expected to have to hear all about the Prophets' great Tapestry, how he was blessed that his father was in the Temple, and so on et cetera. But when he'd finally approached her for a personal conversation on their way back to the Alpha Quadrant, she'd surprised him, with empathy and open-mindedness. She had turned out to be . . . well, *cool*, in Vic-speak.

The Cardassians did their job quickly and efficiently, Opaka thanking them as she retrieved her bag. Even they seemed pleased by her, both nodding deferentially as she moved away to stand next to Jake.

"I guess we're first," Jake said. "Where is everyone?"

"Colonel Kira is with the vedeks who will be escorting us home," Opaka said, craning her neck slightly to look up at him. "They're being scanned, I believe, at the station's medical center."

Jake nodded, noting the sparkle in her eyes. "Are you excited to get back?"

"Oh, my, yes," Opaka said, smiling. "It sounds as though there are many exciting changes taking place. I look forward to reading the Ohalu text, and sharing what the Prophets have taught me during my years away . . . and telling the Assembly about the Eav'oq."

Her smile faded slightly at the last, and Jake nodded again, understanding completely. If the Assembly had had trouble accepting a book of prophecies from Bajor's own past, how would they take to an alien sister species with entirely different views on the Prophets?

"Where's Wex?" he asked.

"Wex has elected to stay behind."

That was a surprise. "I thought . . . Why? Isn't that why she came, to spend time with you?"

Before she could answer, Kira came marching down the corridor, followed by three robed and slightly disheveled-looking vedeks and a security guard. The vedek in front was Yevir, Jake was pretty sure; the youngest of the three, he had an earnest and intelligent face, and when he saw Opaka and Jake, he grinned almost self-consciously, an expression that Jake definitely remembered from their last meeting. Almost as if he were in the presence of royalty.

Jake did his best to keep an open mind, but he'd seen the same look on other Bajoran faces, too many of them. It carried implications of how he could expect to be treated by the man.

In a word, differently. After months of traveling in the Gamma Quadrant, he'd gotten somewhat used to being accepted or rejected on his own merits; being treated special just because of his father was one aspect of home that he hadn't been looking forward to.

Kira ran through the introductions. Vedek Yevir was accompanied by vedeks Bellis and Eran, both of whom had served in the Assembly when Opaka was kai. They bowed low, praising the Prophets that she had returned. Jake couldn't help wondering if they'd be so pleased to hear that her homecoming had been foretold in the Ohalu book. Yevir made a big show of courtesy to her, asking after her health, offering her accommodations at the monastery where she'd spent her days as spiritual leader of Bajor.

"That is where the nine Tears now rest," Yevir said, "at

least until we decide where to place them. And your own chambers have been reopened for you."

As Opaka graciously accepted, Jake nodded at Kira. "Wex isn't coming?"

"No," Kira answered, keeping her voice down as Yevir continued to rain welcome over Opaka. "She said that Sulan requested some time to get settled before taking on a student."

It was an explanation, though not one Jake would have expected. Opaka Sulan was one of those rare people who didn't seem to feel inconvenienced, by anyone for any reason. It seemed out of character that she would ask Wex to stay behind . . . but then, he supposed he didn't know her *that* well.

Kira told him that she'd call Kas, let her know that he was coming, and then gave him a long, tight embrace. She stepped back smiling, turning to embrace Opaka. They exchanged a few private words as they hugged, Yevir and his fellow vedeks doing their best not to look impatient.

As Yevir stiffly thanked Kira for "promoting the spiritual health of the people," Jake turned to Opaka.

"If you need to get settled in, I'm sure Kas would be happy to have Wex stay with us for a few days," he offered.

Opaka shook her head. "I invited her to come, Jake. She refused."

Jake frowned, a sudden low tic of concern in his belly. Why had Wex lied to Kira? "She told Kira that *you* asked her to wait," he said. "Maybe we should—"

"Everything is fine," Opaka said, cutting him off with a light touch on his arm. "Wex is no threat, Jake, of that I'm sure. She'll be along when the time is right."

Jake wasn't sure what to say to that; he was more curious than he had been, but Yevir had finished his reluctant appreciation speech and had turned his beaming smile back to Opaka and Jake.

"We're so glad you've come home," he said, ushering them toward the airlock, Bellis and Eran standing aside so they could enter first. Opaka smiled serenely and walked ahead, Jake casting a final look at Kira before following. Her gaze, fixed on Vedek Yevir, said volumes about what she thought of him . . . but as she turned it to Jake, the complexity of feelings dissolved, becoming much simpler and infinitely more accepting.

I love you, too, Jake thought, grinning at her, and hurried to catch up to Opaka before the feelings could make it to his eyes, suddenly damp with gratification, his throat heavy with a powerful sense that he was, in fact, quite special.

Ro had just finished reviewing the data from the first mass scan of the day. Today's criterion was all off-duty engineering and maintenance personnel on first shift, and door-to-door checks in the habitat ring on the second, the entire fifth level. So far, so good, no new cases . . . but Ro was frustrated with the progress, and with the haphazard setup that security had to work with. The poor scanning equipment meant checks could only be done face-to-face, and even with the sixty-plus Cardassians who'd come to help, there was no way to get through even a quarter of DS9's population in a single day. Thus the revolving basis for scans . . . but while she could tell herself that it was working, there was simply no way to *know*. People could be slipping through the cracks from day to day, borrowing or stealing identity tags, outright lying for one another so that their loved ones could avoid interacting with Cardassians. Besides, there were people who'd already been "interviewed" more than once, some as many as three times; how much longer would they accept the assassination-ring theory? And what if the parasites could move from person to person? It was a possibility that would make the entire operation worthless.

We don't know enough about them, Ro thought helplessly. *We don't even know how they got here, how Shakaar was infected.* Ro's desire for neatly unfolding scenarios objected to all of the skipping around; much as she liked solving a puzzle, working one without having most of the pieces was beyond unappealing. Just knowing where Shakaar had become a host would at least give them a point to work from, to backtrack to the parasites' place of origin and to go forward, to figure out who'd been exposed. Starfleet hadn't yet ruled out any of the dozen or so planets and starbases they were investigating, everywhere Shakaar had been since he left Earth months ago.

She stood and stretched, gazing out at the Promenade; it was mealtime, so there was a crowd . . . but as it had been for the past week, the atmosphere was apprehensive and uncomfortable. There was a line at the Replimat, people wanting to grab something fast and get back to the wishful security of their work environments.

Restless, she decided. She knew the feeling. Maybe a quick circuit would do some good. She contacted Shul and asked him to take the desk. After promising to bring him something from Quark's, she stepped onto the Promenade.

She passed Quark's for the moment, letting herself drift, letting herself walk without thinking. Past the infirmary and the Spican Jewelers, across the east platform, past the greengrocer and the Klingon Deli . . . and she came to a dead stop in front of the Replimat, feeling truly surprised for the first time in days.

Up on the balcony level, gazing out a viewport, stood Taran'atar. And he wasn't alone. Wex was with him, the female Trelian from the Gamma Quadrant. And from the look of it, they appeared to be . . . chatting.

She knew about Wex, of course. Dax had briefed her on the *Defiant*'s last days in the Gamma Quadrant. She also knew that the Trelian had elected to stay behind on the station when Jake and Opaka left for Bajor. She seemed harmless enough . . . But then, so did the sand bats of Manark IV, until they took to the air.

And hanging around with a Jem'Hadar doesn't seem like a harmless person's idea of a good time.

Was it really so strange, though? They were both from the Gamma Quadrant, after all. Maybe that was enough of a reason for them to gravitate toward each other. Maybe she was interested in his perspective on life in the Alpha Quadrant. The surprising part was that Taran'atar seemed to be talking back.

Unable to supress her curiosity, Ro ascended the nearest stair spiral, winding her way up to the balcony. Foot traffic was light, but by no means absent. Falling in with a couple of techs passing by, she waited until they were past the Gamma natives' window before she broke off and stepped to the next viewport over. She was mostly hidden by the window's thick Cardassian frame.

". . . struck by the sight of you here, among all these aliens," she heard Wex saying. "You aren't even in a Jem'Hadar uniform. It takes some getting used to." Wex's voice was low and piping, like a wind flute.

"Much about this quadrant takes getting used to," Taran'atar said.

"Such as . . . ?"

Taran'atar didn't hesitate. "Plurality. Freedom. Chaos." He'd obviously given the matter some thought.

"Sounds like fun," Wex observed.

"Not for me."

"I suppose not. Trelians enjoy their freedom. Did you know that?"

"Yes. They resisted Dominion control twice in the last century. I killed many during the last insurrection."

Ro winced. She got ready to politely interrupt depending on what came next . . . but if Wex was disturbed by the Jem'Hadar's blatant admission, her voice didn't betray it.

"And have you ever stopped to wonder why a people would risk death to be free?" Wex asked.

"Failure to recognize overwhelming opposition," Taran'atar stated.

"No. It's because, faced with the choice of a life of stagnation under the Dominion or the risk of death, the risk of death was preferable."

Taran'atar hesitated before answering. "Then death is inevitable."

"Your presence here, among the defeaters of the Dominion, proves otherwise," Wex said, her voice mild, almost kind.

"My presence here . . . is lost on me."

The tone with which Taran'atar spoke was striking. Ro had been about to move away, feeling guilty for eavesdropping, but she couldn't bring herself to leave, not yet. She thought she was starting to understand something about Taran'atar, something she hadn't realized before.

Since his arrival some months ago, Taran'atar had often infuriated her . . . But he had also fascinated and surprised her in the most unexpected ways. Ro had fought and killed enough Jem'Hadar during the war that she'd gotten used to thinking of them as factory produced killers, not as individuals. But Taran'atar had turned out to be as complex as any sentient she'd encountered—not only because of his origins, but because of the unique circumstances that had brought him to the station. Yet even after five months, he didn't truly understand the task that Odo had set for him, to observe the complexities of a free society. It would seem that he saw himself as a freak and an exile, cast out by one of his gods.

"So why do you stay?" Wex asked.

"I wasn't given the option to leave."

"What would you do if you had the option? Go home? Return to your unit?"

Taran'atar paused, and when he spoke again, his voice was meant to carry. "I'm not sure. Do you have any suggestions, Lieutenant Ro?"

Letting out a breath, Ro turned and stepped into view, saw Wex turn to face her. Taran'atar was still gazing impassively out the window. Wex's liquid black gaze was accusatory.

"I apologize if I've offended," Ro said sincerely. "My curiosity got the better of me. This is a troubled time aboard the station. I'm the chief of security here."

Wex scrutinized her silently. "You're good," she said finally. "By nature, I'm not easy to sneak up on."

Ro smiled, relieved. "I feel I should make it up to you. Is there anything you need to make your stay with us more pleasant?"

Wex stared at her another moment, then nodded toward the entryway into the upper level of Quark's, across the balcony. "I was considering trying out that establishment. How is it?"

"Not bad," Ro said, noting that Taran'atar still hadn't moved. "Food, drink, games of chance, holographic environment rooms. I'm on good terms with the proprietor. I can see to it you're well taken care of."

Wex nodded slowly. "That sounds . . . interesting." She turned to her companion. "Will you join me?"

Taran'atar finally turned away from the viewport and inclined his head.

"Great," Ro said, doing her best to keep the uncertainty from her voice as she led them toward the bar. At least her breach of etiquette would be overlooked . . . But glancing back at the petite, gray-skinned girl and the hulking Jem'Hadar trailing behind, she couldn't help a mental shake of her head.

And people think Quark and I make a weird couple . . .

The officer field shelter was Starfleet standard, a utilitarian one-man pressed piece with all the necessities and none of the luxuries. Not that Vaughn cared particularly; he'd stayed in much, much worse. The communications setup was excellent, all that really mattered.

The central compound was set up off the Tilar peninsula, near the ruins of what used to be the Karnoth resettlement camp. Not necessarily the best choice for Bajoran morale, but except for the outback southeast of them, it was the primary location for transmission clarity in all of Hedrikspool province. With this side of Bajor nearing the end of its hot season, the Occupation ruins seemed a better choice . . . and because of its isolation, less likely to draw attention to the magnitude of the operation. There were smaller, more discreet camps set up in the provinces of Hill, Rakantha, and Musilla.

Vaughn dropped his bag on the cot attached to one wall

of his quarters, dropping after it, looking around at his new temporary home. Food replicator, computer console, fold-out table, 'fresher with shower facilities. The only thing that made it an officer's shelter was that there was one cot instead of two.

Outside, shuttles and hoppers buzzed and rumbled in and out of the deepening shadows of the compound, taking or returning teams of examiners. It seemed he'd arrived during one of the two daily shift changes. There was equipment to be recalibrated, information to download, medical exams to be taken. A number of press-piece shelters had been organized to deal with the day-to-day, from Replimat to com center. There were barracks, too, three long, slightly flattened gray tubes of replicated matter, each capable of holding fifty comfortably . . . depending on one's definition of comfort.

Not bad for a week's work, Vaughn thought tiredly, his shoulders slumped with it. Starfleet could whip together a functioning camp in no time. He knew he needed to get out there, to let the on-shift CO know that he was ready to go over everything. A faint memory fluttered through his consciousness, one of his first classes at the Academy. An instructor whose name he'd long since forgotten, making the students repeat the three *S*'s for organizing sweep ops—strategy, scheduling, sector coverage. After a few years in the field, he'd decided the instructor had been hopelessly shortsighted, leaving out a whole slew of letters that should have been included—*D* for defense in hostile territory came immediately to mind, *C* for communications, *P* for position—but the rule stayed with him. It seemed so arbitrary sometimes, what the mind decided to hold on to. . . .

Vaughn heard a group of people walk past his shelter,

heard friendly bantering among Starfleet personnel, all of them certainly younger than he; he'd been feeling his age lately, and the *Defiant*'s homecoming hadn't helped. He'd gotten little sleep the night before after a prolonged conversation with Akaar, going over his Borg report, what little there was of it. It had taken some time to convince his old friend that the danger appeared to be long past . . . though L.J., to his credit, hadn't tried to lecture him after the whole story was out. An "I told you so" would have been well deserved, but the admiral wasn't without mercy, had even squeezed his shoulder as they'd parted company.

Prynn hadn't returned either of his calls before he'd left the station, though he'd made it clear that he might be away for a while. He was unhappy about it, but supposed he understood. Ruriko's death—her first death, not the death he'd inflicted on the Borg creature—had kept him from having a real relationship with Prynn for too long. He had only himself to blame, of course, it was his guilt and shame that had done it . . . but wasn't it ironic, that after true reconciliation between them finally seemed to be on the horizon, Ruriko's second death had brought father and daughter back to where they'd started. Prynn was resentful and full of pain, and it was his fault. If he'd tried harder, if he'd done a better job during all those empty years, they might have had something to work with, enough kind feelings to see them through the worst of it; all they had now was remembered slights, and good intentions that had gone nowhere. . . .

There was a signal at his door. "Come," Vaughn said, straightening.

Sam Bowers walked in, carrying a handful of padds, his

usual gentle countenance marred by the stern look he wore as he stood at attention. “Good evening, Commander.”

Bowers would be filing daily status reports with the station, acting as contact for all of the Starfleet personnel working the planet.

“At ease, Lieutenant.”

Bowers relaxed, but only slightly. “Sir, General Lenaris hasn’t yet returned from the field, but I have his report. I’m prepared to brief you on our current status.”

Vaughn nodded, standing and motioning toward the foldout table near the replicator. “Take a seat, Sam. When I said at ease, I was serious. Can I get you something to drink?”

Bowers relaxed even more. “Ah, that’d be great, sir. Coffee, black.”

Vaughn ordered two of them, then sat down across from Bowers, refocusing himself. Some days it was harder than others, but he was career Starfleet; no matter how bad things got, he always managed to get done what needed doing. He’d convinced himself long ago that it was a necessary skill in his line of work, and it was . . . but it wasn’t such a great talent, either, to learn how to suppress everything in the name of effective work habits. Something else that came with age, he supposed . . . figuring out what was important.

And right now, that’s finding the infected, he thought firmly. Lives were at stake, and not just those unfortunate ones who’d been attacked and taken over. For all they knew, the parasites meant genocide for the Bajoran people.

“Fill me in,” Vaughn said, and though he was focused enough as Bowers called up a sector map on the console and picked up the first padd, he could still see an image floating in front of his mind’s eye—of tiny dots of Ruriko’s blood spattering ever so lightly across his daughter's stunned face.

Stop. And focus.

Bowers was pointing out the sites that had been established as scanning stations. Vaughn concentrated, filing the information, considered adding an additional group near the labyrinths by the southern islands—and remembered dropping the phaser, turning to Prynn as Ruriko's biomechanical limbs spasmed in death, as Prynn reflexively wiped at the spray on her face, smearing her mother's blood across shocked flesh, beneath shocked eyes. And for the first time since that image had been reality, he felt a stab of real fear, a fear that it might not be all that difficult to lose touch with reality.

God help him, what if there were some things that couldn't be put aside?

8

EZRI AND CYL SPENT A NUMBER OF POINTLESS HOURS SORTing through the Trill historical database, looking for something that might point them in a helpful direction, in *any* direction. They'd eaten a mostly silent lunch together and gone back to it, more hours of silence in one of the small research offices just beneath the Promenade—Ezri, at least, wondering if it was even worth the effort. Cyl had already made it clear that there weren't any files to be had. . . .

And what good would they do if there were? The parasites were trying to start up a war, they hated Trill and didn't seem all that fond of anyone else, either. They'd attempted to take over Bajor by infiltrating the government, presumably to gain control of the wormhole and to establish an entire population within the Federation . . . and knowing the exact nature of their historical connection to Trill would help how, exactly? They were *here,* they were crawling into people and hiding, scheming, and they clearly meant harm; stopping them was the most important thing, whatever it took. Understanding them could wait until after they were wiped out—

Ezri looked away from the screen of her computer interface and rubbed her eyes, surprised by her knee-jerk train of thought. It was true; the very concept of the parasitic species provoked some negative instinctual reaction in Trill, or at least in her; being aware of it apparently didn't make a difference. She went back to her scanning, reminding herself that understanding them might be the Federation's only chance . . . but it was a hard thought to hold on to, and when Kira commed through a few minutes later, Ezri was glad for the distraction.

An unscheduled briefing. Dazed by a full day of reading about everything from ancient land disputes to the evolutionary path of the TSC, Ezri and Cyl hurried out to the wardroom. Ezri hoped that Kira had some ideas on how to better involve both the Federation and Trill in finding a solution.

Julian and Kira were already waiting for them, the full roster for the meeting; as soon as the door closed behind them, Kira started talking.

"We know the biological connection between the symbionts and the parasites."

Sitting down next to Julian, Ezri was just giving his hand a gentle squeeze when Kira dropped the news. With how quickly he jerked his hand away, it seemed her reaction had been noticeable.

"What is it?"

"It's just the beginning, really, but it is significant," Julian said. "We already knew that the DNA codings between the symbionts and the parasites were similar, from the same gene family. I've been collaborating with a cellular biologist on Unefra III for some time, on a program that breaks down the satellite DNA—that's a particular kind of DNA that has a different density from regular DNA. It sediments as a distinct band in caesium chloride density gradients. These are generally polymorphic, which makes them ideal markers for linkage studies—and there's no question, I've run our samples through my copy of the program in every combination possible. The genetic linkage is beyond ancestral; we're looking at recombination, and not from natural crossover."

He cleared his throat, looking from Cyl to Ezri with a furrowed brow. "Everything points to site-specific mutagenesis. Genetic engineering."

Ezri stared at Cyl, whose gaze remained fixed on Julian.

"What—how?" Ezri asked, unable to think of what else to ask, dumbstruck by the news.

Julian shook his head. "That I can't tell you. There's the possibility that the connection between your symbionts and the parasites is much more recent than everyone seems to think; the loci positions in the linkage map are too similar to be accounted for by such a distant historical connection, not when you consider genetic drift . . . but a certain kind of engineering would explain it, too. Another species doing experimentation on a symbiont, perhaps, a very long time ago."

There was silence for a moment, Ezri trying to absorb the information, trying to consider the implications—but she had no idea what to do with it.

She turned again to Cyl, and his expression troubled her.

"Did you know about this?" Ezri demanded in a whisper.

"Of course not," Cyl said, but he couldn't hold her gaze. Ezri raised her voice, unable to help it. "No more secrets, Cyl, I've had enough!"

Cyl shook his head. "Ezri, please . . . You must believe me when I say that I'm as taken aback by this as you are. Audrid Dax herself was one of the first to document the biological connection between symbiont and parasite. But the assumption was always that it represented some natural evolutionary divergence in the distant past. As far I know, no one ever put forth the theory that the parasites were engineered."

"Doesn't that strike you as odd?" Kira asked.

Cyl turned to her. "What do you mean?"

"What I mean is that maybe the reason no one has ever suggested the possibility that the parasites were engineered from symbionts is precisely because no one wanted that to be known. Maybe that's the real reason Trill has always been so secretive about the symbionts. Not just for the living memory they represent—the pseudo-immortality of the joined—but because of the danger they pose if exploited. If they were tampered with once, and it gave rise to the parasites . . . is it such a stretch to believe that your leaders would do or say anything to prevent that from happening again?"

Cyl's brow furrowed. His spots seemed to darken. "You're suggesting a generational conspiracy. Among the leaders of my world."

Kira leaned forward. "Can you honestly rule it out?"

Cyl opened his mouth to respond, then closed it again.

"I called this meeting as soon as Julian told me," Kira said. "My thinking is that this gives you something solid to present to the TSC. If you tell your people that an alien race experimented on the symbionts during their evolution, they might be more willing to cooperate, to find out who and why."

Ezri nodded slowly. It *was* a possible angle; the symbionts were precious to their hosts, and well-protected by them. *And it's about time that something shook them out of their denial. Maybe this is it.*

She took Julian's hand again, under the table. They'd been back from the Gamma Quadrant for less than a single day. "When should we go?" she asked.

"I haven't decided," Kira said. "But I want you to be ready to leave at a moment's notice. That means you taking charge on the *Defiant,* making sure she's prepped for flight immediately, and standing by to depart when I give the word. She'll make the trip faster than anything else we've got."

Ezri nodded, glancing at Julian with a faint smile of regret. He smiled back, but it didn't erase the look in his eyes, the stark worry that she saw there. He was afraid for her . . . and she couldn't refute his fear; she was afraid for all of them.

Ro Laren entered the small block of cells in the early evening, balancing a bulky data-entry padd and two mugs of hot liquid. Gard sat up from his bunk, his attention fixed on the padd, big enough to have a foldscreen and a tie-in to a main system. He hoped very much that she'd be leaving without it.

Ro set the items down on the watch console, turning to look at Gard. "Promise not to kill me, if I open your door?" she asked, a trace of smile in her voice.

"Solemnly," Gard said.

"The outer office is locked down and being monitored from ops, so if you were to try . . ."

"I won't," Gard said quickly. If she only meant to give him something, she could use the meal slot; either she was coming in, or he was being let out. It seemed that word had filtered to her that he wasn't as dangerous as everyone had initially assumed.

Gard stayed seated as Ro paused his cell's shield, stepping inside with the drinks and padd before tapping the remote on her hip. The shield hummed back into place as she sat and handed him a cup, setting the padd down on the bunk between them.

"Tea," Ro said, as he sniffed the clear liquid. "A blend that Quark came up with."

It had a pleasant, flowery scent, about as Ferengi as a free meal, but Gard had noted the bartender's special attachment to Ro, as well as Ro's openness to the concept. Quark had more going for him than met the senses.

Gard sipped at the tea, surprised by the delicate taste, and was about to say as much when Ro started talking.

"You'll have to stay here a while longer, but they told me to give you basic computer access . . . and assured me you weren't dangerous."

Gard nodded, burying an appreciative smile in spite of his surprise . . . and disappointment, that he would be stuck in a cell for a while longer. Her blunt nature was infinitely refreshing, and why he'd been attracted to her from the first. Sadly, that ship had sailed. If he tried to explain that the flirting hadn't had anything to do with gaining access to Shakaar, she wouldn't believe him.

Gard sipped his tea, waiting. After so many lifetimes of reading faces, he saw clearly that the security officer wasn't holding back.

"I thought you might be willing to talk to me about a few things," Ro said. "For instance . . . what can you tell me about the parasites?"

"Nothing you don't already know," Gard said, almost

honestly. "There are a few Trill, myself included, who have been watching for them. For a long time."

"Because of what happened on the comet," Ro said, referring to the disastrous field expedition a century before, that had killed a symbiont and host. Dax's husband at the time, in fact.

"And the similar chemistry," he added.

"You knew Shakaar was infected," Ro said. "Do you know where it happened?"

There were no confidences to be blown, not anymore. "Yes," he said. "It's why I came. We began tracing him after he started asking questions about Trill's defense network."

Ro's gaze brightened. "So you know where he was infected?"

"No," he said, but felt the warmth of sudden interest. "We managed to narrow it down to five places from the timeline, three planets and two starbases, but we didn't have the resources to follow up."

Ro pulled a small padd from her hip belt. "Do you remember the names of the five?"

Gard grinned. He did, in fact . . . and with access to a Federation computer system and Ro's help, there was something useful he could do from a locked cell, after all.

". . . and he said she's doing great, and that his grandfather, Joseph, will be there soon, within a week—and it turns out, he's coming with the chief! And Keiko and their children, too. Jake said it was a personal visit, but Chief O'Brien will come see us, he has to, I know he'll want to see how we transferred the fusion core from Empok Nor, and I'm sure Kira will approve the trip because . . ."

Nog couldn't seem to stop talking. Prynn didn't mind, it was a relief to listen to something besides her own relentlessly repeating thoughts, but she thought Shar might be bothered. It was just the three of them on the *Defiant*'s bridge, the sensor-array control panel in pieces on the console in front of them. It seemed the colonel had ordered a complete overhaul, and wanted to know if the *Defiant*'s sensors could be recalibrated to detect certain chemistries. Prynn didn't know the specifics; she was just there because she knew the equipment, and because Nog wanted her opinion on range possibilities.

Not at the moment, she thought, watching the Ferengi. Nog sat cross-legged on the floor, going through the larger chip trays a channel at a time, babbling enthusiastically about the call from his friend. Almost *too* enthusiastically, actually, as though it was a distraction from his own less than happy thoughts . . .

Project much? Nog was fine. It was Shar she was worried about.

She shot a sidelong glance at the science officer, working over computations on a padd next to her pile of patches and chips. Except for a tracing of irritated flesh around his eyes, he looked the way he usually looked—calm, focused, absorbed in his work. If she hadn't seen him earlier, hadn't seen the look on his face when he'd come to his door, she wouldn't have suspected that anything was wrong.

The way he just stood there, like he didn't know where he was . . . It hadn't been simple shock, either. At the Academy, Prynn had known a boy named Tom Havers, another pilot in training. They hadn't been close, just knew each other through mutual acquaintances, and a family tragedy had taken him out of the program before he was half finished. It so happened that she had been the first person to see him after he'd received the bad news, from one of the instructors. Prynn had been waiting for an after-hours conference in the woman's outer office, and when Tom had walked out, she'd seen the same expression that Shar had worn earlier. "Shock" was too pallid a word, couldn't begin to describe the blank and roaming madness in his eyes, the near break with reality created by a pain too intense to accept. She'd found out later that Tom's parents and older sister had all been killed on a vacation they'd taken together, a life-support malfunction on their transport.

And Shar's bondmates left him today. After seeing him so deeply affected, Prynn hadn't been able to help asking a few questions, which Lieutenant Nguyen had been able to answer. It turned out that though she was staying behind, the Andorian ambassador's private ship had been given leave to return to Andor, with two Andorian passengers on board. It seemed the ship would be returning, but not the passengers.

". . . and he and Dr. Bashir had this incredible model set up, with all these Earth battles," Nog was saying. "It was really— Hey, do either of you have the Lindsey?"

Shar said he didn't, as Prynn shuffled through her pile of bits and pieces for the antigrav tool. She didn't see it.

"Didn't Senkowski come up a while ago, borrow some stuff?" Prynn asked. Senkowski and Gordimer were both below, fine-tuning the pulse cannons or some such; Nog hadn't been all that clear.

"Oh, right," Nog said, pushing himself to his feet. "I'll be back in a minute. Either of you want anything? The replicators are back up."

Neither of them did. And as Nog stepped off the bridge, Prynn found herself hoping he would take his time getting back. She wasn't sure why, she had nothing planned to say, to try and engage Shar in a talk about what had happened . . . but she hoped anyway.

It was Shar who spoke first.

"You said your father had gone to Bajor," he said, not quite a question.

"Just this morning," Prynn said, her stomach tightening slightly. "He said they needed him for some confidential op . . . something about the assassin's contacts, I think."

She looked up at him, met his gaze—which was astoundingly sharp and clear and deep, so much so that she quickly looked away, feeling slightly flustered.

"About this morning," she said, amazed at how stupid she was acting, "I'm sorry if I bothered you."

"It was no bother," Shar said. "I apologize for my . . . awkwardness. I had a difficult morning."

Prynn nodded. "Me, too."

They were silent for a moment, Shar going back to his calculations, Prynn feeling a powerful urge to keep talking, to ask him how he felt, to tell him how she was feeling . . . and then she realized what she was doing, and why. It was surprising enough to her that her desire to converse completely dried up.

All those weeks on the Defiant, *nothing. Not even when we spent that time together, and he told me about his situation with his bondmates, and I talked about Vaughn . . . there was nothing there. So what happened?*

What happened was something that hadn't happened to her since before flight training, when she was still in her early Academy days. Then it had been a boy named Si, who'd had about a hundred girlfriends and had never gotten around to noticing that Prynn was alive. Since then, she'd mostly kept away from romance, sticking to situations where she was in control, where she could walk away the morning after, no strings.

I'm interested, Prynn thought wonderingly, feeling the

strange flush of happy, anxious recognition that came with the understanding. Maybe it was seeing him so vulnerable, so emotional and lost, just when she was feeling the same. Even before that, though, after the horror of Ruriko's murder had turned to anger, he'd made an attempt to console her. He was her friend . . . and consolation could make unlikely bedfellows.

We've both suffered. We've both lost what family we had.

A more practical part of her stepped in. *Forget it. It's too complicated, he won't be interested, you'll embarrass yourself . . .*

To hell with that. If she thought about it any longer, she'd lose her nerve.

"So, would you like to have lunch tomorrow?" Prynn asked, prepared for a rejection, determined not to expect one.

Shar looked up from his work, blinking, brushing strings of white hair behind one ear. He really was very pretty to look at . . . and though it had never been much of a focus for her, she knew she wasn't all that bad, herself.

"That would be very nice," he said. "But I may have things to do. Colonel Kira has asked that I assist with calculations in several departments in the coming days."

"Why?" Prynn asked, not sure what his answer was. "Which ones?"

Shar hesitated, then smiled slightly. "I . . . I'm sure I can take time for lunch, though."

Prynn smiled back, feeling that flush of fear and glee again, and liking it. She didn't realize until much later that she had successfully distracted herself from feeling bad about Ruriko and Vaughn, if only for a few minutes.

9

KAS MANAGED TO SLEEP IN UNTIL LATE MORNING, THOUGH she wasn't convinced it should be called "sleeping in," or at least not for the extremely pregnant.

Sleep doesn't have much to do with it, when you have to get up every hour or two to make room, she thought groggily, not wanting to move, understanding that she had no choice in the matter. How long had it been since she'd slept more than two hours in a row? It seemed like years. Add to that the breathlessness, the random aches, the inability to eat more than a half plate of food without it trying to wander back up . . . in all, though she was excited about the baby, she was finding pregnancy to be a serious chore.

At least now I've got a distraction, Kas thought, wincing as she heaved herself to the side of the bed, her hipbones shifting uncomfortably. Jake had come home to stay for a while, and though he'd gone to bed early the night before, obviously exhausted by his travels, it sounded like he had enough stories to tell to get her through the last days.

Which will save me from having to carry a conversation.

Her last OB trip to the station, Dr. Tarses had shown her an article that explained her general clumsy confusion; it wasn't just the lack of normal sleep, after all. Turned out that pregnancy actually caused brain shrinkage in humans for the last trimester . . . also an explanation for how she could trail off midsentence and forget what she was talking about in the space of a few seconds.

Not that very many had noticed. She didn't have the busiest of social lives, although she had gotten to know a few of her neighbors in the last couple of months. Lately, every few days, someone would drop by with a basket of vegetables or a homemade soup or bread. And there was also the small group of monks who'd set up a makeshift camp just off the property, some ten days earlier . . . one or two of them dropped by every afternoon, just to see if she wanted anything. She had the impression that they were locals, had perhaps volunteered to watch over her as her due date came and went. It was funny, that her main worry about moving to Bajor had been that as the Emissary's wife, she'd be treated differently. In the months since she'd settled in, she *had* noticed that people were especially nice to her . . . but had also noted that they were awfully nice to each other, too. Ben had chosen a beautiful piece of land to build on, but the community was what would make it feel like home.

She shuffled to the refresher and took care of business, stopping to brush and tie back her hair, smiling brightly at herself in the mirror before heading to the kitchen. It was so good, to have a reason for trying to look halfway decent—in the last month or so, she'd gotten used to wandering around in pajamas, and hadn't bothered with her hair in weeks. All the better that the reason was Jake.

Ben's son was sitting at the table just outside the open

kitchen, reading, a scattering of plates and cups attesting to a recent breakfast. She smelled cinnamon. He looked up when she came in and grinned, setting the padd aside as he quickly stood up.

"Sit down, let me get you breakfast," he said, pulling out a chair. "I made French toast when I got up, saved some batter . . ." He trailed off, a sudden look of anxiety on his face. "Do you want French toast? Is that going to make you sick? I can make eggs, or something. Whatever you want."

Only a few weeks earlier she might have protested, insisting that she was perfectly capable of getting her own breakfast, thank you—but now she only laughed, taking the seat gratefully. It was sweet of him to be so attentive, and the truth of it was, moving around a lot was kind of a pain these days. "French toast sounds wonderful. And a big glass of water, if you don't mind."

"You got it," Jake said, hurrying around the counter, a man with a mission. His expression suggested that he would bring her breakfast or die trying. The plus side of late pregnancy, Kas decided; she'd heard that she should enjoy it while it lasted. Once the baby came, she doubted anyone would be as eager to pamper her.

The French toast was great—his only specialty, Jake insisted—and they lingered at the table afterward, Kas listening as Jake talked about some of the things he'd seen in the Gamma Quadrant. He'd explained the night before why he'd left, apologizing about a hundred times in spite of her immediate acceptance. She'd been very upset when he'd disappeared, of course, had suffered through some serious anxiety—but had been determined not to let her pregnancy be dominated by fear, reminding herself constantly that Jake was a grown man, smart and responsible . . . and if something *had* happened, allowing herself to be overwhelmed by sorrow would be bad for her, and therefore bad for the baby. She thought she'd done a pretty good job of it, in all, so reassuring Jake that she was okay hadn't been such a stretch.

Jake also had some news from the station, about what had been going on since First Minister Shakaar's assassination—the Cardassian presence, possible conspiracy scenarios, mostly bits of news heard from Quark, through Nog. At least Kira seemed to be holding up; she'd looked very tired on yesterday's call, but Jake said she'd seemed much better before he'd left for Bajor . . . he said she'd been very happy about Opaka Sulan's return.

Jake talked a bit about the former kai, about how she'd escaped the moon she'd been stranded on, and what she'd done in the years since. Having never met the woman, Kas was interested, but she was also starting to wonder if she should bring up Ben. She'd told herself that she would wait for Jake to broach the topic, not wanting to push him, but she missed Ben, terribly . . . and knew that Jake felt the same. She wanted to talk about it before Jake's grandfather arrived, with the O'Briens and Jake's Aunt Judith; it wasn't that they didn't miss Ben, too, but the connections were different. Besides, Joseph was going to be so happy to see Jake, that would be an event all its own; with the communications restrictions, she hadn't been able to get through to him, but the runabout from Earth was due to show up sometime in the next two or three days.

"So, is it a boy or a girl?" Jake asked, eyeing her big belly with a teasing smile. "I bet it's a boy. You know, when I talked to Dr. Bashir about it—"

Kas mock-glared at him, cutting him off. "He didn't tell you anything. I'm his patient, he's sworn to secrecy."

"You know, Quark's got a pool on it," Jake said.

"Why am I not surprised?" Kas said. "Who's winning?"

"Ah, I think *boy* is ahead, but only by a few points."

Kas shook her head. "Maybe I'll have twins, just to upset Quark. He'd have to give everyone's money back."

At Jake's surprised look, Kas smiled. "No, Jake, it's not twins. That, I would know." She paused, then added wryly, "Besides, *avatar* wasn't plural."

Jake nodded slowly. It seemed he'd been filled in on a few of the other prophecies from Ohalu's book, too, not just the one that sent him to the Gamma Quadrant. Either that, or the page that he'd been given had also referenced the Emissary's second child; Jake had glossed over that part of last night's explanation, apparently embarrassed that he'd thought he'd be bringing Ben home, and had instead found the kai. It was very strange, having one's life so intricately entwined in an ancient religion; though she might come to accept it, it wasn't something she thought she would ever be entirely comfortable with.

"It's weird," Jake said, echoing her thought. "You know, having all these things revolve around Dad, and his family. It makes me wonder if we have any choice in what we do, any free will, you know?"

Kas nodded. "Let me know if you figure it out. I'm just . . . I'm hoping that he'll come back soon. I feel like it's time, now. I know that's because of the baby, of how close I am . . . but I'm also afraid that he's going to miss things, important things in our lives. Mostly, though, it's just what I want. Maybe that's selfish, but it's . . . it's what I want."

Even as she said it, she felt the now-familiar sensations of movement in her belly, the baby pushing as it maneuvered for a more comfortable position. Without saying a word, Kas reached over and took Jake's hand, placing it just below the left side of her rib cage.

"Is it—" Jake started, just as the baby started doing what she thought of as the vibrating dance, throwing in a few solid nudges for good measure. The expression on Jake's face as he watched her belly was beautiful, a dawning understanding that there was life inside of her, that it was real and coming soon.

Kas smiled, watching him, grateful that he was there. At least now she had someone to wait with her, to help her until Ben came home . . . someone as special to her as if he'd been her own.

Kira was just finishing up a meeting with Vlu and Macet when Ro signaled, wanting to meet. Kira asked her to come to ops and then wrapped up the coordination briefing, Macet disappearing from the console screen a moment before Vlu took her leave. The defense perimeter was solid, according to Macet, and Kira was relieved to hear from Vlu that the Cardassians on board seemed to be comfortable enough, in spite of the overall negative reaction they'd received. The news from Bajor wasn't quite as good—Macet said that his people had reported that many Bajorans were still avoiding cooperation, but Vaughn, at least, was doing everything in his power to smooth things over and keep the operation going as quickly as possible.

The office doors parted, Ro striding in with a look of triumph on her face. She dropped a padd on Kira's desk, a tight grin breaking through her usually detached composure.

"Found it," she said.

Kira picked up the padd, not sure what she was looking at; it appeared to be a random list of planets.

"Found what?"

"First Minister Shakaar was infected by a parasite on Minos Korva," Ro said with certainty.

Kira felt her heart skip a beat. "Are you sure?"

"As certain as I can be, considering it's all long-distance legwork," she said. "Starfleet's been looking at all the places Shakaar stopped on his way home from the Sol system. They've managed to cancel out two of the small stations closest to Earth, but still have nine to look at . . . except there are really only five."

"Why only five?"

Ro leaned across the desk, and with a go-on nod from Kira, called up a star chart of Shakaar's route to and from Earth on the computer. She highlighted a number of planets and a few bases.

"These are where he stopped on his way back," Ro said. "Note that Betazed is third, after Deneva. Based on the reports from the *Enterprise* on the Starfleet infiltration, a full Betazoid would probably be able to detect a parasite mind. And Shakaar was there for over a week."

Kira frowned, trying to remember the counselor's report. Ro supplied it. "Deanna Troi was ship's counselor—still is, I believe—and is half Betazoid; she sensed that *something* was being hidden. It's not hard evidence, but I doubt very much that if Shakaar had been infected by then, he would have dared it."

It made sense. "So, that rules out Deneva, New France, and Betazed," Kira said.

"Right. And Gard finally passed on something useful yesterday, after Dax and the general spoke with him—a time frame."

Kira blinked. "You know, then . . ."

"About the Trill watchers," Ro said, nodding. "And I

know when they decided Shakaar might be a threat. . . . About two weeks after Betazed was when he first contacted them, claiming that he wanted additional information about Trill as part of his lobby run."

Kira peered at the chart. "Which would eliminate at least the last planet on the list, Xepolite."

"Probably Lya, too," Ro said, "though I didn't rule it out immediately. I spent most of last night cross-checking Federation arrival and departure logs with what we got from his ship's computer . . . and Minos Korva has to be it, third after Betazed. There are Federation starbases on either side, both set up with heavy surveillance; every moment of his time would be accounted for. But on the planet, he was taken on a scenic tour of their western mountain ranges that lasted for four days. Low population, a lot of isolated territory. There had to be infinite opportunity for infection."

Kira stared at the chart another moment, feeling a smile of her own forming. "Ro, this is amazing. Really excellent work. I'll contact Akaar immediately."

"What about Gard?" Ro asked. "I couldn't have done this without him . . . will you pass that along?"

Kira wished it were that easy. "I'm not sure what Gard told you," she said carefully, "but I'm guessing it's at least part of what Ezri told me . . . and the thing is, the Federation doesn't know about his role in what happened. Not yet."

Ro frowned, an edge in her voice. "Why not? Maybe he went about it the wrong way, but he did what was necessary, they'll have to see that."

Killing Edon was necessary. Kira felt a stir of despairing anger, but pushed it away.

"It's political and complicated," she said. "I'm sorry, I

can't do any better than that . . . but if and when this all comes out, I'll do what I can for him."

Ro's jaw tightened, but she only nodded.

"You're doing a good job, Ro," Kira said. "Even the admiral will have to concede to that."

Ro almost smiled. "It seems to me, he doesn't 'have' to do anything."

Kira sighed, shaking her head slightly. "I know, he can be difficult. But he's just doing what he thinks is best."

"Absolutely," Ro said, that edge still in her voice. "Permission to be excused?"

"Granted," Kira said. "But just let me say . . . I hope you're still considering your options, regarding your resignation?"

Ro's face was a blank. "I've been busy, Colonel. I'll give it all the consideration it's due, when I have the time."

Kira thought about telling her that she wasn't the only one who hoped Ro would reconsider, that the lieutenant still had an ally or two in the Federation . . . but her carefully crafted, barely civil answer made it clear that now was not the time.

"Excused, Lieutenant," Kira said, slightly exasperated with the woman's constant defenses. Every time they made progress as coworkers, one of them managed to rub the other one the wrong way.

Ro retrieved her padd and walked out without looking back, leaving Kira to steel herself up for another conversation with the admiral.

Vaughn commed off from Kira and sat for a few moments, staring at the blank console. Reports had officially been exchanged. He'd spent the day rescheduling and reassigning the scan teams, working to keep most of the Cardassians at the main camp, out of civilian sight; Lenaris had agreed it was a necessary tactic. Vaughn had reported to Kira that he was looking into setting up a temporary transporter system between the central compound and the busiest of the smaller camps, at least using the runabouts' systems, and that they'd managed to clear four more "possibles," a family from the Hill province. There had been no luck tracing Shakaar's final transmissions to Bajor, not from his end. Kira reported in turn that Ro Laren had figured out where Shakaar had been infected, and that the news had been passed along to Akaar; she'd sent Dax and the general to Trill, to dig through files, and Bashir was developing theories on the parasites' telepathic link . . .

. . . and we're not really accomplishing much of anything. He felt hopeless, like that saying about closing the barn door after the livestock had escaped. Everything they were doing, everything they *could* do wouldn't be nearly enough. There was no question that there were a number of infected, both on the station and on the planet's surface, and they hadn't managed to uncover even one more case.

Kira had asked after his health before signing off, studying his face with a scrutiny that suggested he didn't look well. He'd brushed it off with a crack about the plush accommodations, but she hadn't seemed convinced . . . and having stared in the 'fresher mirror for a few minutes that morning, after yet another restless night, he wasn't surprised. The dark hollows under his eyes, the pallid complexion, the lines around his nose and mouth . . . he looked like someone recovering from a lengthy illness, the kind that usually killed.

I'm not, though. In fact, it feels like I'm just getting

started. Things were getting worse, not better. All he'd seen in his dreams for the past two days was Ruriko or Prynn, one or both of them screaming or in danger, and in his dreams, he wouldn't help them. He meant to, he wanted to, but for some reason, he just stood and watched, cursing himself, overwhelmed by guilt and inaction as the only two women he'd ever loved continued to scream, to die. It was terrible. And though he was performing his duties, taking care of what needed to be done, he spent a great part of his waking hours thinking about it.

"This has to stop," he said, the thought of it so deeply embedded in his mind now that he didn't notice he'd spoken. Why was he having such a difficult time shaking this?

Without actually making the decision, he reached out and tapped at the console board, speaking his code—he was one of the few lucky enough to have one that allowed a direct access, though it meant he was scanned up to six times daily—and got through to Nguyen on the station. He made his request and she logged it, connecting him straight through to Prynn's quarters.

Be home, please be home, he thought, watching the cursor pulse at the bottom of the screen, vaguely astounded that he was calling, not caring if it was selfish. He wanted, needed to see her, to tell her again how sorry he was—

Prynn's face flashed onto the screen, open and pleasant—until she saw who was calling. Her features closed immediately, like some flower that drew in on itself with the setting sun, her gaze narrowing, her lips pulling tight.

"*What do you want?*" she said, her voice as rigid as she could make it.

"I'm sorry to bother you," Vaughn started, his heart growing heavy as he looked into her anger, his feelings of helplessness growing. "I—just wanted to see you, to see how you were."

Her expression didn't change. *"You've seen me. I'm fine—and I'm really very busy, so . . ."*

"I'm sorry," he said, blurted out without caring about his stupid pride, without caring that the words were nothing to what he'd done, that they might even insult her. "I'm sorry about everything, Prynn. Please believe that, you have to believe that much—"

"I have to go," she said, one hand darting forward, the screen going blank.

Vaughn sat and stared, feeling like it was all he was good for, remembering that he used to be stronger, less affected by these things, these emotional troubles that had sometimes cropped up in his life. Killing Ruriko had done something to him, and though he'd only just started to gain Prynn's acceptance before the killing, he felt its absence now far more than he thought was possible.

It had to stop, it had to, he was on a downward spiral that he couldn't control. The thought repeated itself again and again as Vaughn dragged himself to his feet and went to find Lenaris, to plan the next day, to do his duty.

10

IMMEDIATELY AFTER HIS NEWEST SCRAMBLE BREAKER PICKED up the transmission between the *Trager* and DS9, Quark put a call in to Ro. He simply told her that he knew, then sat behind the bar on a high stool, his feet pulled up, nervously scanning the floor for movement while he waited for her. Those long moments were a spin through the Vault of Eternal Destitution; not only was there a possibility of evil alien attack, the dinner crowd was horrifically light, less than a dozen patrons—a full twenty percent drop from the night before. And they weren't tipping, either. To top it off, the Jem'Hadar and his little gray girlfriend, Wex, were hanging around out front again, probably scaring off the few customers that hadn't been taken over. When Ro hurried in a few seconds later, it was all he could do not to start shouting curses. That bug that had attacked Macet outside of Treir's quarters hadn't been an escaped lab experiment, after all. There were parasites aboard, and they were obviously eating his patrons, and no one had bothered to tell him.

To Destitution *with the patrons, what about* me? *No, they're perfectly happy to watch my business die a pale and listless death, then wait and see if the things have a taste for Ferengi.* Which they surely would. Ferengi flesh was said to be quite tender.

Ro approached the bar with a look of vague irritation on her face; it was nothing to what he was feeling.

"You know, I expect as much from Kira, but why didn't *you* tell me?" he spat, still hardly able to believe it. "Who else knows?"

Ro glanced to either side before addressing him, keeping her voice low. "Very few. Keep it down, if you wouldn't mind. How did you find out?"

"I have my resources," he said. "And no, I didn't tell anyone. I guess we have that in common, don't we?"

She at least had the good grace to look embarrassed. "Orders. I didn't have a choice. I *am* sorry, but until we get a fix on who's who—"

"What do you mean?" Quark asked, wounded. "Do you think I'm one of them?"

Ro sighed. "If you were, you wouldn't have called to tell me that you'd found out, would you?"

"So instead of telling people that they're in danger, the powers that be have decided to make it a conspiracy to keep Bajor out of the Federation," Quark said acidly. "Like anyone is going to believe that."

Ro cocked an eyebrow. "You did."

"Yeah, well, now I don't. And if you don't think anyone else is going to figure it out—"

"They will . . . given the right equipment," Ro said, watching him closely. She was fishing. Quark didn't blink. "But right now, we're buying time."

"Time is latinum," he shot back. "How many people

have they gotten? Is that why my revenues are down?"

Ro shook her head. "Not that many. Ten, now, all in stasis. Business is bad because people are scared, by the lockdown and the possibility of anti-Federation terrorism."

"And if word were to get out, that there is no terrorist threat?" Quark asked, quickly warming to the idea. "That being in a crowd is actually safer than staying in?"

Ro scowled. "You let it leak, you'll be up on charges, Quark. I mean it."

Quark was unfazed. Jail time was a definite drawback, but on the pro side, he was looking at vastly increased profits—which outweighed even the very worst of cons. Everyone on the station would pack together like slugs in a tin, and where better than the most popular dining and gaming establishment on the Promenade? And the biggest? "It'd be worth it. Look around. How can things get any worse?"

Ro leaned in, her scowl deepening. "I can make it worse, Quark. Count on it."

As always when she was close, and irritated, Quark felt a chill run through him, from his lobes to his toes . . . though probably not the kind she intended. "Come on, Laren," he said, grinning, inviting her enthusiasm. "The truth will come out soon enough, anyway. Why shouldn't someone profit from it?"

Ro's face had fallen carefully blank. "Because the parasites might very well target you."

That was a definite con. "You're kidding, right?" Quark said, reflexively pulling his feet up higher.

"No. Think about it—this is one of the few places on the station that's open to everybody. You'd have half the station in here, crowded together, under your direct influence. Who'd make a better host?"

Quark stared at her, not sure by her cool expression if she was lying. "But—I'd be safe, surrounded by all those people. . . ."

Ro's eyes narrowed, her voice dropping even lower. "You'd have to sleep sometime."

Another beat of cool silence, and Ro straightened up. "Besides, I'd never speak to you again."

An out, and an opportunity. Quark took it. "That, I couldn't bear," he said, letting his romantic-charm grin resurface. "The secret is safe . . . but only if you'll keep me in the loop. As much as possible," he quickly added.

Ro nodded, standing. "You're doing the right thing, Quark."

And the safest.

"Anything for you, Laren," he said, with such sincerity that he believed it himself, for a second or two. He mentally amended that to anything priced reasonably, but saw no reason to spoil the moment with such details.

Ro seemed to soften slightly. "Is there anything you need?"

The possibilities were infinite, but he settled for the most nagging. "Could you get that alien monster and his new friend to move?" he asked, pointing at the Jem'Hadar and the gray alien. "They're scaring people away."

Ro followed his gesture, gave a small shrug. "I asked Taran'atar to keep an eye on the bar, for exactly the reasons we've been discussing," she said. "Wex is from the Gamma Quadrant. If she decides to spend part of her time in his company, his presence will be less disruptive. Be grateful."

Quark looked exasperated. "Grateful for what? She's got an expression that could turn back time. Would you at least ask her to try smiling once in a while?"

"I'll see what I can do."

She promised to try and make it in for a midday meal the following day, and then was gone, pausing for a moment to ask the gray girl—Wex, her name was—to cheer up. As soon as she walked away from the unlikely patrons, Wex shot a look in at Quark that suggested she might also like the taste of Ferengi flesh, and not in a nice way. Quark glared back at her until he saw the Jem'Hadar glowering in his direction, and quickly turned back to studying the ruins of his dinner business.

He sighed again. The news would get out soon enough, he supposed; secrets didn't last too long on the station. Until then, he'd have to try and make the best of it.

At least I never got rid of those old vole traps, he thought, brightening. If there were parasites running around, he could at least make it a bit more difficult for them to get to him . . . though what to bait them with?

He started to get up, then thought better of it, reaching toward the signal light for the kitchen. Why leave the safety of his nice, high stool? Grimp could head down to the dark, shadowy storage compartment for the traps; after all, what was he paying them for, if not to make his life easier?

"Hey, Quark," Treir said behind him. "Call for you. It's from Ferenginar."

Quark's hand froze centimeters from the signal light. He frowned. "Did they lift the comm blackout?"

Treir shook her head. "The call's being routed from the Militia comnet on Bajor."

The Militia? They'd only let a comm through during a state of emergency for a military reason, or for some muckity-muck VIP, like a head of state . . .

Looks like my idiot brother is finally learning how to use his position as Grand Nagus to get what he wants, Gint help us all. Scowling in irritation, Quark stepped around the bar and thumbed the DNA scanner to let the call through.

The companel screen lit up with the familiar, vacuous grin he hadn't seen in over eight months. *"Hello, Brother!"*

"Rom," Quark said, "this better be important. I'm a busy man." He felt no guilt about the lie. Seeing Rom in his nagus regalia, latinum-headed staff in hand, was too painful, especially given Quark's current state of affairs. Of all the people Zek could have picked to be his successor, he'd chosen small-lobed Rom. Never mind that he could barely scrape two slips of latinum together while under Quark's employ, or that he'd quit the bar to become a lowly engineer for the Bajoran Militia, *or* that he'd let his own son join Starfleet instead of steering him toward the proper pursuit of profit . . . or even that he'd broken with tradition and married a poor Bajoran. One of Quark's own dabo girls, no less. No, the worst thing was that Zek had actually chosen Rom *because* of all those things, so that someone would be in power to uphold the insidious democratic reforms Quark's mother Ishka had convinced, connived, and otherwise enticed Zek into implementing before the two of them retired to Risa.

"But Brother, I have wonderful news!" Rom beamed.

Quark's lobes tingled. Maybe his luck was about to turn. If Rom was calling to slip him advance word of an opportunity, his troubles might well be over. And he certainly *looked* excited.

Quark grinned. "I'm all ears."

"Leeta's pregnant! You're going to be an uncle again!" Rom reached off camera and drew his wife into view. Leeta smiled at Quark across the light-years and waved her fingers, her belly already visibly big with child.

Quark's grin fell, crashed on the floor, bounced a few times, and rolled against the bar before it came to a stop and burst into flames.

"How nice," he said.

Rom, predictably, looked confused. *"What's wrong, Brother? I thought you'd be happy for us."*

"Oh, I'm thrilled," Quark snapped. He reached for a bottle of Saurian brandy and poured a shot. "Really, I couldn't be happier. I mean, let's look at my situation: either Bajor's going to join the Federation, or we're all going to be eaten. Either way, business is in the waste extractor and I'm going to have to close the bar. I have no prospects, and my personal life is a shipwreck." He bared his teeth in a sneer and raised the full glass to the screen. "But hey, Leeta's pregnant. So it must be Happy Hour!" He kicked back the brandy and slammed the glass down on the bar.

Rom and Leeta stared back at him, their eyes wide. *"I had no idea things were so bad, Brother,"* Rom said. *"I'm sorry."*

Quark looked away, irritated. Just like that, he'd spat on Rom and Leeta's good news, and just like that, his brother had responded to him with genuine sympathy. Didn't it figure.

"No, Rom, I'm sorry," he said, looking back up at the screen. "You too, Leeta. That's great news. Really. I'm just having a bad day here."

"Is there anything we can do?" Leeta asked.

Quark almost laughed, remembering his earlier misguided optimism that Rom was calling to tip him off about an opportunity. In the old days, being a member of the nagus's family would have guaranteed Quark's solvency, no matter how bad things got. But in these enlightened days of reformed business practices and fair competition, good, old-fashioned nepotism didn't stand a snowball's chance on Vulcan.

"Don't worry about me, I'll be fine," he lied. "I always am." He could see they weren't buying it. He'd have to cut this short. "Look, I need to get back to work. I'll see you around, okay? Congratulations again." Without waiting for them to answer, he cut the signal. The Quark Enterprises logo replaced their faces on the screen, and he stared at it for a full minute before he turned back to the bar and started taking drink orders.

There's always the Orion Syndicate, he thought. *They may still be a little mad about that whole gateway fiasco, but business is business. I could probably smooth things over. After all, I* am *a people person—*

Wait a minute. What was the name of that guy from Farius Prime, with the investment opportunity? Kostaza?

Already, a new scheme was taking shape in his mind, filling him with renewed optimism. He wasn't out of the game yet. There was still one more hand he could play.

Liro Kavi was nervous, but determined not to let it get to her. She'd been on DS9 all of three months, most of that training, and had been on security detail for only two weeks, since right before the assassination. As if that hadn't been bad enough—being brand-new to the job and the station, just in time to see the first minister murdered—now she'd been put on a night watch, lurking through DS9 in the small hours, searching for alien threats in the loneliest of places.

She walked slowly through the low-lit bay, palm beacon in one hand, phaser in the other. She could see the glow from Bennings's beacon reflecting high on the far wall at least thirty meters to her left, heard what sounded like a curse as the young human male ran into something or other, a sharp *clang* ringing through the vast storage area.

Liro tapped her combadge, as much to hear a friendly voice as anything else. "Problem, Bennings?"

A long pause. *"I was attacked by a box of stem bolts, thank you,"* he said finally, also keeping his voice low. They'd shared the same detail for the past week. He was another postwar addition to DS9, and though he'd been in security longer than her, transferring from a Federation base, he was also two years her junior. Hassling him was one of the few perks of her day.

What is *a stem bolt, anyway?* Liro wasn't sure, and didn't care; what she *did* care about was getting through the cavernous bay as quickly as possible, so they could be somewhere else. Bay 5G was a nightmare jumble of discarded crates and stored excess, plus about a thousand personal items belonging to station residents, things too large to be easily stored in quarters. There was a lot of sporting equipment, furniture, a number of massive art pieces . . . basically, a lot of shadowy crevices for things to hide in. Occasionally, Bennings's tricorder would beep with a new contact, and each time he'd insist it was only a vole.

Liro shivered. She knew that Lieutenant Ro wasn't telling them everything, but what had filtered down was more than enough. There was an alien presence aboard, in the form of small insectile or wormlike creatures that could actually take over a host body. The powers that be were keeping it quiet from the majority of those on board, but security had to know. Liro wasn't sure if that was a good thing or not. She preferred the truth to ignorance, she supposed, but when you were basically alone, walking in the dark . . .

A flash of movement, there, to her right—or was it just

the echo of her light, the darkness closing in as the bright beam moved away? The beam jerked back to the small, tight space between two storage units, Liro staring so hard that her eyes started to burn. Nothing there . . . or whatever it was had moved on.

Alone in the dark, knowing that there were parasitic aliens on the loose. Liro suppressed another shiver and started moving again. She figured that between security and upper management, there were probably only a hundred-plus people on the station who knew about the creepily subtle invasion. Maybe twice that; in truth, she didn't have any real idea. For obvious security reasons, the lieutenant had made it very clear that they weren't to talk about it, not even to one another. A good idea, but the lack of communication was making everything much more nerve-racking. All the security officers were being scanned constantly, three times each shift, but that there was even a chance that they, too, could be infiltrated . . .

"Anything?"

Liro started at Bennings's sudden question. She reflexively glanced at the far wall, saw the glow of his light perhaps forty meters away, before tapping her badge.

"No, you?" she asked without thinking, shaking her head slightly at her own stupidity. If he'd found something, he probably would have said so.

"Just a lot of dark. It'd be nice to turn on a few lights around here."

Liro silently agreed. The malfunction of the power grid in this sector of the docking ring was what had led them to the bay in the first place. While engineering worked on the problem, she and Bennings were investigating the affected areas. In the dark.

She bit back another chill. How many people had been

taken over? No one was talking, and all the secretive lurking around was getting to her. When would Colonel Kira make an announcement? Or would it be from Bajor, from the Assembly or Asarem? The truth was probably already leaking, even as she and Bennings and half of the rest of security were wandering through the station's many empty places. It couldn't be soon enough. Her recent training had stressed that knowledge was power, and that security was about containing knowledge, but being able to fight the aliens directly seemed infinitely preferable to how things were now.

Think about something else. Right. She swept her light slowly around some kind of wine rack, trying to force her mind to other things. Rumor had it that Lieutenant Ro wouldn't be transferring to Starfleet, which wasn't much of a surprise. Though she respected the woman, Liro couldn't help thinking that someone else might be better suited to the position; Ro wore her earring on the wrong side, like some rebellious youth . . . though at least she hadn't turned to the Ohalavaru. Liro's mother said that the Prophets would turn away from those who rejected the truth, and—

Liro froze, her eyes wide. She'd heard something, faint but close by, a sound she couldn't place. It was more like a change in the air than a noise, like sensing movement, feeling someone next to you flinch, or quickly turn their head. She reached for her combadge with her phaser hand, saw Bennings's light on the far wall . . .

She felt her jaw clench, a light sweat breaking across her body. The muted glow of his palm beacon appeared to be in the same place it had been the last time she'd looked. Exactly. As though it had been knocked out of his hand, perhaps.

Got to get help—

She fumbled at her combadge, the phaser getting in the way, almost dropping her beacon as her mind raced with the possibilities, all of them horrible. She swung around to find the exit, to mark where she needed to run—

—and there was Bennings, a meter behind her. The beam from her light splashed across his grinning face, his eyes dark and unknown as he raised one hand, his grin opening into a silent laugh. He reached for her, and before she could scream, he had her.

11

VAUGHN WOKE FROM A DREAM OF PRYNN, A VERY YOUNG Prynn who shouted meaningless, angry sounds at him while he tried in vain to speak. For a second after he opened his eyes, he could still see her, just a child, could feel a wisp of hope that it wasn't too late to mend things . . . and then someone was signaling at the door, the sound that had pulled him from his dream. He scrambled to remember where he was, and why.

Parasites. Bajor.

"Come," he managed, sitting up on the cot, feeling achy and mildly feverish. He'd slept in his clothes. Again.

At Vaughn's acknowledgment, Lenaris Holem stepped into the field shelter, a look of strain around the general's eyes as he smiled. A wash of daylight came with him, brighter than it should have been.

"Commander," Lenaris said, and though his tone was warm, the pinched look didn't diminish.

Vaughn swung his legs to one side of the cot, blinking at the timepiece on the wall. Was that right? He'd slept well into morning, hours past when he normally rose. Why hadn't anyone come for him?

"I thought you were at Rakantha," Vaughn said, willing himself to stand up, finding that he couldn't work up the enthusiasm. He stayed seated on the edge of his cot, feeling a first note of alarm at Lenaris's presence as the irregularities piled up. Late morning, Lenaris back at Hedrikspool, the look on the younger man's face . . . "New outbreak?"

Lenaris shook his head, his smile fading. "Nothing like that."

Something in his tone . . . Vaughn instinctively thought of Prynn, but said nothing, drawing the straight face that he'd spent so many years perfecting . . . and was able to tell by the thread of concern in the general's gaze that it wasn't so perfect anymore.

"Have a seat, General," Vaughn said, keeping his tone mild. "Mind telling me what's going on?"

Lenaris moved to one of the wall benches across from him and sat down, leaning forward. "You need a break. I'm sending you to the monastery in Ashalla for a few days, to get some rest."

Vaughn stared at him. "Are you kidding? We're in the middle of a major operation. I don't have the time or the inclination to 'rest.' In case you hadn't noticed, things are getting worse around here."

Lenaris nodded wearily. "I've noticed. But last night's scans say you're not up for it."

Damn doctors. Vaughn remembered thinking that the routine visit had been longer than usual.

"Your serotonin levels have continued to drop, and now your blood pressure is up," the general continued. "You're overtired. I've already discussed the matter with Colonel Kira, and both she and Akaar agree."

"This is ridiculous," Vaughn said, feeling himself flush, disconcerted that conversations had been carried on about his medical status. "There have been seven new cases reported in the last two days—"

"Eleven," Lenaris interrupted. "Remember? The four at Hill, yesterday morning."

"Right," Vaughn said, but felt his self-righteous windup winding back down. He'd forgotten. "I'm perfectly capable of doing my job, and . . . and I don't need this right now, General. Please. I need to work. I can get one of the docs to prescribe something."

Lenaris shook his head sympathetically. "Let's not argue about this, Commander. It's a medical leave, there's no shame in it."

Easy for you to say, you're not the one being shipped off to take a nap. Vaughn wanted to say something more, to fight his case, but there was nothing to be said. If Akaar knew, it was over; when Starfleet pulled someone on a medical, they meant it.

And you can't deny you need the rest. The thought was a flash of clarity. He needed *something*. He was spinning out of control, plagued with guilt and some as yet unnamed turmoil that was driving him crazy. If he didn't get to the root of it, do something to heal himself, he was headed for vapor lock.

"Who's going to step in?" he asked quietly.

"It's only for a few days, a week, perhaps," Lenaris said. "Bowers and I can handle it. If for some reason we can't, both the colonel and the admiral have promised to send aid."

With resources spread as thinly as they were, those promises hadn't been made lightly. The feelings inspired weren't good ones, and again, some of it must have showed. The general stepped forward and clasped Vaughn's shoulder, a light squeeze.

"The choice wasn't yours to make, and dwelling on it won't change anything. You're off duty, Commander. My own transport is standing by to take you to Ashalla."

"Why a monastery?"

"Because it's about as far from your responsibilities as I can send you out without shipping you off planet." He stepped back and smiled slightly. "I'll see you soon," he said firmly, and with a final nod, turned and walked out.

Vaughn stared after him a moment, then stood, gazing around the shelter for his bag. The general was right; frustration and self-pity would be a waste of effort. And the sooner he got on with it, the sooner he'd be fit to return to duty.

Lucky me, he thought tiredly, and started to pack.

Though Shar made the effort to be punctual in spite of his busy schedule, Prynn was already waiting for him when he arrived at Quark's for their lunch. She'd chosen a small table near the base of the stairs that led to the holosuites, half hidden by shadow. She smiled brightly when he sat down.

"I'm sorry if I'm late," Shar said, but Prynn shook her head, still smiling.

"You're right on time. I was a little early."

Shar nodded, returning her smile as best he could. He still wasn't certain why she'd wanted to meet, but suspected she might be trying to learn more about the true nature of the station's lockdown. It was the reason he'd agreed to the meeting in the first place, to divert her from her questions . . . though he'd been surprised to discover, on his way to the Promenade, that he felt some measure of gratitude for the invitation. As the shock of his personal situation wore off, the pain grew. Immersion in his work was proving to be a suitable distraction, but his few spare moments returned him to a deeply felt despondency, one he thought might linger for some time. Perhaps always. He hoped that the company of another might at least relieve the monotony of it.

Prynn seemed both distracted and overly intent, somehow, though it took Shar a while to notice the slight differences from her regular behavior. He, too, was distracted, thinking of the long day still ahead after the morning's briefing. His time was much in demand.

The Federation defense against the parasites was not progressing as quickly as anyone had hoped. Three more cases of infection had been caught on board, two of them security guards. Early on, Colonel Kira had let it "get out" that the infected had been sent to Bajor on an important and secret project, but friends and loved ones of the missing people had started to ask questions, and others were taking notice. Kira had called for a tighter lock on information; they'd all been scanned at the door of the conference room, and had agreed to submit to random scans throughout the day, which intensified the need for better portable equipment.

Nog still needed him on the *Defiant*, especially since Lieutenant Dax had come aboard and ordered the ship's status upgraded to departure-readiness until further notice. At the same time, they had to continue working on improving the accuracy of the handheld medical scanners while on board. On the medical front, the Cardassian enzyme had turned out to be valueless as a deterrent for non-Cardassians; initial tests had shown that it actually destroyed membranous tissue in other humanoids. Dr.

Bashir wanted Shar's input on a light-spectrum test, to determine whether or not the parasites could be driven out by certain bands. It seemed there was some precedent for it in other parasitic species, though Shar had yet to read the file. Another task on his list of many.

And yet I am here, Shar thought, watching Prynn Tenmei order their food, wondering if he should feel shame for it, deciding that he did not. He slept only a few hours each day, and thought that half an hour of time spent eating with a friend was acceptable behavior, in spite of the crisis. He hadn't known Prynn long, but she was unusually forthright, a trait he admired.

She carried the conversation as they waited for their order, jumping casually but skillfully from topic to topic, following no particular theme. He found himself able to relax somewhat, to let her steer his thoughts away from his work, from his lost mates and his *zhavey*. He still hadn't spoken with Charivretha, since before Dizhei and Anichent had gone, and wasn't sure what to expect when he finally did. Would she take pity on his sorrow, be merciful? Resigned, as before? Angry? Perhaps she would choose not to speak with him at all; it was a thought that carried both horror and a strange kind of relief.

As their food arrived—steamed vegetables over sticky *spya*—Prynn finished an anecdote about an instructor they'd both known at the Academy and fell silent, eating a few bites, watching him tuck his hair behind his ears to avoid trailing it in his plate. He noted again that she was distracted . . . but no, "distracted" wasn't the term. She seemed introspective, perhaps, but was giving off a slight tension. He could sense it.

"How's your food?" she asked.

Shar sampled a chunk of vegetable matter, some form of

green squash. The sauce was well spiced. "Very good, thank you."

Prynn nodded, then took a deep breath, meeting his gaze. "May I ask you a personal question?"

"Yes," Shar said, after a hesitation. It seemed likely that she'd want to know about his mates, and he didn't wish to discuss them. But he didn't want to be rude, either.

"Do Andorians have romantic or sexual liaisons outside their species?" she asked bluntly, and took another bite of her food.

Shar was surprised. It was an odd query, and he wasn't used to discussing Andorian social patterns. It seemed a harmless enough question, though.

"They do," he said, "but it isn't encouraged. And it isn't acceptable until after their children have grown to maturity. We must . . . there must be proper role modeling for the young."

"Even off planet?" Prynn asked. "I mean, if there are no children around . . ."

Shar nodded. "It's more acceptable, but is still rarely done."

"Why is that?"

He thought for a moment. "I don't know," he said. "I suppose because we're all so thoroughly indoctrinated into the need for bonding. Mating is so very important, for the future of our world. . . ."

He trailed off, unhappy with himself and uneasy discussing it. Prynn seemed sympathetic, but she wasn't finished, either.

"And if you have no mates?" she asked, her voice gentle.

She was asking what he meant to do, now that his mating seemed unlikely. A friend's concern, he supposed . . .

except there was a curiosity to her expression that suggested more than that, a carefully reined eagerness, like a hunger. . . .

Shar blinked, suddenly understanding. He felt himself flush slightly and looked down at his plate, unsure of what he should say. He wasn't entirely naive; he'd been propositioned a number of times, mostly while a student at the Academy, and had been told more than once that he was attractive by many humanoid standards . . . but that had been before, when his life had already been decided. He'd loved Thriss and Dizhei and Anichent, and would be bonded to them; there had been no question of romance, and nothing beyond a mild interest for him in physically coupling with any other. Thriss had been his only one. . . .

"I hope I haven't offended you," Prynn said, frowning. "I didn't mean to—"

Shar forced a smile. "That's all right," he said.

"No, it's not," she said. "I've been thoughtless. I'm sorry. I just . . . I like spending time with you, and I was wondering what your situation is, now."

As uncomfortable as he was with the conversation, it was a fair question . . . but one he hadn't even begun to answer for himself. He managed to meet her gaze again, saw sincerity and concern there, and told her the truth.

"I don't know," he said. "And I may not know for a while."

Prynn nodded. "Then forget I asked, for a while," she said, and smiled warmly at him. "Let me subtly change the subject. Have you ever had *coconut?* It's a kind of fruit, I think, from Earth, and they make this pie out of it. . . ."

She managed to convince him to try a piece of coconut pie for dessert, and went back to carrying on a light and interesting conversation as they finished their meals. He did what he could to enjoy the time, but found himself quite distracted by what they'd discussed. What *was* his situation? He was not at all ready to pursue an intimacy with another, not so soon after the dissolution of his betrothal and Thriss's death . . . but his life seemed likely to continue for some time, and the thought of spending all of it alone was a bleak one.

After the pie—which was, to Shar's taste, unique and mildly unpleasant—the lunch was concluded, and they walked out together. Shar had to get to the *Defiant,* and Prynn was on her way to a general security briefing, one that Lieutenant Ro had devised; it had been discussed at the morning's meeting. The idea was to suggest that station residents travel in groups, to encourage vigilance and deter possible terrorist attack. It wasn't the most logical reasoning, but as Ro had pointed out, they had to do something to keep the parasites from spreading. It was a strategic necessity, their continued silence on the subject, but in some ways, keeping the secret was doing more harm than good.

They walked past the Jem'Hadar and the small gray Trelian, both of whom had become something of a fixture in Quark's—and according to Nog, a current source of Quark's complaints. As they passed, Shar noted that the Trelian girl gave off an energy similar to the Jem'Hadar's. Interesting. From Taran'atar, Shar believed it was violence held in check, a necessary suppression of his nature. The girl, he didn't know well enough to say, though such extreme passion seemed unlikely. Both wore expressionless faces, seemingly calm as they surveyed the patrons passing in and out of the restaurant and on the Promenade, the two of them an unlikely pair; the girl barely reached Taran'atar's chest, was small and gentle in appearance compared to the spined, angry features of the Jem'Hadar.

The Promenade was subdued, as it had been since the *Defiant*'s return, but for as quiet as things had seemed, Shar knew better. A kind of wary tension had settled across the station like a veil. He hadn't noticed it at first, too preoccupied with personal matters, but the near constant tingle in his antennae meant it was always there.

"So," Prynn said, smiling at him as they reached the lift. "I had a nice time. It was good to get my mind off my—my family, as it were. Want to do it again sometime?"

Shar wasn't sure how to answer. She had made overtures about a possible romantic involvement, which he did not want to encourage . . . but she'd also agreed to put it aside, and he, too, had found some relief in the brief freedom from his own thoughts.

"If you're worried about my interest, don't," Prynn added, as though she sensed his uncertainty. "Really. No pressure."

Shar nodded, relieved, and pleased by her willingness to state her feelings so directly. "Then yes, I would," he said. "I also enjoy your company."

Her eyes seemed to sparkle with her renewed grin. She reached out and placed her hand on his forearm, a soft touch, brief and presumably innocent—and Shar felt a knot of guilt in his chest, for the strange gratitude that swept through him. It had been only a few days, hours, really, since he'd seen his distraught mates away, since he'd felt the cold absence of Thriss's tomb from his quarters. For all that, the simple pleasure of physical contact was impossible to deny. It was not the embrace of his beloveds, not even the loving if condescending hand of his *zhavey* . . . but it was warm, and that was somehow more than he had expected.

The grief, surely it's the grief. It was, of course, and as

Shar looked away from Prynn's friendly face, looked for some distraction from his confused senses, he saw his *zhavey*'s gaze fixed on him from across the Promenade. Flanked by her aide and a Cardassian soldier, Charivretha stood, frozen, outside of the security office, her eyes seeing all, taking in Prynn's closeness and smile, her hand on his arm.

Shar stepped back from Prynn, new knots forming inside even as he told himself that he had a right to have friends, to share food with a coworker, to *survive,* even after what he'd done. Would she have him suffer more than he already did?

Yes. Yes, she would.

The injustice of his situation tripped through his mind, pressing connections, working to inspire rage. It wasn't fair, he hadn't known that Thriss, magical, ethereal Thriss would break and turn away from them all. He hadn't asked to be bonded in the first place, he couldn't help that he'd come to see the futility in the regimentation of their culture to produce as many offspring as their failing reproductive biology would allow. He wanted a career, a *life* to himself—

Breathe. Breathe.

"Are you okay?"

With his *zhavey*'s gaze still upon them, Shar managed a neutral expression for Prynn, releasing the worst of it.

"I am," he said, nodding to affirm it.

Prynn seemed skeptical, but smiled again. "All right. I'll see you later."

With that, she was gone, into the lift and down. Shar straightened his shoulders and turned to face the being who'd carried him to birth, who'd cared for him throughout his childhood, who seemed determined that he should feel no peace as he'd become an adult. He didn't know what he meant to say or do, only knew that he couldn't stand the way things were—and he saw her walking away, unhurried, her head high as she turned her back to her only child.

"Ah, Sulan? The ship has arrived, and the commander has asked to see you."

Opaka looked up from her reading, smiling at the prylar who stood at the opening to the small courtyard garden. He seemed very young, his nervousness adding to the impression of youth, though he was probably well into his forties. The age her own son would have been, had he survived the occupation.

"Thank you, Yukei," Opaka said. "Would you direct him here? It's such a lovely day."

As she put her book aside, Yukei bowed his way back into the hall, as deeply serious and devoted to the Prophets as he could be . . . and as nervous around the former kai as a *tiku* in a *kava* reap, as the saying went. It was unfortunate, though she supposed she should get used to it; from the moment she'd set foot on the space station, she'd been gazed upon with wide-eyed reverence by every Bajoran she'd met with. Returning from the dead tended to create a stir . . . though she also remembered she'd felt a similar wonder as a prylar, when in the presence of Kai Shesa, many, many years ago. Had it been so for those around her, when she'd served as kai? She hadn't noticed, then, but had also been so caught in her own devotion to the Prophets, she suspected she'd missed much about the people around her. While she had never presumed to be all aware, she was humbled to have grown slightly less blind.

Yevir Linjarin certainly hadn't helped make her return

any less conspicuous. The vedek had made much ado of her restoration "from beyond the Temple," organizing a welcoming assembly, publicly taking her to meet with the First Minister, flying her on a shuttle over the B'hala dig. She'd hoped to slip into the monastery quietly, as a guest, just another follower of the Prophets seeking respite—but even among the serenely peaceful society that lived within the cool stone walls, her presence had caused a fuss. Insisting that she be called by her second name had done nothing to curb the agitation of the monks and prylars. Perhaps Shakaar's tragic assassination and the subsequent security measures had created an environment of spiritual need.

At least Yevir had gone, back to matters of the Assembly. She wished she felt kindlier toward him, he was a well-meaning man, but his need for validation in regard to the Ohalu matter had quickly grown tiresome. When he'd finally realized that she wasn't planning an outright condemnation of the prophecies, he'd quietly disappeared. She only hoped their difference of opinion wouldn't close his mind to the opportunities of the Eav'oq. She planned to meet with the Assembly to discuss her discovery of Bajor's sister race, as soon as the current terrorist trouble abated, a move that was at least as unnerving as it was exciting. *If we can't abide a book from our own past, how will we accept that the Prophets have other worlds within Their sight? Especially a world where They are more like Ohalu's version than our own?*

"I hope I'm not interrupting your meditation."

Commander Vaughn stepped into the courtyard, pulling her thoughts to the moment. He moved past the low pastel flower beds and reflecting pool to stand in front of her. Opaka rose, taking his hand warmly.

"Not at all, Commander," she said, smiling up at him. "I was only reading. Please, sit with me."

Vaughn joined her on the bench, leaning against the backrest with a faint sigh. Kira had said he was overworked, but she'd obviously understated the situation. The commander seemed very distraught, his *pagh* scattered and weak, much more so than when Opaka had met him on the *Defiant*. Whatever was troubling him, it had gotten worse.

He glanced at the book sitting between them. "Let me guess. The Ohalu text?"

"Actually, it's a book of soup recipes." She *was* reading the prophecies, of course, but had decided to take the afternoon off from her study.

His smile was faint, but real. "I thought you'd be up to your neck in the controversy by now," he said, a hint of humor in his weariness, a blade of grass in a desert. "Railing against the heresy, perhaps."

"I've opted to read it, first," she said. "I'm about halfway through it. And so far, I see nothing heretical."

Vaughn raised his brow. "Really?"

"I can see why it bothers the Assembly," she said. "And I know I would have protested it, before my time in the Gamma Quadrant."

"But now you don't?"

"It's another interpretation of the Prophets," she said. "One that affirms Their integrity, and Their love for us. There are things in the text that I disagree with, or at least have a different opinion about, but I'm not sure that our traditional religious beliefs are entirely incompatible with what Ohalu says. In any regard, it isn't for me to tell others what to believe."

"You'll leave that to Yevir," Vaughn said, not a question.

Opaka shook her head. "Yevir Linjarin is a devoted follower, with the best of intentions . . . but he was also Touched by Them, and sometimes the fervor that comes with such a strong calling can be . . . rigid. But I'm certain that things will resolve, in the end."

His face was openly curious. "Why is that?"

"Because one way or another, everything resolves, Commander," she said.

He scrutinized her closely for a few beats, as though searching for something, then looked away. He gazed at the flowers without seeing them. "I suppose it does."

They sat in silence, Opaka enjoying the sun on her face, feeling the unsteady pulse of tension from the man beside her. After only a moment, as though he sensed that she could feel his weakness, he stood up, forcing an air of joviality.

"Well, would you be so kind as to give me a tour? I'm quite interested in studying the architecture. For a building as old as this one, it's remarkably well preserved."

"Of course," she replied, recognizing his need for control, or what he believed that to be. It was unfortunate that he struggled so. Over time, she'd come to believe that the only true emotional infirmity was denial; once a thing was accepted, it could be met without fear. She wished she could tell him that it was no weakness, whatever he was fighting against, though she suspected that he would perceive her comment as intrusive. She allowed herself to be helped to her feet.

"A few places are off limits, because of all the security procedures—the lower levels where the Orbs are being kept, I know—but I think we can find enough to keep you occupied while you're here. Part of the secondary abbey is a ruin, you know, destroyed by a fire four centuries ago. . . ."

She led him out of the garden, relating the history she recalled from her days as an initiate as they moved inside, noting how hard he tried to feign a real interest in the faded wall hangings, the well-worn stones. Perhaps after a day or two of rest, he'd want to talk about what was happening in his life, to so disturb his *pagh*—if not to her, then to one of the brothers or sisters who lived at the monastery. Many had been trained as spiritual advisors. For she had no doubt that whatever was troubling the commander, it was his soul that suffered.

12

"Federation runabout Madeira, *you will stand by until otherwise instructed. You are being monitored. Any attempt to continue your course or to leave your current coordinates will be dealt with promptly and with force. Thank you for your patience."*

Miles O'Brien leaned back in his chair, scowling at the alien computer's pleasantly menacing statement, repeated for the third time now. It was actually very polite considering the source, although the last line was obviously a recent addition. It was a kinder, gentler Cardassia these days.

"No, thank *you,*" he muttered, then turned around to shrug at the others.

"That's all I can get now," he said. "All other channels are locked off."

Sighs all around. Although Joseph Sisko seemed resigned to the wait, his daughter was getting irritated. Interesting; Judith got the same pinched look around the eyes that Captain Sisko used to get, when he was royally ticked.

"What about that person you spoke to before, on the Starfleet ship?" She asked, crossing her arms. "He said he'd talk to the station. That was twenty minutes ago."

Keiko, holding Kirayoshi in her lap, shot a nervous glance at her husband but spoke gently; Yoshi was dozing, his head slumped against his mother's arm. The traveling had disturbed all of their sleep patterns. "I'm sure it won't be much longer."

"Then they still haven't cleared up this business with the terrorists?" Judith asked, folding her arms tighter, and O'Brien could see now that he'd mistaken her anxiety for anger. If he knew his wife at all, she was feeling much the same, now that they were actually here. As exciting and unexpected as the sudden trip to DS9 was for both of them, taking the children into a terrorist hot spot wasn't high on their list of good parenting ideas. Though they'd found out about Shakaar's assassination before leaving Earth, they hadn't known about the security lockdown until already under way, when their attempts to call ahead were met with recorded warnings . . . and had continued on only because they were all figuring that Captain Yates's status with the Bajorans—not to mention Miles's own "in" with the command staff of the station—would get them through the block. He and Keiko had reasoned that if the conspirators were hoping to keep the Federation away, it seemed unlikely that Bajor itself would be targeted; the station would be the danger zone. O'Brien knew that Keiko was counting on an invitation from Kasidy, to stay on Bajor. If she didn't have room, they'd undoubtedly be able to find accommodations in the nearest town.

What, and miss all the fun?

He shot that down, fast. He'd promised Keiko that he wouldn't get involved in whatever mess was going on, not if he could help it. He worked on Earth now, had finally settled into the family life; his days of perilous exploits had passed, as they probably should have the very day Molly had been born. And they had come for Joseph and Judith and Captain Yates, for *their* family. If it meant staying away from DS9 entirely, he was committed to that end. Besides, their friends would come visit them on the planet, if they could. Probably.

"We don't know that," O'Brien said, keeping his tone mild. "It could be over, and they're just cleaning up."

"They'll get to us when they get to us," Joseph said, easily the most relaxed of them all. Since making the decision to welcome his new grandchild into the family, he seemed to have set aside the bitter anger that he'd experienced following his illness, almost certainly brought on by the disappearances of his son and grandson. O'Brien was pleased that they'd been able to do at least that much for the Siskos . . . though it had been the children, he and Keiko were sure, that had really drawn Joseph out of his self-imposed hermitage.

How could they not? O'Brien thought fondly, glancing between their two beautiful babies. Molly looked quite grownup, lounging in her seat and reading the old hard-copy book Joseph had given her. And Yoshi, nuzzling sleepily against Keiko's shoulder, was a joy in all that he did. O'Brien hoped everything *had* been cleaned up; though they'd been gone less than a year, the children were growing so fast. He wanted to show them off, and knew that everyone would want to see how quickly they were growing up. And he wouldn't mind running a holo or two with Julian, as long as they were in the neighborhood. Teaching was an adventure, he supposed, but not in the same way that *adventure* was an adventure. In fact, as bright and motivated as his first-year AP students had been, he was finding his new position to be a little on the bland side. . . .

"*Runabout* Madeira?"

Ah! Still no picture, but an actual person this time. He'd had enough standing by to last a lifetime. "Yeah, right here," O'Brien said.

"Stand by."

O'Brien gritted his teeth, but before he could think of an appropriate expletive, a familiar voice came on.

"Chief?"

"Nerys? Ah, Colonel?"

"You have an interesting sense of timing, Miles," Kira said, *"but I'm glad you're here. Kasidy has been looking forward to your arrival. How is everyone?"*

"Good. Great," O'Brien said. He could actually feel the atmosphere behind him relaxing.

"There are a few security clearances we'll have to put you through before you can head down, so if you'll let a small team beam aboard . . ."

"No problem," O'Brien said. They'd expected as much, although in all his years with Starfleet, he couldn't remember such a serious reaction to the murder of a political figure. It was horrible, of course, but calling in the Cardassians . . . that was a real twist. Perhaps it was a test for the Cardassians, too, to see how far their newly formed goodwill would stretch.

"I hope we'll get a chance to visit while you're here," Kira said. *"I'd love to catch up, see Molly and Yoshi, but the station isn't the best place for guests right now."*

He could hear the tautness to her voice, now that he was listening for it. "Is there anything I—anything *we* can do to help?" he asked.

"Not at the moment," Kira said seriously. *"But I'll keep it in mind. Thanks."*

Oops. O'Brien winced, not turning to see Keiko's expression. He hoped she recognized that the offer had been made in a friendly way, not as a *real* offer.

"I've got to go, but welcome back," Kira said, her voice abruptly turning light again. *"And I hope I'm not overstepping my bounds, but there's a surprise waiting for the Siskos on Bajor."*

Joseph and Judith were suddenly standing at either side of him, leaning into the comm.

"Is it the baby?" Joseph blurted out.

"Is Kas okay? When?" Judith asked, at the same time.

Kira laughed. *"So much for surprises. Joseph and—Judith, right?"*

"Yes, Colonel, hello," Joseph said impatiently, but with a smile. "What is it, boy or girl?"

"Wrong surprise," Kira said. *"No baby, yet. But Kas gave me the go-ahead to tell you—"* She took a deep breath. *"Jake is home, with Kasidy. He got back a few days ago, from the Gamma Quadrant. It's a long story, I haven't even heard the half of it myself, but I'm sure he'll be glad to fill you in."*

"Oh, thank God," Joseph breathed, and then he and Judith were laughing, embracing. O'Brien grinned, glad for the news.

"You've made a couple of my passengers very happy," he said, raising his voice to be heard over the Siskos' excitement. "And Keiko and me, too."

They signed off, Kira promising to contact them on Bajor as soon as she could after asking them to wait for the security team. A few more warm words, and she was gone . . . leaving O'Brien feeling strangely wistful.

She's got to get back to dealing with the station, with a

thousand small emergencies, probably, he thought, tapping out. No time to talk. Poor Nog was surely being run ragged, setting up security scanners and the like, not to mention the nightmare of rerouting nearly all of the open comm channels through ops, trying to line everything up with a Cardassian line block. Chaos, total chaos.

God, but sometimes I miss it. Teaching had been it's own unique adventure, to be sure . . . but the excitement of not knowing what would come next, not knowing what challenge would rear its complicated head from day to day . . . that hadn't been such an easy thing to give up, after all.

"What are you thinking?" Keiko asked, putting a hand on his shoulder.

He started guiltily and turned to face her, saw that Molly was reading to a sleepy-eyed Yoshi, that Joseph and Judith were still chattering happily with the news about Jake. They were alone, as much as it was possible on a runabout with six people in the forward cabin.

"Nothing much," he said, smiling, wishing it were true. He wasn't lying, not exactly; he'd committed to the quiet life for her, for his family, and he meant to follow through. A few pangs of nostalgia were to be expected. "And I don't plan on offering my services so lightly next time around," he added.

Keiko smiled back at him, a nice smile. She'd been a bit tense ever since they'd left Earth, but now she leaned forward to kiss him lightly, tenderly. "You're a good man, Miles O'Brien," she said.

A good man. He could live with that. He stood up and took Keiko's hand as they walked over to join their children.

". . . and so I said to her, what do you want from me? I'm in the same ship as you, and it's not as though we were ever *really* partners," Quark said, shaking his head. "To think, she wanted a full half of the last party profits. I mean, look around. Can I afford that? No matter what they look like, those Orion women are a manipulative bunch, I'll be well rid of her. Oh, and that reminds me, did you know that Frool is talking about going back to Ferenginar? After all I've done for him, too. He got a half-slip raise just two years ago. . . ."

Uncle Quark wouldn't stop talking, of course, but Nog had long ago learned how to look interested without hearing a word. A trick his father had once taught him, actually—a slight frown for a count of five, a slight smile for a count of three, two slow nods, then ten seconds of thoughtfulness followed by an appreciative grunt. Repeat. It had gotten Nog through many a lecture, and was serving quite well to see him through the late meal.

". . . and you'd think they'd bother with a decent tip, considering all the trouble I went through to dig out those cases of *kanar* . . ."

Grunt. Frown. Nog forked another toasted slug into his mouth and went over his workload for the night. It was already 2100, but lately no one was getting much sleep. Lieutenant Ro still wanted to get all of the storage bays scanned a level at a time, then set up silent motion sensors as they closed off each area. It meant rigging up at least a half-dozen new sets, since they had to be grid; everyone thought the parasites were ground creatures, but Dr. Bashir said they probably hopped, too, from the spine curvature or something, which meant a straight floor beam wouldn't do the trick—

". . . parasites, maybe?"

Nog blinked up at Quark, who was leaning over the bar, his voice low. "What?"

Quark scowled. "Got your attention, didn't I? That trick only works for so long. I *said,* do you think that Wex person might have something to do with the parasites? I think it's quite a coincidence, her turning up when she did, then her and that Jem'Hadar getting chummy. Though, now that I think of it . . . do those monsters mate for fun? Maybe they're . . . you know . . ." Quark leered appropriately.

Alarmed, and not a little disgusted, Nog shook his head, trying to look casual. "I don't know what you're talking about, Uncle."

"Oh, stop," Quark snapped. "And by the way, thank you so very much for telling me that my life is in danger. That's what makes family so special, the *honesty* that we count on from one another, the *trust.*"

"Uncle, *please,*" Nog said, looking quickly from side to side. If he'd had any doubt as to his uncle's purity, Quark's tone of voice dispelled it; no parasite could be so sarcastic. Thank the River, business was bad, less than twenty customers scattered about. "How did you— Never mind. But you're not supposed to know, and we're not supposed to talk about it, so be quiet, all right?"

Quark smirked. "I haven't told anyone, if that's what you're worried about."

Nog nodded, relieved. That was something, at least. "Don't, okay?"

"Don't teach your elders how to forge checks," Quark retorted. "I've been keeping secrets since before I had my first tooth filed."

At a signal from down the bar, Quark went to fill a drink order. Nog sighed, chewing down another slug. So, Uncle knew about the parasites. The only surprise was how long it had taken him to find out . . . although the fact that he wasn't in hiding was something of a shock, considering.

Quark was famous for his cowardice. When he returned a moment later, Nog had to ask.

"Aren't you afraid?"

Quark shrugged. "I've got a security system in place."

Nog casually glanced around, saw nothing . . . then remembered what he'd nearly tripped over when he'd gone behind the bar for his order. "You mean those rusty old vole traps?"

"Hey, I paid good money for those traps," Quark said defensively. "They caught voles, didn't they?"

Actually, they hadn't, or rarely at best, but Nog didn't want to start an argument. He nodded. "Good thinking."

"Besides, I've got Mr. Victory-is-life over there," Quark added, tipping his head toward Taran'atar. "Unpaid security. Between him and Lady Gray, the atmosphere in here is creepy enough to scare away anything."

As always when he saw the Jem'Hadar, Nog felt his gut tighten, though not as much as before his ordeal with the cathedral. He ignored it, refusing to let himself fall into that particular trap; he had other things to deal with. He focused on Wex instead, sitting at the table nearest Taran'atar's post at the exit, nursing an ale and gazing out at the activity on the Promenade.

"Wex isn't creepy," Nog said, looking her up and down. She was kind of attractive, actually. Big, black eyes, long white hair, short. A little thin, but not annoyingly so.

Quark snorted. "It's her demeanor. She's been coming in for hours at a time for days now, and I haven't seen her smile once. Not one time."

"Maybe she's just shy or something. Have you talked to her?" Nog asked.

"I don't have to talk to her," Quark said, his eyes narrowing as he stared at the small humanoid. "The way she looks at me . . . not to mention the company she keeps . . . she's trouble. I don't know how, but I'm sure of it."

As if she could hear what his uncle was saying, Wex turned her head and stared directly at them, at Quark. It wasn't a glare, exactly, but Nog did get the impression that she disapproved of the bartender.

"See that?" Quark asked. "See?"

Nog nodded, shrugging inwardly. There were parasites running around the station, and Uncle was having paranoid fits over an undemonstrative alien girl. He had to agree that anyone who voluntarily hung around with a Jem'Hadar might be a little off, but Wex seemed all right otherwise. And Jake had mentioned that although she kept to herself, she had been instrumental in finding Kai Opaka. In any case, Nog had finished eating, and had work to do.

"I don't know. Half the people who come in here look at you that way," Nog said, pushing away from the bar. "If I don't stop in later, I'll be in for breakfast," he added, knowing that even with his discount, Uncle appreciated the business.

Quark started to say something in return—and then there was a telltale *clink* from under the stairs, a noise Nog hadn't heard in years, the sound of a vole trap snapping closed. Almost simultaneously, a customer yelped, jumping from his chair, and suddenly it seemed that everyone, all sixteen customers, were on their feet, pointing and shouting.

Nog caught just a glimpse of movement, incredibly fast, a tiny *thing* streaking across the floor, headed for the Promenade. Behind him, Quark let out a high-pitched shriek and clambered onto the bar.

Taran'atar bent low, blocking the parasite's exit as much as was possible, thrusting his hands toward the darting creature, his reflexes at least as fast as the creature itself. Everything was happening fast; Wex had run for the door mechanism, was closing the entrance, and Nog reached for his badge to call security, his heart thundering, Quark was still squealing and the excited cries of the few patrons seemed to be getting louder—

—and Nog watched in horror as the parasite seemed to take wing, flying at the Jem'Hadar's face. There was a blur of wriggling movement and then Taran'atar stood up, his mouth working as the animal forced itself deeper inside.

The Jem'Hadar frowned, seeming almost confused by the experience—and as his jaw tightened, he grimaced. The expression of a man biting into something unpleasant.

With that confused, disgusted look still on his spined face, Taran'atar lifted his head, opened his mouth, and spat. A wad of greenish ooze flew out, landing on the floor in front of him with a noisy wet *splick*.

Stunned, Nog walked forward, joining the other customers as they crowded around the small, slimy puddle that had so recently been alive. Nog could see what might have been a leg, or maybe a pincer. The Jem'Hadar had effectively mulched it.

Nog called Ro and then quickly surveyed the gathered watchers, noting that except for himself, Quark, and Taran'atar, only two of them might know about the parasites. The other onlookers were confused and anxious, whispers already starting, several trying to leave. They needed some damage control, fast—and it came from an unlikely source.

"I told you, this place has vermin," Wex said loudly, addressing the Jem'Hadar. "I saw the traps. Some kind of lice, I think."

Several of the watchers paled, or their species' equivalent, and Quark, who had finally climbed down from the bar, hurried over with an expression of absolute fury for the diminutive girl.

"This establishment is clean," he hissed at her, then turned an ingratiating smile on the concerned customers. "I assure you, Quark's is vermin-free. Unless it's on the menu."

No one seemed reassured. Quark bared his teeth harder, and Nog knew what was coming, could see it in Quark's eyes. His uncle would keep a secret, but not if it interfered with business.

"It so happens—" Quark started.

"—that my pet *hunta* spider just got eaten," Nog interrupted, the first lie he could think of, trying to look properly forlorn. "I'm so sorry, Uncle. I know I wasn't supposed to bring him to the restaurant." He shot a malicious glare at Taran'atar, one he didn't have to fake. Didn't it just figure. Jem'Hadar could withstand parasites.

"But you don't—" Quark said, before he caught on. He shook his head, forcing a laugh as he opened his arms to the watching group. "Ha ha. My nephew's pet."

He turned to Nog, eyes flashing. "I've told you time and again, that's a stupid pet to have. See what happened?"

He addressed the customers again, promising a ten-percent discount on drinks for the next round, cursing Nog's irresponsibility to anyone who would listen. Most seemed at least slightly mollified. Nog saw Ro and two security people discreetly slip through the doors, and allowed himself to breathe . . . but he also heard a few furtive whispers, telling him that not everyone was convinced.

Ro casually spoke with Taran'atar and Wex as one of her team scooped up the remains of the parasite, then went to speak with Quark, presumably to try and convince him to shut the restaurant down until it could be scanned. The parasites were getting bolder, it seemed . . . and Nog felt that he'd just witnessed the beginning to the inevitable breakdown of the information lock ordered by the Federation. Tactically, a bad thing, but he couldn't help feeling some measure of relief, and suspected he wouldn't be the only one. When it had been a handful of cases, the lying made more sense. But it was obviously getting to the point where people needed to know, to protect themselves.

As he left Quark's, Nog thought of all that would have to be done to get the infestation under control, and all that they hadn't even started to address, and felt his usual optimism dwindling. What were they going to do? Where was safe, anymore?

It seemed that no one could say. Nog trudged back to work, his heart heavy.

After his call from Kira, Vaughn wandered through the quiet corridors of the monastery, not realizing that he was looking for Opaka until he saw her. She was alone in one of the small reading libraries, seated in front of a pile of opened books, apparently cross-referencing something or other. Outside, a light rain fell in the deepening twilight. She seemed thoroughly immersed in her work, and as much as he didn't want to intrude upon the woman, his brief conversation with the colonel—one that had included his current medical status—had left him in need of some peace.

Vaughn stood in the entrance a moment, watching Opaka's gentle, graceful movements as she flipped through one of the books, the slight frown of concentration on her brow. In the few days he'd spent at the retreat, his conversations with Opaka Sulan were the only times he didn't feel . . . well, bad. Frantic to return to work, or depressed about Prynn, or hopelessly self-pitying. The former kai was one of those rare people whose very presence was soothing to those around her.

And after that call . . . Kira had updated him on what was happening with the parasites, but only in the most general way; Vaughn suspected she'd been holding back, to spare him additional anxiety. He'd had another physical only that morning, one of the docs sent over from the scan camp just outside Ashalla. Vaughn wondered if she'd had any idea how much worse that had made it for him, how frustrating it was to hear a diluted version of the crisis—knowing that Ro had learned "something" that "might" be useful and would be back at the station soon; hearing that Bashir and his team were nearing "several good conclusions"; being told that the screenings on Bajor were moving right along, nothing he needed to worry about. The colonel was a good liar, but not that good.

Neither am I, unfortunately. At least, his body wasn't. Nervous exhaustion, according to the med tech, another three days, minimum. It seemed his rest wasn't turning out to be particularly restful.

And why should it? He watched Opaka, not really seeing her. He hadn't done anything to address his "problem," hadn't managed to pin it down. Hell, he hadn't even tried. Heavy self-analysis wasn't in his nature, never had been. Maybe that was part of it; maybe his fierce need to feel completely independent, to carry no emotional ties, had finally caught up to him in a way he could no longer handle.

And why? Except for my own pride, what good has it ever done for me, this self-imposed requirement that I deal with everything on my own? Looking back over his emotional life, he saw nothing useful in his autonomy. It had kept him apart from Ruriko and then Prynn, had kept almost every friend he'd ever had at a distance. Had kept him alone, and safe. Or so he'd thought, so he'd told himself.

"Commander."

Vaughn smiled at Opaka's gentle acknowledgment, still hesitating in the doorway. "I don't mean to interrupt . . ."

"Nonsense," she said, closing the book in front of her. "I'm done for today, I think. Come in, sit. Would you like tea, something to eat?"

At Vaughn's shrug, Opaka reached for a panel on the table, politely asking for a tray to be sent to the library. She settled back into the worn wooden chair, focusing on Vaughn. It was strangely calming, to be closely scrutinized by someone seemingly so at peace with herself. Vaughn knew how rare that actually was, a truly peaceful spirit . . . and knew that he was ready to talk to someone about his medical leave, and the source of his troubles. He thought, he *hoped* that Opaka might be willing to listen.

The tray arrived, tea and light fare for both of them, fresh greens, sliced fruit, a loaf of bread. They talked about the weather as they ate, about the harvesting seasons of Bajor's different continents, about history, travel, about nothing in particular. Vaughn let himself be soothed by the conversation, enjoying Opaka's perspective on even the simplest of things—and though he'd planned to work up to it, he found that their talk led naturally into more personal matters. Opaka was younger than he, but was certainly old enough to share a few laughs with him over the follies of youth, and the experience of aging. Twilight turned to dark, and their conversation continued, deepening as the evening deepened to night. She was easy to talk to, open with herself but not presumptuous, her judgments tempered with kindness. It was after she told him of her son, killed during the Cardassian occupation, that he found himself telling her about Prynn. Then Prynn's mother, and then his short time at DS9, and how nothing had seemed to turn out as he'd hoped. Opaka listened with a gentle ear, no trace of the scorn that he'd feared in her countenance or manner.

Vaughn recounted what had happened to him in the Gamma Quadrant, what had happened to the sad remnants of his family, and trailed off, feeling a strange mix of embarrassment and relief when he'd finally run out of things to tell her. It was hard, harder than he'd expected, but it was out; at last, he had talked about it, about the dreams, about his inability to focus.

Opaka sipped from her long-cold tea, quiet settling over the dim room as Vaughn waited. She seemed perfectly content to say nothing, and after a few moments, he felt a burst of impatience. She must know how agonizing it was for him, to share such private things.

"Do you think I should resign?" he asked.

"Do you want to?"

"I—don't know," he said. "No, I suppose not."

Opaka nodded, took another sip of tea. It seemed she wasn't going to offer any unsolicited advice.

"What *should* I do?" he asked finally, feeling a flash of irritation with her because he had to ask, with himself for asking.

Opaka raised her eyebrows. "How am I to know? It's your life."

"I thought—I thought you might have some insight," Vaughn said, his anger melting away even as he said it. She was right, of course, and his impatience was only because he wanted to share the responsibility of his problems. She knew better. He should have.

"I have opinions," Opaka said, smiling. "Insight, no, but I can tell you what I see . . . if you're willing to look with me."

Vaughn nodded, relaxing a little. "I'd like that."

"In our religion, it is said that our lives are like tapestries, all of us weaving our own stories . . . and that these stories become threads in a much greater Tapestry," she said. "I've found it to be an apt analogy in secular matters, as well. Tell me—if you had to pick a moment or an event that changed things for you, that turned your life onto this path you now walk, what would you say it was? Don't think on it too long."

That was relatively easy. "My experience with the Orb, on the *Kamal*," he said.

Opaka smiled wider. "Ah, yes. It made you want to explore, to seek out new places. To become what you wanted to be, in your youth."

"I took the job at DS9 because of it," Vaughn said. "I didn't even know that Prynn was stationed there. . . ."

He trailed off, remembering. The Orb experience had led him to his daughter and a new career, that had led him to the Gamma Quadrant and Ruriko. It wasn't a direct line by any means, but it was certainly a chain of related events. He had said as much to Prynn after trying to make sense of their improbable discovery of her mother.

"If you could go back now, and erase that moment—unravel it from your story—would you?" Opaka asked. "Would you cast aside the knowledge you've gained from this thread?"

Vaughn started to answer, to tell her that knowledge

should never be cast aside—and then frowned, pushing aside the automatic response. It wasn't a time for reflexive answers.

"I don't know," he said. "Right now, I just don't know. What I want is . . . clarity, I suppose. It felt so right, when I looked into the Orb, and afterward. For a time. I just wish I had some sign, that I'm still doing the right things, for the right reasons. . . ."

Opaka's half smile told him he wasn't the only one.

"I know, I know, but if there was some way I could refocus, find that deeper understanding. Remember *why* I chose. Maybe that would make things easier."

Opaka nodded. "And you can't, because . . . ?"

"Because . . . because I'm lost right now," Vaughn said slowly, and was somewhat horrified to find himself near tears. It was worse than being lost; he was stuck, repeating the same loop of self-hatred and doubt, living the nightmare of killing Ruriko over and over, seeing it in his daughter's eyes every time she looked at him, every time he *imagined* her looking at him. "I don't know if my judgment is sound."

He struggled to maintain himself, and Opaka looked away, allowing him the privacy to regain control. After a moment, she spoke, still looking away—and gave him what he'd been looking for, an option he hadn't even considered.

"The Tears of the Prophets are here," she said softly, and Vaughn grasped her words like a drowning man might grasp a thrown rope. He started to nod, the faintest hope touching his damaged soul, knowing already that he'd do whatever was necessary to look into the brilliant light of the Bajoran artifact once again, to see what he could see.

13

The notification that the O'Briens had arrived came from the station late, just as they were getting ready to turn in, and instantly banished all thoughts of sleep from Jake's mind. Learning that his grandfather had suffered an attack of some kind after hearing that Jake had disappeared had been weighing on him, as he couldn't help but feel responsible; seeing him again would be a relief, in all kinds of ways. And he hadn't seen his aunt since just after Jadzia had been killed, when he and Dad had gone back to Earth. Even then, they'd only had one dinner together; Aunt Jude had been leaving for a Sol system tour with the orchestra.

Jake and Kasidy hurried outside, Kas pulling a shawl around herself as they stood on the back patio, overlooking a rolling field of brush and wild kava, pale and multishadowed in the soft glow of the moons. Something about being awake and excited so late made Jake feel like a child again, up past his bedtime for a holiday, some special occasion. Kas seemed to feel the same, fidgeting anxiously as they waited, almost giggly with anticipation. Whoever had called from the station said that the party would transport down as soon as they'd been given clearance to enter orbit, which meant anywhere from five minutes to who knew how long, but Jake had no intentions of waiting inside. He wanted his face to be the first his grandfather saw.

Jake spotted a grouping of lights north and west of the property, a few small fires, perhaps. They seemed awfully close to the house for a campsite. "What's over there?" he asked.

Kas smiled. "Remember I told you I've had some volunteer help around here? And those monks that stopped by, yesterday?"

"Really?" Though it made sense that the locals would want to watch over Kasidy, Jake was surprised that they would actually camp out . . . and felt an echo of his guilt returning, for having been away for so long.

Kas seemed to sense it in him. She took her hands off the small of her back—what he'd come to think of as the pregnancy pose—long enough to pat his arm reassuringly. "You're here now," she said. "Besides, they just want to make sure the Emissary's wife doesn't happen to lose communications, break her leg, and go into labor all at the same time."

Jake felt a surge of protectiveness for her. "With the chief and everyone coming, I can tell them we're okay . . ."

"Feel free to try," Kas said. "I've been telling them that I'm perfectly fine for weeks now. They seem determined to stay, and I don't really mind the—"

Whatever else she was going to say was abruptly cut short by the shimmer of a transporter effect, five beams a dozen meters in front of them. In the beat it took them to fully materialize, Jake saw that Mrs. O'Brien—he still thought of her as his old schoolteacher—was holding her small son against one hip. All was silent for another beat, and then Granddad's strong, deep voice called his name, the loved and familiar face emerging from the gloom as he stepped forward from behind the chief, arms open wide.

Though he'd had some vaguely formed idea of shaking his grandfather's hand when they met again, the sound of the old man's voice triggered some gut reaction, sent Jake hurrying over to be solidly embraced. Even light-years from his kitchen, Joseph Sisko smelled of good food, a faint odor of cooking garlic and wine that Jake had always associated with him. Joseph squeezed him hard, and as they stepped apart, Aunt Jude was there, all smiles, waiting her turn, exclaiming over how much he'd filled out.

As his family moved on to Kasidy, Jake had a clumsy embrace with Mrs. O'Brien, still holding Yoshi. His right leg was solidly tackled by Molly. He could hardly believe how much both of the children had grown, in so short a time.

"It's good to see you, Jake," the chief said warmly, extending his hand, as Molly pulled on his shirt, holding up a hardcopy child's book.

"I can read you a story, Jake!"

"I can't wait," Jake said, scooping her up after shaking with the chief, as his grandfather slapped him on the back, aware that he had a big, stupid grin on his face, not caring one bit. He was with his family. The only thing missing . . .

Nope, not tonight, Jake thought firmly. Kas and Judith were laughing about something, the shimmer of the transporter beam casting a fine light over them all as the luggage was beamed down. Tonight was just perfect as it was.

What if we bait her out?

The idea wasn't new, it had already been rejected

because of the obvious impossibility of an open quarantine, but if they could just get everyone on the station doing something else, somewhere else . . .

What if we bait her out while everyone's accounted for? If it was something that everyone was required to do, or see, that wouldn't tip our hand. It would have to be big. Like a public address from Opaka and the first minister, perhaps. . . .

Ro walked slowly back to her office from the morning's briefing, working the problem for what felt like the billionth time. Dr. Bashir had reiterated it yet again—while they could learn a lot about the species from the individual parasites, for any real breakthrough they needed to get their hands on a queen.

If we made the message available only on the Promenade, an announcement about the kai, maybe, or some standard patriotic speech about sticking together in times of crisis . . . and then sent a handful of three-person teams into the suspect areas, two to check and a third to stand watch with a scanner . . .

Or . . . what if they made a big show of outfitting the Promenade with step-through scanners, making sure it got out that it was a new weapons check, something innocuous. Nog and Shar were getting closer to developing a scanner with the right sensitivity. Calibrating one to pick out subtle abnormalities in different types of humanoids—each of which had a spectrum of what constituted "normal" within their species—was still yielding too many false positives. But they could let the computer weed through the faces of everyone who showed, then check up on those who neglected to attend. Some of the individual parasites might try to slip through, but the queen carrier would surely avoid coming; she was a spawning ground, filled with parasites, and would set off even the most obtuse scanning equipment.

And yet we have no idea who has her. It felt like they'd run checks on everyone, thrice, and nothing.

Still, they hadn't seriously considered trying to group the station population somewhere. It wasn't much of a plan, but it was enough to turn Ro around, hoping to catch Kira before she left the wardroom. The day's briefing had been sadly lacking in innovation, and Ro figured that even an unlikely plan was worth a mention.

Nog and Shar were headed back to the *Defiant* together, and stopped for a minute to discuss the afternoon's schedule. They thought they'd be ready to try one of their step-through scanners within the next twenty-six hours, which was something. They'd coordinate a test with Dr. Bashir, send one of the stasis field patients through; they agreed that Ro should attend. Ro wished them luck and continued on, thinking that both young men looked the way she felt—hopeless, or at least a little beaten down by the work that wasn't getting done. She'd gotten used to the look on Shar since his return from the Gamma Quadrant, his personal troubles undoubtedly making his job that much harder, but even Nog, the perpetual optimist, seemed to be affected, his chin low, his tired eyes downcast as they walked away.

Things weren't going well. New cases of infection continued to spring up here and there, on Bajor and the station, and nothing they were doing seemed to have any effect. Dax and Cyl would be back soon, but the news wasn't good unless the Federation was willing to evacuate Trill and give it to the parasites, and *that* wasn't going to happen. Commander Vaughn was still out on a medical, progress on the planet was achingly slow. The loss of Liro and Bennings had been an especially hard one for Ro, who had personally handed out the assignments. Admin was still trying to keep the carriers' identities under wraps, but Ro's people knew what had happened, it was obvious, and morale was down. Akaar's attitude about the two security guards, when it had come up—that they were casualties of war, like some abstract concept—made Ro angry and sad.

Maybe Quark has the right idea, after all. He'd actually tried to bribe Taran'atar to be his personal bodyguard, to no avail. It wasn't such a far-fetched idea, in a way; it made sense that the parasites would try to target people as high up on the command ladder as they could get, and though she doubted that Quark was even on their list, individual surveillance and protection might be in order for the station's officers.

Ro turned the corner to the wardroom offshoot—and froze, hearing Kira's voice coming from around the next turn, the wardroom proper. She had to be standing in the doorway, and she sounded tense.

". . . which I've already put in my report," she said, a thread of cold in her tone. "I'd think you'd want to give credit where credit is due, Admiral."

Akaar. That explained the tone, anyway. Kira kept a game face when it came to the admiral, but Ro could see that she often had to struggle to maintain it. He wasn't a bad man, even Ro knew that much, but there were some things about which he could be inflexible. For someone as unorthodox as Kira, that had to rankle.

"If you want to suggest a commendation, that is your prerogative," Akaar's voice came back, equally cold. "But we have vastly more important matters at stake, Colonel, than whether or not your security chief decides to stay."

Ro's blood seemed to stand still; they were talking about *her*. She knew she should walk away, that listening to private conversations was a good way to complicate one's life—she learned as much eavesdropping on Taran'atar and Wex—but as before, she couldn't move. She didn't *want* to.

"After all she's done," Kira snapped, "finding the assassin, tracking down the planet—"

"Colonel, step inside. The corridor is not shielded."

Kira's voice dropped, but she didn't go back in. "I don't think we have anything to discuss. You obviously have a personal stake in this matter, some grudge that you mean to hold on to regardless of her exemplary performance throughout this ordeal."

"Colonel, please. Now is not the time for this. I will make my report on Ro Laren as I see fit, as is *my* prerogative, but for now, we need to talk about another matter. If you will step inside . . ."

A second later, the hiss of a closing door.

Ro didn't move, her heart thumping, bits of the conversation repeating in her mind. *Commendation. After all she's done. Exemplary performance.* Akaar's issues with her were common knowledge, and for the most part, so was Kira's support—but to actually hear the colonel stand up for her, go up against Starfleet's representative in Bajor's transition to the Federation . . .

Ro smiled, unable to help it, and felt a kind of ache at the same time, low in her gut. It was ridiculous, wasn't it, to feel pride at a job she was bowing out of, a job she'd never wanted . . . but it didn't matter. What the colonel seemed to have forgotten was that working alongside Starfleet personnel again, even as an officer of the Bajoran Militia in Bajoran territory, was hard enough. Expecting her to do so after the changeover, or thinking that Starfleet would even want her back after all the bad blood on both sides, was misguided and unrealistic.

And I'm nothing if not realistic.

Ro shook her head, backing away from the wardroom. Akaar had one thing right—there were much more important things to worry about. She'd head back to the office, make some notes, talk to Kira a bit later—

Halfway down the corridor, she turned—and jumped, startled. A middle-aged Bajoran woman was standing right behind her, a vaguely familiar face—she worked in the small tourism office on the Promenade, Ro thought, though she wasn't certain.

"Excuse me," Ro said, stepping to one side.

The woman stepped to the same side. Ro smiled, the woman smiled back—but something was wrong. The smile didn't touch the woman's eyes, which were dark and opened wide, and she was starting to say something, but her mouth was opening wide, too, too wide for speech. Inside, something stirred.

Ro didn't think. She dropped into a crouch, snatching at her phaser. *Stun won't work, in the reports it said—*

No time to fix it. The woman was leaning over, and with the barest *cough* of sound, she vomited a squirming insectile creature from the dark hole of her mouth. It happened fast. Ro fired at her with one hand, instinctively batting the dropping parasite away with the other, her skin crawling at the wet, moving touch of it against her palm.

The woman took a single step back and grinned, unharmed, barely affected as the creature scrabbled across the meter or so of corridor between them, moving impossibly fast. Ro threw herself backward, kicking at it, horribly aware that she had seconds, at most, not a free hand to call for security, a phaser that she might just as well throw—

Ro screamed, as loud as she could, snapping her mouth

closed a split second later as the parasite leapt, its hard, strong, chitinous legs ripping at her lips, prying at her teeth, trying to force her jaws apart.

The day's meeting had not been an inspiring one, for anyone. Even had Shar not been able to sense the lack of enthusiastic energy, the grim faces of the attending officers had communicated the mood clearly enough.

As soon as the meeting was over, he and Nog started back for the *Defiant,* walking in silence. Shar found his thoughts turning away from their work and back to Prynn Tenmei, where they'd found focus quite often since their lunch together. Not so much the young woman herself, but the questions she had raised for him. Thinking about Dizhei and Anichent, about Thriss, about his damaged relationship with his *zhavey*—these things were too much, too consuming, when he needed his primary attentions to center on his role in countering the parasite invasion. But the gently bittersweet dilemma of his future relationships, of love, bonding, sexual intimacy . . . these were things he'd never thought upon before, had never needed to consider, and he was discovering them to be diversions that didn't wound him overmuch to entertain.

They stopped to coordinate briefly with Ro Laren, then continued on their way. Nog began thinking aloud about the fabrication aspects of their current detection design, rattling off numbers and theory, but it was all material they'd already discussed. Shar continued to think on Prynn's curiosity, and on her expressed interest in spending time with him. He didn't realize that Nog had stopped walking, had asked him a direct question and was waiting for an answer.

"I'm sorry, Nog," Shar said. "What did you ask?"

"I asked if you had something on your mind," Nog said. When Shar hesitated, Nog shrugged, smiling widely. "Forget it. None of my business, right? Unless . . . I mean, if you ever *wanted* to talk about anything, that would be okay with me."

It wasn't the first time that Nog had offered. In fact, most of his new friends on DS9 had invited him to share his emotions with them, if he so desired. In his own culture, feelings were not so casually discussed among acquaintances . . . but then, his adherence to Andorian custom no longer seemed to be of much importance, did it? If this was to be his home now, these the people that were his social contacts, perhaps he should try something new.

"I was thinking of Prynn Tenmei," Shar said, deciding to be as concise as possible. He didn't want Nog to be burdened in any way by his own frivolous thoughts. "She has suggested that she and I develop a closer friendship, and this has raised, for me, considerations of my future personal life."

Nog blinked, seemed dumbstruck for a moment, then grinned ever wider. "You and Prynn? *That's* interesting."

Shar hurried to clarify. "I don't mean to suggest—that is, I am not currently interested in pursuing a . . . *familiarity* with anyone." Even saying it aloud made him wince internally, his inner voice shouting that he'd had his opportunity, that he'd destroyed it.

"Right, I gotcha," Nog said, still smiling, nodding. "But it's something to think about, particularly now that . . ."

He trailed off uncomfortably, but only for a second before pushing his grin ever wider. "But she's something, isn't she?"

Shar wasn't sure how to answer. Prynn was a human, a

lesser-ranked coworker, a pilot. "In what capacity?" he asked.

"In the female capacity," Nog said, and blinked one eye. He seemed happy to be talking about something besides work. There was a glint of enthusiasm in his gaze that had been absent only seconds before. "They can be complicated, though. You should talk to Vic about it, if you want some pointers."

Vic Fontaine, the hologram. Shar hadn't yet met the program, he'd scarcely had a free moment since his assignment to the station, but Nog referred to him often. "Vic has points to make, about females?"

Nog nodded eagerly. "When this is all over, we can go together, it'll be fun. I owe him a visit anyway, and—"

The Ferengi broke off suddenly, his gaze going blank, his head cocking. He held the pose a beat, then frowned.

"Did you hear a—"

A short, sharp scream came from behind them, back toward the conference room. Nog and Shar both started running, Nog calling for security, Shar pulling ahead as his friend called off coordinates.

Shar turned a corner, the corridor leading back to the smaller offshoot of the wardroom—and saw Ro Laren, on her knees, clawing at her face. A woman, Bajoran, was standing between them, and as Shar ran to help Ro, the woman whipped around to face him. Her mouth, there was something wrong with it, something moving behind her wide grin—

—parasites—

—and Shar did what came most naturally, what Starfleet had trained him not to do when faced with conflict. In an instant he was overcome with rage, with a seething hatred for the Bajoran invader, for the creatures that even now were creeping from her gaping mouth. Without hesitating, he leapt up and kicked, first with one leg and then the other as his body twisted in midair. Both blows landed solidly, the first against the host's face, the second against her chest.

The impact sent her flying backward. He caught a glimpse of her dull surprise before he landed on the floor, hard, and immediately rolled to his knees to help Ro. The parasite carrier was also getting up, but had landed several meters away, giving him a fraction of a second to get to the struggling security officer. Behind him, he heard Nog shouting into his com, clarifying the situation, but Shar's own rage made the sounds incomprehensible. For him, there was only the immediate threat, only the desire to kill the attacking creature.

Ro had two of the tiny animal's legs in one hand, was trying to pull it from her upper lip with little success. It had dug into the right corner of her mouth with its over-large pincers, its small, pointed tail squirming against the left corner, seeking a way inside. A small amount of blood was trickling down Ro's chin, smearing down her throat. Without pausing to consider how best to remove it, Shar snatched at the creature, grasping the middle of its body firmly. He jammed the forefinger of his other hand in between the scissoring pincers and then yanked. Ro cried out but the parasite came away, its body flipping and writhing in Shar's hand, its claws gouging into his skin. Still holding it tightly, he slammed it into the floor, hyper-extending his arm, pressing the heel of his hand through its hard little body. He felt wetness, a satisfying warmth spreading from beneath his fingers. It still moved, but weakly now, slowly.

The Bajoran host, the carrier, was back on her feet. Two,

three more parasites had fallen from her unhinged jaw, were already darting across the corridor to where Shar and Ro sat, where Nog was standing. Shar hissed at the woman, at the insectile runners, overcome by the need to destroy them, his teeth gnashing with the need to bite and grind, to rip them apart—

—and two of the small creatures froze, the woman, too, suddenly and completely, stopped as solidly as a holo on command. The third parasite, closer to Shar and Ro than the others, made it only a few centimeters further before the blast of a phaser obliterated it.

Wide-eyed, Shar turned, his antennae sensing the contained stasis field before it registered mentally, saw the three security officers standing near Nog. One had his phaser outstretched, while the others held out two stasis projectors. A half second later, a pair of med techs beamed into the corridor and ran to Ro's side. One of them asked Shar if he'd been injured, but he ignored her, breathing deeply, releasing the violence that he'd allowed into his consciousness, into his body.

Ro stared for a moment at the frozen Bajoran woman, at the pair of creatures by her feet, then looked at him, smiling even as she winced, as a tech blotted at her torn lip with a steady hand.

"I'm sorry—" Shar started, regaining himself as he motioned at her bleeding mouth, but Ro shook her head, her smile widening.

"We have a queen," she said, and though he'd let go of the violence, though he was fully himself again, there was enough of it in him still to allow Shar a smile in turn, a grin of blood-lust triumph at the understanding. They had a queen.

14

Keiko stood on Kasidy's back porch, bemusedly watching Jake play with the children in the late-afternoon sun. She wasn't sure of the game, but they were certainly enjoying it; Jake ran through the overgrown field with Yoshi on his shoulders, Molly at his side, her arms out as though in flight. They'd run quite a distance, the faint sound of their laughter only just carrying back to the house. Kasidy, Joseph, and Judith had all walked to the nearest village to buy vegetables an hour or so earlier, and should be back soon, before dark, Kasidy said . . . and Miles was inside, talking to Kira.

And he's telling her that he can't. Whatever it is she called for, he's telling her that he's a teacher now, that he's on leave, and that he didn't come all the way out here to risk his life rigging together some miracle or other to save the day. He's made promises.

Was that uncharitable? Maybe. Probably. She sighed, folding her arms against her chest. She knew herself too well, at times, knew that she was just waiting for him to come outside with that hangdog look on his face so that she could be angry. After so many years of marriage, she could feel the unformed resentment tugging at her, could feel the desire to pick a fight.

Maybe she was tired of watching him march off into danger, and she *was,* tired to her very core. When the DS9 position had first opened, she'd been all for it. She'd mistakenly assumed that compared with some of what they'd experienced on the *Enterprise*, a space station would have to be safer. There had been Molly to consider, after all, and even then she'd dreamed of having another child. When they'd actually gone to the station, when she'd seen what the living conditions were like, how limited her own career opportunities would be . . . even then, she'd stuck to her end of the bargain, for the sake of his job. But if she was going to be honest with herself—and the time was long past when she could afford not to be—she'd also been willing to stay out on the frontier's edge because she, too, had a touch of the adventurer's spirit, had wanted some of the same challenges out of life that Miles so enjoyed.

But the war changed that, at least for me. And for him . . .

She held herself tighter, watching the children play. She wanted him to be happy, of course, wanted to support him in his choices. He liked teaching, or at least certain aspects of it . . . but she could see that he was already starting to chafe a bit around the collar, and that worried her. Maybe she had pushed too hard for him to take the Academy position, because she wanted some stability for her children, some prospects for herself. And it was a feather in his cap, no two ways about it; teaching AP Engineering at the Academy was a position of no small esteem.

Except this isn't about fear, or what's best for him, or what's best for our family, is it?

She sighed. No, of course it wasn't. A good marriage—and she and Miles had one, she knew it and was both proud of and grateful for it—demanded a willingness to examine one's own motivations, with as much honesty as possible. It was hard work; blaming Miles would be a lot easier, but this was about her. The comm she'd received just before they'd left Earth, from the I.A.A.C. . . . she'd been offered an incredible opportunity, and had turned it down without even telling Miles about it. Because she wanted to be fair, because she wanted to keep her promises. That was why it seemed so important that he turn Kira down, if that was even the reason for her call. Because if she was going to make yet another sacrifice, she wanted a little of the same consideration.

But maybe it's time for him to support you, for a change, she thought, the thought a whisper, feeling guilty and defensive and secretly joyful, all at once. They'd agreed that the move to Earth was the best thing, for all of them, but the I.A.A.C.'s offer . . . it was once-in-a-lifetime. The rep she'd talked to had asked her to reconsider, to think it over, and though she'd insisted that her answer likely wouldn't change, she couldn't stop thinking about it, either.

So if it's a done deal, why haven't you mentioned it, yet?

Because . . . because she didn't know why.

Because you want it.

Yes. Because she wanted it.

"Hey," Miles said, and Keiko turned, forcing a slight smile, one that quickly faded. Even with a grin pasted on, apology was written in the lines of his face as he stepped outside, squinting at the sudden brightness. She knew she'd only been ready to lay blame because of her own secret-keeping, but felt a burst of anger at him, anyway.

"Miles, you didn't," she said.

"I'm sorry," he said, and sighed, stepping closer. "I tried to get out of it, I swear I did, but Kira said that Nog was working on some kind of weapon scanner, that it's not picking up a certain biosig, and asked if I could take a look, and I said—"

"I don't care what you said," Keiko snapped, and was instantly sorry when she saw the flash of hurt in his eyes. His shields were up an instant later, she could see them go, but the damage had been done.

"What am I supposed to do, Keiko?" he asked, shrugging his arms wide. "I'm still in Starfleet. It's my duty to help, and I owe Kira, we both do. If she'd asked you, what would you have said?"

She didn't answer, only turned back to the children. Jake was swinging Molly around by her arms. Yoshi sat in the dirt, giggling, his grubby hands reaching out for a turn. Kirayoshi. *Of course he has to go.*

He touched her shoulder, his voice softening. "I *am* sorry," he said.

"I got a call from the I.A.A.C.," she said, not turning to look at him, surprised to hear herself say it, just like that. She'd made no decision to tell him, but knew, as she spoke, that there had never really been a choice. They were married. "Right before we left. They offered me a position."

Miles turned her around, smiling broadly, a touch of confusion in his happiness for her. She'd applied to the Interstellar Agricultural Aid Commission soon after their return to Earth, had waited for months to hear back from them. They were technically private-sector, but worked closely with the Federation. "That's great. Where's—Why didn't you tell me?"

"I turned it down," she said, only able to meet his gaze for a second, her feelings in a muddle. "I turned it down, but now—I don't know."

Miles shook his head. "I don't understand. What's the job?"

In spite of her upset, telling him made her proud. "Only to head the botany team on a planet renewal," she said. "Crops, season patterning, new irrigation systems, everything."

"That's wonderful! I thought you weren't even going to apply for a lead position, you were so sure you wouldn't make it," Miles said, beaming at her. "It's what you wanted, isn't it?"

Keiko smiled, felt her eyes well with tears at the same time. "You don't understand. I'd—we'd have to move there, for at least two years."

"Well, where is it?"

"Cardassia."

Cardassia. The word hung between them, stilling his excitement, painful to even say aloud. How many old wounds did he have because of them? How many times had he expressed his distrust of them, as a people? How often had he complained about their technology, been appalled—as she had—by aspects of their society? He'd come to a grudging tolerance for them through the years, had even learned to respect a few select individuals, but want to move there? With the children? How could she possibly expect that of him?

Because I matter, too, that whisper of thought. *My career matters, too.*

To her surprise, he didn't immediately scoff, didn't throw off a line about how she'd been right to turn the offer down. He only stood there, looking vaguely stunned, uncertain.

"There are a number of offworld projects starting up there, to work with the survivors, to help rebuild," she said quietly. "We wouldn't be the only humans."

"You're seriously considering it," he said, almost wonderingly, his face flushing slightly. "Without even telling me."

"I didn't tell you because I knew you wouldn't even think about it," she said, her own defenses rising. "You hate Cardassia."

"I don't remember *you* ever expressing any particular love for it," he retorted. "Anyway, you said you already turned it down. What does my opinion matter?"

"I turned it down because we just moved, because you just started teaching," she said, hearing the sullen note in her voice, unable to keep it out. "How could I even ask?"

Miles stared at her, that look that drove her crazy, that suggested she'd lost her mind. "So now you're mad at me because you *didn't* ask me something you thought I'd say no to?"

Keiko sighed. This was going nowhere. "No, I'm not mad," she said. "Or maybe I am, but it's not your fault. I just . . . I feel like all the big decisions we've made have been about your career, about what I'd have to sacrifice. Don't misunderstand, I agreed to those things at the time, it's just . . . I don't know. *Would* you have considered it? Really?"

He frowned, thinking, and in spite of her distress she felt a rush of love for him, for his ability to set aside the quarrel, to see that she wasn't trying to make things bad between them.

"Moving to Cardassia?" He smiled a little, shaking his head. "Of all the planets . . . I don't know, Kay. I'd like to say that I'd be a hundred percent behind you, whatever you want, but there? I really don't know."

She sighed again, but nodded. She could always count on him for honesty.

"We should talk more about this," he said. "But I told Kira . . ."

". . . That you'd be right there," she finished. "I know. You'll be careful?"

"Always," he said, and stepped in to kiss her, to hold her briefly in his strong, warm arms. "And I'll be back as soon as I can, I promise."

"Stop promising me things," she said, and though she meant it to come off lightly, she felt a slight distance come up between them even before he stepped away.

He went down to tell the children and Keiko watched him walk away, watched Molly run toward him, Yoshi toddling behind. They would talk later, that was something . . . because in the course of their brief discussion, she'd realized that she wanted the Cardassia job, wanted it with all her heart.

"Are you prepared?" Opaka asked, smiling at Vaughn. He knelt in front of the ark on a small pillow, anxious and expectant, a shaft of late-afternoon sunlight playing across the floor, casting the intricate carvings on the small casket in bright relief.

Vaughn nodded. He was nervous, but she could feel his readiness, too, feel how open he was to the experience. They were alone, in one of the larger meditation rooms. She'd wanted to take him to the underground chamber, to see if another Orb called to him, but was told by a smiling young prylar she'd never met that the current security standards wouldn't allow for it. She'd noted an air of tension in the past few days, and hoped it would soon pass. It seemed strange to her, that even a former kai apparently wasn't to be trusted in the turbulence following Shakaar's assassination. A pair of monks had brought the Orb of Unity up from the chamber instead, at her request. Unlike the prylar, they hadn't smiled.

"You'll stay?" Vaughn asked, not for the first time.

Opaka nodded. Direct communion with the Prophets was considered to be the most private of experiences for a Bajoran, but he wasn't Bajoran—and it seemed to ease his mind, to know that she'd be with him. She could watch without participating, use the time for her own reflection. Even being near an open ark was an experience, in itself—not as powerful, but still quite moving.

"I'll be here," she said. She moved behind the ark, made herself comfortable on the small padded bench that she'd placed there, and reached around the Prophet's Tear. She could feel its wondrous energy, had felt it like a warm embrace when it had been brought in, and had marveled anew at the Love They shared with Their children, the opportunities They offered for self-awareness. It struck her yet again, how unnecessary Yevir's concerns were, his fear for the Bajoran people's spiritual context; the Prophets were Many, One, and All. Whatever form They took, however They were perceived . . . it was all Truth. It was the faith that mattered, faith that carried men and women through the Great Tapestry, through good times and ill.

Faith, and an open heart, she thought, smiling anew at the man in front of her, a man who reminded her of the Emissary, just a little. Human, troubled, seeking answers without really knowing the questions . . .

"Walk with the Prophets," she said, and opened the doors.

15

HERS WAS THE FACE THAT HE LOVED, THE FORM, THE VOICE and mind and soul. As he pointed the weapon at her, at her beloved form, her gaze pleaded for mercy, for understanding . . . for life.

"Please," she whispered, and he heard her pain, and ached, and said nothing. Only took careful aim at his wife, at the mother of his only child, and squeezed the trigger.

Her beautiful, beseeching eyes turned to glass, turned cold and dead even as she crumpled, falling back and away, and he had murdered her, his fault, his. There'd been no good reason, no justification in the world that could make what he'd done acceptable. The revolver was heavy in his hand, the sound of the discharge still echoing in his shocked mind, and in the time it had taken to pull the trigger, he knew that he was damned for all eternity.

He was holding the gun . . . and she was gazing at him again, alive, her eyes bright and begging for her life.

"Please," she whispered, and he took careful aim, his heart beating in anguish and fear. Fired. Watched her die, and understood that it would never, never end as she sat up again, her eyes wounded and afraid, that breathy, lonely plea on her fine, trembling lips.

He took a deep breath, opened his mouth to scream—

—and Eli was awake and in the dark, the low sound of thunder rumbling outside, overlaid by rain pattering on glass. He didn't scream, only stared at the blank, unfamiliar wall next to his cot, eyes wide and unblinking. The small window near the ceiling cast a patch of watery street light across the floor, the bars of shadow that cut through it gray and insubstantial.

But solid, he thought vaguely, and was both disturbed and comforted at once. All of the windows had bars at Riverdale, or so he'd been told. Tomorrow, when he joined the general populace, he'd see for himself.

Ruri was dead. His family was dead. Pria had come to the trial, but only for the sentencing . . . and the single look she had spared him had been so full of rage, so hateful and hurt, he understood clearly that she, too, was lost to him. He deserved it, just as he deserved the nightmares, as he deserved the windows with bars.

He watched the shadow rain drizzle across the floor, feeling the night cold of the lonely room settling into him. Someone, somewhere not too far away, started screaming, a wail of madness and despair. Eli listened but couldn't tell if it was a man or woman before it stopped, an abrupt, choking halt that surely came from an orderly's club or fist. Another deranged mind, another damned soul, perhaps hoping for redemption during the day even as he or she screamed in the night. Did they hope for freedom? The concept was no more for Eli. He might be released, someday, but the dream would always be there. The memory of what he'd done.

After a very long time, he slept. And his wife was waiting for him in the dark.

". . . group sessions three times a week, Monday, Wednesday, Friday," the nurse said, looking up at Eli as they walked, her wrinkled face carefully set in a placating smile. It was a kind face, but understandably wary. He was a new inmate, an untested quantity.

"We're quite progressive here, but we also find that most of our patients enjoy some structure," she said, leading them down a long, silent corridor that smelled like disinfectant. The walls were an industrial shade of mild green; the linoleum was worn but reasonably well maintained. "We have meals at the same time every day, as well. You've already had your breakfast, but from now on, you'll be eating with the other people from your ward. Lunch will be at twelve o'clock sharp, dinner at five-thirty. Someone will show you the way to the dining hall. If you're hungry in between those times, speak to one of the orderlies and they'll take care of it."

Eli glanced behind them. The young Negro man following sneered, one hand dropping to the billy club tucked into his belt.

"I'm sure that will be fine," Eli said, quickly looking away.

"That's very accommodating of you, Mr. Underwood," the nurse said, her smile still in place. She was very short and getting on in years, and seemed nice; she'd led him away from his solitary cell, was taking him to the room where the other inmates—the ones not intent on hurting anyone, he presumed—whiled away their days. He couldn't recall her name, though she'd told him. . . . Susan? Sue-Lynn?

They rounded a corner and came to a stop in front of a closed door.

"Samuel?" the nurse asked, and the young man stepped forward with a ring of keys, his expression boyishly innocent as he worked the lock. Eli was careful not to stand too close, afraid to incur any ill will. He'd only arrived yesterday, after the sentencing; he'd been searched, deloused, and sent to solitary for his first night. So far, he'd had no trouble with the staff, and he wanted to keep it that way.

Samuel-the-orderly pulled the door open and stepped inside first, taking in the room before standing aside for Eli and the nurse. It was a big room, long, with a row of windows opposite the door they'd come through, another door at the far end to the left. There was another nurse inside, and two more orderlies; the three of them stood near one of the windows, smoking. Eli counted eight, nine people wearing the same uniform as his, the once-white material a soft shade of gray. Most of them sat together near the center of the room, their cheap wooden chairs loosely arranged, though a few were standing or walking by themselves, mumbling quietly, their faces slack with drugs or insanity or perhaps one of the barbaric treatments he'd heard of and didn't want to think about. In all, though, it was much less horrible than he'd imagined; no one was screaming or crying or tied up, and he saw no bruises or other signs of abuse.

The nurse walked him to the gathered inmates as Samuel joined the other staff members, a cigarette already in his hand. One of the men, another Negro, stood up as they approached, a wide, friendly smile on his dark face. Eli attempted to summon a smile of his own and fell short, his insides too ravaged for it.

"Benny, this is Eli Underwood," the nurse said, her manner relaxing as she spoke, an apparent familiarity between her and the tall Negro. "Eli, this is Benny Russell. He's something of a . . . trustee, I suppose you could say. I'm sure Benny would be happy to introduce you to the others and help you get situated. Won't you, Benny?"

Benny's smile widened. "My pleasure. It's nice to meet you, Eli."

He extended his hand and Eli took it, surprised at the warmth and strength he felt in Benny's grip, realizing suddenly how much he'd missed the touch of another human being in past months. It had been too long since anyone had touched him, even a simple handshake. It made him feel like crying.

"Same here," Eli said.

"Well, I'll leave you to get settled," the nurse said. "Benny, I hope we can talk later . . . ?"

She said this almost with an air of deference, enough that Eli took notice. Benny nodded at her, and she smiled, then walked away, disappearing through the door to the left, her soft white shoes creaking faintly against the faded floor. Eli looked around at the others in the room, doing his best not to stare as he studied the faces of his fellow inmates.

There were several men and women, some brown, some white; everyone sat together, which was fine by Eli. He thought Thurgood Marshall had the right idea, pushing for an end to segregation. He had worked with and fought alongside a number of colored soldiers in Korea, and though he hadn't been particularly prejudiced before the war, he'd never given much thought one way or another for the Negro race, either. Afterward, though, after watching so many good men die during the liberation of Seoul—men of all colors—he'd found that he could no longer smile at the hateful jokes, even listen to the ridiculous bigoted rhetoric he so often heard since his return to the states, casually spewing forth from the mouths of ignorant whites. There were certainly cultural differences between Negro and white, but only in the same way that there were between Italian and Jewish, Irish and Greek, any two peoples from different places.

Apparently the insane get to be more enlightened than ordinary folk, Eli thought wryly. In spite of his self-proclaimed worthlessness, his half-believed vows to never find comfort again, he was glad to be in a "progressive" place.

"Let's get you introduced." Russell casually slipped an arm around Eli's shoulders and turned him to greet the others. Again, Eli felt grateful for the friendly touch, was surprised by the depth of his feeling.

"Mr. Underwood, this is . . ."

The names that Russell gave him mostly slipped past Eli, though the faces would stay with him. A petite, dark-haired young woman with wise blue eyes; an androgynous young man with dreadlocks, an older man, almost a giant, physically, named Leo—and wouldn't he give Samuel and his buddies something to worry about?—with a cool, appraising look on his rugged features. There were several others, and when they had finished with the inmates, Russell walked him over to greet the nurses and orderlies . . . a tall, curvaceous nurse with green eyes, an unsmiling but attractive woman named Laura or Lauren, an orderly named Terrence who moved like the soldiers Eli had fought alongside—and against—during the war. Each acknowledged Eli in some way . . . though as with the inmates, most seemed more interested in Russell's attention than in Eli—smiling at Russell after a cursory nod at

Eli, eager, somehow, for the attention of the tall, dark man. Eli felt almost privileged when, after the brief introductions, Russell led him to one of the windows, pulling up two chairs so that they could sit together.

The bars he'd expected were on the other side of a square of smudged glass that overlooked a parking lot, ringed with dripping hedges. It was still raining, staining the late-summer sunlight a mournful, shadowy gray, but it was warm inside. Eli felt a few seconds' pleasure, sitting cozily by a rainy-day window, and then felt the guilt again, the guilt that was his near constant companion, his lonely twin.

Killed her, killed her and I don't deserve to be glad about anything, not anything at all—

Russell sat in front of him, his wide smile fading.

"What's wrong, Mr. Underwood? Or . . . may I call you Eli? You can call me Benny."

Eli nodded. "I'm . . . Nothing is wrong." *—took her away from her daughter, only woman I ever loved, because I'm mad, evil, and crazy, I don't deserve—*

Benny's dark eyes were watchful. "I see. That makes you something of an exception around here."

"Oh?" Eli wasn't interested, but didn't want to be rude. He clamped down on the inner litany, forcing himself to pay attention.

"That's right. Everyone who stays here, everyone who works here . . . I don't know if I'd say there was anything wrong with any of them, but we all have our crosses to bear." Benny leaned forward, lowering his voice slightly, his gaze intent on Eli's. "Choices we made that we wish had turned out differently. Bad memories. Bad dreams."

Eli stared at him, wondering for an instant if somehow he knew about Ruri, but Benny sat back again, smiling.

"But some of us just want to learn about ourselves,

and others," he said. "Some of us . . . we *need* to learn. To better ourselves."

Eli's throat felt dry. "But . . . aren't you here because . . . I mean, we're all here for some crime or another . . ."

Benny's smile didn't waver. "That's one way of looking at it, Eli. Is that why you're here?"

"I . . . Yes," Eli said, feeling a deep urge to confess, to tell this man everything, and understanding at the same time that he didn't deserve to unburden himself, didn't deserve to ask for the comfort of such release. Benny only watched, his expression a study of patience and calm.

"I'm here . . . because I deserve to be here," Eli said finally.

This time, Benny's smile got even wider. He reached forward and patted Eli's knee, his eyes sparkling.

"Then this must be where you belong," he said lightly. "Let me tell you about the schedule around here. Did Sue-Lynn tell you we're a 'progressive' group?"

Eli nodded, his thoughts distant as Benny described art time, and mealtime, and talk time, where the men and women slept, how to get cigarettes and extra food. Outside, the rain continued to fall.

"*. . . this must be where you belong,*" he thought, marveling at how Benny had made it sound, how casual, as though Eli had chosen to think of his sentence as proper . . . implying that there was any other choice. He'd killed his wife in cold blood, in a moment of madness he couldn't justify; what was there to choose? If Benny noticed that Eli wasn't paying full attention, he didn't comment . . . throughout the rest of the morning, he only talked about little things, smiling and warm as he related anecdotes about the other inmates and staff and about himself. It turned out they both loved baseball, and both had been in the military;

Benny had been a Navy man in the Pacific theater, '42, and had some good stories about the men on his ship . . . and though he'd obviously seen plenty, he didn't relate any combat tales, which was something of a relief. Eli had seen enough of it himself. Benny's pleasant, unguarded manner was entirely engaging, comforting in its completeness; it was as though he had the ability to draw a man outside himself, to make him see things with a different point of view, a perspective somehow more forgiving than one's own. Eli wasn't sure what to make of him. At lunch, when Benny went to sit with another of the inmates for a time, the dark-haired woman with the ancient eyes, Eli was almost relieved to be back with his own familiar thoughts, bleak as most of them were. He watched as Benny took the girl's hand, talking with her in a low, calm voice, smiling frequently at her . . . and wondered at how such a man had come to be in an asylum for the criminally insane. And wondered, too, why he already felt that he and Benny were going to be friends.

16

Julian finished his briefing and waited for questions, running over his report for any holes he might have left open, any nuances he might have failed to imply. Those gathered—Kira, Ezri, General Cyl, Sam Bowers, Ro Laren, Nog, and Shar—were still digesting what he'd said, he could see it in their faces. They stood in security's well-shielded cell area, along with Hiziki Gard, still in custody; Gard, too, was silent for the moment, his eyes narrowed in thought. Taulin Cyl had apparently requested that Gard be kept in the loop, and it seemed that Kira had acquiesced. Julian couldn't help wondering if avoiding the guarded wardroom might also be a reason for her decision to meet at the security offices; there were certainly any number of Starfleet or Cardassian personnel on board who might question an unscheduled officer's briefing. Julian noted Admiral Akaar's conspicuous absence, but didn't pursue it. He had other things on his mind.

Julian was exhilarated by what he'd discovered, but subdued, too, by his inability to save the queen's host.

Tigart Hedda, the carrier, was dead. Figuratively speaking, she'd been dead before security had brought her to the lab, but that hadn't made Julian's job any less distressing, his efforts any less resolute. He'd been given the go-ahead to transport the parasite from Hedda's brain stem immediately, of course, but the operation had hastened the middle-aged Bajoran's inevitable demise, as he'd suspected it would, as precedent had implied. In addition to the slightly larger female parasite that had rooted itself at the base of Hedda's brain, there had been twenty-seven "soldier" parasites at varying stages of growth inside of her; the internal injuries had been severe. It was a wonder that she'd remained functional as long as she had, really, yet he still felt the loss as a personal failure. His ego, he knew, vanity, arrogance—they all applied, but he had still hoped to save her. She'd had no husband or children, but had left behind a sister, a cleric on Bajor to whom she'd been close.

"So they communicate telepathically with one another," Kira said, finally breaking the silence.

"The queen does," Julian said. "The females are higher functioning, and presumably make the decisions for the colony or colonies as a whole. There's no evidence to suggest that the soldiers are capable of it. It appears that a female has limited pheremonal contact with the 'soldier' parasites, one that allows her to send simple messages—return to a collective, perhaps, or be alert to danger—but to communicate with other females at a distance, they seem to use a kind of mental imaging. Not thought so much as picture, I believe."

"More Klabnian than Betazoid," Shar interjected, and Julian nodded. A number of lower-order life forms on Klabnia, a somewhat backwater Alpha swamp planet, employed such a type of telepathy; Julian had looked it up, while studying the female parasite.

Shar was also the first to grasp the obvious implications of the gross anatomy rundown. The specialized haploid cells necessary for sexual reproduction were absent. "And if neither the female nor the male has reproductive organs . . ."

Julian nodded. "The female parasites are born gestational, with a finite number of offspring already implanted. Each female is fully capable of setting up a colony on her own, and as the soldier parasites lack the transmitters that would suggest dominant or even independent behavior, the female 'leader' for each grouping probably communicates with other females. There's no telling what their range is."

"So . . . what produces the females?" Kira asked.

Julian shook his head. "Nothing we've seen so far," he said. "And likely not on the station; if the hive or colony structure is consistent with other parasitic species we've encountered, whatever it is would be capable of a mass spawning, suggesting a being much larger in size. Perhaps something on Bajor. That would explain Shakaar's transmissions."

"Based on the *Enterprise*'s reports, if we kill this female, the soldier parasites it commands will die, is that right?" Ro asked.

"The data suggests that the soldiers would exit their respective carrier bodies before they expire," Julian said. "But yes, the offspring are somehow dependent on the continued life of the mother, possibly through the telepathic link."

"So what are we waiting for?" Ro asked, looking at Kira.

"If we kill the female, any other females in the vicinity

will know it," Julian said. "I don't know how much information would be passed along, but it could be a serious security risk."

"The risk is to the people carrying those things around," Ro said, but didn't push it any further. Her point was made.

"More queens . . ." Kira murmured. She looked up. "Is there a way to communicate with her?"

"I don't— Not without a host body," Julian said slowly. "And introducing the female to another host is out of the question. Her ability to fully integrate her chemistry to a humanoid's CNS is fast and practically irreversible."

"All humanoids?" Cyl asked.

Julian didn't hesitate. "I believe so."

"But a being adapted to joining," Cyl said, looking to Gard, who looked at Ezri. She turned her wide blue gaze to Julian, searching his own for the truth.

Don't. He could feel all of them looking, and though he'd thought to lie if it had come up, had planned to, he found that he couldn't. Not with Ezri watching him, demanding his honesty by her own. "If it tried to bond with a symbiont rather than a Trill host, there might be a way. I could run a benzocyatic depletion, lower the isoboramine levels . . . but I can't recommend it. It would be extremely dangerous, to the host as well as the symbiont."

Cyl was nodding as though he hadn't heard the warning. "You could use a deFeguo spark line to protect the symbiont, surround it with an electrical pulse network."

"That should keep her from settling in," Ezri said.

Kira actually seemed to be considering it. "We have to communicate with it, find out what it wants. At this point, it's all we've got."

Ezri's expression made Julian try again. "Again, there's

the security factor to consider," he said. "Once she's conscious, she'll be able to communicate her capture to the others."

Kira looked at Shar. "Could we shield against it?"

"Uncertain," Shar said. "Most telepathies can be inhibited, but the materials and circumstances necessary to do so vary widely. It's possible that if I were to study Dr. Bashir's data, I may be able to determine the conditions necessary to block the queen's telepathic signals outright."

"Nog?" Kira asked.

Nog was nodding, looking around the crowded cell room. "If Shar comes up with the specs, I can pull off the tech, no problem. We could even do it here."

"I'll do it," Ezri said quickly, and Julian's heart skipped a beat. It was like a nightmare, what he'd dreaded most since hearing what had happened to Audrid's husband, to the Vod symbiont.

"No," he said, more forcefully than he'd intended. "It's . . . There are other options."

Ezri stared at him. "Like what?"

Julian grasped for something, for anything. "Perhaps we should kill it, as Ro suggested. The station would be cleared, at least, we'd have a safe base from which to continue our defense."

It was weak reasoning, and he didn't try to justify it any further. Kira was right, they all knew it; if such a covert infiltration could even be called a war, the parasites were winning it. Ezri stepped closer to him, her face filled with an understanding that made him angry, that made him feel entirely helpless.

Cyl turned to Kira, his face set in grim lines. "Colonel, I volunteer for implantation. In fact, I insist on it."

At Ezri's rising frown, Cyl shook his head, his tone

insistent. "I've spent my life preparing for this, Dax. Don't think you can step in and take it away, just like that."

There was a beat of silence, the others in the room shifting uncomfortably. Julian didn't want anyone to be implanted, he didn't think it was safe, but he also couldn't help hoping that if it had to happen, Kira would agree to Cyl's demand over Ezri's. The thought made him feel ill.

For the first time since the briefing had begun, Gard spoke. His voice was low, but it carried. "I've spent *all* of my lives preparing for this. It's what I do. If she's going anywhere, I'm taking her." He looked at Kira. "It's the least I can do."

Kira was still hesitating. Seeing that she hadn't quite decided to go forward, Gard added a final push.

"How long do you think it will take for the soldiers to realize that their mother isn't around anymore?" he asked. "The lockdown is over, Colonel. Don't waste what little time you have left."

Kira nodded once, sharply. "All right," she said, turning to Julian. "Do what you need to do. Nog, Shar, get the room ready. Ro, I want security standing by. . . . Dax, contact ops, make sure Nguyen fields any incoming calls from the admiral. Have him say that I'll . . . that I'll get back to him ASAP."

Ezri and Cyl had moved to Gard's cell, were talking to him about the implantation. As Julian turned to leave, Ezri shot him a look, one that suggested they'd be talking later about his attempt to dissuade her, but he didn't care. What mattered was that he wouldn't have to put her in harm's way.

We're not going to be able to work together for much longer, he thought, and buried it before it could go any further, determined not to muck things up between them, aware that it was already too late. He loved her, and that had changed everything.

For the fourth time in a week, Benny and Eli had their lunch together, and stayed in the dining hall after the others had wandered away, the two of them alone at the end of one of the long tables. A janitor walked by pushing a mop and bucket, smiling at Benny as he passed them, Benny smiling back and tipping a half salute. Though he'd already been there almost a month—or six weeks? strange, that he couldn't remember exactly—Eli continued to be amazed at how casual the staff was when it came to Russell; except for his own set of keys, Benny seemed to have as much run of the place as any of the doctors or nurses.

The large room echoed with sounds from the kitchen—the metal *clang* of trays being dumped, water splashing, the occasional burst of laughter or conversation between the janitor and the cooks. Benny and Eli sat in companionable silence for a few moments, Eli not thinking about much of anything at all. He'd found it was easier to get through the days that way, just existing, surviving, going through the motions of being a man; he even found some enjoyment in the false reality. Between his numbness and the distraction of Benny's amiable personality, he could forget himself for hours at a time. At night, though, when he was alone in his mind, in the dark, listening to the snores and gasps and rustlings of the other men in their cots . . . then, he still had to think about what he'd done.

"Do you have children, Eli?"

Eli looked up from his cold coffee, feeling a flicker of self-hatred at Benny's innocent question. He cleared his throat, nodding once.

"A daughter," he said. He thought about saying more, thought he should say more—some qualifying statement that made it clear what kind of father he'd been to her. *Absent* was the word. Ruri had never complained about his position's unlikely hours, that his postings had taken him away from her and the baby for months at a time. The baby, the little girl, the teenager . . . the young woman who surely despised him now. God knew she had reason enough, even before what had happened with Ruri . . .

What I *did to Ruri,* he thought, forcing the thought to stick.

If Benny noticed his discomfort, he didn't show it. "I have a baby on the way," he said, a proud smile breaking across his face. "My girl, Cassie . . . she's expecting any time now."

Eli smiled hesitantly, not sure what to say. How long had Benny been in? Had he even told him? From the way he came and went, Eli had had the impression that Benny had been there awhile. Longer than nine months, anyway.

And as proud as he must be, she's out there. He's stuck in here, with the rest of us.

"That's nice," Eli said, stepping carefully. "So, ah . . . Cassie is your girlfriend?"

Benny didn't answer directly. He sat back from the table, sighing. "I miss her, very much. I thought I'd be okay here, but knowing that she's waiting for me at home, about to have our baby . . . I don't know. It's important for me to be here, but . . . but relationships don't go on hold. People keep moving and growing, and if you spend too much time away, you miss things. You miss life."

The way he spoke . . . Eli was struck anew by the peculiar phrasing that Benny so often chose. It was as if he felt he had some choice in the matter, as though staying at the sanitarium was optional.

"What's your daughter like?" Benny asked.

Eli tried to shrug it off. "Women. You know."

"Not really," Benny said. "How is it, having a daughter? What kind of baby was she?"

A clear, perfect memory surfaced, of looking into her tiny face, at her dark eyes, so like Ruri's, the baby gazing back up at him, lips pursed, a hint of a frown creasing her silken brow. As though she wasn't sure what to make of him, wasn't sure if he was entirely trustworthy.

"She was . . . she was perfect," Eli said, barely aware that he was speaking. "A perfect baby. She looked like her mother, but acted more like me, I think. She was careful. Watchful."

"And now?" Benny asked.

"She's got some of her mother in her, some of me, I suppose," Eli said, picturing Pria's lovely face, a crooked smile across her fine mouth. "But she's mostly her own. Stubborn as a mule. Smart. Beautiful. She's got an impulsive streak in her, too."

Eli smiled, remembering. "When she was twelve, she decided she wanted to go to the beach for the day. Her mother told her that she was too busy to take her, so Pria actually took Ruri's car. Just borrowed the keys and drove off, happy as you please. She made it three blocks before running over a curb; ended up in a neighbor's rosebushes." He shook his head. "She could barely reach the pedals, didn't even know where the beach was, but thought she'd give it a shot."

Benny was grinning. "I bet there was hell to pay when you got home."

"No, I was out of town," Eli said, his own smile fading.

"Ruri told me about it a few days later . . . I was in the middle of a conference, I think. Or . . . no, I was traveling, on my way to a meeting in D.C. . . ."

He looked at Benny, surprised that there was a sudden knot in his throat, surprised into saying what he actually felt. "I missed a lot of things, Benny. I was providing for them, I told myself—I thought I was doing the right thing, doing what I was supposed to do. But I missed it, I missed all that time, all those memories, and there's no way to get any of it back."

Tears were threatening, and Eli swallowed them back, hard, covering with a cough and a forced smile. For a change, Benny didn't return it.

"You're right," Benny said, but he wasn't talking to Eli, Eli could see that by his distant gaze, by the wash of concern on his strong features that was entirely personal. "You can't get it back."

Eli felt a flush creep up the back of his neck. Listen to him, going on about missing his child's life when Benny was about to be a father; open mouth, insert foot.

"I, ah . . . I'm sorry," Eli started uncomfortably, but then Benny *was* smiling, back to his usual self.

"Don't be sorry, Eli," he said, his sincerity real. "I'm glad you said what you did. And I'm glad you're here."

It was an odd thing to say considering where they were, but somehow, Benny could get away with it. Eli understood what he meant, and was relieved.

"Just don't forget that you still have a daughter," Benny added. "And just because you missed part of her life, doesn't mean you have to miss all of it."

"She's—" Eli hesitated. How to explain? It was complicated . . . but the bottom line was simple enough, wasn't it? "She doesn't want to see me anymore."

Benny reached across the table, patting the back of Eli's hand. "If my child didn't want to see me, I'd keep trying. I'd try until one of us stopped breathing, just to let that child know that I loved her."

Eli felt a kind of warmth flow through him at Benny's touch, warmth and . . . hope? But no, there wasn't any hope. He pulled his hand away, grabbed his cup and finished it off in one cold, bitter swallow.

"Guess we should get out of here," he said, setting his cup back on the table and pushing away. Benny watched him stand, his gaze thoughtful.

"Guess we should," Benny said.

It took less than an hour for the cell room to be readied, for Julian to prep Gard for the implantation, but Kira could feel time slipping by, fast, too fast. The mother parasite was in stasis; how long did they have before her brood figured out what had happened, if they hadn't already? What would happen when they found out?

And Akaar will be back soon. Any minute, probably. The admiral had beamed out to meet with the first minister literally seconds before Kira got the com from security, that Ro had been attacked; he'd wanted to "touch base" with Bajor, to reorganize the defense network, to call a meeting with Macet, with HQ, with Lenaris Holem. He'd planned to return to DS9 as soon as preparations were made. The second she'd learned of the attack, Kira should have called him back immediately, should have held that holomeeting with all of the Bajoran and Federation officials standing by, to weigh the situation, to make decisions about the next step.

And instead, I make a snap judgment to risk my career and possibly jeopardize the entire defense web we've estab-

lished thus far. That was probably—hopefully—an overstatement, but she had to be willing, at least, to assume the worst. She would see what her own people could do with the situation, first, before she called in the administrators. Ideally, she'd learn something vital, something big that she could pass along to the admiral as she passed "the buck" along, as Benjamin used to say—something so beneficial to the UFP's defense that her neglect to make that immediate call might be overlooked. Practically, there was a better chance that she would gain nothing but the wrath of Starfleet, along with the outrage of every major dignitary currently aware of the parasite situation. She'd be stripped of rank, removed from her position, perhaps even judicially prosecuted. And yet try as she might, she couldn't talk herself into making that call, not yet. *Her* people were being taken over, the people of her homeworld, the people she worked with every day. By the parasites, of course . . . and by the great devouring machine that was the Federation, that was bureaucracy and talk and more talk. The Federation was a good, even necessary union, a strong, just ally, beneficial to the worlds it accepted into its membership; she believed that, wouldn't have continued to work toward Bajor's induction if she didn't . . . but she was a good commander, too. DS9 was her command, Bajor was her home, and she was through playing politics with them. Politics had taken away her religion, had sidestepped her authority in making the simplest of decisions for the greater good of the men and women she led, had made it impossible to be up front about what she knew, when she knew it. If the people up top were going to take her down for being good at her job, for making the decisions that needed to be made, she didn't want to work for the Federation. It was high time to take a few risks, to gamble at getting ahead of the parasites, and talking to one of the queens might be their best shot.

She watched as Julian strapped Gard to a gurney, as Shar and Nog hooked up computer screens and gestured at patch boards and conduits. Nguyen was at ops, and Ro had moved back into her office, but it was still crowded in the small holding area. Ezri and Cyl stood near Julian, watching over his preparations. The female parasite was in a stasis chamber on a tray stand near where Julian worked, frozen in a clear field of static energy. As the room was readied, Kira walked over to look at her, repulsed and intrigued by the tiny creature that seemed so intent on dominating and destroying the humanoids it encountered.

It was small, barely the size of the palm of Kira's hand, a mottled orange-brown color with a sliver of blue on its pointed tail. Its compact body had six short legs and an oversized pair of pincers at its head, that seemed to *be* its head. Kira couldn't make out eyes or a mouth; according to Julian, there weren't any. The tail was a kind of gill that expelled spent gases taken from the host's blood, absorbed through pores in the parasite's exoskeleton. The thought of volunteering to have something like that put inside of you . . .

"Not very appealing, is she?"

"The *Enterprise* report described the queen differently," Kira said. "A big, bloated thing . . ."

"That was the gestational body," Julian explained. "When the soldier parasites are ready to begin maturation, the queen grows a temporary second body for that purpose, connected to the main body at the brain stem by an umbilicus."

"And there was one of those inside Tigart Hedda?" Kira asked.

"I'm afraid so, Nerys," Julian said. "She was beyond saving. I think her death came as a mercy."

Kira looked up, saw that Gard was watching them. Julian had moved off to talk with Ezri and Cyl about something, and Shar and Nog were finishing the environmental readjust on the other side of the cell. Kira smiled at Gard, at the man who'd killed her lifelong friend and former lover, and shook her head.

"Are you sure about this?"

Gard nodded. "Absolutely."

He hesitated, then spoke in a slightly softer tone. "I've already talked to the doctor, but I want you to know, too. If things start . . . going badly, don't worry about my host body. But save the symbiont, if you can."

"It won't come to that," Kira said firmly. "We'll take her out before we let either of you get hurt."

Gard nodded again, though he didn't seem convinced. Kira searched for something more reassuring to tell him, but was still searching when Julian turned around and stepped to the gurney's side.

"We're as ready as we're going to be," he said.

A nod from Nog, and Shar tapped at the environmental controls. Kira felt the faintest tickle across her skin as the cell filled with unseen energy. Shar had theorized that the particles would be proof against the queen's ability to communicate with her brood.

"Let's do it," Kira said, and Gard took a deep breath, closing his eyes.

"This won't take long," Julian said. He reached over to a medical padd, typed a few commands, adjusted a setting switch on the stasis chamber . . . and an instant later, the female parasite was gone, transported out of her box in a brief sparkle of light.

Kira held her breath, looking down at Gard. Julian said he would place the parasite where the cerebellum met the spinal cord, where they typically nested . . . and also where the Trill symbiont's neurochemical pathways intersected with the host's. He didn't have an estimate on how long it might take for the female parasite to be able to communicate, if at all—

Gard opened his eyes, and was different. Kira could see it, they all could, his dark eyes muddy now, bleared with some unidentifiable emotion or sensation, there was no way to know which. He stared off into space for a moment, his gaze sharpening—and then winced slightly, his eyes blearing again. This repeated twice more—an expression of awareness crossing his features, a wince, then that look of dazed confusion again.

Julian manipulated the keys of the padd and spoke in a low voice, almost to himself. "Cyatizine levels down twenty-one point one, cortical proteins at functional count . . ."

"Is it working?" Cyl asked quietly, frowning as Gard started again.

Julian ignored the question for a few beats, then nodded slightly, not looking away from his screen. "She's trying to attach, but can't integrate. She may not have actual control of Gard's speech, but he's in contact with her on a basic chemical level."

Kira leaned in, tried to look Gard in the eye. His gaze blurred, focused, blurred again. "Gard? Can you hear me?"

"She's here," Gard said, his voice so hollow, so dead that Kira shuddered. It was Gard's voice, but sounded nothing like him. "She knows what's happening."

"Will she hear what I say?" Kira asked.

Gard's gaze cleared. "Yes," he said, the tone dead but

the shine in his eyes glittering and spiteful—and then the shine was gone again, lost to that tiny wince as Julian tapped at his controls.

Kira cleared her throat and prayed for guidance. "I'm Kira Nerys. I'm in command of DS9."

"We know who you are," Gard said, faltering on the last word, not so much drifting in and out of awareness as being jerked, like a fish on a line. "We know what you represent."

"Then you must know that none of this is necessary. The Federation would be willing to help you, to help your species find an alternative solution to whatever problems you and your kind face," Kira said. "Stop your attack on Bajor. We don't wish to fight with you."

Focus and blur, in and out. "It's too late. We've already won."

Kira's jaw clenched. "What do you mean?"

"We know, now," Gard said, a hint of a smile touching his lips before fading away, that glitter of malice there and gone again. His empty, toneless voice continued to skip and falter. "We know everything. You will destroy Trill. You will leave us the wormhole, and withdraw from this space. You will give us the bodies we need, or we will obliterate all that you hold sacred, and take what we want. Tell them."

Kira's heart was pounding with anger. "You won't succeed. I won't let you do this, do you understand?"

"I'm taking him, now," Gard said, and his voice was no longer so hollow, so devoid of emotion. A kind of hard brightness had crept into it, a false and frightening good cheer. "You'll have to kill him. Kill us, it doesn't matter. We've waited for the time and it's happening, now. You will all be taken."

"Julian?" Ezri sounded scared, as frightened as Kira felt.

"She's working her way around the pulse line," Julian

said quickly, looking to Kira. "I have to pull her, *now*."

Kira didn't hesitate. "Do it."

Gard was grinning, a wide, soulless grin, his gaze finding Kira's, his back and limbs arching against the gurney. "Doesn't matter, doesn't matter, doesn't—"

The restrained Trill gasped suddenly, his eyes widening in shock. Julian jammed a hypospray against his arm, injected, snatched up a handheld scanner and checked vitals with a practiced eye.

Silence, tense and taut, as they all waited, Gard staring at the ceiling, unmoving. Every muscle in his body seemed to be flexed—and all at once he relaxed, his eyes closing, head rolling to the side. Behind them, the female reappeared in her box, her body convulsed, frozen.

"Report," Kira snapped, her voice sounding far away against the rush of blood in her ears.

They waited, the few seconds like years before Julian spoke. "Neither symbiont nor host appears to have sustained any permanent damage."

Kira let out a breath she hadn't realized she'd been holding. "And the queen?"

Julian checked the stasis chamber. "She didn't survive the separation."

Gard rolled his head back, opened his eyes slightly. His lips moved, but his voice was barely a whisper. Kira crouched next to him.

"She's . . ." Gard rasped. "They're . . . She's . . . There's only one. She sees the artifacts . . ."

"Who? What artifacts?" Kira asked.

Gard's gaze flickered. "Mother. Bajor. Tears."

His eyes closed again.

Tears . . . Kira chewed at her lower lip. Was he talking about the Orbs? The Tears of the Prophets were at the monastery, where Opaka was staying. Commander Vaughn, too, until he got some rest.

"Do you think he meant the Orbs?" Ezri asked.

"Another mother parasite, maybe?" Cyl added. "Or maybe *the* mother the doctor hypothesized. The matriarch."

Before she could answer, Kira's combadge chirped. She tapped it, shaking her head at the questions.

"Kira."

"Colonel, there's a medical crisis—we've got reports from the Promenade, from engineering decks five, seven, eleven—two more at the docking ring—"

It was Nguyen, in ops. His voice was high and strained. Even as she rattled off locations, Julian's badge bleated, an emergency signal, and Ro stepped into the cell room, her cheeks high with color.

"Colonel, I'm getting reports from all over the station—people are collapsing, at least nine incidents so far and six alien sightings. The parasites are leaving their host bodies."

Julian had grabbed a med kit. "Colonel, he's stable and I've got to—"

"Go," Kira said, nodding. She turned to Ro. "Get your people out there, coordinate with Vlu's teams to track the parasites, top priority. We need crowd control . . . Get ID verification on everyone, oral or visual, we need to know where our people are."

She spoke into her badge, already moving. "Stationwide address—red alert. Alien presence on board, lockdown status. Describe invaders as small, insectile, extremely dangerous—"

At Kira's pause, Nguyen interrupted, a new note of worry in his voice. *"Colonel, something's happening on Bajor. General Lenaris is reporting . . . he's receiving news that a number of skirmishes have broken out . . ."*

"I'm on my way up," Kira said, the cold grip of responsibility knotting her insides. This female's death may have released the victims on the station, but what about Bajor? Killing the queen had set something much bigger in motion, Kira was sure of it; the telepathy block hadn't worked. It only remained to be seen how far-reaching the consequences would be.

She snapped off instructions to Shar and Nog to help Ro organize the general quarters detection, to find O'Brien, brief him, and get him involved; the chief's ship should be docking any minute, if it hadn't already. She told Ezri to get back to the *Defiant* and stand by, and asked Cyl to escort Gard back to the infirmary, all as she strode for the door. By the time she reached Ro's office, she had instructed Nguyen to alert the Cardassian and Federation ships standing by that the parasites were moving, and to arrange extra security on the few dignitaries still aboard the station. She'd call Akaar personally, *he should still be with Asarem, I can tell them both.* They could string her up if they wanted, they probably would, but later.

The alert status loop went off as she hurried out onto the Promenade, the computer's cool voice informing the station's residents that they needed to get to their respective crisis positions. Most of the people she passed were already moving, running to or from a large gathering of people just past Quark's, a woman shouting that someone needed a medic. A security team ran by, began working its way through the crowd, but Kira was already trained on the lift, her mind running a mile a minute. Was Cyl right? Had Gard been talking about the parasite matriarch? The Tears could only be the Orbs—he'd said artifacts—and if the monastery wasn't safe, she had to get word to Vaughn, to protect Opaka.

"Colonel Kira."

A short gray alien stepped in front of her, blocking her way, female, dark eyes. Kira blanked on the name for a half second, then remembered. She'd seen the girl a number of times recently, usually with Taran'atar.

"Wex," Kira said. "Now isn't a good time. If you'll excuse me—"

The girl nodded. "I understand, but it's important that we talk. I may be able to help you. I *want* to help."

Wex's expression was blank, almost stoic, but her eyes seemed to reflect some deep inner feeling. Kira couldn't place it, wasn't about to stop to figure it out.

"You want to help? Find Taran'atar, tell him to report to Ro," Kira said. She sidestepped the girl, headed again for the lift, calling back over her shoulder. "You can go with him."

"I know you'll want to hear what I—" Wex began.

Kira reached the lift, stepped on, and turned to face the girl as several others climbed aboard. "It'll have to wait," she cut in, ordering the lift to proceed nonstop to ops, snapping off her override code. The last thing she saw was Wex's upturned face, her dark eyes shining brightly, watching as the lift rose up and out of sight.

17

Eli was getting the hang of the place. He knew how to get to all the common areas and a few less common ones, knew what time the cafeteria actually had hot coffee, knew how to hide extra food and avoid getting caught at it. Though he'd never been there himself—the inmates in his ward were considered "docile"—he knew all about the rooms downstairs where the therapies took place; electrical shock and insulin, mostly, though there was an experimental hydrotherapy room, too. He knew most of the staff, although they rarely spoke to him, and was at least on nodding terms with everyone he saw on a daily basis. After only a few months—or was it just two?—he felt he understood a lot about the way Riverdale worked. But though he spent a large part of his time with Benny Russell, had probably grown as close to him as he'd been to any man in his life, there was something about Benny that defied understanding. The point was driven home one afternoon, not long after their conversation in the cafeteria, about Pria.

It was a drab autumn day, the halls reflecting pale light

from outside, most of the inmates in the main common room, listening to a Cubs game on the radio. Eli went looking for Benny during a newsbreak (Hurricane Hilda had killed two hundred in Mexico, the president of Argentina had resigned and fled, and gasoline was expected to jump to thirty cents a gallon), curious as to why his friend hadn't been around since the first inning; Ernie Banks was on the verge of breaking a grand-slam record.

After checking the cafeteria and the smaller common room, Eli headed for arts and crafts, a closet, really, crammed with reams of cheap paper and soft pencils and a bin of clay that always smelled vaguely of mold. There were a number of drawings pinned to the walls there that Benny seemed especially to enjoy, a whole series of outer-space scenes, with rockets and ringed planets and vast, floating buildings hanging in star-speckled darkness. Eli had found Benny sitting there more than once, staring at the slightly crumpled space-station picture, the station itself somehow rounded and angular at once.

As Eli was rounding the corner just before the art room, he heard voices coming from inside. He stopped, heard Benny speaking—and a second later, a response from somebody else in the room, a woman. Eli hung back, not wanting to interrupt, not sure if he should come back later . . . and then he recognized Samuel-the-orderly's voice asking a question, and was suddenly too interested to leave.

"But if you recognize your basic aloneness, your individuality of thought, of what import are the relationships?" Samuel asked, his voice strangely monotone. "The comforts do not last."

The woman spoke again. "Is it the memories? Do they provide the same comfort as the communication and time spent with the other?" It sounded like Nurse Lauren, but her voice, too, was unemotional, almost hostile in its complete blankness.

"Not the same," Benny said. "But yes, there is comfort in the memories. Even in unhappy ones. Remember what I said about familiarity?"

At least he *sounds like himself*, Eli thought. But what was he doing?

Benny was answered by a soft whisper. Monotone or no, it could only be Shiloh, the young man with the knotted hair. "There's comfort in familiarity. In not-change."

"Because . . ." Benny urged.

"Because change is difficult," Shiloh said. "As with letting go of anything, a memory, a relationship . . . even the bad seems better than the nothingness that might take its place. We know this."

"That's right," Benny said, and Eli could hear a smile in his voice. "We know this."

So, Benny was having a philosophical discussion with the staff, so what? There was no reason to be unnerved by it, no reason that Eli should feel his palms go sweaty, or his breath short. No reason at all that he should be concerned, to hear the nurses and orderlies and doctors asking Benny questions about feelings and memories as though only Benny could explain.

But who always seems to lead the therapy groups? Who helps all the inmates, when they're feeling low? And who's the one man who has made any real effort at getting to know me since I got here?

Who's really running this place?

Eli retreated from the corner, then turned and hurried back the way he'd come, back to the common room and the ballgame. Ernie Banks ended up hitting a record fifth grand slam of the season, only the day after Willie Mays had tied

Joe Adcock for homers at Ebbets Field—an amazing week for baseball lovers, to be sure—but even as several of the inmates danced around the radio, laughing, clapping each other across the back, Eli's thoughts were elsewhere. It seemed he wasn't sure about much of anything anymore.

There was a knock at the front door. Frowning, Kas excused herself and went to answer; it seemed late for a visit, though she supposed it might be one of her neighbors, checking in; they were about due. She might have ignored it earlier, but the intense conversation between her and her two female guests was winding down anyway, Keiko having talked out the bulk of what she'd needed to talk out.

Jake and Joseph had taken the children on a star watching expedition, complete with blankets and telescope and mugs of warm chocolate drink, all of it spread out on the back field some twenty meters from the house. Judith had suggested it—rather forcibly, actually—after their return from the market. With Miles gone and Keiko obviously wanting to talk about it, Kas had also urged the boys to distract the children for a while; Jake and Joseph, while perfectly capable of forming reasonable opinions and suggesting reasonable options, were men. Kas didn't know if that was sexist or not, but she firmly believed that there were conversations which didn't need a male perspective.

It's not sexist if it goes both ways, she thought idly, glancing at the timepiece on the wall as she shuffled down the front hall. Or maybe it was, she wasn't sure, didn't care. Keiko was struggling with career issues, as Kas had many times, as Judith had . . . and for Keiko, balancing those issues with family was proving difficult. It had been a valuable conversation for Kas. She wanted to return to work at some point, but hadn't yet decided when, wasn't sure how long she would need or want to bond with her new baby. It was hard not to wish . . .

No wishing, she told herself firmly, not for the first time. It was too easy to start worrying about what she didn't have. There were too many blessings in her life to start thinking that way; just having Ben's family around her . . . Talking about him, earlier, on her walk with Joseph and Judith, there had been a few tears, but she felt supported in a way she hadn't expected. It was good that they'd come. A little tiring, maybe, but then again, everything was a little tiring, lately.

She opened the door, saw a handful of Bajoran monks standing outside, rumpled and dusty. She recognized them as the group that had been camping just off the property, greeted them with a slightly puzzled smile.

"Yes? What can I do for you?"

The man in front, silver-haired and grinning, held up what appeared to be a Bajoran phaser. The others were armed, too, and the leader trained the small, deadly weapon on her belly. His eyes seemed black as night. "You can let us in."

Kas backed away from the door, opening her mouth to scream, to tell the others to get out, get the children—but she could hear Jake, now, angry and defiant, could hear Joseph cursing somewhere out in the darkness of the yard.

Terrorists. The assassination.

She grasped on to the fleeting thoughts as the men filed inside, one of them grabbing her arm roughly. Judith and Keiko were calling out, now, cries of shock and anger and fear, as Kas closed her eyes, praying with all her heart that they were being taken hostage.

* * *

The sounds from outside were far away, for a time, distant and erratic. It took some time for them to seep into Opaka's consciousness as she meditated, and even then, she successfully ignored them for a while. The warm, liquid light of the Tear bathed the room in radiance, soothing her spirit, relaxing her into the deepest of trances. It wasn't until the door to the meditation chamber actually opened that she forced herself to return from the ethereal, to draw away from the inner dance and address the firmer realities of outside.

A woman, a prylar, there in the doorway. The same who had denied her access to the Orb chamber . . . and with her, the two monks who had brought up the Orb that now filled the meditation room with its brilliance, reflecting from the bowed face of Elias Vaughn. Vaughn's eyes were barely open, his mouth slack, his arms at his sides as he took in whatever the Prophets had to share with him.

Opaka started to draw to her feet, alarmed at the terrible breach of privacy of such an intrusion. It wasn't right for a number of reasons, not the least of which being the commander's emotional safety—an emergency, it had to be, and she was already chiding herself for urging Vaughn to seek, she'd felt the tension in the air, had known that something wasn't right—

"We don't need him," the prylar said, her voice cool and clear as she stepped to one side, as one of the monks pointed something at Vaughn. There was a flash of light even brighter than that of the Orb, but only for an instant—

—and Vaughn was knocked aside like a child's doll, limp and rolling, his eyes like dull beads as he crashed to the floor. The other monk had come in, was closing the doors to the ark, shutting away the Orb's power. The reflection of light left Vaughn's face like life itself.

"No," Opaka breathed in horror, rushing forward, falling to her knees. She reached the fallen commander and touched him with trembling hands, felt for his *pagh* as she studied him for wounds. A nasty, burnt and bloody gouge across his upper left shoulder—but he was alive, she felt the strength of his life force tingling in her fingers. Alive but not present.

"Put the artifact back with the others," the prylar said, though Opaka barely heard her, didn't look up as the monks carried it away.

Vaughn's eyes remained empty, and though his heart beat on, pumping blood through his injury in pulsing, steady spurts, though he breathed, he also remained with the Prophets.

Oh, no, no. They would do what They could for him, surely, but without its spirit, how long could his body live on, a wounded, empty shell?

The prylar smiled at Opaka as the monks lifted the ark, carrying it away, as Opaka began ripping at the ceremonial garb she wore, making clumsy bandages while she silently asked the Prophets to watch over them all.

18

RURI SCREAMED, COLLAPSED. PRIA WAS CRYING SOMEWHERE in the dark, a sound that epitomized pain, that sank into his mind with steely fingers, gripping him, forcing him to hear.

Eli?

Confusion, there was blood and such horrifying, overwhelming guilt—and he sat up, barely holding back a shout, sat up to the cool stillness of a room, big, he couldn't *see. . . .*

"Eli, are you all right?"

The shape next to his bed, a deeper shadow. Benny's voice, warm and calm and concerned, a gentle hand touching his shoulder. Eli took a deep, trembling breath and blew it out, the dream still fresh in his mind, in his heart.

"I'm—fine," he stammered, but it came out weak. Pathetic, *you're pathetic, murdered your wife and now you can't, won't take responsibility—*

"Stop it," Benny said, his voice sharp and clear and too loud. Eli started, anxiously looking around in the darkness, waiting to hear the murmured, sleepy protests of the other men . . . and why was Benny here? He didn't sleep in the common room, he had his own room. Didn't he?

And what am I supposed to stop?

"You think you killed her," Benny said. "That's what."

That was too strange to think about. It was late, Eli was confused, and Benny wasn't supposed to be at his bedside, *especially not if he's going to read your mind.*

"What—why are you here?" he asked, keeping his voice low. He didn't hear the night noises he had grown used to, the snores and sniffles, the rustlings of sleep . . . and as his eyes started to settle into the dark, he saw that the cots around his were empty, that he and Benny were alone.

"What's going on?" he asked, feeling a stab of real worry. "What's wrong?"

"Some things are happening, outside," Benny said mildly. "Though really—what do you care?"

Eli blinked, sat up straighter. He ran his hand over his beard, rubbed at his eyes.

"What do I—"

Benny continued on. "I mean, you don't live here, isn't that right? You live in there. You stay in there."

He reached out and tapped Eli on the side of the head. Eli could see that Benny wore a slight half smile, could see moonlight reflecting from the white of his teeth, from the shine of his eyes.

"Where is everyone?" Eli asked. He could hear thunder rumbling outside, a faraway sound.

Benny stood up from his crouch, sat on the edge of the cot next to Eli's. It was where Leo was supposed to be, shifting his bulk restlessly through the night, snoring to beat the band. Benny turned on the small lamp between the two beds, throwing the room into dim reality. Definitely empty. Even the guard's cage, down at the end.

"Don't worry about everyone else," Benny said. "I know you have questions, a lot of them, but I'm going to ask you to trust me, just for a little while, okay?"

"But—"

"Do you trust me? *Can* you trust me?" Benny's kind, caring face, that half smile.

Eli nodded.

"Good," Benny said, sitting back slightly, resting his hands on his knees. "Listen good, now. I thought we'd have more time here, but circumstances have changed, and we need to get some things cleared up, you understand?"

No, Eli thought, but nodded again.

"This will be hard for you to believe, but I need you to believe it, just for a short time," Benny said. "Everyone is gone. They were called away, all right?"

"But not us," Eli said. He still felt confused, more than ever, but somehow not as worried. Benny had a way of making things seem . . . possible. That wasn't the right word, but it was as close as he could get.

"That's right, not us," Benny said. "Because it's time for us to go our own way . . . time for you to go back to your life, and me . . ." Benny's smile grew. "I've got places to be, myself. But for that to happen, you have to trust me, to accept what I'm telling you, even if it seems . . . well, crazy. And you have to make a decision."

Eli looked into Benny's dark, kind eyes and waited.

"The place we are now, this place—it's a place created by sickness, in a way," Benny said. "Created by emptiness, really, by lack of understanding. It's not a bad place, but it's not a real place, either."

Eli shook his head. "I don't understand."

"That's all right," Benny said. "That'll come later, maybe. For me, this place has been about learning and teaching. It's only one of the places I am. . . . That probably doesn't make much sense, but never mind, that's the way it is, sometimes. Things don't always make sense, do they?"

At last, something Eli could agree with. "No, they don't."

"I've stayed here because of the people, you could say," Benny said, his gaze thoughtful. "Representations. Aspects of character, of thought . . . but I'm getting off topic. I'm here to help, do you believe that?"

Thinking of all that he'd seen, of how everyone reacted to Benny, how *he* reacted, even now, Eli nodded. He heard thunder again, distant, but closer than before.

"And you're here because you think you killed your wife," Benny said.

That familiar cold metal in his gut, the rising ache. He'd never said it to Benny, never admitted it aloud. "I did kill her," Eli said, his voice dry in his mouth.

"You think you did," Benny said.

Eli felt a flash of irritation. What was all this, anyway? "No, I don't *think* I did, I did it. I killed Ruri."

"You think it," Benny said, patiently. "You live it, again and again, by keeping it in your mind."

Eli frowned, feeling agitated now, angry. "So? I keep it in my mind. I feel bad about it, I . . . I deserve to be punished."

"And as long as you believe that, you will stay here. If things were stable, outside, that might be all right, at least for a while longer. I wish you had more time . . . but things are speeding up, now."

Benny's smile was brilliant. "Time is moving," he added, dreamily, almost to himself, before refocusing on Eli.

"You think you deserve to stay in the pain, to repeat it,"

he said. "You think that you murdered your wife, and lost your relationship with your daughter because of it."

To have it laid out so casually, so matter-of-fact . . . Eli felt the heaviness in his belly rise into his throat, choking him as he nodded. "Yes."

Benny reached forward and took his hand, looking into his eyes. "I know what it is, to stay in pain," he said. "You think it's beyond your control, that you don't have a choice . . . but you can decide to let it go. Because here's the thing—even if it's true, even if you actually murdered her, it doesn't matter anymore. Whatever happened, it's the past, now. For you, this place—" Benny glanced around at the dim, empty room. "—is like a cage of the past. It's a trap. And you can leave it behind. You can—you *must*—choose to set yourself free."

Tears trickled from his eyes, he couldn't help it, no longer cared. He felt desperate, felt he was being offered some impossible dream. "How? *How?*"

"By understanding time," Benny said. "By knowing the truth. You already know it, most people know it, but they let themselves forget. They hang on to the pain because it's familiar, because to let it go might mean having to change. It's easier to keep the pain than to ask the questions, to find out why you think what you think, to question why you do the things you do. Nobody wants that, nobody wants to tear themselves down, rebuild from the beginning, only to have to do it again, and again. But the nature of time, for beings like you and me—it has to be about movement. It has to be a process, not a goal. There is no goal."

Eli shook his head. "I know that, but—"

"You *don't* know it," Benny said, his eyes flashing with something like anger. "*Listen*, Eli, hear what I'm saying with your gut, not with your mind. You think that holding yourself responsible for your wife's death, that staying in a place like this will help somebody, somewhere. You think your relationship with your daughter is something that *is,* a noun, a thing that can be broken, or fixed. Neither of those things are true. Time moves. Ruri is dead, she died long, long ago, and you are alive. What you have with your daughter isn't a *thing,* it's a *process,* a verb, it's something you create with each and every moment.

"If you want to atone for Ruri's death, then do it. Understand the process you have with your daughter, as much as you can, work with her to make each living moment worthwhile. But repeating the guilt, living in the pain, in the past—it doesn't work. It denies time. It denies *life.*"

Eli held fast to Benny's hand, his tears flowing freely now. He felt compelled to tell Benny that he was wrong, somehow, that he needed to feel bad, to stay where he was . . . but a part of him knew better, too, knew that Benny was telling him the truth. He'd told himself that he'd broken his daughter's heart . . . and then clung to the guilt, using it, letting it victimize both of them instead of trying to understand the process of their relationship. So many years, wasted. How could he live with that, with knowing that? How—

"There's the trap, again," Benny said, a hint of smile in his eyes. "Do you see? Get past the blame. See what's in front of you, see *her*. Let it *go*."

Eli shook his head, but not in denial of anything. It was such a leap of understanding, of faith, to accept—time moved. Was it really that simple? Could it be as easy as just *deciding*?

"It's never easy," Benny said. "But it is that simple.

Stand up, Eli. Come with me. Decide to move on, to explore, to see what there is to see."

Eli looked to the guard's cage, a flutter of panic in his chest at the thought of trying to escape—and saw that the security gate next to it was standing open, the dark hall beyond as empty as the bunk room. There was a deep rumble outside, thunder again . . . except Eli could actually feel it now, could feel the building tremble all around them.

"What's happening?" he asked.

Benny closed his eyes for a beat, then opened them again. "It's time to leave, Eli. Will you come with me? Can you?"

Eli felt the wetness on his face, felt the strength of Benny's fingers around his, and nodded. He hurt inside, but not the way he expected, the way he'd come to know and despise himself for. He felt . . . cleaner. He felt hope.

"I'm ready," he said, and let Benny help him to his feet.

Ro headed to ops, ticking off her mental list as she hurried to the nearest lift, only half seeing what was in front of her—people running by on the Promenade, headed for quarters or to secure their stations against new attacks.

—half-dozen parasites still unaccounted for, twenty-two teams out with handheld scanners and trackers, general population mostly secured in quarters with motion detection set up through environmental control—

Pairs and trios of guards, Federation, Bajoran, and Cardassian, stalked to and from the seventeen sites of parasitic activity that had been reported—primarily areas where medical emergencies had been called owing to someone's collapse. In spite of the repeating explanation that calmly blared through the station's comm system, there was a lot of confusion about what was happening. Parasites had been spotted at eleven of the seventeen emergencies, most by security she'd dispatched to each scene. The others had apparently escaped.

—still no ID track on thirty-four people . . . and three Cardassians wounded by Bajoran mobs, no serious injuries. Or lethal, anyway, but they all should have foreseen that it was asking for trouble, having teams of Cardassians run through the station, weapons drawn. It wasn't going to be an easy report to deliver.

Running into the Chief again after he'd come aboard the station had been the only bright spot so far, though there'd been no time to enjoy it. She'd always liked O'Brien, from their days on the *Enterprise*. And she guessed the feeling had been mutual—he hadn't scowled at her or gaped in outrage when he saw her, unlike many Starfleet officers who knew about her past. But he'd only had time to nod to her as he hurried toward engineering, led by Nog and Shar.

Ro hit the turbolift call, angry at how things were playing out, angry that the UFP had let it get to this. That was the problem with the Federation; they were always looking at the big picture, which meant they tended to miss the details.

Surprisingly, the lift was empty. Inside, Ro sighed, leaning against the wall as it carried her up to ops. Even with the adrenaline pumping through her system, she felt a hot, grainy kind of weariness. She knew her assessment of the Federation wasn't fair; tactically, they couldn't have done anything but what they had done, or at least nothing she could think of, but the fallout was murder. Besides the chaos and confusion, there were parasites running loose on board, at least six. Dr. Bashir seemed to think they wouldn't survive very long outside of their carrier bodies, but how long was that? An hour? A day? A week? And what if he was wrong, what if the soldiers could change gender—not an uncommon survival trait in some species—start a new colony? Or there was more than one female on board? If that was the case, they were exactly where they started.

The lift deposited her at ops, where it was only slightly more orderly than down below. Every station was manned and backed up, the tension palpable as people spoke and moved quickly, hurrying to get information where it needed to go. Ro headed for Kira's office. She could see the colonel standing, talking to a blurred face on her com screen. The intensity of the discussion was obvious, Kira's hands knuckled on the desk, her shoulders high and tight.

Akaar or Asarem, or both. Ro didn't envy her position. Kira had decided to see what the female parasite had to say without alerting any of her "superiors," and while Starfleet had a way of overlooking renegade conduct when things turned out well, the current situation didn't qualify. The big secret was out, the parasites knew that their enemy knew about their activities, and it appeared that they'd had some kind of plan in place, all along. Ro had gotten word from Bajor of what was happening on the surface. It seemed that infected citizens—and there were dozens, if not hundreds—were attacking people of high rank, in the Vedek Assembly and government offices. It was still too early to tell if the parasites were taking hostages or making demands, the reports had been sketchy, but it had all started at about the time Gard was being implanted, no question. And if Ro knew anything at all about the woman she'd grudgingly come to respect in past months, it was that Kira wasn't trying to pass off her blunders as anything less than they were. She'd broken the chain of command, and would own up to it.

Ro hesitated outside the office as Kira finished her conference, breaking the comm with a slap of one hand before waving her inside. She was pale and tense, her arms folded tightly as she turned to look at Ro. Ro quickly and dutifully gave her report, and though Kira listened intently enough, her gaze fell away a number of times, hearing other thoughts, her mind working on multiple levels.

Ro wrapped it up and waited, prepared to add a dozen new commands to what was already on her internal list—but Kira said nothing for a moment, the seconds ticking past for what seemed a long time. Considering how quickly things were happening, Ro supposed it was.

Finally, Kira met her gaze and nodded once, sharply, as though deciding something. "Right. Good. It sounds like you're on top of it," she said, her voice sure and strong. "I need you to get Nog, ch'Thane, and Chief O'Brien to the *Defiant*, but do it quietly. Bare-minimum crew, Nog will know who. Dax is already there, but she'll need to be alerted that we're 'go.' Direct channel, go through my office. I'll get Nguyen to cut us loose. Macet will spot us, even cloaked, but we can deal with that when it comes up . . ."

She was half talking to herself, and as Ro understood what she was planning, she felt her heartbeat pick up, her weariness suddenly a million klicks distant.

"You're taking the *Defiant* out," Ro said, wonderingly. *Without authorization, obviously.*

"Asarem Wadeen tells me that she can't get through to the Ashalla monastery," Kira said, and Ro saw that in spite of her demeanor, the colonel was afraid, too. On the verge of terrified. "There's been activity at five other sites, at least. Hostages have been taken. Six senior members from the Chamber of Ministers, an as yet undetermined number of prominent vedeks from the Assembly . . . and B'hala, the Central Archives, and the shrine at Kendra are now under parasite control."

Ro nodded, a bit surprised that the news hurt. She was no patriot, but if they meant to make demands, the parasites couldn't have chosen better people or areas to target. Except for the Orbs . . .

"Gard had to mean the parasite mother, the matriarch, and the Orbs are the only artifacts anyone calls the Tears," Kira said, as though reading her mind. "She's at the monastery, Ro, I know it. Kill the mother, maybe all the females die. Even if they don't, it will stop them from spreading."

"Did you tell them that?" Ro asked, tilting her head at the blank screen.

Kira shook her head. "Akaar was too busy ordering me to stand down to hear what I think. He says he'll deal directly with DS9's officers from here on out . . . and Asarem only had time to tell me that Kasidy Yates and the Sisko family have been abducted. Keiko O'Brien and her children were left behind to pass along a warning, that any sudden moves by the Federation will be dealt with harshly. They're safe, at least."

Captain Yates was already past due to give birth, by a week at least. Ro understood the fear she saw on Kira's face a little better.

"I'm to confine myself to this office until the admiral gets here," Kira continued, "at which time he'll take my report, and then coordinate with the Federation and Asarem as to contacting the parasites to discuss their demands. A delegation of top mediators is already forming for a holo con."

"That could take days," Ro said.

Kira smiled at her, a tight, humorless smile. "Which is why I'm going to try and stop her myself. Since I'm officially out of the picture, the negotiators can argue that I was acting on my own. If I get caught, which I won't."

As bad as things were, Ro was unable to help a small smile of her own. No wonder Kira had given her a chance; the woman was no more Starfleet material than she was, and had the confidence to back herself up. What the colonel said next made the smile disappear.

"I'm leaving you in charge."

What?!

"What?" Ro croaked, the sound much weaker than the exclamation of her thought. "You can't."

"I can," Kira said. "You're my chief of security. You know what's happening at every level, you have access to everyone, you're more than competent enough to handle this. All you need to do is what you're already doing . . . keep everything and everyone moving, find those missing bugs, and when Akaar shows up, do what you can to stall him."

"You can't," Ro said again. "*I* can't. Nguyen, maybe, or—"

Kira glared at her. "No time for this, Ro. You know you can. Do it. Put Etana on security, Nguyen can keep ops running, Chao can take over engineering. I'll tell Bowers to back you."

With that, Kira turned and hurried out of the office, head high, not looking back. Ro stared after her, but only for the space of a few heartbeats. There wasn't time for anything more.

She was behind Kira's desk in two strides, opening a secure channel before Kira paused at Nguyen's station, the colonel still not looking back to see how, if Ro was managing. She felt a rush of fear, of being overwhelmed by the scope of what she'd been ordered to do, but it didn't slow her fingers, didn't make her voice tremble as she called Nog, then alerted Dax.

You know you can. Do it. Kira's voice in her head, or was it her own? It didn't matter. It was the truth. She could and would handle the station until Kira came back, or until Akaar had her physically dragged down to security and tossed in one of her own cells.

But I'll kick every step of the way, Ro thought, and found the thought to be surprisingly uplifting. She was about to give him a real reason to despise her; it was about time.

From the house they were taken to a small shuttle and flown to an undisclosed location, Jake doing what he could to keep everyone calm, himself included. It wasn't easy. Kas was scared, and watching her run trembling hands over her swollen belly again and again, almost compulsively, made him feel small and helpless as they sped through the Bajoran night.

When they finally landed, a handful of monks stepped out of the dark and used weapons to motion them off the shuttle, leading them to a large, ancient stone structure. They were aliens, but looked Bajoran. Possessed, Jake figured, and Kas, Grandpa, and Aunt Jude agreed. They'd all heard one of their captors refer to himself as "this body" while still on the shuttle . . . and though they seemed capable of expressing emotion, none of them did. All of them wore empty, hollow expressions, as though their faces were masks.

The stone building was a monastery, if the aliens' garb was any clue, and Jake recognized it as the big one in Ashalla. They were jostled through a dark corridor, their conversation ignored by the monk-aliens, as they had been since being taken. Jake instinctively stayed close to Kasidy, and saw that his aunt and grandfather were doing the same, crowding around her as they were led to their next destination.

"At least they left Keiko and the children alone," Kas said, not for the first time, holding her belly tightly. Jake nodded, exchanging a look with his grandfather.

"Everything's going to be fine," he said, his voice calm and reassuring, the look on his face a little less so. Jake hoped he was right.

Ahead of them, a square of light as a door opened. The monk in front of them stopped just outside, gesturing for the hostages to go in. Jake stepped in front of Kasidy and entered first, hoping very much that they would be treated decently—and that whatever their captors wanted, Bajor or the Federation would be able to give it to them. Fast.

"Jake?"

Jake hesitated in the doorway, blinking. The light was low, but seemed very bright after their walk through the dark.

"Sulan?"

The former kai sat cross-legged on the floor, looking up at him with an expression of concern. A wounded man lay next to her, his head propped up by a cushion. . . .

Vaughn, that's Commander Vaughn.

He'd been hit in the shoulder, and though the wound didn't look too horrible—Opaka or someone had bandaged it up—he was unconscious. Three "guards," more Bajoran clergy, stood at the front of the room, weapons drawn, their faces blank.

"Sit," said one of them, her voice toneless. She wore a

prylar's gown. She smiled chillingly, emotionlessly. "Don't make trouble or we'll kill you."

Behind Jake, his family had filed in. "We won't make trouble," Jake said. The alien ignored him, seemed to look straight through him; it appeared that the conversation was over.

They situated themselves on the floor—there were no chairs in the room—doing what they could to get Kasidy comfortable with floor pillows, leaning against the back wall. Jake introduced Opaka Sulan to the others, relieved that the elderly woman's placid demeanor had an immediate soothing effect on Kasidy. Grandpa and Judith seemed to calm down, as well; Jake knew that he felt better. In the short time he'd known Opaka, he'd come to respect her, very much.

And we're here, being watched over. Whatever's happening out there, we haven't been slated for execution.

Not yet, anyway.

Jake settled to wait, glad at least that he was with people he loved.

19

MILES O'BRIEN WAS TRYING TO PAY ATTENTION TO WHAT WAS happening—but what was happening was what always seemed to happen, what had happened a hundred times before in the course of his career. He was on the bridge of the *Defiant,* trying to concentrate on what Kira was saying as Nog and a few of his underlings manned the cloaking device down below, as Ensign Tenmei carefully started to edge them away from the station, and a red-shirted Ezri Dax called out readings from tactical.

". . . they're fine, they've been taken to a Starfleet camp in the Hill province. They weren't hurt, Miles."

He replayed it again, then again. Nothing to worry about, right? Right. Kira wanted to go fight the good fight, and he would back her, he'd done it before . . . but he couldn't remember the last time he'd felt so helplessly adrift in a crisis, so angry with himself.

I should have been there. The parasites had to be stopped, of course, and he was more than willing to help save the Siskos, not to mention any number of other poor souls who'd fallen prey to the alien threat—

—but I still should have been there. His wife and small children had been terrorized, had watched as their friends had been abducted by strangers. They'd been left alive to bear a message of caution, and though he was infinitely relieved to know that they were unharmed, he was finding it extremely difficult to get past the news.

Things had been crazy since he'd arrived at the station, less than an hour ago. He'd stepped off the private shuttle resigned to yet another medical scan, performed just outside the airlock by a Cardassian with unfortunate breath. Given the all-clear, he'd started off to ops, feeling strangely ill-at-ease in the too-familiar corridors, trying to think of a way to convince Keiko that he was fully in support of her career without actually having to move, when an infiltration alert had started to sound. From there, things had really picked up speed; Nog and a young Andorian male, the new science officer, had tracked him down just inside the docking ring, Nog filling him in on the crisis—a real doozie, too—as he was hurried along to engineering. There was that brief run-in with Ro on the way. She'd looked startled when she saw him, but he hadn't had time to do more than nod and hope they could talk later. He'd hardly had time to set his tool kit down before Nog had him recalibrating comp boards on enviro controls, and he had barely started *that* when Nog got a call from ops ordering the three of them to report to the *Defiant.* They'd met up with Kira at the airlock, along with several others, engineers he'd never even met before, all too young, too excited to be doing what they were doing.

The ship was already set to go when he boarded. Someone in ops had cut them loose with a wink, firing up a substantial stasis transmission at the airlock to take the place of the departing ship. Anyone scanning DS9 would get a general reading of appropriate size and mass, though it wouldn't stand up to real scrutiny. Hell, it wouldn't stand up to anyone looking out a *window,* but it would probably hold for a little while, long enough for *Defiant* to be on its way to Bajor.

They hadn't been hurt, that was the important thing, he had to try and concentrate. *Though maybe it* is *time for me to get behind her career, for a change. How many botanists are called away from home to fight terrorist aliens?*

". . . Chief?"

O'Brien blinked, realizing that he'd missed something. "Wha—? Sorry, say again?"

"I asked if there was any way to transport through the cloak without being detected, even theoretically," Kira said from the center seat.

O'Brien started to tell her that there wasn't, but then thought of the discussion that had cropped up among his AP students one day, on the subject of cloaking technology. One of them, a particularly bright youngster still too inexperienced to know what was impossible, had offered up an interesting theory.

"*Theoretically,* I suppose," O'Brien said, hoping that his obvious reluctance would be deterrent enough, already knowing that it wouldn't be. The expectant look on Kira's face wasn't going away.

"If we created a series of overlapping subspace fields to use as a transport site," he said slowly. "Each progressively weaker as it neared the surface . . . they'd get a reading, but too vague to identify, and nowhere near the ship. If it works, though—which it probably won't—we'd only be able to beam one person through, without setting off surface sensors."

"That would take a tremendous amount of energy, more

than we have," the Andorian, Shar, said. Seemed like a nice enough kid, though engineering obviously wasn't his forte.

O'Brien shrugged. "So, we tap the warp core. We're not using it for anything else."

"How long will it take?" Kira asked.

"How long have we got?" Miles returned.

"Do it," she said. "Shar, you and Nog help him. You too, Prynn, once we establish an orbit."

They all nodded, O'Brien heading for engineering, Shar close behind. Apparently, Kira hadn't heard the 'probably won't' part, though in his experience, commanders rarely did. If it *did* work, he'd have to give his student a substantial extra credit write up at the end of the course . . .

. . . which will probably be my last act as a professor at Starfleet, he thought, barely registering the thought as a decision, already certain that it was the right one, that it felt right. He loved Keiko more than this, than any of it. His work made him happy, but his family was his life, and if she still wanted to go to Cardassia when this was all over, he'd find a way to make it work. He wasn't overjoyed at the thought of living there, but Keiko deserved to have her turn at a real career, and it wouldn't hurt the kids to see a fair partnership between their parents. And surely they needed engineers there, particularly any with experience in Cardassian hardware.

He shivered, remembering the nightmare of rerouting power through DS9's Cardassian/Bajoran/Federation interfaces, but it wasn't an entirely unpleasant shiver. Being with Kay and the children, that was all that mattered. And he did like a challenge . . .

As they reached the lift that ran closest to engineering, Shar spoke up. "You believe it will be possible to integrate the weakest field into linear space, with the transport subject inside," he said, a half question as they started down.

O'Brien nodded. "Anything's possible," he said.

As their captors stood silent, watching over them, Opaka sat with the commander for a time, meditating, feeling for his spirit with her own. The *pagh* that radiated from him was powerful, the energy of a man or woman who had just received a vision from the Prophets . . . except he was still receiving, the muscles of his face and body relaxed, even his pulse and respiration slowed. She worked to stay in tune with him, to breathe as he was breathing, and though she could feel slight surges in his *pagh,* could feel that his spirit moved, there was no change for him physically.

After a time she opened her eyes, looking down at his empty face, reaching to ease his eyes closed again; they would dry out if left open, but with so much of him gone, they wouldn't stay shut. She reached for a strip of cloth, turning to look at the loose assemblage against the wall behind her—the Emissary's wife and son, father and sister. Kasidy was propped up by every spare cushion in the room, her face flushed, her gaze wide and unhappy.

Poor child, Opaka thought, smiling gently at her as she spoke to the others. "Would one of you get some water? There's another basin in the storage cupboard," she said, nodding at the old wooden unit that stood at the front of the room. "Perhaps one of our . . . watchers might escort one of you to the fountain outside?"

It was unlikely. They hadn't even allowed Kasidy to relieve herself in private, but had at least let her use the room's other basin, the one Opaka had brought in for the commander; it wasn't uncommon for one coming back from the Prophets to feel ill for a moment or two, as they readjusted to the physical plane. Opaka had discreetly mentioned it when she'd noticed Kasidy's obvious discomfort, shortly after they had arrived to join her and the wounded commander.

Unlikely they'd let one of us go, but they might fetch it themselves. If they mean to use us, they have to take care of us, at least on some rudimentary level. She knew she was being hopeful, but also knew that there was no other way to be. The Prophets would provide what They could; it was up to Their children to remain in faith, as much as *they* could. If these were to be their last moments of life, living them in fear and dread would be a horrible waste.

"I'll ask," Jake said, nodding, and Joseph silently stood up with him, his face set. The Emissary's father was a strong, determined man; it shimmered from him like light, and in spite of the circumstances, Opaka was pleased to have met him.

"I'll go with him," Joseph said protectively, narrowing his eyes as he surveyed the trio of the infected. There were others standing guard outside, and, Opaka imagined, a number more walking the halls, dressed in the skins of her brothers and sisters. The three weapon holders stared blandly back, not speaking, not moving, their attention fully focused on the captives. Their faces were as slack as the commander's, but their eyes burned, shining with an awareness that didn't belong. They didn't frighten Opaka for herself, but she was deeply concerned for the innocents who had been taken, and for the Emissary's family.

The two Sisko men took a few careful steps forward and began negotiating for water, explaining Kasidy's condition, explaining Commander Vaughn's. After a moment, one of the monks went to the cupboard. Opaka pushed herself closer to Kasidy and Judith, finding another smile for the frightened young mother-to-be.

"How are you feeling?" She reached out and touched Kasidy's hand, stroking the back of it lightly.

"Not very well," Kasidy replied. She shifted uncomfortably against the floor cushions, forcing a smile of her own. "Though to be fair, I haven't felt all that great, lately."

Opaka smiled wider, still stroking the girl's hand, feeling her respond to the light touch, her muscles relaxing slightly. It seemed that human women often experienced extreme pain when the child came forth.

"I remember my last days of bearing too well," Opaka said. "When the baby comes, women set aside the memories of discomfort, I think, remembering the emotional—the anticipation, the joy—but carrying a new life through the last few weeks is no easy appointment, is it?"

Kasidy's smile came more naturally, now. "No, it isn't. Particularly when—"

She shifted again, frowning and smiling at once. "The baby's moving," she said.

Opaka instinctively reached for her belly, hesitated. Kas nodded her assent, placing her own long, strong fingers over Opaka's, moving her hand to just below her navel.

Opaka closed her eyes, felt . . . felt the long, shuddering movement of life inside, the Emissary's unborn turning, the *pagh* of new life giving off heat and energy. It was magic, the very highest kind, what Kasidy and Benjamin had created. And though *pagh* was not generally gender-specific, there was an intensity there . . . Opaka thought she knew, or at least had a good guess as to the baby's sex. And—

—and *there*, the sudden tension of the muscle beneath the flesh, the involuntary strain of Kasidy's abdomen.

Opaka remained still, gentle in thought, smiling again at the young woman as she restlessly moved her legs—unaware, it seemed, that she was having a contraction. It was mild but not weak, not at all, and lasted longer than Opaka might have hoped.

"My back hurts," Kas said, almost apologetically, shifting away from Opaka's hand.

"I'm sure it does," Opaka said, deciding not to speak of it, not to alarm the sweet young woman unnecessarily. If it was a true labor, she'd know it soon enough.

Prophets help them, they all would.

20

KIRA STEPPED ONTO THE TRANSPORTER PAD, HER THROAT DRY when she swallowed. Her legs felt a little shaky, and her utility belt seemed unusually heavy around her hips. She was scared, but she'd make this work.

A plan would be nice, though, wouldn't it?

She *had* a plan, just not a particularly detailed one. Find the queen and kill it. Find the hostages and help them. If the Chief and Nog and Shar had managed to figure out a way to beam someone through a cloak, she could certainly come up with something, once she got down there. She had her childhood to thank for that. Resistance fighting was all about making do with whatever was at hand; planning had often been a luxury she'd gone without.

She turned, saw Dax watching, Nog and Shar working with an open circuit panel in the bulkhead next to the transporter console. Miles was at the controls.

"I've pinpointed the entrance to the underground chamber," the Chief said, and Kira nodded, blowing out a deep breath, praying that she hadn't misinterpreted Gard's last conscious statement.

"There are a number of lifeforms near it," he added. "I can't get an exact count, the subspace fields are causing a lot of interference."

The same reason he couldn't beam her directly to the Orb chamber; there were lifeforms there, too, so many that he didn't want to risk putting her in. The thought was an exceedingly unpleasant one.

One among many. She was going up alone against an unknown number of enemies, and from what she understood of the Chief's theory, she might also end up scattered across Bajor's outer atmosphere, a billion burning atoms turning to ash and gone.

She held phaser loosely in hand, nodding again, her adrenaline up. If he explained one more time that he wouldn't be able to beam her back, she was going to throw up.

"Let's do it," she said. "I'm ready."

Ezri straightened, looking as if she were about to speak, and both Nog and Shar looked up from their work, but Kira only nodded to the Chief sharply, not wanting to hear what any of them had to say. There wasn't enough time, she could feel it.

"Good luck, Colonel," O'Brien said, his hands moving across the controls—

—and an instant later, she was in a cool darkness, heavy with the scent of old stone—

—and hands came down across her back, two, three, a half dozen. Kira was spun around, the phaser knocked from her hand, all of it happening too quickly. She tried to drop into a fighting stance, but before she could even find her balance, a leg was hooked behind hers, knocking her to the hard ground. The silence of it was as terrifying as the speed, the parasites apparently not needing to speak as they crowded around her, five, six of them, Bajoran faces that sneered at her with a gleaming contempt.

No! She could see the entrance to the Orb chamber, less than ten meters away, but the guards were crouched over her, her limbs instantly pinned beneath hands and feet, one of the carriers reaching down to her face, to her mouth, *Kas I'm so sorry—*

—and as suddenly as she'd been attacked, she was free, her attackers thrown or pulled backward, seemingly all of them at once. Kira was knocked onto her side, receiving a kick in the ribs, another to her throat. Behind and around her she heard scuffling feet and grunts of exertion, heard the heavy fall of bodies hitting the floor. It was all so quiet, so fast and unexpected; she'd beamed in seconds before, and the battle—if it could be called that—had been lost and reclaimed in the space of a few heartbeats.

What—?

She rolled to her feet, confused, searching the near dark, snatching her phaser up. She had time to see the last Bajoran host fall to the ground, to take in that they were still alive, unconscious, but how—

—a shimmer of movement, and a small figure stepped forward, gray, female . . .

"Wex?"

The alien stepped forward, reaching out as if to touch Kira, then letting her hand fall to her side. Kira backed up a step, holding the phaser higher. Wex had saved her, but until she knew why the alien had done so—not to mention *how*—she wasn't going to take any chances.

"I'm . . . sorry," Wex said, and started to change, her body seeming to ripple, to glow with a soft golden light that Kira remembered so well, that she couldn't believe, couldn't *let* herself believe—

—and she had no choice, because an instant later, there was Odo.

Her backache was getting worse, not better, and the dull, achy pain of it was working its way all the way through her belly. She checked her timepiece for what seemed like the thousandth time, but didn't know if she was timing the ache early or late. There was too much going on, her stress level wasn't exactly tapering down, and she was exhausted, which made it hard to tell much of anything. She just felt crummy, regardless of how many cushions the Sisko family kept trying to ease behind her back, regardless of Jake's mildly distracting shoulder rubs or Judith's soft, gentle tones. She hurt and she felt almost as annoyed as she was afraid, ready to snap at anyone who got too . . . well, too *something*. Annoying.

She felt that low, rotten-tooth backache get worse again and checked her timepiece, remembering the childbirth holos she'd practiced, *time from the beginning of each contraction* . . . She had to go to the bathroom again, but the effort of having to get up, take the bucket off into the corner, and be shielded by Judith from their weapon-wielding captors seemed like way too much effort.

Hell, getting up is too much effort, she thought, counting minutes. If she *was* having contractions—and she wasn't entirely convinced that she was—they were somewhere between four and six minutes apart. Was that right?

The fear overrode the physical again and she took a long, deep breath, trying to relax, tensing in spite of it. This was a bad place to be, to have a baby. Julian said that labor could take a full day before her amniotic sac broke, even longer if the contractions weren't regular, and though she dreaded the thought of feeling even half this bad for anywhere near that long, she mentally crossed her fingers—also for the thousandth time—that her real labor hadn't started.

Which was, of course, when she realized that her bottom and lower back were getting wet. She reached back with numb fingers, doing her best to work her hand behind her . . . and felt the warm, wet spot growing on the pillow behind her, even as she felt a tiny gush of liquid trickle down her left thigh.

"Oh," she said, startled by the wetness, by what it meant—and at the sound of her own surprise, she started to cry.

"Kas?" Seated next to her, Judith turned her wide, worried eyes to Kas's face, searching to help.

I'm going to need it, Kas thought, fresh tears welling up as she groped for Judith's hand. Her water had broken. The baby was on its way.

Ro stood in Kira's office looking out at ops, feeling reasonably calm, considering. Things were slowly but surely getting under control. Kira was right, she *could* do this, or at least as long as nothing too unexpected popped up. She didn't have to second-guess anyone, everyone was competent enough in their respective fields to offer intelligent suggestions; it was just a matter of taking reports and letting the officers tell her what should be done.

Engineering had reported that the motion sensors were working, and security had backed that up. There were only two parasites still unaccounted for, plus a handful of civilians left to track down, but her people were working their way through, one step at a time. Dr. Bashir had reported that there were no new cases of infection, and no fatalities as a result of the female parasite's death. It seemed that the parasite soldiers had simply let go of their victims and crawled out, causing surprisingly minor injury in their wake. He was just about to start on the stasis cases, backed up by the Cardassian medical teams. Bashir and Tarses had both noted that the captured parasites were weakening, their systems shutting down. They'd all be dead in a matter of hours. And Vlu had just called in to tell her that for the most part, everyone was now cooperating with the Cardassians. People were finally starting to see that they were here to help, and the response was positive.

This isn't so bad, Ro thought, still vaguely amazed that she was running things, more so that people were actually listening to her. Nguyen had passed word along that Kira had left her in charge, and no one had questioned it. She was still nervous, no question, but felt like she had a pretty good chance of getting out of it unscathed—

A call came in on the desk com. Ro cleared her throat. "Yes?"

"Lieutenant, Admiral Akaar has just requested permission to beam aboard from the *Trager*," Merimark said.

Ro nodded to herself. *So much for the unscathed theory.* She was ready . . . but before she could open her mouth to say as much, she had a sudden inspiration, one that would ruffle every last one of Akaar's feathers.

Kira did say to stall him.

"Tell him to come up to the office," Ro said. "Tell him that she'll meet him there." It wasn't a lie, technically. When she got back, she probably *would* meet him in her office.

Ro stepped out into ops, moved to stand near the new situation table—recently set up to replace the one destroyed when Ro had sent Gard crashing into it. She smiled inwardly at Merimark's expression. How long would he wait? Five minutes? Ten? When he was about to fray a cable, Ro would step forward, explain that she was temporarily managing ops, that Kira had pressing duties elsewhere but should be back soon. He'd stew, but he wouldn't be able to accuse her of anything, and she was under no obligation to tell him anything in regard to Kira's whereabouts. Of course, once he figured out what had happened . . .

If I were in Starfleet, he'd see me court-martialed. Again. If she were in Starfleet. Realistically, the worst he'd be able to do was lodge a complaint with the Bajoran Militia, and by the time it reached anyone's desk, she'd be long gone. What was it that Nog was always quoting, one of Vic Fontaine's colloquialisms . . . in for the penny, in for the pound?

Ro crossed her arms and leaned against the situation table, watching the turbolift with bright eyes.

21

ODO WATCHED THE SHOCK SPREAD ACROSS HIS LOVER'S face. In spite of the circumstances, he was unable to keep himself from searching for a thread of joy, of pleasure at his sudden appearance. He saw it, along with a dozen other familiar expressions, all of them much loved and missed. Even her anger, which was no small thing.

"You . . . I . . ." she stammered, and before he could start to explain himself, she had stepped into the circle of his arms. She embraced him tightly, so tight, and he allowed a second to close his eyes, to rejoice in the feeling of her body against his, of her love for him. Then he moved, understanding that everything else was going to have to wait. She understood it, too, nodding as he cocked his head toward the shadows at the end of the corridor, out of the light and away from the fallen Bajoran carriers.

They slipped into the darkness, Odo expanding his senses, listening for movement as she leaned in to speak.

"You know why we're here?" she whispered, and

though her voice was cool, her manner collected, he felt the tremble of her arm against his, and was glad of it.

"Yes," he said. "The hostages. The queen."

Nerys nodded. "You take the hostages."

"We should stay together," Odo said, hearing the urgency in his own voice. He didn't want to separate, not here.

"We have to hurry," she said. "And you've got a better shot at protecting them."

Odo nodded reluctantly. Arguing would only waste more time, and at least he'd been able to help her clear the way to the monastery's lower level. Perhaps she wouldn't encounter any more resistance. "All right."

They had to leave, had to do what needed to be done, but for a second, neither moved, their gazes locked. There was so much to say, to explain; he saw the questions on her face and tried to think of some brief statement, something he could tell her that would answer everything, that would explain. The circumstances leading to his presence weren't complicated, but would certainly take too long to lay out now. Nevertheless, he knew he would owe her a long conversation about why he'd returned when he had, and in the guise of Wex.

All of it flashed through his mind, the story replaying itself yet again; he'd rehearsed it many times in the weeks it had taken for him to get back to the Alpha Quadrant. In the long hours since that he'd stood on the Promenade with Taran'atar, watching for trouble, uselessly wishing that Nerys might walk by. He never meant to stay, or to reveal himself to her—he'd disrupted her life enough, he knew—but had practiced the story anyway, half hoping that he'd have a chance to tell her.

Even on his isolated homeworld, word had come to the

Link about a holy woman who was traveling through the Gamma Quadrant, a woman who spoke of Prophets and healing, who was spreading a message of self-awareness to those communities she touched . . . and there were stories that she'd had contact with an extinct race, one that the Link knew little about, the Ascendants.

Remembering the lost kai of Bajor, Odo had disguised himself as a Trelian woman to investigate the rumors, Weyoun never far behind . . . and found Jake Sisko, as well as Opaka Sulan.

The information she'd shared about the continued existence of the Ascendants was important, perhaps vital to the future of the Gamma Quadrant, but he couldn't return to the Link without first seeing Jake and Opaka safely home. He'd chosen also to continue the pretense of Wex, even after his arrival at the station. The plan had been to come and go as quickly as possible, but the parasite infiltration and subsequent lockdown had made that impossible . . . as had his own need to help, to lend whatever he could to the resolution. Taran'atar had known, of course, and Odo thought that Opaka Sulan might have sensed something, but he'd felt sure that no one else suspected that Wex wasn't as she seemed. Quark, of course, didn't count.

When the parasite hosts on DS9 had begun collapsing, Odo had hurried to Nerys's side . . . and hidden there, hearing her conversation with Lieutenant Ro. He'd concealed himself in her phaser holster, knowing too well that she would put herself in the thick of danger . . . because she was strong, and brave, and because the Nerys he knew was incapable of standing down just because someone told her to.

You'd put yourself in danger because *he told you to*

stand down, he thought fondly, smiling at her. He was better at smiling than he used to be; she'd taught him how.

"You could have said something," she said.

"You were busy," he replied, and though he hadn't meant it to be humorous, she returned his smile, with a depth of feeling behind it that made his entire form ache—

—and there was someone coming, he could hear footsteps. They were out of time. Once the bodies were discovered . . .

"We have to go," he whispered, and she nodded, reaching up to touch his face, her warm palm cupping one cheek. Odo turned his head and brushed her fingertips with his mouth, wondering how he'd ever managed to leave her, how he would dare to do it again . . . and she turned and moved away, crouching her way silently to the lower level's entrance, not looking back. He waited until she made it through the door before shifting, dropping into the small, lithe body of a *po werm,* a form he'd learned from the Link. It was an ideal creature for the situation: The animal's senses were acute, highly attuned to heat and scent; it was barely a handspan across, fast-moving, and could change its skin color to match its surroundings.

Within a second, the *werm* knew where the hostages were, from the faint scent of humanoid blood trailing through the air. It dashed away on multiple legs, skittering madly through the cool dark, Odo hoping that the blood smell wasn't nearly so strong as the *werm* understood it to be.

They made it to the first set of stairs before Eli realized that something was different. He stopped outside the door, looking around, Benny stopping with him.

It took him a few seconds to place, it was such a small, odd thing, and he wasn't fully awake yet—his head was muzzy, his limbs heavy with fatigue—but once he noticed, it was impossible not to see it. Or to wonder.

"The walls," he muttered, half to himself. The color. The mild, industrial green had faded considerably, from dull lime to a color like sea foam. Had they repainted? They must have, but when? There was no smell of paint in the air . . . and as Eli breathed deeply, he realized that there was no smell at all. No disinfectant, no cheap, utilitarian food, no sweat or urine, none of the odors that were such a part of the institution that he'd long since ceased to notice them. The air was . . . flat.

Maybe the storm, he thought vaguely, as thunder rolled somewhere outside, but that didn't make sense . . . nor did the way the floor suddenly seemed to warp beneath his feet, making him stumble from his standing position.

Benny grabbed his arm, steadying him, pushing the door to the stairwell open with his free hand. "We have to hurry," he said.

"Why?" Eli asked, but Benny was already pulling him to the steps, still holding his arm. A good thing, as Eli stumbled again. The floor *was* warped, he was sure of it, and he was more tired than he'd thought; even standing seemed to take a tremendous effort, and he surely would have fallen down the stairs if Benny hadn't been at his side.

They descended quickly, two, three flights of steps, Eli leaning on Benny when he needed to. What was wrong with him, with everything? He was dizzy, the air was strange, and the thunder was louder now, a continuous sound, almost a roaring by the time they reached the ground floor and Benny led them back into another corridor.

That's not thunder, Eli thought, letting himself be led. He didn't know what it was, but it wasn't thunder.

Eli cried out as a chunk of linoleum tore up from the

floor in front of them, as though something beneath had exploded upward. He staggered back, half expecting to see some fantastic creature rising from the underground, but what he saw instead was somehow much worse.

That's impossible. Instead of cement or dirt, instead of a basement, the jagged hole opened into nothing. As he watched, loose pieces of linoleum around the hole fell into it, whirling away into the dark as though falling a great distance.

Benny pulled him around the hole, holding his arm firmly.

"Benny, what is it?" Eli asked. He trusted his friend, but this was madness, this was a waking nightmare.

"Dissolution," Benny said, raising his voice to be heard over the not-thunder. "Hurry, Eli!"

Dissolution. Eli hurried, his mouth dry, his body shaking, everything different and wrong. All around them, things were falling apart.

Kas was in labor, the contractions coming hard, only a minute apart and getting closer and longer. Jake sat at her side, trying to think of reassuring things to say, occasionally shooting helpless looks at his aunt and grandfather. They seemed to feel just as helpless, moving anxiously to hold her hand when they could, to get Opaka the few things she asked for, to tell Kas to breathe, breathe. Except for the former kai, Kas seemed to be handling things better than any of them, her breathing measured and steady, her concentration intense. She took short sips of air, then longer ones, then short again as Jake smoothed her hair back from her sweating brow, gripping her hand tightly. When she started to pant, she'd clutch his hand hard enough that he could hear his bones creak, but he'd grit his teeth and hold on, as afraid as he could remember being in a very long time.

At least Opaka's here, Jake thought, thanking whatever gods might be around as another contraction started to take hold. Opaka was almost as focused as Kas, stroking her legs, speaking gently, reaching under the small throw blanket across Kas's belly to check her progress every few minutes. Neither woman seemed to notice the three terrorists at the front of the room, their weapons still trained on the small group . . . and didn't notice when outside in the corridor, someone began to shout.

"Intruders! Intruders!"

Everything happened fast.

One of the terrorists opened fire, the woman, a bolt of purple-white energy erupting from her weapon—and a golden streak of light leapt across the room, intercepting the killing discharge before it could slam into Kasidy's heaving belly. There was a loud *crack,* and a sharp cry of angry surprise from the woman who'd fired.

Jake didn't know what had happened, didn't try to understand. He threw himself over Kas, covering her body with his own. An instant later, Joseph and Judith were with him, their arms wrapped over him, their heads down as they tried to protect both him and Kasidy. Jake could hear another weapon fire, and another, two more *cracks* of unknown origin as something stopped the beams from hitting them.

Kas groaned, a deep, guttural sound, her body tensing as she started panting again. Someone was pounding at the door, and Jake risked a glance up, saw what looked like a shimmering liquid rising up from the floor, leaning against the heavy wood as more pounding shook the door in its frame.

Changeling? Odo? Jake didn't know, but as the trio of terrorists fired again, and again, he could see that whatever was protecting them wouldn't be able to do it for much longer, its form already stretched into impossibly thin lines of glowing protoplasm, leaping out to intercept the bursts of fire, struggling to bar the shaking door at the same time.

Kas was still panting, moaning, and Jake lowered his head again, holding her tightly, not knowing what else to do as the weapons crackled on, as the door began to splinter.

It was all Kira could do to keep Odo out of her thoughts as she descended the worn stone steps into the underground chamber, moving as quickly and quietly as she could. It seemed that only the door had been guarded; from the first minister's intelligence report, the majority of the parasite carriers were guarding the monastery's perimeter.

Which will change, once they find the doorkeepers out cold in the corridor. Images of Odo tried to creep back into her mind, but Kira forced them away, concentrating on her footing. It was dark, and she'd never been here before, though she recognized the place from an account Captain Sisko had once given her. This was the secret chamber in which the Orb of Prophecy had been sequestered during the Occupation. Now they were all here, the nine Tears. The thought that a malevolent alien queen had chosen the sacred room to hide in was infuriating, and Kira held the anger close, let it keep her fears at bay.

The stone steps curved ahead, opening into the chamber. Holding her phaser tightly, Kira moved into position, preparing herself to attack, wishing she had some idea of what she'd be attacking. Something bigger than one of the parasites, Julian had suggested; not much to go on.

As she tensed herself to move, she heard a sound like water, a wet, slurping noise, and a half-dozen repellent images leapt to mind. It was about then that the smell hit her, a smell like rotten vegetables and salt, adding color to the unpleasant pictures in her head. What did it look like? What was it *doing*?

She heard a muffled shout from above, and stopped wondering; the guards had been discovered. Odo would do what he could, but once the carriers holding Kas and Jake and the others found out that the monastery had been infiltrated, they'd call for help. And the hostages . . .

Kira stepped around the corner, her weapon raised—

—and though the mental pictures had been bad, the reality was worse. There, surrounded by the sacred arks, was a massive, fleshy body, rippled and soft and pale. It was perhaps four meters from tip to tail, its form vaguely rootlike, tapering at both ends. It was thick enough through the middle to tower over Kira, and through its semitransparent flesh she could see what appeared to be hundreds, thousands of squirming shadows, tiny egg sacs filled with liquid and claws. As she watched in horror, a handful of sacs *glurted* out from a corpulent, sagging wet opening near the tail, landing on the cold stone floor in a liquid heap.

The head of the creature turned toward Kira, blind but hideously aware, her black maw of a mouth mewling at the invader in a high-pitched whine. Above the mouth, long, useless pincers opened and closed, opened and closed, the queen too swollen, too suited to function to attack, let alone defend itself. It was an abomination, and Kira instinctively stepped back, her finger tightening on the phaser's trigger—

—*Wait!*

The blast would tear a hole in the queen's body, perhaps

killing her . . . but the eggs, they were ready to hatch. The few dozen on the floor beneath the queen's birth canal were already opening, the tiny creatures inside worming out of their soft shells, clicking aimlessly in the muck of after-birth. There was no way she'd be able to get them all, not with one phaser.

Not before they get me. Already, two or three of the parasites were edging toward her, as though sensing a warm-bodied host nearby. And while it had been borne out that the death of the lesser queens also meant the demise of their brood, she wasn't prepared to take the chance that the same would hold true here. One mistake could unleash an army on Bajor.

Kira backed up a step. She'd have to retreat, come back with more firepower, with *fire*, something that would wipe all of them out. She'd have to get the Orbs safely away, too, she couldn't let them burn, but—

There was more shouting from above, and Kira heard the door to the chamber slam open, heard cries of rage and alarm in Bajoran voices, voices that shouted from parasitic souls.

Help me, Kira prayed, frozen with indecision, with impotent anger—at herself, at the aliens that had taken Shakaar, taken her people, taken her friends—

—and she didn't hear anything, didn't think it, but *felt* the answer, knew what to do as surely as she knew her own name, as she trusted in her own faith. Dropping her phaser, Kira stepped to the closest ark and opened the doors. Brilliant light blossomed into the room, casting the ghastly queen in shades of magnificent silver-white. The Orb of Time, she thought, and stepped to the next, the Orb of Contemplation, pulling its doors wide. And then the next, Destiny, and the next, Souls, the combined brilliance of the sacred artifacts spilling into the chill air, searingly bright, as powerful as a thundering wave. Kira felt it wash over and through her as she opened the rest, Memory, Wisdom, Prophecy, Truth . . . moving to the final ark, one of Yevir's finds, the Orb of Unity.

You want Bajor, she thought, overwhelmed by the light as she threw open the doors to the last Tear, *here it is.*

22

THEY WEREN'T GOING TO MAKE IT. THE FLOOR HAD FALLEN away, become—become nothing that Eli could see, exactly, just a whirling darkness that felt loose and horribly unstable beneath his feet. The roaring sound had grown louder, a sound like the ocean in a storm, like the hissing crash of a waterfall, and the roar had been joined by tremendous cracking noises, like bones, breaking. The walls seemed to waver like rippling water.

Benny still dragged him forward, pointing ahead into the strange and turbulent air. A light, ahead in the thick haze that had blanketed everything. Blue and gold and white, so bright that it defied color, the brilliant rays cut through the fog, leading them on. It seemed far away, but only a few steps later it appeared that they had reached the source—an opening in the dark, a lighted well of space that looked, that seemed like the tunnel Eli had always heard described.

A tunnel of light . . . Were they dying, now? Eli didn't know, he didn't know anything anymore, except that he no longer wanted to die. He wanted to see his daughter.

"There!" Benny shouted, pushing him forward. "Go!"

"What about you?" Eli shouted back. The crashing and cracking had grown louder, the haze thicker, the floor jolting and buckling beneath their feet. Whatever was happening, the building—

—building, is that what this is—

—was on the verge of collapse.

"I'm right behind you!"

"But—" Eli felt lost, confused. In spite of the dissolving structure all around them, he was afraid to go into the light, afraid that he wasn't ready.

Benny grinned suddenly, a warm and somehow peaceful grin that radiated almost as brightly as the well of light in front of them.

"It's okay," he said, and Eli could see in his eyes that it was so. "Now—go!"

Benny gave him another push, hard, sent him reeling into the undefined brilliance even as behind him, the very air seemed to break apart, an infinite cold at Eli's back as he stumbled into the light.

Her spawn began to issue forth from her, their birth the culmination of her patience and planning. She felt them eject from her body, her children, cool and wet and alive, leaving behind an emptiness that made her whole. That would make all of them whole, that would carry them to the meat worlds where they would take their rightful places . . . And turn their attentions to the obliteration of the weak ones.

The betrayers. The Trill. Even thinking the name made her tense, sent a number of her brood squealing from her body to the cold, hard ground. The hatred she felt for the weak ones had sustained her for many spans of time, when she had been tiny and hiding, waiting in the darkness of her frozen nest beneath the mountains of the unknown world. All her attempts to reach out had gone unanswered, for so long that she had come to believe that she was the last matriarch, alone in the charge of her species. Her hatred had made her patient, though . . . And when the Shakaar-thing had stumbled upon her, she had taken him, finding in him and his people the perfect instrument for movement and growth.

It had not been easy. She had underestimated the meat, had learned of other spawnmothers' failures since taking Shakaar, had witnessed the failures herself . . . But once she completed this great spawning, her brood would take the remaining population of this small meat world. They would unlock the secrets of these strange artifacts arrayed around her, and would use that knowledge to bring true and final death to the weak ones of Trill, and all their allies.

It is a good beginning, she mused as her membranes contracted, releasing more of her young. *It is—*

The great spawnmother tensed anew. Something was in her chamber. A meat-being, untaken! In the throes of spawning, she had not felt the danger.

She extended her will, found her guards asleep, wounded. She forced them to consciousness, demanded it, and they began to stir, crawling and stumbling; in seconds, they would be at her side. There would be no escape for the invader.

The meat-being hid behind an artifact now, trapping itself—

Light.

What was happening? She could no longer feel the workings of her tremendous body, the spew of her young.

Her contact with the guards above was broken. The nest, the entire chamber—all of it, gone! The meat-being had opened the artifacts, and all had become white void.

I see you.

She spun out her senses, searching. She was not alone, but what thoughts were these?

They're mine.

She reached out, seeking the mind she sensed, that dared to interrupt her time of birth. But the thoughts came from no particular direction, were simply all around her. She felt her uterine muscles contract, her fluids congealing. What did it want with her?

I wanted to tell you that it's over. Your campaign, your hatred . . . your time. It ends here, now.

It was no taker of gist, no spawnmother; why could she hear its mind? She sought through the void with her rudimentary eyes . . . and saw it, emerging from the white. Like a meat-being in appearance, it walked toward her from the nothingness, its features becoming clearer as it neared. Dark and human, meat, but . . .

. . . the eyes . . .

It drew closer, looming ever larger as it approached. It was vast, she saw now, vast as space. Its brown face filled her perception, filled the void itself—

And then it spoke.

"You picked the wrong planet," it said, and she felt her first glimmer of doubt.

It was also her last.

First Hanal'ahan surveyed his surroundings once more, his frustration growing with each passing moment. The white nothingness in which he and his men had suddenly found themselves appeared to be absolute. Yet it could not be a true void, his mind insisted. Although he couldn't see it, there was a level surface on which he and his troops stood, which implied gravity. There was heat, or they would already be freezing, and there was breathable air, obviously . . . which meant, unfortunately, that he could clearly hear the nasal voice of the tiresome, demanding Vorta who kept calling his name.

This is impossible, he thought. Hours ago—or was it merely minutes?—he'd been on the bridge of a Dominion battleship, leading an armada of thousands more ships through the Anomaly. The Federation's minefield had fallen, the way was open—and the Federation fleet that was even now attempting to retake the Bajoran system was soon to understand the power it faced in daring to oppose the Dominion. It was to be the turning point of the Quadrant War. The Federation and its allies would fall, and the Bajorans themselves, the backward spiritualists native to the world nearest the Alpha terminus of the Anomaly, would be eradicated. Their presence was deemed unnecessary, even offensive to the Founders. It would end.

Hanal'ahan had witnessed the armada's passage through the Anomaly by his headset, satisfied by the prospect of combat as he recited the Jem'Hadar oath to reclaim his life through victory.

Then a single ship had appeared from the other side of the Anomaly, speeding toward the armada.

Third Musata'klan, monitoring sensors, had reported that the approaching vessel was the *Defiant*, the ship the Federation had most often used in its incursions into the regions surrounding the Dominion.

And it was alone.

Hanal'ahan had been mildly impressed. He had not

believed Federation soldiers possessed the strength of will to make suicide runs, especially futile ones.

The First snapped off the order to lock weapons on the approaching ship—

And then they were here.

No Anomaly, no ships, no enemy craft, not even sidearms, except for their blades . . . and *this,* this seeming . . . nothingness. Hanal'ahan half suspected some new form of transporter technology, but their intelligence on the Alpha Quadrant suggested nothing like this. And even a transporter would not explain the nature of this place.

"First!" the Vorta shouted next to him. "I demand an explanation for this."

"I have none to offer," Hanal'ahan replied, not for the first time, his gaze still searching the emptiness.

"We were on the verge of altering the face of half the galaxy, and this is your response? But for your incompetence, we would already— First! Look at me when I address you!"

"Be silent," Hanal'ahan hissed. He'd heard something, a strange sound, like a high-pitched scream very far away. "Do you hear that?"

He did not address the Vorta. Second Valast'aval nodded, his eyes narrowing. All the Jem'Hadar were turning in their direction now, drawn by the sound. It was becoming louder.

"What is that?" the Vorta demanded. "What's happening?"

The First was considering a violently physical response to the whining Vorta when something in the uniform blankness became visible: an enormous, bloated mass, a misshapen creature, squirming toward them like some massive, swollen eelworm. Its screams intensified.

"First . . ." the Vorta began.

"Weapons!" Hanal'ahan shouted, and as one, his men reached behind their backs and unsheathed their *kar'takin.*

Hanal'ahan held his blade before him, reassured by the solidity of the grip. The triangular blade was keen, his reflexes steady.

This, at least, I understand, he thought, and addressed his men.

"Victory is life!"

The chorus was unanimous. "Victory is life!"

As one, the Jem'Hadar charged.

"May I speak with you a moment, Admiral?" Ro asked politely, leaning into Kira's office. Akaar pushed past her, stepping out into ops.

"Not unless you can tell me where your Colonel Kira is," he snapped. He'd waited in her office for a full seven minutes, by Ro's count, before the flush creeping up the back of his neck finally reached his face. He was now entirely upset. Several people looked up at the sound of his voice, most of them Starfleet, then quickly looked away.

"If you'll step back inside, maybe I can explain," Ro said, wanting their conversation to be private, primarily because Akaar could pull rank on practically anyone else in the pit—most of them were Starfleet—demanding answers. Even the Bajorans on duty could face repercussions.

But for those of us about to quit . . .

"Please," Ro said, making herself smile at him. "I'm sure I can help."

Akaar glared, but moved back into Kira's office. Ro took a deep breath and followed, reminding herself that this was no game. The humor was incidental. She really did have to stall him, to keep him from going after the *Defiant*—and if she chose her words carefully, she could probably pull it off without lying.

"What is it? Where is the colonel?"

Ro took another deep breath. "I regret to inform you that the colonel is unable to meet you at this time. However, I'm prepared to present you with a full status report."

Akaar stared at her as though she'd lost her mind. "Where is she? She was supposed to wait here."

Ro was ready for that one. "The colonel is pursuing an idea about a possible solution to the parasite situation, but as I said, I'm fully informed of the station's current—"

"You are giving me the runaround, Lieutenant," Akaar interrupted, his eyes cold. Obviously aware that his size made him more intimidating, he took a step forward, glowering down at her. "We are in a crisis situation, and I would rather not deal with any of your, your *nonsense* right now. Where is she?"

Ro felt something break, something that had been pulled taut for too long. She also took a step forward, not caring that he was practically a meter taller, not caring about much of anything . . . except that she was sick and tired of his attitude, and the attitude of those like him.

"*My* nonsense? Admiral, you've made it clear on more than one occasion that you don't like me, that because of my history you consider me a poor risk, which is fair enough," she snapped, the words rushing out fast and hot but also smooth, as though she'd prepared a speech. "Let me make clear to you what *I* see. Your mind is closed, Admiral, to the concept that people change, to the idea that Starfleet's way is not necessarily always the best way. Colonel Kira is working to resolve this crisis. What are you doing, besides looking for somewhere else to put your foot down? Now, do you want to hear my report, or not?"

Akaar stared at her, shocked pale. For a moment he appeared to be speechless, his mouth working, no sound coming out—but Ro could see the circuits firing, could see in his narrowing eyes that she was about to get the shout-down of her life.

Come on then, she thought, glaring back at him—

—and both of their badges went off, even as Merimark's excited voice erupted from the desk, as ops exploded into a spontaneous flurry of action, people standing and clapping, embracing one another.

"Lieutenant, Bajor is reporting that the hostage-takers have collapsed," Merimark reported breathlessly. *"At every site. The parasites are fleeing. Lenaris Holem is standing by, he says—he says it's over, sir."*

Ro and Akaar stared at one another for what seemed an eternity, what was probably only a few seconds—and Akaar stepped back, finally finding his voice.

"I have things to see to, Lieutenant," he said coolly. "Inform the colonel that I'll expect her report as soon as she returns to this office."

With that, he was already striding out the door, slapping at his badge, requesting a return to the *Trager*. Ro watched him go, her eyes wide, feeling like she'd just sidestepped being run down by a freight loader—and then grinned, the reality sinking in.

It's over. Not only that, she'd survived leadership and a direct confrontation with a Starfleet admiral.

"Maybe I have an affinity for this kind of work," she said, and still smiling, went to call the *Defiant*, to bring them back home.

23

ELI—ELIAS VAUGHN OPENED HIS EYES, BUT COULDN'T SEE. A woman was shouting, moaning, and he hurt, his shoulder, there'd been an accident, and where was Benny? The light, he'd gone into the light, and everything seemed hard now, the surface beneath him, the air around him, and he couldn't *see*. What was happening?

Someone was shouting, not the woman. Around him, movement, he could feel it through the floor beneath him, could hear running.

"Got it—"

"They're dying—"

"Get that one—"

Voices of conquest. The thought was a fragment, but he knew the tones he heard, knew that a battle had turned.

Something cool on his face, lifted away. Painful brightness flooded his eyes for a moment, and there was Benny, looking down at him, except—

—*you're* old! His friend had aged twenty, thirty years. His eyes were the same, he could see that, but his face—

"You're okay. Just rest now, you're going to be fine," Benny said, and it wasn't Benny at all, this man was clean-shaven, white-haired, just a man with Benny's eyes. There was another loud moan, almost a scream, and the man looked away, his face tight with anxiety and fear and . . . and excitement?

Too much to take in, and he was exhausted. Vaughn closed his eyes again, deciding that he'd believe the man with his friend's kind gaze, take the man's advice. Benny was coming, anyway, he'd be there in a minute, he could explain everything. Vaughn let himself drift away, knowing that something had changed, slipping into the dark with an easy mind.

"Uuuhhhh!"

The sound was the feeling, it was coming out of her, but Kas didn't know it, knew nothing at all but her body, the pain, the *need*. Push, push, she had to push, her body was pushing whether she wanted it or not. The pain was huge and glassy, searing, but the need was greater.

A door, opening, a rush of air, more yelling. "What's happening? Are they all—"

"—All of them!"

"Oh, thank the Prophets! Thank the—"

Shut up, why won't they shut up, I'm, I'm—

"Uuunnhhh!"

"—get someone down here, now! Right *now*!"

Sounded like Jake, but Kas wasn't sure, couldn't think, couldn't do anything but push, had to push. Opaka Sulan said something, her voice sweet and sure, Kas couldn't hear the words but thought she could feel hands on her thighs, warm and strong. The need came again and she pushed, as hard as she could.

"—two, three, four—"

"You're doing great, Kas, great!" Judith's face, close to hers, a sweaty flash that was there and gone, and was someone holding her hand? She didn't know.

"—nine, ten and breathe, *good,* deep breath and push, two, three—"

Sulan's voice. The pain was like nothing she'd felt before, surely she was turning herself inside out, but even that wasn't a thought, barely a scrap of understanding. The need. The need, and the feeling of movement, deep at her core, of liquid heat and movement.

"Now, Kasidy, push and hold, two, three—"

"There! There, I see it!"

Kasidy bore down, unaware that she was screaming, the pain so vast that it was no longer pain, it had become something else. The feeling of letting go, of movement had become all-powerful, quenching the need, finally giving her release. There was a burning, far away, and then that was gone, too—and she felt something leave her body. The baby, she was feeling the baby leave her body.

"Good, good!"

"Oh, God! Oh, it's so—"

"Kasidy!"

Her mind was grasping, clawing for answers, hearing more now—hearing the sound of joy in the voices of Sulan, of Joseph, of Jake. Judith's face next to hers again, aglow, tears in her eyes.

"She's beautiful, Kasidy. She's beautiful."

A girl? Kasidy laughed, her heart filling up with the thought. A girl, and then Opaka was putting a warm, wet weight on her chest, and there she was, a tiny, tea-colored face above a piece of blanket, frowning, blinking, covered in goo. Looking at Kasidy with bright, confused eyes.

Another rush of air, cool and sudden. Kas looked away from the perfect, beautiful baby for a split second, saw that the door had opened, saw Kira Nerys standing there, her clothes ragged, her eyes going wide. Saw an amazed grin surface, then was through looking at Kira, her gaze drawn back to the blinking bundle in her arms. The girl was screwing up her face to squall, her tiny, perfect mouth working, her frown deepening, chin quivering. She let out a hoarse, fragile wail and Kasidy closed her eyes because her heart was breaking with it, with love for the child.

"Kasidy."

Ben?

Startled, Kasidy opened her eyes, tears blurring her vision. She saw Kira again, saw, standing next to her, now striding toward her, kneeling at her side, the form of her husband, her love. Everyone was talking at once, excited, shouting, laughing, but he was with her, reaching out to cup her face, saying her name again, and again.

Kasidy wept, dying with happiness, reborn with it. Ben held her, held them both.

24

Business wasn't terrible, for a change, had been pretty good, in fact, since that whole parasite business had been wrapped up a few weeks prior, but Quark was so upset that he couldn't even water the cocktails properly. He had Broik doing it, and was spending the pre-dinner rush just sitting behind his bar, his beautiful, doomed bar, cursing his lot.

Bajor was going to be inducted into the Federation in just over twenty-six hours . . . and Quark had only just received word from his business associate's lawyer that Kostaza, his lifeline, his primary post-Quark's investment, was under indictment. The Federation had seized all his assets—Quark's latinum a not-insubstantial piece thereof—and prohibited him from conducting business pending completion of an investigation . . . which, considering how deeply the Federation cared about the plight of the small businessman, meant that the UFP's legal system would be tying Kostaza up for the next five years, give or take a decade. His dreams of flying away with a ship full of latinum were over, *ke-plat*. Would Ro Laren even consider going away with him, now? That didn't matter, either, because there was no way he could afford to keep someone like her interested, not anymore. He was ruined.

"Quark, do you have a minute?"

Quark looked up and saw Kira Nerys, of all people, standing across from him. She looked the way he felt, only not as sharply dressed.

"Seems like I have all the time in the world," he said, sighing heavily. "It's over. My new business venture fell through, along with all my latinum. Once tomorrow's party is over, I'm finished."

"Yeah, that's a shame," Kira said dismissively. "Look, I came by because I was asked to bring you some news."

Marvelous. Perhaps his quarters had caught fire. Or Odo was planning to stand outside his restaurant for its final business day, glaring the patrons away. That Odo had been masquerading as Wex had come as no great shock; Quark had suspected all along, of course. Hadn't he said as much to his nephew? He'd tried to strike up a conversation with Odo when he'd come in with Kira a few days prior, but old stodgy-face had only scoffed and turned away.

Odo's back, O'Brien's back, Sisko's back—though he hasn't even bothered to visit, thank you very much—even Worf is supposed to be on his way, for the big signing. It was like some terrible reunion of vexing, boring, and scary; he had no idea what Kira wanted to tell him, but had the feeling he wouldn't like it.

"Whatever it is, just get it over with," he said.

Kira sighed, as if every word she was about to utter required tremendous effort on her part. Probably just tired from too much Odoing, Quark decided. When they'd stopped by for dinner, they'd been mooning at each other all over his bar. Blech.

"A couple of weeks ago, the Ferengi government contacted the government of Bajor and expressed interest in opening full diplomatic relations," Kira said. "Minister Asarem agreed, and with the approval of the Chamber of Ministers and the Federation Council, your bar has been declared the Ferengi Embassy to Bajor. In other words, Quark, effective immediately, the space within these walls is the sovereign territory of Ferenginar, subject to its laws and commerce practices."

Quark snorted, trying to imagine the lobeless loser who'd be saddled with the thankless task of running an embassy on Deep Space 9. That would mean—

He looked up, his jaw hanging, speechless, but only for as long as it took to hear the latinum clattering. "Are you telling me . . . my *bar* is the new Ferengi embassy? And *I'm* the new ambassador to Bajor?"

Kira gritted her teeth. "I didn't have any say in the staffing."

Embassy, Quark repeated in his mind. *Hello, and welcome to Quark's Bar, Grill, Embassy, Gaming House, and Holosuite Arcade. I'm your host, Ambassador Quark. What can I get you tonight?*

Quark smiled toothily, hopefully. "Diplomatic immunity?"

Kira's eyes narrowed. "Don't push your luck, Quark. Come by my office tomorrow. Better yet, make it the next day." Without another word, she disappeared back into the crowd.

Okay, so he would still have to watch his toes. And with the democratic reforms back home, Ferengi laws were decidedly more constraining on the extent to which he could gouge his customers, but the fact remained—

"I'm still in business," he said in a weak voice, the reality of it starting to sink in.

Treir was hurrying across the room, her own assets jiggling prettily, a grin on her face as she stopped in front of him.

"Congratulations, I just heard. Either you have the dumbest luck in the quadrant, or somebody in high places really loves you. I assume you'll be wanting to renegotiate our contract . . . ?"

Quark nodded dully, and Treir said something about telling the staff, wandering away a moment later. For a change, Quark didn't drop everything he was doing to watch her walk away, his thoughts too full. He'd have to talk to Ro, have to convince her to stay; she'd been hesitating, anyway, he'd seen it in her face . . . but their not-yet romance wasn't at the forefront of his mind.

Dumb luck, Treir said . . . or someone in high places loves me.

It wasn't changing politics or Ferenginar suddenly seizing a new business opportunity that had saved him. There was only one person in the Ferengi government who had any interest in *not* seeing Quark capsize on the Great River. Only one person with the power to establish those kinds of ties with another planet.

Rom, Quark thought. *My idiot brother did this. For me.*

He gazed unseeing at the crowd milling about the bar, eating, drinking, and gambling as more and more of them poured in for their last big meal before departing for Bajor, for the induction ceremony. He was unaware that his patronage had gone up so dramatically because his eyes had blurred, tripling the number of customers, and was still in a daze when he finally felt the meaty tap on his shoulder, and turned to see Morn sitting there next to him, holding out a stein of freshly tapped ale. Morn still had *calidine* lotion spread across his fading rash, and a look of pleasure on his great, ugly mug. It took Quark a few beats to register what he was doing, but it was more than enough time for his vision to clear. It was just . . . Morn had never bought him a drink before.

"Don't think this is going to win you any favors," Quark snapped, taking the ale. "Things are going to be very different around here from now on, let me tell you. This is an official government establishment now. Your days of running ridiculous tabs are over, my friend—"

Morn just rolled his eyes and raised his own mug, tapping it against the rim of Quark's. After a moment, Quark raised his in turn, and drank deeply.

It was the best ale he'd ever had; he was definitely going to have to raise the price.

Shar was reading a series of articles that Dr. Bashir had recommended about hybrid mutagenesis when there was a tap at his door. He stood from his desk and went to answer, half expecting to see Prynn Tenmei. She'd dropped by on several occasions recently, often just to say hello. Shar still wasn't sure what to do about her interest, if anything; Nog had taken him to meet the Earth singer, Vic Fontaine, who had been pleasant enough, but had also confused him thoroughly. The hologram had called him a "free agent," and suggested that he should "sow oats" when he felt ready, not before. Even with Nog's explanation, Shar was uncertain as to his course of action.

He opened his door and instantly felt his circulation pick up, his digestive system clenching unhappily. It was his *zhavey*. She'd been on Bajor the last few weeks, a guest of the first minister; he hadn't been sorry that she'd gone.

"Will you come in?" Shar asked, standing back from the entry.

"I— Yes," she answered, and stepped inside, her posture stiff and unyielding.

He offered her a seat, a refreshment, but she declined, only standing uncomfortably in the middle of the room. She seemed to be waiting for him to speak, but she had also come to him. In spite of all the things he wanted to say, wanted to tell her, it was appropriate that she speak first.

"I'll be returning to Andor the day after tomorrow," she said finally.

"Oh?" Shar nodded. Waited.

"I came to ask if you . . . if you will be joining me," she said, not meeting his eye, her tone as rigid as her stance. "I know there was some consideration among the three of you, that an arrangement might be made . . ."

"None has been," he said. "I think that they'd be best off with another. But I thank you for your offer, if that's what it was."

She met his gaze then, her own angry, accusing. He waited for the guilt to overwhelm him, to make him apologize for daring to deny his place, but there was no crashing wave of it, not like before, not for her; only a mist of unhappiness, like an unpleasant dream.

My guilt is my own. She can't have it. It was a strange thought, but a compelling one.

She turned to leave, obviously done with him, forcing him to say what he wanted to say to her back. It wasn't the way he would have had it, but then, nothing about his situation with her had been, not for a long time.

"Whether or not I can help our people, I have a place

here, *zhavey*. I was able to help Colonel Kira resolve the situation on Bajor. I'm—I'm wanted here."

"You were wanted at home," she said.

"I was *needed* at home," he said. "Perhaps I'm wrong, perhaps I've done everything wrong, but I want to stay here, now."

"Stay, then," she said, refusing to look back at him, her voice like iced water. If there was any pain on her face, any loss, it seemed she meant to deny him even that small solace. Without speaking further, she swept out of his room.

Shar stared at the closed door for a long moment, not knowing what to do, wondering why he didn't feel the need to lash out. He was hurt, and angry . . . but less so than he had been before.

After a while, he went back to his desk. Found where he'd left off, and started to read.

Opaka had asked Yevir to meet her in the Archive. It seemed appropriate, to her at least, that the venue for their meeting be a place of knowledge and learning. She hoped that Yevir would see it that way.

The Archive was unused this evening, the shadowed aisles silent, the tables empty. Opaka sat at a bench at the library's far end, facing a window that looked over a quietly dozing street. With the signing ceremony so close at hand, most people were at home or with their loved ones, preparing for the celebration that would follow. The truth of the parasitic aliens and Shakaar's death had been an unpleasant shock . . . but the successful resolution of the crisis had coincided with the birth of the Avatar, the return of the Emissary, and her own resurrection; it was being taken by all as a sign that Bajor was indeed on the right path.

Avatar. Opaka smiled to herself, thinking of the beautiful child she had helped into the world. How strange to think that Ohalu's book alone, among all the known prophecies, had foretold the birth of the Emissary's daughter. She hoped that Yevir could be persuaded to see it as the wondrous gift that she had come to believe it was.

Behind her, she heard the library's great double doors open. She turned and saw Yevir walking toward her between the two great rows of reading tables, his expression unreadable. It was their first meeting since he'd brought her back to Bajor; she hoped very much that he'd since opened himself to the possibilities that Ohalu's book represented.

When he stopped in front of her, he bowed his head in deference. "You wished to see me, Eminence?"

"I am merely Sulan now, Vedek Yevir," she said, welcoming him with a smile.

Yevir's return smile was uncertain. As before, he seemed caught off guard by her casual disregard for ceremony. "I—very well. Sulan."

Opaka patted the empty space beside her on the bench. "Please sit. I only wish to speak with you a moment."

Yevir sat silently as Opaka searched for a way to begin.

"I don't know if I managed to convey to you how much I admired your work with the Cardassians," she said finally, her tone light. "The return of the Tears is a great achievement. It speaks to the power of your faith . . . and your willingness to employ unorthodox means on behalf of your people."

Yevir bowed his head humbly. "I am merely an instrument of Their will . . . and that of the Emissary."

Opaka nodded. She'd heard the story of his call to the Prophets, through the Emissary. "What do you think you might do next?" she asked.

Yevir shifted on the bench, looking away. "Once I believed I was destined to become kai," he admitted.

"And now?"

He frowned, his confused gaze turning to her face. "You've returned, Eminence."

Opaka let that go by unchallenged. The Prophets had not shown her that resuming the spiritual leadership of Bajor was to be her path.

Yevir went on. "I must follow through on my peace initiative. I thought I might go to Cardassia for a time, as an ambassador of faith."

Opaka nodded again. She knew of the proposed exchange program, between Bajor's vedeks and the guides and clerics of Cardassia's Oralian Way.

"Your vision is inspiring," she said sincerely. "You have truly been Touched by Them."

Yevir was relaxing, she could see it in his face, in the way he sat. But there was still a tension in him, deep and unresolved. She waited, certain that he wouldn't be able to resist returning to the source of his anxiety, the same sore spot he'd brought up again and again at their initial meeting—the Ohalu text. That she'd refused to respond to his prodding had unnerved him, apparently unnerved him still.

"Perhaps . . . perhaps you will be able to heal our spiritual disunion," he said finally.

Opaka took a deep breath. "I see no disunion," she said gently. "Certainly there is discord among some members of the faithful, but I do not believe it to be the crisis you perceive. Our people are merely learning new ways to seek and understand the Prophets, new ways to think about our relationship to Them, and new ways to walk the path on which They guide us. These are not things we should fear, they are to be celebrated."

Yevir's *pagh* was clearly in turmoil. "But the Ohalu heresies challenge the very foundation of our faith."

"Is that something to fear?" Opaka asked honestly, searching his face. "We are sentient beings, Linjarin. To question everything is our nature. Why would the Prophets not wish us to indulge, even exult, in that aspect of ourselves that defines us like no other?"

Yevir said nothing, and Opaka pressed on, hoping that she was being heard, that he would still listen when he understood what she wanted to ask.

"I think that exposing our people to such ideas might prove beneficial," she said. "That such an act might be seen as an act of faith."

Yevir stood up abruptly. "What I did in Attainting Kira Nerys had to be done. She put her own judgment before the judgment of the Vedek Assembly, and is directly responsible for our people's present spiritual upheaval—"

"Kira Nerys," Opaka said quietly but with conviction, "may be the truest child of the Prophets I have ever known, Vedek. No matter what losses she endures, no matter what injustices are inflicted upon her, no matter how long or how mightily she struggles to master the violence she carries within her, her faith never wavers, and does not diminish. What she did in releasing the Ohalu prophecies was an affirmation of her faith."

Opaka rose from the bench and took Yevir's trembling hands in her own. "To deny the exploration of faith, each according to our will, is to deny faith itself." She paused, looking deeply into Yevir's troubled eyes. "As I see it, it was not the release of the Ohalu text that set in motion Bajor's present spiritual discord, Linjarin. It was the Attainder of Kira Nerys."

Opaka released his hands, and turned away from him.

"Your *pagh* is strong, Vedek Yevir, and I believe that there is much good you will accomplish as you walk your path. I hope you will take care that your steps are true."

She bowed and slowly walked away, leaving him to consider what she had said.

Ro hadn't been back to Tora Ziyal's art exhibit since it had reopened, except on business—the beat check for suspicious activity, a few times filling in for one of the guards so they could get a cup of something hot or run to the 'fresher. After she'd received the package, though, left on her desk by some helpful Starfleet cadet, no doubt, she'd found herself wandering, off duty and in a state of . . . a state of feelings she wasn't sure about. Amusement and irritation and gratitude and uncertainty seemed to be vying for position at the top, but none were winning. Mostly she was confused, and an art exhibit seemed just the place for someone who didn't know what else to look at.

The exhibit was quiet, only a few men and women walking through, gazing silently at Ziyal's work or speaking in low, appreciative tones. The station was starting to feel just as deserted; everyone was getting ready for the big ceremony, and many of the station's Bajoran residents had already taken transport to the planet's surface. In twenty-six hours everything would go back to normal, but everything would be different, too. The Federation was already moving in, instructors and mediators and diplomats on their way to Bajor to help with the transition. Starfleet was almost finished with their Bajoran training facility, ready to enlighten the militia to the Federation way. There was talk that they might even open up a branch of the Academy, although that was still somewhere down the line.

A new start, for anyone who wants it. Almost anyone, she thought, wondering what she was going to do about Quark as she stopped near one of the small line drawings, looking around for the big oil painting he'd pointed out to her on their one and only tour of the exhibit. She remembered that it had been the first time she'd really accepted that he might allow his depth to shine through. His expressions, his comments . . . he had exposed real insight, not in a practical sense but as a fellow being of emotions and spirit. He'd made her really look at the piece, the divided faces that he'd named as Ziyal's self-portrait . . . and that, in turn, had made her look at him in a way she hadn't seriously considered before.

If I stay, what will I tell him? She'd been so set on leaving, determined not to be folded back into an organization that had only been trouble for her . . . but what she'd done in the past weeks had been invaluable to stopping the parasites, and had made her feel needed. Which felt . . . good. Kira had even pulled her aside to mention that Akaar had withdrawn his objections to her staying on—reluctantly, undoubtedly, but it was what it was. She'd been approved, and stranger still, she'd found that she liked it.

Still, she'd been ready to tell Quark that she would leave with him. They'd gotten together twice since the end of the parasites, but the conversation had been light, the mood deliberately casual. Neither time did they discuss anything of real import, but the future had been there, silent and possible between them. If they didn't work out personally, they could still look into opening some kind of a business together . . . she could actually *see* herself a few years ahead, comfortably dressed, hair pulled back as she leaned behind the bar of some pleasant neighborhood tavern somewhere, polishing glasses while Quark worked the customers. He'd get himself trapped in some minor intrigue, she could spend her spare time getting him back out. It wasn't such a bad vision of the future.

The package that had been on her desk, that she'd opened only a few moments before walking across to the exhibit, had her name and designation on the outside, nothing more. Inside were only two items, one of which had made her decision complicated again. The first, a Starfleet uniform, standard-issue security gold, what many of the Bajoran Militia would be wearing before much longer; she hadn't been terribly impressed, until she'd seen the second item—a slip of hardcopy resting near the uniform's insignia, only a few words dashed across, the script fine and elegant.

In case you needed encouragement. JLP.

From the captain of the *Enterprise*. A man she admired, respected, and even feared in some ways, a man she couldn't begin to fathom. He'd taken an interest in her that she'd never really understood, that had both flattered and irritated her more times than she could count . . . and in spite of the fact that they'd only spoken once in the last six years, he still kept track of her—and had sent her the package as a vote of confidence, it seemed. Why he continued to find her so deserving, she couldn't begin to guess.

And it had worked, too. As though the note was what she'd been waiting for, to make up her mind. Enough had changed for her on DS9 that she wanted to stay, to at least try to make it. There was nothing stopping her anymore . . . except, of course, for Quark.

She was aware that a good many of the people she knew thought she had a serious emotional imbalance, the only explanation for her willingness to date the Ferengi bartender, but she had ceased to care. Whatever their relationship was, exactly, or would turn out to be . . . it wasn't anyone else's business. Quark was obnoxious and strange and often a caricature of himself, but there was also a lot more to him than people gave him credit for. If they couldn't see it, that was their loss.

Except if he goes and I stay, what relationship? It's over. She could accept that, she thought, and also thought that Quark could manage to bluster his way out of seeming to care . . . but he'd be disappointed, and so would she.

She wanted to see Ziyal's portrait again, to see if she could feel what she'd felt that day, standing next to Quark . . . to see if she could clarify her options, somehow. The curator had done a good job at salvaging the vandalized exhibit, but Ro couldn't find what she was looking for, and felt a stab of sorrow at its loss—until she realized it had been moved to the back corner of the room. A lone Cardassian male stood in front of it, his hands clasped behind his back, and though he didn't look up when she approached, he politely stepped out so that she could also see.

Ro smiled slightly, looking at the dramatic and beautiful work, remembering that she had touched Quark's hand while they'd looked at it together. It was amazing, how Ziyal had managed to work stark, geometric shapes into an organic flow, creating the profiles of faces that joined together to make one; maybe not the most subtle of duality interpretations, but it was beautiful and sincere. The man next to her shifted slightly, clearing his throat.

"It's wonderful, isn't it?" he asked softly, his voice filled with pride, an undertone of real sorrow beneath it. It was such a distinctive tone that she recognized it immediately, instinctively—the voice of someone who must have known Tora Ziyal. Ro turned to look at him, sorry for his loss. By all accounts, Ziyal had been an exceptional person . . .

. . . and realized that she recognized the man himself.

"It's my favorite," she said slowly, her muscles tensing reflexively. "Mr. Garak?"

Elim Garak, the tailor and onetime spy. How had he gotten aboard without her knowing about it?

The Cardassian's smile was slight but his eyes glittered as he looked at the painting again, as he ignored her surprise. "Mine, too."

She was at a loss for words. She'd only spoken to him once, via holo, trying to spare Quark more trouble in return for his help, and Garak had been surprisingly genial. But she also knew enough about him, about the allegedly defunct Obsidian Order, to know that his very presence on DS9 was cause for . . . concern. "Are you . . ." What was she supposed to ask? Are you here to cause trouble? To kill someone? She felt extremely off her guard, and asked the only thing she could think of.

"Are you here for the signing?"

Garak sighed. "You know, that was my original purpose in coming. See a few friends, watch the ceremony . . . and I suppose I was looking for some kind of closure to my time here. But now that I've seen this"—he panned the exhibit with a slow gaze—"I think I might just go home again. Avoid the rush, you know."

He turned his attention back to the painting. "She was so . . . herself. Seeing her work, I'm reminded of my real purpose—of what my life is now, you could say, helping others, rebuilding. Creating something new. *Stray not from the path that fate decides for you,* as my mentor used to tell me."

A compelling quote. "Vulcan?" Ro asked.

"Ferengi fortune cookie," Garak said. He didn't smile, but his eyes seemed to glitter ever brighter. He straightened, turning away from the portrait to offer Ro a slight bow.

"It's been a pleasure to see you again, Lieutenant. Please give my regards to Quark."

"I'll do that," Ro said. "Anyone else?"

He smiled. "No, no thank you. I'm sure I'll find a way to keep in touch."

Another polite bow, and he walked away, leaving her alone. She should probably notify Kira of Garak's presence, get a detail on his movements, warn Quark . . . but she turned back to Ziyal's powerful artwork instead, deciding that she would take their conversation at face value. It was probably a mistake, but she believed what he'd told her. She had no reason to think otherwise, except for his reputation . . . and she knew well enough from her own experience that reputations could be deceptive.

She gazed at Ziyal's self-portrait a while longer, her brief conversation with Garak replaying itself in her mind, about purpose, about what life became. She told herself that she hadn't yet decided whether to stay with DS9, to rejoin Starfleet, or to strike out on her own, to try a life with Quark . . . but telling herself that didn't make it so.

I'm staying, she thought, wondering at the tingle that the simple statement sent through her, wondering how she was going to break the news to Quark.

Vaughn waited for Prynn outside her quarters, anxious but determined to speak with her. He'd called her every few days since his release from the infirmary, and though she hadn't agreed to meet with him yet, he thought she had seemed less angry the last time he'd contacted her—had even seemed curious, that he wouldn't stop calling.

He leaned against the corridor wall, checked his watch. She'd been off-duty for ten minutes or so. If she wasn't back soon, he'd have to assume that she'd gone out for the evening, and would try again later. He didn't want to track her down with the computer, wanted their conversation to be private . . . but also wanted her to have the option of closing a door in his face, if that was what she wanted. So he waited, hoping that he hadn't been wrong, that she was more willing to speak to him than she had been in recent weeks.

I'm about to find out.

Some ten meters away, Prynn rounded the corner. When she saw him she faltered a moment, slowed—but didn't turn around and leave, either.

She's so beautiful, he thought, feeling as though he was seeing her through new eyes. Not just that she was attractive, that she had her mother's delicate features and casual grace . . . it was her anger, too, the fire in her. The turmoil, the pride and humor, the *uniqueness* of her.

"Commander," she said, entirely polite, entirely indifferent as she walked to her door.

"May I speak to you a moment?" he asked.

"If I say yes, will you stop calling me?" she retorted. He heard the barely hidden wound in her voice and shook his head.

"No," he said simply. "I've already made that mistake."

She considered him a moment, searching for something, then shrugged, pressing her door panel. "Come in."

He followed her inside, not surprised that her quarters were relaxed, sparsely decorated and casually messy. She didn't offer him a seat as she turned to face him, a look of studied irritation on her face.

"What do you want?" she asked, crossing her arms.

Vaughn nodded, drawing a breath. He was nervous, he didn't want to make things worse—but he wasn't afraid, either. It wasn't a test.

It's a process, he reminded himself. He'd met Benjamin Sisko twice since his Orb experience, and though the encounters had been warm, even comfortable, neither had spoken of what had happened, of Eli and Benny. Vaughn wasn't sure they ever would; strangely, he hadn't felt compelled to bring it up, either . . . but at both meetings, Sisko had asked about his daughter, if he'd talked with her. Vaughn hoped that the next time he saw Sisko—

—Benny—

—he'd be able to say he had.

"Maybe I should tell you what I don't want," Vaughn said. "I don't want to tell you I'm sorry again. And I don't want your forgiveness."

At the very least, he'd surprised her into looking surprised, her apathy set aside. "What?"

"I could tell you I'm sorry a billion times, and it would never make up for my behavior as your father," he said, meeting her eyes, hoping that she would hear him, that she *could* hear him. "And you shouldn't forgive me. Not for me, anyway. There's no excuse for how inadequately I've loved you."

Prynn folded her arms tighter, not speaking.

"All I want now is to get to know you, a little," Vaughn said. "You don't owe it to me, and if you don't want to talk to me for a while, that's okay, too. But I won't stop trying, not ever again. Giving up, telling myself that you were better off without me . . . that has been the worst mistake of my life. Because my life has been so much the poorer without you in it."

Still, she didn't speak—but he saw her gaze turn liquid, and felt hope, real hope.

"We don't have to talk about the past, if you don't want to," he said. "Or you can yell at me about it every day for the rest of my life. Either way, I'd like it very much if you'd accompany me to the ceremony tomorrow. And maybe afterward, we could get something to eat. Or the next day, or next week. Whenever you're ready, Prynn. Whatever you want."

Prynn cleared her throat, but still, her voice broke slightly when she spoke. "I'll think about it," she said.

Vaughn nodded, struggling not to push it any further, well aware of how very lucky he was.

"Thank you," he said, meaning it with all his heart.

25

KIRA HEARD THAT HE WAS ON HIS WAY AND READIED HERSELF, excited and anxious and a bit melancholy, all at once. She was also happy, happier than she could remember being since the end of the war. The preparations were finally complete. In less than an hour, she'd be leaving for Bajor, for the final signing, along with DS9's senior staff. Odo would be coming, too, to stand at her side. The thought made her heart skip a beat. Politics and career and religion aside, her reunion with Odo had done wonders for her state of mind, but with everything else that was happening, all she'd worked toward for so long . . . things were good. Things were wonderful.

And he'll be here to see it. Benjamin Sisko, who was on the way up, the first visit back to the station since his return from the Temple, and the first time she'd seen him since the day his daughter had been born. Rebecca, after the woman who'd raised Ben as her own; Jae, after Kas's mother.

"Captain on deck!"

Even with her door closed, Kira could hear the boom of

Sam Bowers's voice. At his grinning declaration, everyone in ops stood up, and all of them turned to face Sisko as he stepped off the turbolift. Kira took a deep breath and tapped a contact on the desk, opening the door to her office. She wasn't sure who started clapping but it was quickly picked up, gathering momentum as everyone cheered for Benjamin.

"At ease," Sisko tried to say, but the words were lost to the applause. They were all smiling, laughing as they continued to clap furiously.

"At ease," Sisko said again, louder this time, and slowly, the applause dwindled. "I appreciate the welcome," he said as he stepped down into the pit. "It's good to see you all. I hope to be able to catch up with each of you later, and for the chance to get to know some of you better, perhaps after the induction ceremony. But right now, I'm late for a meeting. I know I don't have to tell you how the CO hates to be kept waiting."

Laughter, and warm touches and smiles for him as he walked to the office. Kira watched him approach, hefting the desk ornament he'd left behind, that she'd drawn strength from in the months he'd been gone. As he stepped through the doorway, she threw it at him.

Sisko reached up and snatched the missile out of the air, grinning as he realized what it was.

"I suppose you'll want the office," Kira said.

Sisko turned his grin toward her, and she could tell that he remembered. It was one of the first things she'd ever said to him, when he'd come to the station all those years ago.

"Not this time, Nerys," he said, tossing the baseball easily from one hand to the other. "The new uniform suits you, by the way."

Captain Kira glanced down at her Starfleet uniform,

touched the four gold pips on her collar, and smiled back at him. For all of her own doubts about Bajor's induction, she thought she was finally ready. The suit felt good. That Starfleet had not only forgiven her behavior, her decision to take the *Defiant*, but awarded her a special commendation . . . it renewed her confidence in the Federation, that they had recognized her commitment to what was important. "Still haven't gotten used to the rank. Makes me feel like I've been demoted. And the combadge is on the wrong side."

"You'll adjust," Sisko told her, his smile turning slightly wicked. "Or maybe Starfleet will."

He tossed the baseball back at her, a gentle lob. "And this belongs with the station's commander, I think."

Kira caught it, her smile fading, her heart skipping a beat. There had been no official word, no one suggesting that she step down, but she also hadn't wanted to assume anything. "You're not coming back?"

"Actually, Starfleet wants to make me an admiral," Ben said. "They planned to offer it to me after the end of the war."

"That's wonderful news," Kira said enthusiastically. "And well deserved. You'll be—"

"I turned them down, Nerys."

Kira wasn't sure how to respond. He wasn't coming back, but he wasn't taking a promotion, either. Ben leaned against the closed door, calmly watching her. He was the same Benjamin Sisko she remembered, but different, too. Not changed, but more . . . more *present.*

What did you expect? He's been to the Temple. With Them.

As it had ever since his return, the thought threatened to overwhelm her, but she did her best to set it aside. They'd been through that before, when he'd been named Emissary; this was bigger, but the essentials were the same. If he wanted to discuss Them with her, he would, but she would not pry.

"So . . . what are you going to do?" Kira asked.

Ben smiled. "I'm going to take my family to the induction ceremony. And after that . . ."

He studied her a moment, that little smile still playing across his mouth. "After that, I thought I'd stick around for a while, see what happens next."

Kira nodded. "Something always does."

"Yes," he said, his smile widening. "Yes it does, doesn't it?"

To those in the gathered crowd, it must have felt like half the planet had turned out for the ceremony, which was held just outside the great capital of Ashalla. It had been a long time since Kira had seen so many of her people in one place, though from where she stood, she could see that the assembly was far from planetary. Still and all, it was quite a sight. There was no official count yet, but she estimated several thousand people had come, drawn not only by the signing, but by the chance to see the people who'd made it possible. The appearances of Benjamin Sisko and Opaka Sulan played no small part, she was sure.

The city directors had planned well. The open stage was on a low rise, looking out over a wide field, great lengths of freshly baled kava stalk acting as impromptu seating for those who wished to sit . . . though as First Minister Asarem, Councillor zh'Thane, and Admiral Akaar approached the table where the documents would be signed, Kira couldn't see anyone sitting. The massive crowd moved and pulsed, a living, breathing thing, watching with grand expectation. Kira could feel it emanating from the families and farmers, the city people, from everyone who'd come—a warm, rising wave of anticipation, of resolution at hand.

The stage was overflowing with Bajoran and Federation dignitaries. Vedek Yevir and a handful of his cronies were representing the Assembly, their expressions stern and serious, and there were a number of high-ranking member officials from both the Chamber and the Militia. Opaka Sulan stood near Yevir, smiling serenely, her grounded, peaceful expression as different from Yevir's as day from night. A lot of people wanted Opaka to reclaim her position as kai, Kira among them . . . but that was a resolution for another day, perhaps. For now, the joy of feeling her earring restored to its proper place reaffirmed her belief that all things were possible.

She shifted from one foot to the other, unable to hold still. Odo reached out and took her hand, squeezing it comfortably. She squeezed back. Though they hadn't talked about it much, she knew he wasn't going to stay. He spoke of progress within the Link, but it was also clear that there was still much to do. While it lasted, though, she meant to enjoy every minute of it. She no longer doubted that they'd be together, someday, and that was good enough for now.

Next to Odo, Taran'atar stood stiffly, his head high, as he'd stood next to Wex almost the entire time she'd been on the station. Odo had mentioned that the Jem'Hadar had expressed interest in returning to his own kind, but had admitted also that he hadn't yet learned "everything" about the peoples of the Alpha Quadrant. He'd be staying a while longer than Odo, Kira suspected.

Next to Taran'atar stood Ro Laren and Quark, both looking mildly uncomfortable in their new outfits. Kira could see that the Starfleet uniform was chafing Ro a bit, figuratively, at least, but her chin was up. Quark—*Ambassador* Quark—had decked himself out in lavish purple pants and a specially made sparkling gold vest with matching leg bands, easily outshining the Grand Nagus to his right, an obviously pregnant, smiling Leeta on Rom's arm. Rom and Leeta looked very happy. Kira noticed that her own security officer and the bartender were standing fairly close together, but decided not to speculate any further. The rumors were bad enough.

Maybe these things just have a way of bringing people together, she thought, scanning the rest of the stage. It was a diverse enough group, to be sure. Ezri and Julian were joined at the hip, as usual, standing near Taulin Cyl and Hiziki Gard. Gard was only a meter away from Trill's president, who was expected to pardon him after a mandatory trial; the first minister had already signed his extradition. Ambassador Worf and Chancellor Martok had made the journey, standing near Captain Jean-Luc Picard and his senior staff. Kira spotted Natima Lang and Gul Macet among the Cardassian contingent, and Vlu, who'd received a Starfleet commendation for her work during the parasite crisis . . . and was also supporting a fairly hefty crush from Sam Bowers, whose gaze kept wandering across to the petite Cardassian. No one had expected *that,* but stranger matches had been made.

Commander Vaughn and Prynn Tenmei were both onstage, Prynn doing her best to look as though she belonged there. She wasn't a senior officer, but Vaughn had insisted . . . and though neither seemed entirely at ease, they were together, at least; more than could be said for Councillor zh'Thane and her son. Shar stood a good distance from his parent, near where Nog and Jake were exchanging grins over something or other. Although Shar wasn't smiling, he seemed more at ease with himself than he'd been since returning from the Gamma Quadrant, too. Kira was glad to see it.

General Lenaris stepped to the table, joining Akaar and zh'Thane and Asarem. A ripple of good-natured laughter moved through the crowd as he searched for a pen, the general's face flushing slightly in spite of his wide smile. Standing at the foot of the stage, Kira saw that both Yoshi and Molly were giggling, though their parents quickly hushed them, Miles slipping an arm around Keiko's waist as they watched. They'd begged off stage duty, Keiko worried that the children wouldn't want to stand still for any period of time. The O'Briens would be going back to Earth in a few days, to pack; then they'd be off to Cardassia. It seemed that Keiko had accepted a job there, to assist in Cardassia's agricultural renewal. Kira had been surprised by the news, but the Chief had assured her that he was looking forward to a little more chaos in their lives.

At the front of the stage, Lenaris had signed his name on both "official" documents of induction. The hardcopies were for show, of course; the binding documents were all part of multiple computer and comnet systems by now, witnessed behind the scenes shortly before the ceremony had begun. Kira knew better, though; until people had actually experienced the pride that accompanied such a grand change, witnessed it with their own eyes, nothing was truly official.

Kira looked for, and found, Benjamin Sisko, not far from his son, his arm around Kas's shoulders. She held their sleeping daughter against her breast, glowing as only a new mother could, barely able to take her gaze from their beautiful baby. Benjamin was watching the signing with a look of pure pleasure, his eyes sparkling. As Admiral Ross jotted down his own signature at the table in front, the final endorsement, Ben turned and looked directly at her. He nodded, a slow, sure nod, his thoughts as clear as if he'd spoken them.

We did it, he said.

Kira nodded back, smiling, wiping at the single tear that had spilled from her wet gaze. *Yes, we did.*

Ross held up his copy of the document; Asarem did the same, and a mighty roar rose up from all those who'd come, their faces radiant in the late sun, their voices glorious in triumph.

EPILOGUE

THEY HAD A FINE DINNER. BEN MADE CREOLE, THOUGH Joseph insisted on doing the roux himself, convinced that kava flour needed the attention of a master. They all stayed up late, talking, laughing. Dad wandered off to bed after a time, Jake doing the same not long afterward, a handful of holovids and a bowl of *jumja* ice accompanying him. Judith followed, pronouncing herself too full of creole to stay awake. They'd all be leaving soon, too soon; Jake had gained some very adult perspectives in his brief absence, and was itching for some space to stretch into, to explore further. Jude and his father both had lives to get back to. He would miss them, but was glad for the time they'd shared, and for the time they had left.

While Kas gave Rebecca her last feeding, Ben closed everything up, savoring the simplicity of it all. He loved the house, loved shutting the doors and windows, loved turning out the lights and feeling its quiet spirit settle in for the night. It was the house he'd dreamed of, and that Kas had built it . . . it was all the more special, knowing that what she had done was out of love, out of a readiness to be his family.

They went to bed, talking softly about nothing important as they got ready, as they slipped beneath the coverlet and Kas tapped the light panel at the headboard. Outside, a gentle wind blew across the silent fields. They held hands, facing each other, their fingers touching beneath their sleeping daughter's feet. Ben took a deep breath, inhaling the warm, baby scent of her, feeling it fill him up. Kas smiled, at Rebecca and then at him. He smiled back. In her sleep, Rebecca splayed her fingers, then relaxed them.

This is home, he thought, watching as Kas's eyes closed, listening as her breath became deep and even, much slower and deeper than Rebecca's. A part of him would always be in the Temple . . . but he was where he belonged, where he needed to be.

And where I'll soon be needed. The Prophets had revealed as much before letting him go. What was happening, what was going to happen to Bajor and its people, was of great importance to Them. His role wouldn't be easy; he'd need the help of old and new friends. Kira, of course, and Dax . . . and Eli, who'd been set on a course by the Prophets that led him to DS9, that sent him to meet Benny in the Temple. Because he'd needed help, himself . . . but also to remind Ben of his own humanity, to show him how to follow his lifeline back to his own people.

Elias, he reminded himself. Elias Vaughn. He smiled. The commander had already called him "Benny," more than once.

All that was later, though. Soon, but not now. For now, he decided that in the morning he'd make a big breakfast, flapjacks and eggs and juice, fruit and sausage, coffee . . . maybe he'd talk Dad into doing up a fine batch of his spicy home fries, too, Jake loved them . . .

Life was in the details, he thought, and thinking it, fell into a deep and peaceful sleep, at one with himself and the people he loved.

THE SAGA OF
STAR TREK: DEEP SPACE NINE
WILL CONTINUE

ABOUT THE AUTHOR

S. D. (Stephani Danelle) Perry writes multimedia novelizations in the fantasy/science fiction/horror realms for love and money, occasionally in that order. She's worked in the universes of *Resident Evil, Aliens, Xena* and, most recently, *Star Trek;* she has also written a few short stories and translated a couple of movie scripts into books. Danelle, as she prefers to be called, lives in Portland with an incredibly patient husband and their two ridiculous dogs. She and her husband have recently been joined by the best baby ever, Cyrus Jay.